The Eunuch's Heir

ALSO BY ELAINE ISAAK

The Singer's Crown

The Eunuch's Heir

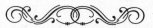

Elaine Isaak

An Imprint of
HarperCollins*Publishers*

THE EUNUCH'S HEIR. Copyright © 2006 by Elaine Isaak. All rights reserved. Printed in the United States of America. No part of this book may be used or reproduced in any manner whatsoever without written permission except in the case of brief quotations embodied in critical articles and reviews. For information address HarperCollins Publishers, 10 East 53rd Street, New York, NY 10022.

HarperCollins books may be purchased for educational, business, or sales promotional use. For information please write: Special Markets Department, HarperCollins Publishers, 10 East 53rd Street, New York, NY 10022.

FIRST EDITION

Eos is a federally registered trademark of HarperCollins Publishers.

Designed by Lovedog Studio

Library of Congress Cataloging-in-Publication Data has been applied for.

ISBN-13: 978-0-06-078255-9
ISBN-10: 0-06-078255-2

06 07 08 09 10 JTC/RRD 10 9 8 7 6 5 4 3 2 1

For my sister, Michelle;
we found common ground in the realms of fantasy

The Eunuch's Heir

Prologue

Year 1236 since the Second Walking
A courtyard, castle of the
Kingdom of Lochalyn

"HOW COME the Goddess didn't touch me, Alyn?" Princess Melody demanded, scowling as fiercely as a six-year-old could.

Her brother gazed back at her with that unsettling hint of knowledge, but what he said was, "I don't know."

Prince Wolfram rolled his eyes at both of them. He saw them maybe a couple of times a year, and they were always having the same argument. "Let's play a game," Wolfram suggested, bouncing up from his bench.

"I don't want to play, I want the Goddess to touch me." Melody crossed her arms more sharply.

"I'm not sure we should play right now. We haven't got our play clothes on," Alyn pointed out, smoothing his silk tabard, blue for Name Day.

"You want to just sit here? It could be hours before they call us for dinner!" Wolfram waved his arms at the courtyard. Alyn and Melody's nurse sat not far off, picking at a bit of embroidery while his own great-grandmother, Duchess Elyn, propped her hands on her cane reading a scroll with a squint that narrowed her eyes even more.

"Alyn could ask the Goddess to tell us."

"That's not funny, Melody. The Goddess is very serious. And what She tells me is really important." Then Alyn's voice fell. "Even if I can't figure it out all the time."

Wolfram grinned. He stalked toward Melody and poked her lightly in the arm. "Touch! I'm the Goddess."

Melody shrieked with laughter, then pounced after him. "No, I'm the Goddess!"

Dodging away, Wolfram ran across the courtyard.

"Children," said Duchess Elyn in a warning tone, not lifting her eyes.

"That's not funny!" Alyn howled, but Melody caught up with Wolfram and slapped his back.

"Touch! I'm the Goddess!"

Both of them laughed, and the chase began again, Melody scooping up her skirts in both hands as she fled. But she couldn't resist glancing back, taunting, "Can't catch me, can't catch me!"

"Melody, watch—" but Wolfram called too late, as Melody sprawled headlong over a loose cobblestone.

She wailed, and the nurse threw down her stitching to hurry over. "Are you hurt, Your Highness?" She gathered the girl into her arms, cooing and wiping away locks of dark hair and the tears that tracked Melody's face. Her cheek, chin, and nose oozed blood through nasty scrapes, and Wolfram winced in sympathy.

"Are you all right, Melody?"

"Don't you talk to her," Alyn said. He pushed his way between them. "That was a bad game, and you shouldn't have been playing it."

"It was just for fun," Wolfram protested.

"You started it. You're a bad boy, Wolfram." Alyn's bright eyes widened, and he seemed to stare through Wolfram and their surroundings as if he could see inside them. "There's darkness all around you, Wolfram, Prince of Lochalyn," he said. "The altar is falling, and even the sun goes dark. There's blood upon your hands." Alyn's own hands rose slowly.

"What's this?" Duchess Elyn stalked nearer, her cane clicking.

"Hush," said the nurse, "Prince Alyn is speaking for Her."

"Blood and dying and darkness, the ground shakes with it. The stars cannot be seen, and a foulness corrupts the Lady's way."

Wolfram's entire body trembled, but he couldn't look away or stop up his ears. Alyn almost glowed before him, his pale skin and golden curls alight. Wolfram thought that beams of light might shoot out from his fingertips. He'd never seen Alyn having a vision before. It felt like the Lady Herself stared back at him from Alyn's vacant eyes, and he wanted to drop to his knees and cry.

"The darkness moves through you. It wants to live in you. *It knows your heart.*" Alyn gasped, and his arms fell. He gave a tremendous shake and gulped a few breaths of air. Wolfram, too, was gasping.

"Sit down, Your Highness," the nurse urged, patting the ground beside her.

"She showed me . . ." Alyn blinked, frowned, and finally focused on Wolfram's face. "I can feel the danger in you. You're evil, aren't you? That's why it's dark and bloody." He took a step back, and his sister whimpered.

Still fighting tears, Wolfram balled his hands into fists. "I am not evil. You take that back."

But Alyn kept shaking his head. "There's blood on your hands, Wolfram."

His hands felt sticky and damp. Quickly, he glanced down, his lips trembling. Nothing was there. "Take it back!" Wolfram jumped toward Alyn, about to snatch him by the tabard. He stumbled, and they both fell in a heap, tumbling together. "Take it back, Alyn!"

Melody shrieked again, and the nurse called out, then a hand grabbed Wolfram's tunic and hauled him upward, carrying him away from the twins and dropping him on his unsteady feet. "You leave them alone, Wolfram," Duchess Elyn hissed. "You were raised better than this. You respect your betters, and you respect the Lady."

"I didn't do anything! He called me evil." At the other side of the yard, the nurse cuddled Melody and Alyn close in her embrace.

Rising away from him, his great-grandmother glared. She

hefted her cane, and Wolfram tried to spring out of the way. He caught the blow across his bottom, and pain exploded through him. Wolfram wailed, tears streaming down his face as his hands flew to protect himself. He dared not turn his back on her again and edged away toward the door.

"Go on, run away. Don't try to tell anyone about this, boy." Elyn waved the cane at him. "I'll give you what you really deserve."

At that, Wolfram did run, his feet pounding the floor all the way to the room where his mother must be. He slipped between the guards and pushed inside, then froze. The room, lined with benches, must hold a hundred people staring at his mother on her throne, but they turned when the door popped open. Seeing him, some of them sighed, some laughed or smiled as they returned their attention to the front. Wolfram clamped his mouth shut so hard that his head ached. His hands hurt from being clenched, and if he pulled them a little tighter still, he could drown out the pain in his bottom. His mother glanced up from the supplicant before her, her crown sparkling, her face creased briefly in a frown.

Then a man rose up from his lower chair, his green tunic fluttering. Fionvar DuNormand, his mother's Lord Protector. Fionvar gave the queen a short bow and came swiftly down the steps of the dais, one hand clapped to his sword to keep it from swinging. His chain of office clinked upon his chest.

At Wolfram's back, the door opened more gently, and a guard's voice murmured, "Forgive me, my lord, he came up so quick. I'll take him—"

"No need," said Fionvar. He dropped to one knee, his eyes searching Wolfram's face. "What's happened, Your Highness?"

Wolfram's lips twisted, and his eyes were burning. If he opened his mouth, he'd start wailing again, and he knew it. But Fionvar did not wait for an answer. He scooped up the prince in one strong arm and carried him back through the doors, Wolfram's small arms wrapping instinctively around his neck. As they walked, Wolfram blubbered out the story of the game and Alyn's words. Fionvar took him to a bench in the sun and sat down, letting the sword hang free while he stroked the prince's back.

"It doesn't mean anything, Your Highness. Nothing at all. Prince Alyn is just a child like you. Do you know everything the Goddess has planned?"

Wolfram shook his head slightly, Fionvar's chain pressing into his forehead.

"No one does, Your Highness. Not even Alyn."

"What's happened?" Wolfram's mother stood suddenly before them, and Wolfram watched her from one eye, tightening his grip on Fionvar's tunic.

"They were playing in the courtyard and Prince Alyn started prophesying again."

The queen's eyes flared. "Prince Alyn had a vision? About Wolfram?"

Fionvar shook his head, his hair brushing against Wolfram's cheek and fingers, soft and dark. "Just a load of nonsense, Brianna. The boy sees things, but he doesn't know what they mean. His parents ought to teach him not to open his mouth until he understands what he's saying."

"He'll learn," she said, patting Wolfram's head. "What did he say?"

"It's nothing," Fionvar repeated.

Wolfram raised his head, his mother's hand warming him and his tears drying at last. "He said I was evil. He could see a falling altar and darkness and blood. He said even the sun went dark because of me."

His mother's hand froze, then lifted away. "I'm sure it's nothing." She swallowed and took a step back. "Nothing at all. I should go."

"Brianna," Fionvar called, but she gave a tiny smile, and a nod, and walked away.

"Mama?"

Fionvar's sigh ruffled Wolfram's hair. "She's very busy, Your Highness. I'm sure you'll see her later."

"You're busy, too," Wolfram said. He could see that Fionvar wanted to deny it, but the man gave another sigh instead.

"I should be, yes. I'm sorry."

Wolfram slid down from his lap, wincing as the impact of the floor sent shivers of pain from his bottom. "But I'm not evil, right?"

"Of course not," Fionvar told him, his hand lingering on the prince's shoulder. "Will you be all right, Your Highness?"

Wolfram nodded. His bottom still hurt, and his head throbbed from crying, but he wasn't supposed to go into court, and they all knew it. "I'll just stay in the sun a little while." He tried to smile. "Then I'll see if Dylan can play instead."

"I'll fetch you for supper. Won't be long." Fionvar bowed and smiled.

Wolfram waved as Fionvar walked back down the hall, then he lay on his belly on the bench, arms folded under his chin, letting the sun from the tall windows warm him. Fionvar's warmth lingered for a while, too, and that felt good. He was not evil, and Alyn didn't know what he was talking about.

Outside, a dark cloud ate away the sun, plunging Wolfram into the cold of a dim corridor, and he squeezed his eyes shut, trying not to be afraid. Clouds covered the sun all the time, it didn't mean anything. His head pounded, and his bottom throbbed with any movement. He wished that Fionvar would come back and find him, but he lay there alone and hurting as the bench grew cold and the sun was hidden in shadow.

Chapter 1

Year 1248
City of Lochdale

In the darkest valley beneath the foot of the castle, Prince Wolfram finally cast the demon from his mind. It would not come tonight, not on his way to visit the best lover a man could find. He slapped Dylan on the back, grinning at him in the darkness, and the restlessness receded but did not disperse. Perhaps another drink would banish it completely.

"How about the Copper Kettle, before we go our separate ways?" Wolfram wriggled his eyebrows.

Dylan laughed, tossing back his head to shout his laughter to the night. "Have you not had enough then, Wolf? Aren't you afraid you'll not—" Dylan broke off, waving a suggestive hand below his belt.

Wolfram growled back at him, teeth snapping the air.

"Oh, no, not you!" Dylan waved his hands a little more broadly than usual, then paused to steady his swaying steps. "I forget myself, my liege!"

Chin held high, Wolfram struck a regal pose. "You do indeed, my good man. Am I not the finest sower of seed across this great city of mine?" He waved a hand and nearly toppled, but Dylan caught him.

"Aye, Wolf, the greatest. You must be the luckiest man I know." He paused to peer at a street name roughly painted on the stone wall.

"I have just been thinking that very thing." Wolfram leaned closer, throwing an arm around his friend's shoulders. "You're not using your wizard-stuff to spy on my thoughts, Dylan?"

"What, me? Would I do that?" Dylan laughed. "I'm just a bloody 'prentice anyhow. What could I do without my master getting on my back? You're the prince, after all."

"'Sright! You can't touch me! Nobody can." He smirked. "Excepting my lady, of course."

"And which one would that be?" Dylan started their steps down a brightly lit street where buxom whores leaned out the windows to call to the pair.

Ignoring them, Wolfram cast his friend a warning glance. Uneasiness began to chill him again, but he shook it off.

"This one tonight, I suppose," Dylan went on, returning the kisses the women threw down to him. "Though I think your mistress touches you more deeply." He poked the prince lightly in the ribs.

Wolfram glowered. "You're not to mention that. I only told you because I can trust you to keep a secret."

"Oh, I'll keep it, Wolf. But every now and then, I take it out and marvel at it. The prince seducing a woman twice his youthful age, a woman who turned her back on marriage, a woman who—"

"A woman of the Goddess, Dylan." Wolfram's cheeks burned, he glanced about wildly, but no one here could listen in, or understand their meaning. "It hasn't happened yet, Dylan, and if anyone suspects, it could ruin her."

"I'm sure it happens all the time, Wolfram, but you and her would be something special—"

Wolfram punched Dylan's side, eliciting a wince and stifling the proclamation.

"Hey, you didn't need to do that," Dylan griped, kneading the bruise and eyeing him darkly. "Tell me you're not getting into one of those moods, Wolf," he added, voice cajoling.

"I'm not." Wolfram stalked on, regretting that he had ever spilled his secret dreams, even to his best friend. Suddenly a rabble of dark faces swarmed down the street, a group of Hemijrani refugees dressed in colorful rags and carrying bundles on their heads. Without their bundles, they would hardly have reached the prince's chin. For a moment, Dylan was lost from sight.

"Watch your purse, Wolfram!"

"I'm watching," came the reply as Wolfram pushed his way through the mob. Most of the men looked down, perhaps ashamed of the eye patches so many wore.

Dylan followed more gently, letting his eyes linger on the dark eyes of the foreign girls, who turned to smile back shyly.

Wolfram dusted himself off. "Bury the lot of them." He checked his dagger, relieved to find it still in place.

"It's war, Wolfram, or so they tell me. These people have no place to go. Your mother's compassion—"

"My father's legend," Wolfram snorted.

Biting his lip, Dylan gave a half shrug, acknowledging that he trod too near his friend's sore spot. "Whatever the reason. They do mean cheap labor, and the women—" He sucked in a breath and let it out slow, shaking his head.

"You think so?" The prince looked dubious.

"Oh, I know, you prefer redheads."

"Watch it, or it's you your father may be finding in the street in the morning!" He raised a threatening fist.

Dylan backed off, holding up his hands. "It's not my fault he dragged you in that time!"

"Well you didn't have to rub it in quite so much." He scowled.

"I was joking!" Dylan's face lit with a smile. "Just a joke."

Wolfram scuffed his boot in the muck of the street. "A joke? 'He's the guard captain, not the garbage collector,' I think you said."

Biting his lip again, and letting it go, Dylan pointed out, "I also said I was sorry."

Glancing away, Wolfram raised one shoulder and let it drop.

Dylan sighed. "Anyway, this is where we part company. If I'm late, the astrologer will have my hide."

"What, you'll miss seeing the moon with one of those gadgets?"

"It's important work, Wolfram," Dylan said, scowling. "We're plotting the most complete map of the stars ever made, and constructing this clock—Oh, you don't care, you're just after the Love Star. When I'm done should I meet you?" He nudged the prince with his elbow, attempting a more cheerful tone.

"No, I might be a while. I'll walk back alone." With a half-hearted wave, Wolfram turned away. "Maybe I'll meet a friendly pickpocket to lighten my way," he called back over his shoulder.

"Goddess walk with you!" Dylan called after him.

Wolfram waved again without turning. Dylan's mind was already off in the stars, he knew, following their patterns and charting the moon. As for himself, Wolfram had more earthly pleasures in mind. He longed for the peace and comfort of a woman who neither knew nor cared who he was, a woman who did not know the darkness that pursued him. He rounded a corner and trotted down a series of short stone steps. At the bottom, his lover's door stood open, as if she knew just when to expect him. She herself stood in the doorway, wearing the linen chemise he had bought for her, her figure outlined through the thin fabric by flickering candles. "My lord, come in out of the dark," she whispered, holding out a warm hand to him.

Smiling, he obeyed.

SOMETIME LATER, Wolfram lay on his belly, his chin propped on his crossed arms, staring vaguely at a scrap on the floor. It almost looked like one of Dylan's star charts. He thought of the Love Star and smiled. His lover slowly drew her long red hair along his spine, eliciting a shiver of pleasure. "I love your hair," he murmured into the semidarkness.

She laughed, drawing her face near to his to kiss him lightly. This close, he could see the fine lines around her eyes—she was old enough to be his mother, but beautiful, and very good at what she did. She treated him merely as a man, like any other—not blessed with a saintly father, nor cursed by the Lady's prophet. With her alone he could shed the weight of his own failings. She twirled a lock of his blond hair around her finger. "I'm glad. I do it for you, my love."

He frowned, tilting his head sideways to look up at her. "Do what?"

"Dye it," she replied, blinking. "But you knew that."

"What do you mean?" The frown intensified as he gazed upon her face. A small, cold doubt began to creep along the spine she had so recently caressed.

She laughed again—and the sound did not seem so light to him—shaking her head so that the red hair rippled about her. "You know it's not natural."

He sat up abruptly, forcing her to move back on the narrow bed, nearly sliding her off onto the rough wood floor. The cold grew inside him, fastening itself with sharp claws of anger where some soft, forgiving organ should have been. The demon defending his heart unfurled. "No, why would I know that? I can't believe you've been deceiving me!"

She stood up, crossing her arms over her still-lovely breasts. "Because you dye yours, silly, that's how. I haven't deceived you, any more than you have deceived me." In the flickering golden light, she appeared suddenly both young and strange, no longer playful, any trace of softness slipping from her sharp features.

Wolfram narrowed his eyes at her. "I don't dye my hair— I'm seventeen, why would I dye my hair?" Tension gripped his shoulders, the demon pounding inside his skull, struggling to get out even as he struggled to contain it.

She shrugged. "Dye, bleach—what's the difference?"

"I don't know what you're talking about," he replied, pressing his palms to his temples, staring at her like the whore that she was.

Her hand flashed out and snatched a lock of his hair, pulling it almost taut between them. In the other hand, she offered a lock of her own. "Feel the texture; it's rough—natural hair doesn't feel like that." The flush of anger lit her cheeks. "If you must use me, my lord, that's fine, but don't think you can deny what I can see with my own eyes—what anyone could see who looked closely enough!"

He jerked his head away, quaking with fury and confusion—anyone? Anyone could see it, she said—anyone but he himself. The pounding in his head cried for violence, destruction, and Wolfram tried to force it down. She didn't know what the problem was; no point venting his fury at her. He flung himself from the bed, shoving his fingers through his hair, then sharply pulling back his hand. He laughed, a dry little cackle. "Of course," he said, "I should have known better than to lie to you." He pushed past her to the table where he'd heaped his clothes.

Above the table, a small mirror flashed. In the dim light, he stared at his own face, at the blond hair tumbling over his shoulder. His hands clenched the edge of the wood, slivers piercing his uncallused fingers.

Slowly, she came up beside him, her pale face joining his in the polished silver. "You didn't know," she whispered.

"How could I not know my own hair was bleached?" he snapped at her. "I'm not stupid." He grabbed a handful of cloth from the table, shook it until it was revealed as his woolen tunic, and yanked it over his head. "What do you take me for?"

"Nothing, my lord," she protested, pulling a little back from him.

Jerking on his hose, he flicked a quick glance up at her. The fine cloth tore beneath his hurried fingers. Her arms pulled tighter over her breasts, her thighs pressed together, her head lowered so that she watched him from behind a curtain of that false red hair. She trembled, ever so slightly.

When he had met her, in the depths of a disreputable tavern, he had seen first her beauty, and only then the marks upon her from another man's hands. From that first night, she had been his alone, he had kept her, paid rent upon this hovel she lived in, bought her the pretty things she admired. Since that first night, months ago, there had been no marks upon her—yet now, she trembled at the sight of him.

Wolfram let out a pent-up breath between his clenched teeth. "I won't hit you."

Defiance and disbelief glittered in her eyes. "You never have, my lord," she replied coolly, tossing her hair back over her shoulder. "But there's always a first time."

With shaking hands, he gathered his belt and slapped it around his narrow waist. Straightening, he caught the flash of his hair again in the mirror and growled at his own reflection.

"Perhaps it's the soap," she said lightly, standing still through some force of will he had not seen in her before.

He eyed her in the mirror. She didn't know who he was; he had been at pains to keep it from her—if he never came back, she wouldn't know how to find him. It didn't matter whom she told about her young lover with the bleached-blond hair. Already, he missed the comfort of her arms. He shoved his foot into a boot.

"You aren't coming back, are you?" she asked. "You're leaving me because of this?"

Wolfram shrugged stiffly, pulling on the other boot, and turning to face her.

"What are you afraid of, my lord?"

"I'm not afraid! It's just the soap, remember? Just a little paler than it should be, that's all."

"I'll bet your mother has a locket," she said quietly, her arms still rigid, gooseflesh beginning to creep along her naked skin.

He glowered. "She may have a dozen, who cares?"

"A locket with your baby hair in it. Many women save the first cutting."

"Do you have any lockets?" he inquired, brushing past her toward the door.

"My lord," she called. "Don't leave without a kiss!"

Wolfram spun on his heel, grasping her face in both hands, and pulling her lips to his. The kiss left her trembling in the doorway as he stormed out into the dark and narrow street.

All the way home, Wolfram turned it over in his head, slapping the treacherous hair out of his face. It didn't matter. It shouldn't matter at all, and yet the darkness he carried with him spoke in whispers of dread. His mother would have a locket—she must. What if it were blond? What if the feel of his hair was just the harshness of the soap, or the bleaching of the sun? Of course it was. His wild imagination had again sprung to the wrong conclusion.

Perhaps the dagger hanging against his hip deterred the pickpockets who slipped in and out in the shadows, or perhaps it was that special darkness he carried with him that night, but he arrived at the little door unmolested. He turned a key in the ancient lock, and it slid without a sound. Wolfram pushed back the door and replaced the key in the cleft between two stones. When he shut the door behind him, even the starlight left him at last. No matter, he had come this way too many times to be uneasy in the dark, even up the narrow stairs, choosing the right passage. On the other side of the wall, voices murmured, chairs scraped—the sounds seeping through to him in the musty little corridor. He came to the temple stairs. He hesitated a moment—he could turn down, descend to the chapel and find Mistress Lyssa. She would know what to do, what to say to convince him that his very hair had not turned traitor. Abruptly, he turned upward, toward his mother's chambers. At this hour, she would still be in the hall, or listening to the complaints of some tedious courtier. He came to the door, pulling it cautiously inward, so that it barely ruffled the tapestry that concealed it. Wolfram stood for a moment without breathing, waiting to hear if anyone moved within. Silence greeted him.

He slipped back the tapestry and entered his mother's room. Some of the anger had worn away along the walk to get here. A hint of apprehension entered in its stead, but he shook it off. Did he not have a right to visit his mother's rooms? Well, perhaps not when she had no knowledge of it. His father would never have done it—not his sainted father. Of course, that other one probably did it all the time, sneaking through this very door to pay his nightly visits.

Wolfram's hands hardened into fists, and he pushed away from the wall, the new anger carrying him to the wardrobe. He popped open the doors and pulled out the first drawer, pawing through the jewels it contained. The search fruitless, he shoved it back again, but it stuck, and he let go, the drawer clattering onto the tile floor. Heedless of the mess, he pulled out another.

When the last drawer had joined its fellows, Wolfram kicked the wreckage out of his way and slumped to the floor. Aimlessly, he kicked another drawer, sending it skittering against the wall. There, it struck, and the bottom cracked and fell away. From beneath the panel, a small ivory box tumbled.

Grinning, Wolfram rose and crossed to the wall in two long strides. He swept up the box and creaked open the lid. His fingers suddenly careful, he lifted out a thin gold chain, letting the pendant twinkle in the light of the lamps his mother always burned. The pendant resembled a shell, two smooth curves of glass bordered in gold sheltering a little curl of hair. Soft baby's hair, as dark as the night around him.

He stood transfixed, his heart lurching within him, throat dry. It could not be. It could not be. Why would she do this to him?

Voices approached in the hall outside, and Wolfram spun, staring at the mess he'd made of his mother's things. Even as he took a step to rectify the damage, he stopped himself, the cold demon anger gathering again inside him. Why should he care? Maybe she wasn't even his mother—maybe everything he knew was a lie.

The door swung open, his mother leaning into it, with her back to the room. "Yes, of course, Grandmother. I'll have it seen to immediately." She raised her eyebrows to the man who accompanied her.

Duchess Elyn, tall and gaunt with age, her white hair piled atop her head, retreated from the chamber, disappearing down the hall.

The Lord Protector, Fionvar DuNormand, let a smile spread across his face, gazing into the eyes of his queen. "Do you remember when we were afraid of her?"

Queen Brianna laughed, pressing her hand to Fionvar's chest. "Terrified," she agreed, then the smile dropped from her lips, for his mouth had fallen open. "What is it?" She swung around, catching sight first of the ruined wardrobe, all her jewels and baubles spread upon the floor like gleaming garbage. "Thieves," she whispered, but Fionvar's chin directed her to look a little farther, and she saw her son.

Their eyes locked, brown on brown, her features pale, lips

parted though no sound emerged. Abruptly, the lips pinched shut for a moment, then she demanded, "By the Lady, Wolfram, what have you done?" Her hands balled into fists, and Fionvar clasped his hands lightly over her shoulders, propelling her forward just enough to shut the door behind them. "What are you doing in my room?"

"I thought I'd pay a visit, Mother," Prince Wolfram replied. "Looking for mementos of my childhood." He held up the necklace, the pendant trembling with translated anger. The anger that tried to conceal his fear.

"Where did you find that? I cannot believe you've been searching my things. Great Lady!" she burst out. Shaking off Fionvar's restraining hands, she made as if to snatch the necklace away, but he kept it from her, swinging it above his head.

"Not so fast, Mother. I have some questions—like whose hair is this? After all, I'm blond, like my father."

"You're nothing like your father! Great Lady, how I wish you were." She slammed her fists onto her hips, glaring.

Behind her, Fionvar winced, shutting his eyes. "Let the boy talk, Brie, let him explain himself."

"Oh, no, I want to hear her explanation. Go on, Mother, is it my hair or isn't it?"

"Who else's would it be? You're my only son." Her closed expression plainly told him what she thought about that.

A twinge of pain shot through the anger, but he pushed it away. He had been evil in her eyes too long to hope for redemption. He held up the dangling glass shell beside his own hair. "Mine? I don't think so. Anybody can look at it and tell."

The flush burned away from her features, leaving her pale. She drew closer to Fionvar. "Lots of babies have different-colored hair. Yours grew in blond."

He shook his head, free hand pressed to his temple. "Why are you always lying? Everything you say to me is a lie."

"That's not true! How could you say that to your own mother?"

"And I'm your son, no matter how much you wish it otherwise." He gathered the chain into his hand.

If he had struck her, he could not have gotten a more satisfying response. She shook, and the Lord Protector slid an arm around her shoulders. "How can you be so cruel?" she murmured.

"I must have gotten it from you, Mother, since my father was a saint, who descended from on high to deliver his desperate people." He waved his arms about, making grand gestures of deliverance. "Oh, and leaving behind a pathetically human son, unworthy to be a prince, unworthy to carry his blessed name—Strel Rhys, wasn't it?"

Fionvar blinked stupidly over Brianna's shoulder. The Lord Protector, too, seemed to have been struck dumb by Wolfram's vehemence. Suddenly, the man laughed inanely, shaking his head, his eyes still wide.

Wolfram clenched the necklace so tightly he felt every link of it jabbing his hand. "Don't you laugh at me," he hissed, shaking the fist at Fionvar. "You have no right, you adulterous bastard."

His words snapped the Lord Protector out of whatever trance he'd sunk into, and he drew himself up to take full advantage of the two inches he still had over Wolfram. His own hair, silvered at the temples, matched the chain of office about his neck.

"Don't act so surprised," Wolfram said, "I could see it in your lecherous stare—even if I hadn't seen it in the garden last spring." He repeated Dylan's below-the-belt gesture.

Fionvar's brows notched upward, and Brianna grew even more pale. "I don't think now is the time to discuss that," Fionvar replied, with remarkable control. "We were talking about why you had broken into your mother's jewelry. The reasons why you did it do not make it right."

Wolfram gritted his teeth. The bastard didn't deny his adultery; then went on to act like he knew exactly what the prince was getting at, why he'd come there—dared to act as if he could possibly understand! "What do you know about right? You're even lower than I am from what I can tell."

"Be that as it may"—Fionvar's voice rose with a satisfying anger at last—"your mother deserves some respect from you; certainly more than you've given her lately."

"Who are you to tell me what to do?" He shook a finger

in the older man's face. "You're not my father! No matter how much you try to be!" His voice had grown shrill, echoing off the stone walls and ceiling.

For a moment, a change passed over the Lord Protector's face. If Wolfram's eyes could be credited, the bastard was going to laugh again. Just as quickly, the expression shifted to one of concern. With a sharp intake of breath, Wolfram realized that his mother had fainted, slumped back against Fionvar's chest.

The Lord Protector gathered up his queen and carried her gently to her bed, touching her wrists and forehead, her son forgotten.

The cold ache of the anger within him roiled and lurched, leaving a hollow place as he looked upon his mother's collapsed body. Wolfram shifted his attention to the man who bent over her. How many times had he carried her to that bed, the royal bed? The anger swelled again. He let out a little animal growl. When Fionvar glanced his way, Wolfram spat on the ground. He pivoted on his heel and crossed the room with pounding strides. He ducked beneath the tapestry and slammed the door behind him.

⚜

FIONVAR TURNED back to his queen. "Brie? Are you well?"

Brianna moaned, her eyelids fluttering open so she could behold her lover's face.

"Don't you agree that it's time to tell him at last?"

"Not now, Fionvar. I can't think about that now." She pressed a hand to her pale cheek. "Would you bring me some wine, something to steady my heart?"

He shook his head. "When can you think about it? Look at your son—he's confused, hurt, furious with both of us. He reminds me so much of—" Fionvar broke off, then tried a new tack. "I know it's making you sick the way he treats you."

"Wine," she insisted, pushing on his chest to get him to go.

His features hardened. "We should have told him years ago. He deserves to know the whole story."

"He deserves the walloping that Elyn is always offering, Fionvar. I can't control him anymore; the past few months, he's just gone wild."

"He was always wild, Brianna; you've just been too busy with the kingdom to notice."

"Well, and isn't the kingdom my first priority, what with these foreigners flooding the city? He's had the best nurses and tutors in the world, he's had you"—this elicited a snort from Fionvar—"and I've been here when I could, I haven't been distant or uncaring. I've tried to forget what Prince Alyn said of him. I've loved him as best I could, Fionvar."

"And hated him, too," he said quietly.

She turned her face away from him.

"I know," he whispered. "I know you've tried." Fionvar stood up and found the wine she had asked for. He settled beside her again, offering the silver goblet. "I'm sorry. You don't need me to attack you when he's already done an excellent job of that."

She accepted the goblet and sipped delicately.

"You know," Fionvar put in, smiling a little, "I wanted to faint, too, when he said that. I don't know whether to laugh or cry."

"Laugh," she said. "There hasn't been enough laughter around here."

Fionvar gazed down on her face. The years of her reign had etched their way into her forehead and cheeks, and the bloom of her lips had withered with age. Still, beneath the face of the queen, he could make out the features of the girl he'd fallen in love with so long ago. "Heart's Desire," he murmured, "I'll bring you bushels of laughter, if you tell me where it grows."

"I wish I knew." She sighed.

The Lord Protector smoothed the silvering hair back from her cheeks and lightly kissed her. She reached the goblet over to her bedside table and set it down to embrace him. "Come on, you adulterous bastard," she said, her eyes glinting so that the girl inside seemed suddenly released from the shackles of age. "If not laughter, at least we have love."

Kissing his queen, Fionvar thought briefly of the young man in the dark passages beneath them, fleeing the sin of his mother's love. He was everything like his father—if he only knew the truth.

Chapter 2

TAKING DEEP breaths, Wolfram huddled atop the altar in the great temple. His arms wrapped around his knees, and he rocked slowly in the gloom, gathering himself. Starlight shone faintly down upon him, gleaming on the dagger he had cast to the floor. He did not yet trust himself to retrieve it, but at least his anger was ebbing away. He thought of the pale figure of his mother collapsed into Fionvar's arms, and shuddered. She spent hours every day presiding over the court, and stayed late into the night, consulting with her ministers—and too much time between trying to school him in the ways of kingship, for the day his time would come. The day she died. Now, with streams of refugees fleeing war in the East, she looked older every day as she walked a path between charity and chaos. If only his father were still here, still exuding his mystic influence, perhaps creating another miracle every once in a while.

Wolfram bent his head back, looking up through the opening in the distant ceiling to the stars beyond, as if this could draw him closer to his father. He snorted. He would never be close to King Rhys, Strel Rhys—who promised mercy for his enemies, who flew through battle, and raised the dead when it suited him. Turning from the starlight, Wolfram rested his chin on his knees, gazing toward the curtain that enclosed an alcove in the outer wall. Beneath the curtain, a narrow band of light showed that Mistress Lyssa still worked. The steady plinking of her chisels soothed the angry pounding in his ears. He feared she would come out and find him there, but he did not move, staring now at the curtain that concealed her.

As if by the force of his will, the curtain parted, and a tall figure emerged, carrying a lantern. Backlit by the lights within, her silhouette seemed strange and foreign, the bald arc of her skull gleaming, her muscled shoulders and back rippling as she snuffed the lights.

She crossed quickly, at first on a diagonal toward the main door, then stopped her steady pace, head turned toward him. She raised the lantern, the planes of her face glowing as her lips curved into a rueful smile, and she changed course to approach the altar. As she drew near, he could make out the deep green of her eyes, the red of her brows arching in question. From the right eyebrow, a tattooed vine meandered in a tracery of blue lines back over her ear to dwindle down her neck.

"Hey, Wolfram," she called. "Didn't expect to find you here."

"Didn't expect so myself." He let out a breath he hadn't been aware of holding.

Then, at the base of the dais where the altar stood, Lyssa froze once more. The red eyebrows climbing, lips parted. "What have you done?"

"Oh, left my lover, given the queen a scare, frustrated the Lord Protector"—he shrugged—"the usual things."

"I meant your head, silly." She gestured, then climbed up and bent over him to see for herself.

On the steps and on the altar itself, the false blond locks lay about him, raggedly cut with the dagger to leave his hair spiky, tinged with red where he had nicked his ear. Wolfram looked away from her incredulous gaze. He shrugged again.

She stood over him a moment longer. "Move over."

He obliged, and she hopped up on the altar beside him, her split working skirt falling away to reveal her powerful legs clad in dark hose. Lyssa gathered a lock of the fallen hair, puzzling over it, waiting.

Breathing carefully, Wolfram felt the heat of her beside him, the brush of her bare arm against his as she reached up to pat his shorn head.

She let out a chuckle, tossing her head as if to cast back her own long-vanished hair. "Well?"

He glanced at her sidelong, eyeing the tight leather bodice she worked in, slowly raising his eyes to her face. "What color is my hair, Mistress?"

The tattooed vine at her brow curled downward as she frowned. "Blond." She flicked the clump of it between her fingers.

Wolfram shook his head, feeling an unaccustomed breeze along his scalp. "No, it's bleached. Every bath with that special soap. I've been using it since I started bathing myself." He uncrossed his arms and let his legs dangle, revealing a pale patch on his tunic. He rubbed his fingers across it as he spoke. "I washed this, just to see."

The last traces of mirth drained away from her face. "So, you tell me."

"That's just it, I don't know. I cut it all off, to see, when it grows back. In a few months, I'll know something I should have known years ago."

Lyssa nodded, less a confirmation than an encouragement to go on. When he didn't, but just kept staring down at the dagger among the blond hairs, she prompted. "Tell me everything."

At last, he did, the words tumbling out for her as they always had since he'd first hidden out in her temple years before. She listened gravely, not judging, not shaking her head at him, but with the sort of concentration she always gave to her work—as if he were blunt stone, and she could tease out the beauty within. As if he contained any beauty. With Lyssa paying such close attention, he wanted to be the hero of his own story, wanted to put himself in the right, but, even as he heard his own words, he saw the ruin he'd made of his mother's special possessions, and the expression on her face when she called him her only son. The hollow place within him returned. "I came in here," he finished, "so that I couldn't ruin anything else." He flicked a patch of his hair off the altar and watched it fall.

When he finished, they sat still for a long time.

"You know she loves you," Lyssa said at last.

He let out a half laugh. "Why else would she put up with me for so long?" This question trailed into a sigh. "Except I am the son of the blessed Rhys," he said bitterly.

Lyssa didn't answer, absently stroking her thigh with a clump of his hair.

Watching the gesture, he shivered. He dragged his eyes away, forced himself to look at her strong profile, the sleek line of her skull, bald as any priestess's. His gaze slid back toward the curtain she had emerged from.

Lyssa tilted her head in that direction. "Want to see?"

He nodded quickly.

She sprang down lithely from the altar, and he followed her across to the concealed alcove. Lyssa brought up the flames on the lanterns set about inside, lighting the little chapel. Given free rein for the project, she had imported lapis lazuli and malachite for slender columns and tiles inlaid with gold. The chapel was nearly done, but her workbench still dominated, holding a few chunks of pale pink marble and her well-kept tools. She turned one of the stones up to face them, her muscles flexing easily beneath the weight. A face emerged from the surface, a face that would one day support the entry arch to this family chapel.

Lyssa stroked her fingers along the nose and cheeks she had so carefully revealed, letting them linger at the turn of an ear where unruly tendrils of hair crept onto the face. Though not yet polished, the lips appeared ready to speak, the eyes about to blink against the settling of dust. It was a kind face, well formed, if not handsome in the classic way. "Wolfram," Lyssa said, and it took him a moment to realize she referred to the stone, not to himself. She glanced back to him. "This is your namesake, Prince Wolfram of Bernholt—as I remember him, anyhow." She smiled wistfully, tracing again the curve of the stone cheek, and Wolfram's throat ached a little, watching her.

Laying the carving back into the rubble of its creation, she raised the other stone, and he knew the face immediately, feeling his own features grow hard. It should have been like looking in a mirror, at least in some small way—the eyes perhaps, or the delicate nose, or the tremulous smile about to spread upon the lips. Instead, Wolfram's eyes were drawn to the curls upon the brow and tucked behind the roughed-out ears.

"Maybe now's not the time," Lyssa said, shifting her grip to lower it to the table.

Wolfram shook his head. "No, now's the perfect time. I've seen the portraits; this just makes it even more obvious that I'm nothing like him." He ruffled a hand over his remaining hair. "I must be some kind of family freak. I guess bleaching my hair was one way to make it seem as if I could follow in his footsteps, but it's a lie." The cold anger began to seep its way up his spine, and he gritted his teeth. He would not let it come, not here, not with Lyssa looking on.

She shook her head. "Rhys was human, too, Wolfram. He made mistakes and drove his grandmother mad when she was trying to teach him to be a king."

"So when I'm king, I'll suddenly be wise and kind and miraculous?"

"No, not that." She frowned at him. "Sometimes we forget the other parts, the human parts, when somebody's gone. We want them to be remembered as perfect, even if they were just like us."

"Yeah? I wish I was dead—like him." He thrust a finger at the stone face of King Rhys. "I wish I were in the stars, and everyone thought the best of me, too, if there is anything worth remembering." The demon anger sprang into him, full-grown and howling.

"You don't mean that, Wolfram."

"How do you know what I mean? Aren't you my friend? Aren't you supposed to listen to me?"

"Bury it, Wolfram, I am your friend. You're angry at your parents, and you're not thinking straight! You don't want to die."

He flung up his hands. "Maybe I do, if it's the only way to be like him, to finally make my mother happy."

"Don't be ridiculous! The Lady would give you pity, not glory for that. Besides, nobody would be happy if you died, Wolfram, least of all Brianna."

"Maybe I would be! Maybe I'd find my saintly father and tell him what I really think of him."

"Tell it to the stars, Wolfram."

He laughed. "You can't yell at a star. You can't beat it, and you can't make it hurt. If he had a grave someplace, at least I could spit on that."

"You dare speak heresy in the Lady's temple?" Her eyes were dangerously dark.

"Oh, of course, we bury criminals, not saints. Chances are, they'll bury me some day—even in death, I won't stand by my father."

"But he's not even dead," she howled into his face.

Wolfram stumbled back a step, fetching up against the table. "He's what?"

"Great Lady," Lyssa mumbled, "now I've put my foot in it."

"He's what?" Wolfram repeated, voice shaking.

"Rhys"—she sighed—"he's not dead."

"What are you talking about?" he breathed. "He was taken into the stars, directly, to the Lady." The anger that had sustained him threatened to let him collapse now, into some weak and crawling thing.

Lyssa shook her head sadly, frowning at herself. "It was magic," she said, "a trick; I don't know all the details."

Knees trembling, Wolfram grasped at that. "But you knew he was alive."

"Yes," she said. "Yes, me and a few other people. Your mother, Fionvar, Elyn—a few others, I guess." She spread her hands.

"I knew they lied to me—they have to—but you?" His tongue wet his suddenly dry lips, retreated into his parched mouth.

"I'm sorry, Wolfram, truly I am. It wasn't my choice."

"It wasn't? Every day I swept up your studio, every day you told me the story of the war—you didn't make a choice every single day, not to tell me my father lives?" He wanted to crush his pounding head between his hands, but he dared not move.

"It's complicated," she replied awkwardly.

"Oh!" he cried. "Oh, I bet it is, keeping the truth from me. Wait a minute!" he said theatrically, thrusting up one finger. "No, it's not hard, not if the one you're lying to is a trusting fool!"

"What can I say, Wolfram?" She took a step toward him, hands out, pleading. "I'm sorry, I really am. I know there's no way to make it up to you."

"Why would you want to?" he shot back. "Why make it up to me, why not just go up and laugh with your brother and the queen? Tell them how well you fooled me." He turned away, arms braced against the table. His chest ached so that he could hardly breathe, and his cherished dream, his star of love plunged into darkness with her every word. His father's stone face smirked up at him, compassion exchanged in an instant for cruelty. Alive!

"Listen to me, Wolfram." Lyssa's voice came low, still pleading.

"No! You listen." A terrible inspiration leapt to his pounding head. The sense of triumph ringing in his ears in a thousand goading voices. He could hurt her as deeply as she hurt him. "Listen to this." With both hands, and a strength almost beyond him, he pulled the stone head toward him, clutched it a moment to his breast and let it fall.

The finely worked stone crashed into tiles of malachite, shattering the swirling green, gold wire springing from the inlay like sharp spiderwebs. The sound echoed its earthquake in the tiny space.

The nose cracked and fell aside on impact, skittering across the floor to tap against the toe of Lyssa's boot.

Echoes reverberated in the temple and died away.

Stone dust disturbed from the table eddied about them, settling again in the quiet.

Wolfram's heart quaked. His hands dangled useless and treacherous at the ends of his wrists. He stared down at the back of his father's ruined head. She had betrayed his secret love; but what he had broken lay at the very center of her being, her own skill used in the dedication of the Lady.

Lyssa did not even tremble. Her powerful hands curled and uncurled at her sides. Her lips pressed together, breathing slow and normal. Over and over, her green eyes traced the shattered tiles, shying away from the instrument of their destruction.

"Lyssa," he whispered, when he regained his voice. "Great Lady, Lyssa, I—"

A hollow, heavy voice answered. "Go." Her lips formed the word with the precision of one of her chisels.

The sound shot through the last of his anger, sending the ragged shreds of it fleeing from him. "Lyssa." His voice close to cracking.

"Go," the dreadful voice repeated. "Now."

He sucked in a deep breath of the dusty air, and, coughing and sputtering, ran as far from her dead voice as he could.

Chapter 3

DRAINED AT last, Wolfram found his way back to his own chambers. As he wearily approached, trying to work out what to do, his manservant Erik dashed up to him.

Erik hovered, opening and closing his mouth several times, unsure what to make of his prince's disheveled appearance. "Ah, Your Highness," he began, blinking rapidly.

Worn-out from his rage, Wolfram couldn't muster his customary annoyance. "I know, I was out, I'm back now, I'm sorry."

"Ah, not that, Your Highness." His stubby legs worked hard to keep up with his master's long strides. "But, ah, thank you, Your Highness."

Wolfram pressed a hand to his forehead. The queen of all headaches was building just beneath the skin. "Then what?" Every motion of his jaw sent a shivering pain through the bone, as if he had been clenching it shut too long—or saying too much.

"Somebody's waiting, Your Highness. Ah, a—ah, a lady, Your Highness." His pale hands flapped through the air like plucked squabs trying to take flight.

"What now?" Wolfram groaned. He stopped before his oaken door, pressing both hands to his head to keep it from popping open and revealing the demon within.

"I, ah, I don't know." Erik hastened to add, "Your Highness. She came an hour ago, maybe more." Perpetual lines of worry tracked his pasty brow, and he whipped out a kerchief to mop the sweat from the wrinkles.

"Who?"

The servant risked a tiny shrug, a roll of the fleshy shoulders. Wolfram nodded once—a mistake. "Where?"

"The parlor, Your Highness."

No chance to prepare himself, he'd have to get by her to change. Straightening his shoulders, Wolfram pushed open the door, trying a mask of casual interest. It failed.

His lover waited inside, seated in his favorite chair by a crackling fire. She glanced up as the door opened, her lips curving into a smile at the sight of him—but not the broad, expectant look he had grown used to.

Then again, his own expression may have precluded any joy on her part. What little color he yet had seeped away, and he coughed again, sharply. "How did you—?"

She did not rise to greet him, but instead lifted his goblet from the table by her side, and took a sip. "How did I find you, Prince Wolfram?" She let out a peal of laughter. "You thought I had no idea, didn't you, my lord?" she added, in a light mockery of her usual subservient tone. When she spoke again, her voice rang with knowledge, power, and a chilling awareness. "I have always known who you were. You are not precisely anonymous, Your Highness." She looked him up and down, her ice-blue eyes sweeping from his mottled tunic to the butchery of his hair. "I take it you have confronted your mother?"

Wolfram shook himself, letting his unsteady feet lead him to a chair. Another lie, another liar he had trusted with his heart. "But what are you doing here? I thought I made everything clear."

"Oh, indeed you did, Your Highness, but you left before I had the chance to make things clear to you." She took another sip. The scent of her wine reached him, a very good vintage.

"Things? What things?"

"Well"—she toyed with the goblet—"one thing really. One very important thing." She met his eyes, her features sharp, as if the skull were closer to the surface and he saw right through her flesh. "I am carrying your child."

The breath rushed out of him, and his head dropped to his hands. "You're sure?"

"Of course I am, Highness."

He frowned briefly at her tone—almost smug. "I understand there are herbs, there are ways, to, well, get rid of it."

"Of our child?" She drew away from him. "You don't understand at all, Highness, I want to carry it. I want to give birth to your baby." Her voice curled around the word as if it were a succulent dessert.

He squeezed his eyes shut. It couldn't be happening, not all of this, not at once. He could not be having a baby. "What do you want?" He sighed. "I'll pay for the house, of course I will, and whatever you need."

"What do I want?" she echoed, and this time, he had to look up to see with disbelieving eyes the change that had come over her. No more the sweet and willing partner, the woman before him sat bolt upright, her voice commanding. "This, Your Highness." One hand swept the room with unmistakable strength. "I want this."

He searched desperately for his fury, but now, when he wanted it, that power escaped him. Too thunderstruck for words, he followed her gesture with wide eyes.

"Now, don't look that way." She patted his knee almost maternally. "This is a royal baby. This baby deserves some love from its father, and some attention from its loving grandmother, don't you think?"

Think? Wolfram had moved beyond thinking, into a shadow world where everyone around him concealed a secret, each more awful than the last.

"I want you to acknowledge this baby, Prince Wolfram."

"I can't marry you," he managed thickly.

"What, am I beneath your station, Highness?" She rose and cast off her cloak. She wore a gown of velvet and silk, vastly different from the woolens he had provided. The style seemed old-fashioned, the colors faded. "But I have been a princess, here in this very place." She held out the skirts of the gown, the gesture girlish, the glee in her face a thing beyond the innocence of girlhood. "This is the gown I wore when I left here; when your accursed saintly father threw me out." She enunciated these last words very clearly. "It amuses me to wear the same one now that I've returned."

She towered over the seated prince, eyes sparkling.

"I don't understand," he protested, watching her.

"Of course you don't, but I think your mother will. Why don't we go see her, and you can explain."

"Oh, no." He shook his head fiercely, despite the headache. "I can't go to her like this. You can't—who are you?" he demanded suddenly.

"A lifetime ago, I was betrothed to that other Wolfram. Ironic, isn't it?" She stood a little taller. "I am Princess Asenith yfEvaine duThorgir. Now there's a name you don't hear very often these days. Thorgir the Usurper was my father. He taught me everything I know." She leaned down, resting her hands on the arms of Wolfram's chair to stare into his face. "Your holy father killed my father but he let me live. If only he were here to rue the day."

Her breath, warm and rich with wine, made a shiver run down his spine. He imagined his mother's face, learning that her son not only had a lover but that his lover was the enemy, the daughter of traitors. But he would never see his mother's expression, he couldn't face her, not with this, his final failure. He studied Asenith up close, in a well-lit room for the first time. The mother of his child if all she said were true. Shame ran together with his anger, overwhelming his own pain and panic. Abruptly, he rose, forcing her back, and walked swiftly to his bedchamber.

"Wolfram!" she snapped, then followed. "You have to listen to me, Wolfram. This life is sacred, and half belongs to you." She pointed toward her belly.

"Good," he replied, "keep it." He pulled open his wardrobe and started piling clothes on the bed, gathering a few things on his arm.

"What are you doing?" Asenith's querulous voice pursued him. "I don't want your clothes."

"So give them away." He left the pile and shoved the few things in his arms into an emptied leather game bag.

"You're not leaving," she protested. "Not when you're going to be a father!"

He whirled to face her. "Yes, I am. My father left; I want to be just like him."

The confusion on her pinched features made him laugh, but she composed herself quickly. "What about the baby? You can't go like this."

He stuck a hand into his pouch and dropped something into her palm, closing her fingers around it. "So let it grow up to rule this cursed place."

Asenith's eyebrows notched upward at the glass locket in her hand.

"Show that to my mother; tell her everything." He shrugged widely, flopping his hands back to his sides. "Tell her whatever you want, I don't care." Wolfram turned back to packing, something like the mindlessness of his anger leading him through. He found his sword by the bedside, and Asenith jumped away from him, but he only swished the blade through the air, remembering how Lyssa's steady hands had taught him. He fastened the scabbard to his belt and slid the blade home.

Shouldering the bag, he turned toward the door to find Asenith in the way. "Move," he ordered.

At the tone, she flinched, but didn't budge from the doorway. "But I wanted—"

"You wanted revenge, you wanted the palace, you wanted to have my baby—well, good, you have it. Now move."

This time, she stepped aside, letting him brush past toward the door. "Wolfram," she called, a sudden warmth in her voice. He stopped, cocking his head, but did not turn to face her. "You were an excellent lover, Wolfram."

He snorted and left, knocking Erik out of his way as he followed the passage toward open air and freedom. Suddenly, the walls pressed on him, gloating, laughing, hiding secrets of their own, and he longed to break into a run. Seething, he mastered himself, pounding down the stairs, refusing to look to the Great

Hall where he'd danced, or the chamber where his mother slept (no doubt twined in her lover's arms), or the vast and glorious temple where Mistress Lyssa mourned her murdered creations. Let them mold his child as they failed to mold him; let the baby carry the weight of the legend of King Rhys; let the baby— please, Great Mother—let the baby not inherit the wrath that tore through him. Let it never be like him.

Wolfram slipped quietly out the little door he had used not long before. He hesitated a moment, not sure which way to go. It occurred to him that he ought to have a plan, a haven in mind. Maybe head over the mountains toward Bernholt. The passes should still be open—the days had been warm. He'd need a horse, though. Turning aside, he followed the quiet alley behind the houses down and toward the outer wall. The guard kept a stable by the western gate where he could snatch a horse without much trouble. In younger days, he and Dylan had plotted to escape their intrusive parents, sneaking the horses out through the western gate.

Paying little heed to secrecy, Wolfram quickly covered the ground and came to the bailey before the stables. A wall as high as his head surrounded the yard, and Wolfram narrowed his eyes, considering. The smell of horses drifted in the air around him, and they snorted and stamped just beyond the wall. The prince slid his bag to the ground, then froze—surely he'd heard something.

He spun, and found nobody there, but his shoulders tensed. The demon pricked his consciousness.

"Wait, Your Highness!" a voice called—Erik's voice.

Straightening from his half crouch, Wolfram turned toward his servant. "What are you—" A chain snapped over his head, around his throat, cutting off words even as it tore into his skin.

His hands flew first to his throat, then to the strong hands of his attacker, flailing. Pain shot through him. Where was Erik? Bury it, he couldn't see a thing.

His fingers slipped in his own blood, couldn't get hold of the wire. His head throbbed.

With sudden ferocity, Wolfram set his teeth and flung himself backward. He landed hard, feeling the crack of his opponent's head against the stones.

A wheezy curse. The hands slipped free.

Wolfram smacked his head against the downed man's nose with a satisfying crunch. Wildly, he fumbled for his dagger.

Suddenly a figure loomed over him—pudgy and pale, Erik's face swam into view. Wolfram heaved himself off his attacker, lunging forward even as the hilt of his blade came into his hand. Roaring filled his ears. Erik's hands reached toward him. Erik's lips moved, his face taut.

In one swift upward rip, Wolfram tore open Erik's belly. Gore spattered his face as he sprang back for another blow.

Even as he shifted his grip, he saw that one slash had done its work.

Voices echoed around him. Lights appeared at windows. Did someone call his name? Wolfram spun around, his pounding head and torn throat protesting. The two ends of the garrote bounced against his rigid shoulders.

A pack of Hemijrani surged up from where they'd been sleeping beyond the curve of the wall. Their shrill voices beat upon him, dark hands waving, pointing, cursing him with unknown signs.

From the other direction, the heavy bar on the gate scraped free. The guards inside called a halt.

Wolfram spun back to Erik. The mouth flapped stupidly as he died. His flabby hands pressed to the wound, struggling to staunch the unstoppable flow, to keep hold of his heaving innards. The servant's eyes rolled about, trying to focus on his master and failing.

Surely the hands had gone for his throat! He had seen a blade, hadn't he? Hadn't Erik cursed him as he came? Wolfram's head roared, his hands beat with the terrible pulse of his blood.

As the heavy gate swung open, the crowd of Hemijrani stumbled over themselves to flee, and Wolfram's legs, as if of their own accord, stumbled with them. He ran, feet pounding, flinging aside the filthy dagger.

Beside him, behind him, a high-pitched voice screamed.

Guards shouted; one of the refugees fell, and others turned back, yelling and pleading. More ran on, but Wolfram quickly out-stripped them in the familiar streets of his city. He let the demon take control, teeth and fists clenched. Suddenly his feet splashed into one of the culverts that flowed out beneath the city walls. Wolfram dashed to the wall and flung himself down in the muck, pulling himself under the bent and rusted grating.

Free of the wall, he sucked in a deep breath and gagged, hands to his throat, as the pain of the injury flared. Staggering, Wolfram made for the woods. By dawn he must be far away. If he kept running, the guards couldn't pursue him. If he only kept up his speed, surely he would leave the face behind, the pale face with its flapping mouth that howled with him into the night.

Chapter 4

BRIANNA GAZED at Fionvar across the little table in the salon adjoining her chambers. She took a succulent bite of plum and let the juice run down her fingers. One by one, she licked off her fingers with long sensuous pulls.

Pretending not to watch, Fionvar cracked the shell of a hard-boiled egg with the butt of his knife. A smile tugged at the cor-ner of his lips, however, and he let his eyes flicker up to meet hers. In the soft morning light, the shadows beneath her eyes faded, the fine lines smoothed into her glowing cheeks.

She slid her little finger between her lips and slowly drew it forth. Fionvar began to consider whether they could go back to bed for just a little while, but even as he wondered, there was a loud knock on the door, and it popped open.

"Your Majesty, Your Lordship," Lady Catherine said, bob-bing a little curtsy. "Lady here to see you." Catherine was a little

younger than her queen, and performed every task with remarkable direction and efficiency. She seemed to know what needed
doing even before Brianna could ask it. "She won't give a name,
Majesty," Catherine went on, anticipating the question. "Somewhat familiar, though." A frown pinched the handsome features.
"Says it's about the prince."

Brianna, seated with her back to the door, rolled her eyes
at Fionvar and offered a wry smile. She dried her fingers on a
cloth, and called over her shoulder, "Very well, Catherine, show
her in."

A rustling of skirts allowed the stranger entrance, and Fionvar
immediately rose to his feet. He still held the knife in his hand,
the naked blade thrust out.

Startled, Brianna, too, rose, clutching the edge of the table in
both hands.

Asenith drew herself up from a slight, but graceful curtsy. She
wore a long blue gown with silver trim and a demure veil over
her hair. Her smile and blush hinted at triumph and secrets, and
Fionvar gritted his teeth. Bury him if he'd greet her as any other
than the snake that she was.

"What do you want?"

"What, won't you offer me a seat, Lord Protector?" Her eyes
sparkled. One hand played with a pendant at her throat.

"You were banished from my domain, Asenith," Brianna replied coldly. Even as she did, though, Asenith's hand fell away,
and Brianna could see the wink of the glass and gold, the twist
of dark hair within. "Where did you get that?" she breathed, her
fingers twisting tighter into the cloth.

"Wolfram gave it to me. He said you would know it, Majesty."
She sneered around this last word.

Brianna sank back into her chair.

"When and why did you have cause to see the prince?" Fionvar snapped, his mind racing. Wolfram must have seen her last
night—purposefully gone to his mother's enemy with this evidence he did not even understand. But Asenith might. His chest
tightened as her sharp eyes sought his.

"Wolfram is my lover, sir, half a year since." She paused to let them understand this, then continued lightly. "He is the father of my child. Your grandchild." She nodded to the queen, but her eyes did not leave Fionvar's face.

Hard as he tried to steel himself to the blow, still it knocked the fire from him. "Won't you have a seat?" He sat heavily in his chair, the knife clattering to the table.

"This is a lie," Brianna said. "Your family is not famous for honesty."

"Nor is yours," Asenith answered. She helped herself to a custard tart from their abandoned breakfast. "Bring on anyone you wish, midwife, priestess, wizard." She scooted her seat toward the queen. "Or place your hand just here—" she caressed her belly—"and you can feel it growing in me."

Brianna stiffened. When she did not move, Fionvar reached for the handle of a silver bell and jangled it.

Lady Catherine instantly appeared from the inner chamber and curtsied.

"Fetch Strelana here, and quickly," Fionvar ordered.

Catherine curtsied again, and exited swiftly.

"Even if it were true," Brianna said, "how would we know it's his child?"

"Wolfram did not think otherwise, Majesty. May I call you Brianna? After all, I am practically part of the family."

"What does he know of such things? Clearly he was taken in by your deceit."

Sighing, Asenith settled back in her chair, fingering the pendant. "Paternity is such a difficult issue, it's true." Her features formed a thoughtful air, but the glinting eyes turned again to Fionvar. "Of course, with his father being so special, no doubt Wolfram, too, is possessed of some little miracles of wisdom."

Brianna sprang from her chair and crossed to the far window, leaning into the frame to watch the garden. Fionvar, with a glance toward Asenith, followed, moving to stand beside the queen though he did not touch her.

"What has the little fool gotten us into?" Brianna murmured. "Am I so terrible that he needed this revenge?"

"We don't know that. We don't know anything for sure, not

yet. Let Strelana examine her, then we can get Wolfram down here and listen to his side."

"His side? He has been sleeping with the Usurper's daughter! He should have known better than to father himself a bastard, never mind with her. Oh, yes, I'll get him down here, but listening will not be the first thing on my mind." Crimson suffused her flesh and her fingers, recently so sensuous, now tightened on the windowpane as if she'd carve through it with her nails.

"He's wild, Brianna, you've said so yourself, but I don't think he's stupid, and I don't think he's so bent on revenge that he'd go this far to get it." Now he pressed his hand over hers. "Not that he hasn't put us in a very tight place."

Behind them, the door swung open, and Catherine cleared her throat. The pair turned to find Strelana the Healer awaiting their command, head bowed, eyes flicking back from a surreptitious view of Asenith. The former princess picked her way through the bowl of fruit, evidently unconcerned.

"Bring my son, would you, Catherine?" Brianna gestured for Strelana to rise and approach. "This—lady—thinks that she is with child. Would you please determine the truth of the matter?" Her voice rang with regal authority bordering on arrogance.

Strelana curtsied to Asenith. "My lady," she said, "I'll need to touch you."

"Of course," Asenith replied graciously. She parted the lacing at the side of her gown and let the old woman slip her hands beneath the cloth. Frowning, Strelana pressed her gentle hands to the other woman's flesh, letting the fingers creep about with cautious prodding.

At last, she nodded. "The lady is correct. About three months, I'd say."

Brianna blanched, then quickly turned away. Fionvar nodded back to the healer. "We would ask for your discretion in this, Strelana," he said carefully.

Her eyebrows twitched, but she curtsied. "Of course, my lord."

When Strelana opened the door, Lady Catherine barreled into her, both women stumbling back, breathless. Strelana edged by, and Catherine entered, her face as white as the queen's. On her heels came Gwythym DuLarce, Captain of the Guard. His skin was gray, eyes red, hands shaking as he bowed. He clenched one fist around his sword hilt to try to regain some measure of control.

"Your Majesty," Catherine began, gasping in a breath, "I found him on his way from the prince's."

"What's happened?" Brianna looked from one to the other, and her hand reached out blindly beside her.

Fionvar squeezed the searching fingers in his.

Gwythym gulped and swallowed, lowering his eyes. "The prince is gone, Your Majesty. Early this morning. His manservant, Erik, is dead, and my son, Dylan—" He swallowed again, tongue darting out to dampen dry lips.

"Great Lady, not Dylan!"

"He's breathing, but he's not opened his eyes." Gwythym shut his own, wincing as he tried to master his breathing.

Releasing Brianna, Fionvar crossed to his friend and took him by the shoulders, gazing on the bowed head, red hair streaked with gray. Asenith shifted back in her chair, trying to look inconspicuous, but Fionvar glared at her. "Catherine, take this lady to a chamber and set guards to watch her there."

Asenith glared right back. "Last night, I stayed in Wolfram's rooms; besides, I have a stake in this as much as any of you." She cupped a hand over her stomach.

"Catherine, get her out," Fionvar growled, and the lady hurried to obey.

Catherine took Asenith's arm firmly, hauling her for the door. At first, she tried to resist, then allowed herself to be tugged into the hall and gathered her skirts in one hand, thrusting her chin up as if it were she who insisted on going.

"Sit down, Gwythym, tell us all." Fionvar gently guided him to a chair and poured out some water for the captain.

Behind him, Brianna came out of her shock to settle back in her chair, pushing away the plate of food. She focused her attention on the captain as well.

After taking a long swallow, Gwythym began. "A few hours

ago, a man came up to me from the western gate. The garrison had been roused by a fight outside, and mustered quickly. They found a rowdy group of refugees and two bodies. My men fought to subdue the easterners, but they were already running away. A few stayed to fight. In the dark, it must've been chaos. When they brought out enough torches, they found Erik there dead, and Dylan among the injured." As he reported to his commander the tremors left his voice, and he straightened. "We lost two men, four wounded."

"What of the refugees?" Brianna prompted.

"Five down, six wounded. They're in the infirmary."

The queen shook her head, and sighed. "Go on. Tell us about Wolfram."

"Seemed odd to find Erik and Dylan there without the prince, Majesty, so we sent up to his chambers. That lady answered. Said he'd gone out with the servant, and she hadn't seen him." Gwythym reddened. "Should've told you then, I suppose, Your Majesty, since—" He broke off.

"Tell me everything, Gwythym. It can hardly be worse than we've had already."

"Well, why'd he go looking for company if he'd already got this lady in his room, that's what I wondered. Must've been some other reason. I didn't worry though, since—" he broke again, shrugged, and went on—"it's like him to be impulsive, begging your pardon, Your Majesty. Wouldn't be the first time I had to bring him in."

Brianna frowned. "I don't recall hearing about this, Captain."

His face reddened further and he shifted uncomfortably. "Some things a young man would just as soon his mother not know, Majesty, even a prince."

"After you've done here, perhaps you'd better tell me about those things."

He glanced to Fionvar but nodded once. "We started to search the city, Majesty, all his places. Anywhere Dylan or Erik might've left him. No sign, not anywhere. We got a chance to ask the injured men this morning, and one of them said he thought he'd seen the prince, just a glimpse mind you, before the battle.

Long and the short of it is"—he met Brianna's gaze without flinching—"either he's gone off with the refugees, or they've taken him and fought to cover themselves."

"Oh my Holy Mother," Fionvar breathed.

"You're saying you think the prince has been kidnapped? To what end?"

"Money, sanctuary?" Gwythym took another swallow of water and shrugged again. "They've been asking your intervention, Majesty, perhaps they thought this'd make sure of it."

"Bury it," she snapped. "What proof? What've we got?"

"Well, we're looking for the refugees from last night, and we've just got an interpreter to talk to these ones in the infirmary. I'm sorry I waited so long to tell you. I just . . ." He slumped in the chair.

"You didn't want to tell us the prince was gone," Fionvar supplied quietly.

Gwythym nodded miserably. "Might as well turn in my badge, Fion."

"How's Dylan?"

"He went down early in the fighting, got trampled, mostly. They say he'll pull through. Erik though—" Gwythym shuddered suddenly.

Fionvar and Brianna waited.

"Some monster left him gutted like a fish, begging your pardon. Most terrible thing I've ever seen." His voice died away, remembering.

Fionvar put a hand over Brianna's, stilling its trembling. The queen whispered, "And these people have my son."

Chapter 5

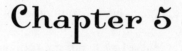

LYSSA KNELT on the floor of her little chapel, carefully scraping away the ruined patch of tiles. She worked in studious silence, her entire being focused on the task. Not far away, the cracked bust of King Rhys lay on the floor beneath a cloth. She had moved it aside but did not lift it from the floor, as if letting it lie in state.

"Lyssa."

She flinched, dropping the fine chisel, and turned her head to glower at Fionvar. "Don't surprise me like that."

He frowned. "I said your name three times, Lyssa; is something the matter?"

She gazed up at her brother, whose dark eyes seemed a few shades darker than they had been. "I think I should be asking you that question." She rose, wiping the dust from her hands upon her work apron.

Fionvar took her place on the floor, touching the bare patch where she had removed the broken tiles and filigree. "Was it the refugees? They've been hanging about the temple lately." His eyes lit upon the covered sculpture, and he twitched aside the cloth to study the damaged face. Suddenly he sprang up, hands balling into fists. "It was that Asenith, wasn't it?"

"Who?" Lyssa frowned her puzzlement.

"Who else would have so much against . . ." he trailed off, looking down at the face again.

"I can name one, Fion."

His shoulders fell. "Oh, Lyssa, we've made a mess of it, haven't we?"

"Some of us have, anyhow." She sighed.

He jerked as if she'd struck him.

Quickly, she touched his shoulder. "I didn't mean you, Fion. Last night, he came to talk to me and—" She broke off, eyes narrowing. "Wait a minute, why did you come down here? Something's happened."

"It's Wolfram," Fionvar began, but she cut him off.

"He's run away, hasn't he? Bury it!" she exploded, pounding a fist on the table.

Fionvar shook his head. "Kidnapped," he blurted, "early this morning."

Lyssa froze. "Kidnapped? But I—" Again, she broke off, considering. "Tell me everything."

Fionvar told her in a rush of words all that they knew—the refugees who had been spotted, then vanished, the terrible death of the prince's manservant, his own visit to the quiet room where Dylan had still not awakened. Lyssa leaned against the workbench, listening, watching Fionvar pace the tiny space behind the curtain. He didn't need to know what she had said to Wolfram; it had become meaningless beside the greater tragedy. Even as that little fear was soothed, the weight of what he said flowed over her. The crown prince—the only heir—missing, presumably at the hands of this band of foreigners. Perhaps he had meant to go, been followed by his friend and servant before being carried off. Perhaps it was not she herself who had destroyed him.

It took her a long while to realize that Fionvar had fallen silent, and stood, eyeing her suspiciously. "Why did you think he might have run away?"

Lyssa gave her one-shouldered shrug. "He was furious with both of you."

"He generally is. It would have to be more than that."

She gestured to the fallen statue. "He cut off his hair, Fionvar, and we fought. With this on top of everything, it seemed likely he'd want to escape."

"He can't escape from everything," Fionvar growled.

"Out with it, Fion. What haven't you said?"

"Wolfram had a lover, Lyssa; she's here at the castle."

"He said he'd left her."

"Not far enough. The woman is with child."

"Great Lady! I suppose it was bound to happen, but—"

"Bound to, you say? I take it you've known about her for some time, then, sister." Fionvar folded his arms across his chest, staring her down. "But wait, I haven't told you the best—or do you already know?"

"Wolfram is my friend. If he wants to keep secrets from you, who am I to reveal them?" She met his steely gaze.

"Asenith," Fionvar said simply, watching for a change in her face, but the name meant nothing to her. "His lover was the former princess Asenith yfEvaine duThorgir."

"I knew we should have killed them all." She smacked her fist into her palm.

"Harsh words for one of the Goddess," Fionvar observed.

Lyssa shrugged again. "We were at war, there were crimes to be redressed. Remember when that Faedre tried to kill the king? She and Asenith were tight at the end. We'd no evidence, of course, but I tend to doubt the little bitch was innocent!"

"She certainly isn't now, Lyssa, she's been knocked up by my—" His face froze a moment, and he finished more quietly, "my prince."

Just for a moment, she saw the anguish on his face, then his eyes snapped away, lips set—the Lord Protector once more. "There's no one to hear, Fionvar," she offered, quietly. "Say what you will to me."

He let out a long breath, arms crossed a little tighter to hold himself in. "It's disaster all over again, Lyssa. I can see it happening, and I can't do a thing."

"Say it, Fionvar," Lyssa urged. "It isn't disaster you're afraid of, big brother." She hesitated a moment, but he did not look up. "It's Orie."

A shudder ran through Fionvar's body. "Brianna won't let me talk to Wolfram the way I need to, the way he needs. Elyn spoils him with one hand and slaps him with the other. And every year, every day, he gets more and more angry. It's like he's trying to live out Prince Alyn's curse. Great Lady, I don't know what to do."

Lyssa straightened. "The first thing is to find him and bring him home." She swept a dagger from her belt, clutching the blade in her left hand.

Fionvar's chin shot up, as Lyssa squeezed her fist tighter. Blood dripped down the metal onto the floor.

"By the blood in my body, Fionvar, I swear to you that I will bring him home." She drew the dagger from the sheath of her flesh and pressed her bloody palm to the gap in the floor. "Let this work remain undone until I have fulfilled my oath. Nothing, and no one, will stand in my way." Her eyes gleamed with emerald fire.

"I do not want to lose you, Lyssa, not like the rest."

She smiled grimly. "But I am not like the rest, Fionvar. I am a lady of the Goddess, I am a Sister of the Sword, and I am sworn to find your son"—she met his shadowed eyes, and repeated—"*your* son, and bring him home. When he gets home, you'll tell him the truth, all of it."

"As I should have done years ago."

Lyssa began to gather up her tools, laying them out neatly on the workbench, covering the lot with a drop cloth. She glanced down to the covered bust but let it stay.

"Where will you go?"

"The infirmary first, and the west gate. After that, to find the refugees." She paused, gazing into the distance. "Across the mountains, or the ocean—all the way to Hemijrai, if that's where he is." To Bernholt first, she thought, in case they were wrong, in case Wolfram were tracking the legend of King Rhys, and their web of lies could lead him there.

EXHAUSTED, HEAD and neck throbbing, Wolfram slowly rose to consciousness. Something damp and dark lay over his head—cold upon the heat within. His palms and knees stung, and he vaguely recalled staggering into the trees, falling more than once, and a final tumble down a rocky slope. As he shifted, the bruises on his back and legs, too, cried out, and he winced. Branches were poking into his shoulders. For a moment, he thought he lay in the gully where he'd fallen. He wriggled his fingers carefully about, and found that the branches beneath him were padded with animal hides of some sort. He raised a hand to his face and pushed aside the cloth over his eyes. More darkness, and a pale, looming shape, its mouth flapping, its guts—

Wolfram screamed and bolted upright.

Hands seized his shoulders, and the figure swam into view. Enough light seeped in around an unseen door that he could make out the rough features, the moving lips, and finally he noted the harsh voice that tried to mold itself into soothing sounds.

Wolfram frowned. Had he knocked his head? He didn't remember—but then, he wouldn't, would he? He focused again on the figure, struggling to make out what it was saying, but he couldn't understand a word of it. Whoever it was backed away and flung aside a flap, letting sunlight stream in.

Blocking his eyes with his hand, Wolfram faced away until he'd grown used to light again. Then he turned to the figure.

The woman, her dark hair braided and falling over her shoulder, smiled. She pressed a palm to her forehead, then to his. She was one of the Woodfolk, the nomads who hunted in the mountains between Lochalyn and Bernholt, and wore a shapeless garment made from leather, with a necklace and belt of beads. She called out the doorway and came back to kneel beside him on the dirt floor.

The hut appeared much larger when she'd settled again. Another pile of branches and hides lay on the other side of a fire pit lined with stones, and several leather bags jumbled together by the doorway. A bow and quiver of arrows fletched with hawk feathers hung from the interlaced branches of the ceiling.

The woman reached out and removed the cloth from Wolfram's forehead, still smiling. Tentatively, Wolfram smiled back. "Thank you," he tried, his voice barely escaping the band of pain about his throat. He touched his neck gingerly. Another cloth wrapped the wound, and his fingers came away smelling of herbs and animal grease.

"You speaking tongue no?" She managed to ask, watching him expectantly. Her face and hands were deeply tanned, her teeth chipped and stained, but she was younger than he'd thought at first.

"Do I speak your language?" Wolfram interpreted. He shook his head, but quickly thought better of it when the pain snapped through him. "No."

She lost her smile momentarily. A shadow crossed the light of the door as a tall man stooped to enter. He and the woman touched each other's foreheads, then he squatted beside her, glowering at Wolfram.

"You are from stone place?"

"Thank the Lady!" Wolfram brightened at hearing his own language. "Yes, from the city, but—" He broke off, considering what to tell them.

"But leaving?" the large man supplied, rubbing his finger on his scarred chin.

"Ah, yes. There are people who would kill me," he finished lamely.

The man grunted. He spoke a few words of their growly language, and the woman answered at length, with many sweeping gestures and an animation of expression that let Wolfram follow the whole story of how she had found him and brought him here to tend his wounds.

The conversation turned quickly to argument, both of them pointing at Wolfram, shouting across the few inches between them. The man slapped a hand to his own throat, his voice a roar, as he jerked upward.

Wolfram realized the man thought he had been hanged. Again, he shook his head, and quickly regretted it. "Excuse me," he said, but the argument rolled over his interruption. "Shut up!" he shouted, thrusting his arm between them.

Both turned to stare, the man glaring in fury.

"I'm not a criminal," he protested. "Somebody tried to kill me."

The woman cocked her head, then, when he gestured to his neck, she seemed to understand. She reached into the empty fire pit, and brought something out of the ashes, shaking it off, and holding it up for the man's inspection. The thin chain glinted dully in the sunlight except where ashes still clung to Wolfram's blood.

This gave the man a moment's pause. He took it between his fingers, turning it this way and that. The delicate golden chain had a large knob of lead on either end, providing a grip for his would-be murderer.

Wolfram shivered, then let out a little ironic grin. At least the bastard had tried to kill his prince with gold, not some base metal or tradesman's twine. Actually, with that chain, his attacker should have had his head off before he could even struggle. He must be quicker on his feet than even he knew.

The woman gestured then to the sky and spoke more quietly.

Eyebrows leaping, the man looked from her to Wolfram and back, his craggy face breaking into a grin.

"Can you please tell me what she says?" Wolfram pleaded, certain these two were deciding his fate.

"Last Fishing Moon, her man die, in that place where she find you. Two years together, and he gives her no baby. No man of our people would have her." The man let out a thunderous laugh. "She think you her new man, give from spirits, to show she worthy."

Wolfram smiled his surprise. "The spirits did not deliver me in good condition."

The woman asked an eager question, and the man replied, gesturing to Wolfram's injuries.

She shrugged.

"What's her name?"

"She called 'Morra.'"

Understanding this, the woman grinned, starting off a wave of excited chatter.

Wolfram waved her into silence. "Morra," he said politely, "I'm Wolfram."

"Wolf Runs?" she echoed in puzzlement.

"Close enough." He turned back to the man. "And you are?"

"Gorn, Great Hunter. Morra is—" he frowned over the word—"sister."

Eyeing the thick features and bushy brows of the Great Hunter, Wolfram muttered, "No family resemblance, thank the Lady."

"You say?"

"Nothing important. Look, I'm starved." He patted his stomach. "Can I get something to eat?"

Morra immediately scrambled up and slipped from the hut.

Once she had gone, Gorn leaned in close to Wolfram. "You from spirits?"

Wolfram considered how to answer this. His only thought last night—or had it been several nights since then?—had been to get out, away, someplace where he could do no more harm. Perhaps this woman's "spirits" had brought him here. Castle folk rarely had dealings with the Woodfolk, and he knew enough about them to know they traveled frequently, packing up their few possessions and trekking miles into the wilderness, far from the reach of Lochalyn's queen, or its justice. He had killed a man, brutally and knowingly, and even a prince could not completely escape a charge of murder. He needed a refuge, a place to heal, plan, and rest. She needed a man, preferably a baby, to appease the tribe. It could be the spirits brought him to her after all. "I don't know," he answered at last, "but will you let me stay until I am sure?"

Gorn leaned back again, rocking slightly, rubbing the tangle of scars on his chin.

Morra ducked inside, carrying a leather skin full of water and the haunch of some small animal, still sizzling from an outdoor fire. She knelt at Wolfram's side, her face downcast as she offered the food.

Wolfram caught her hand along with the meat and flashed his best smile. "Thank you, Morra," he said, "for everything." He gently kissed her callused hand.

Tugging away, she pressed her hands to her face and giggled, watching him curiously. She asked something of Gorn, and he grunted in return, never taking his eyes from Wolfram's face.

"Stay," Gorn said at last, grudgingly. "Five moons," he held up his fingers to demonstrate, emphasizing the point in their language to his sister, who nodded eagerly. "Five moons is Spirit Moon, is gather clans for—" His words failed him, and he shook his shaggy head. "Ask spirits then, if stay longer."

Wildly, Morra grabbed her brother's hand, pressing the back of it to her forehead, head bowed in some ritual gesture. Gorn growled and shook her off, snatching the waterskin from Wolfram and taking a long swallow.

Between bites of meat, greedily lapping the juices from his fingers, Wolfram learned that he had been unconscious for two days. Their encampment had been about to move for the winter, and Morra had had to stay behind to care for her injured prize. Gorn, too, had remained, since she could not be left alone, but he hoped to catch up with their tribe very soon—he glowered at Wolfram as if daring him to lapse back into fever. Once they could travel, they would move west, through the foothills and up, crossing over the saddle that joined two spurs of the mountains and down to the plateau where they would make their winter camp. He used broad gestures to describe the length of the journey, the difficulty of the mountains, and the hardship of life on the plateau.

Through it all, Morra laughed and shook her head, patiently explaining to Wolfram with her mobile face and hands, that Gorn exaggerated everything. He thought she meant to say her brother was jealous, as he seemed to have no partner of his own. Finally, Gorn threw up his hands and left them.

Morra called something after him, then turned back to her new man. Wolfram studied her in the slanting light. She would be no beauty in his mother's court, but hers seemed an open face, her features round and full where Asenith's had been sharp and probing. Besides, hadn't the spirits brought him to the very place where her husband had been lost, where she had gone to pay homage to him before they broke camp? Mistress Lyssa would have seen the hand of Finistrel in that. But Mistress Lyssa wouldn't know. His heart ached suddenly in his chest, and Morra touched his brow in concern.

He looked up into her dark eyes, noting the flecks of gold that glittered in them. Impulsively, he reached for her and kissed her.

Laughing and frowning simultaneously, she broke away, sitting back on her heels. If not kissing, how did these people express their affection? How would he convince her and her family that it was meant to be, that his only wish was to go with them, to be a part of this tribe? Cautiously, he reached out for her hand. As he had seen her do, he drew her hand close, bowing his head over it until the warmth of her skin, the knobs of her knuckles pressed against his brow.

For a moment, she did not move, then, with a tiny cry, she sprang closer to him, gathering him against her breast. He could feel hot tears dropping onto his scalp through the remnants of his hair.

Wolfram could not say what he had done, but clearly, it had been the right thing. Two days later, rested and in high spirits, he shouldered a bundle of hides and followed Gorn and Morra into the mountains, turning his back on Lochalyn, perhaps forever.

Chapter 6

"STEADY THERE," Fionvar said, placing a guiding hand on Dylan's elbow as they crossed the rough ground.

The young man nodded up at him, blue eyes visible above a swatch of bandages. Fionvar felt a twinge as he looked at him. It was too soon—the boy should still be in bed. And yet with Wolfram missing these five days, and no clues to follow, Dylan was their best chance. An awfully slim one, even then.

Gwythym led the way slowly, often glancing back with obvious concern. They worked their way through the narrow streets and down a flight of stairs toward the outer temple wall. There, a small gate led outside to the funeral ground with the broad stone slab where cremations were held. Beyond that, around the curved wall of the temple, lay the refugee camp.

As they crossed the ground, Fionvar looked off to the distant woods. A long time ago, King Rhys had burst from those trees on a borrowed warhorse, leading the charge that regained his kingdom. Rhys and his few companions—Lyssa among them—had come not for battle but to save the life of Jordan, the Wizard's Bane who had once been Rhys's tutor. Fionvar wished he could have seen it. If he had been there for the Charge of Miracles, as the common folk now called it, he would not have been witness to his brother Orie's transformation from man to wizard . . . and madman. In using his magic to murder the Prince of Bernholt, Orie had doomed himself to madness. Rendered helpless by that same magic, Fionvar could only watch the prince die. He dreamed of it sometimes, recalling both the horror and the wonder. From the prince's own diary, Fionvar had learned that Wolfram of Bernholt had known the fate that awaited him, and from the expression in his face as he had died, he had not feared it. It had taken a little doing to convince Brianna to name their son for a foreign prince, but Fionvar had rarely been so serious about anything in his life. The dead prince of Bernholt was as wise and kind as the living prince of Lochalyn was not—but Fionvar still held on to his hopes. Wolfram was his son, what could he do, if not hope?

Also in those woods, Fionvar had met the Hurim—the Woodfolk, as most called them—for the first time, in the person of a man named Quinan, a shaman of his people, and friend to the prince of Bernholt. Quinan had been entrusted with that diary and had given it to Fionvar as the prince's last friend. After Orie's death, and their long wait in Bernholt for King Rhys to recover from his injuries, Fionvar had given the diary to Wolfram's sister, Melisande. He had written out a copy for himself, which he flipped through when he was in need of wisdom. He imagined himself speaking to the dead prince, asking him questions, finding the answers as if by magic in the pages of the diary. It had become his oracle, and the one thing he kept private even from Brianna, his queen-lover. He wished it could tell him where to find his son.

The small party entered the makeshift courtyard of the refugees' village. On all sides, the Hemijrani had erected tents of poles and brightly colored fabrics—many of them the veils and wrappings of their women. From the fires before these tents rose exotic scents of cloves and cinnamon, though the beasts they cooked were squirrels and rabbits. From one pot, Fionvar thought he glimpsed the tails of rats protruding, and he quickly turned back to his charge. The dark inhabitants of the camp scattered before them; the few women turned their faces away, and the men retreated, heads bowed. In this sea of dark-skinned, bowing figures one woman stood conspicuously tall, making her way back toward the gate.

"You!" Fionvar shouted. He crossed toward her in long strides, leaving Dylan with his father. "What are you doing here?"

"I don't see that my business concerns you, Lord Protector," Asenith answered, starting to brush by.

Fionvar caught her elbow and spun her toward him, her face looming dangerously near. He could see the age lines she sought to hide with powders and paints—she looked like an artwork in need of restoration. At least the child would be beautiful. "I am the Lord Protector, as you say, my lady," he said, giving her a smile, "and you may be carrying the future heir to the kingdom. That makes your safety my business. What are you doing here, and where are the guards assigned to defend you?"

"Defend me?" She jerked away. "Spy on me is what you had in mind! It didn't take much to addle them, did it? And I'll thank you to keep your hands off me!"

"Considering your recent occupation, my lady, I can't imagine you have much objection to being touched." A sound beside him distracted him, and he found that Dylan had come up, his mouth curled into a frown beneath the bandages. "Sorry," said Fionvar, "I thought Gwythym was with you."

Bandages muffled Dylan's voice, giving it a nasal whine. "Better things to do, I guess."

"Fare you well, sir," Asenith spat, gathering her skirts to sprint out of reach.

Nearly colliding with Asenith, Gwythym trotted up, hand on his sword, his face red. "Thought I'd lost you, lad. All over again."

"Bury it," Fionvar muttered, watching Asenith's escape. He turned to look where she'd come from, but could see no difference between those tents and any others, except that area looked even more dirty. He recalled his sister's remarks, linking Asenith with her old friend Faedre, a native of Hemijrai herself. Faedre had escaped justice for her attempt upon their king, and none knew where she'd gone after that. Fionvar shook off the past and studied the present. A group of men squatted outside a small, well-made pavilion, dirty hands dangling toward their laps as if they had tried farming recently. One of them even held a small shovel. What if they had been burying their dead? Fionvar didn't mind the refugees sheltering so close to the funeral ground; after all, the Lady's mercy and kindness should extend to them as well, but they shouldn't be profaning Finistrel with burials so close to Her temple. "I need to talk to these men, Gwythym, I'll be right back."

Fionvar started purposefully toward them, but the little group scrambled away, bowing their heads. He pursued them through the twisting lanes of tents until he came up against the curtains closing off a large area. Women's voices could be heard within. They had built a special place for the women, protected by a row of armed and dangerous-looking men. Fionvar nodded to them, and they stared back with an insolence he found disturbing in a displaced people. Quietly, he took his leave.

When he had returned to Gwythym and his son, he found them exchanging greetings with a small, lithe Hemijrani. The clothes he wore were faded but of fine fabrics, and the tattoos on his feet formed the intricate patterns reserved to priests. He turned toward Fionvar as he approached, revealing sharp features, the flash of gold in his smile as he bowed over his hands. His long hair was piled atop his head in a style more suited to women, but held in place with slender knives. The medallion at his neck showed their god and goddess entwined in love, and Fionvar winced, averting his eyes from the heathen display. He recalled the man from one of Brianna's recent courts.

"Greetings and greetings again, good sir," the Hemijrani called, tucking the medallion under the crossed wrappings of his clothes. "I would be Ghiva, and would be the representative of my people here in your great country."

"Oh, would you?" Fionvar folded his arms, gratified by the small man's hesitation. "Then would you explain why your people have been digging here?"

Ghiva blinked, his hands still pressed together, fingers to wrists. "Digging."

"Shovels, dirt—digging! If they have been—" Fionvar sought a way to say it that wasn't a curse—"if they have interred any . . . remains, I'll have to throw the lot of you into the dungeon, you know that."

"I believe it is burials that you mean."

Fionvar and Gwythym made the sign of the Lady.

"But we do not bury our dead," he continued, apparently oblivious to their distaste. "They would be enshrouded and left for the vultures; I have seen vultures here, so this is not a problem, this ritual of ours." He smiled again, showing his gold incisor.

Gwythym and Fionvar exchanged a look. "We don't speak of that here."

"You do not speak of burial." They flinched. "Then you will please forgive me, for I sought only to soothe what I anticipated was your concern."

"Only one of our concerns," Gwythym growled. "We're looking for Crown Prince Wolfram. Have any of your people seen him?"

"I have heard that he has left the city, but I do not know that any of us shall have seen him go. I have been visiting your infirmary and spoken with our wounded there, as I am sure you will recall, sir," Ghiva said, inclining his head toward Fionvar.

"Yes, I do. We need to ask some questions, and we'd rather do so without bringing in the guard, do I make myself clear?"

Losing his smile, Ghiva nodded vigorously. "We are here only on your sufferance and the generosity of your queen, may the Two defend her. Of course I will be happy to assist you in any way. You will be needing a translator for instance, sirs."

"Are you ready for this?" Fionvar asked Dylan, who shrugged.

"I've not been practicing long; you should get someone more experienced."

Gwythym patted his shoulder. "You'll do fine, lad. And we're hoping the sight of you might shake loose some secrets."

"This is Dylan DuGwythym, who was injured in the fight by the gate. He also happens to be a wizard—"

"In training!" Dylan modified quickly.

"In training," Fionvar allowed. "Your people will need to ask him a question, to allow themselves to have a small spell cast on them. If they lie to us, Dylan will know."

Ghiva rubbed his amulet beneath the cloth which concealed it. "I do not know if they will submit themselves in this way. Many of us are apprehensive about your magic, and I believe that this fear is justified, sir."

"They will have your example to follow—"

"My lord," Dylan said, tapping Fionvar's arm.

Fionvar gave him a pointed look.

"I haven't cast the spell—he hasn't asked any questions." Dylan spread his hands in a helpless gesture.

"But he—" He faced the little man. "Ghiva, what do you know about our magic?"

"I am sure that I am ignorant, good sir, being a foreigner and a humble man."

"In order to cast a spell on someone, the wizard must have an invitation, as it were. The person has to be open to receiving magic, he has to ask a question of the wizard. Since we've been standing here, you've made several inquiries without actually asking a question. That makes me suspicious, Ghiva."

Putting up his hands, Ghiva said, "It is a habit of speech only, sirs. What would you have me ask?"

"That will do." Fionvar raised his eyebrows at Dylan, who mumbled a few words, then nodded. "So, Ghiva, I ask you again, have you seen Prince Wolfram?"

"I have not."

"Do you have any knowledge of his whereabouts?"

"I fear that I do not, much as I would wish to assist you directly, sir."

"Did any of your countrymen have any part in his disappearance?"

"Not that I am aware of." Ghiva stood carefully under their scrutiny, appearing at ease, and eager.

"Dylan?"

The young man hesitated. "He hasn't lied to you, my lord."

"You don't look convinced."

"I felt something ... strange, on that last answer." He lifted his hand to rub his bandaged nose, then stopped and lowered it again.

"Have you an explanation, Ghiva, or should we invite the guards in to ask a little more forcefully?"

"No, sir, that would be most unnecessary. If my answer were doubtful, it is only that my countrymen were at the gate where the Highness was last seen. I am not aware that they had any involvement, but I was considering more carefully, that is all."

One by one, they questioned most of the men in the camp. The few women they saw immediately turned away, or hid inside their tents until the strangers were gone. By the end of the long afternoon, Dylan began to droop, and Gwythym's attention strayed between the matter at hand and his concern for his son. Finally, Fionvar agreed they should let it rest: these ragged people had nothing to hide. Living as they did under the scrutiny of the city watch and subject to deportation, they had every reason to cooperate.

"I'm for the barracks, then, talk to the scouts." Gwythym paused before he left them at the gate. "I am sorry about this, Fionvar, I had hoped ..."

"Me, too. I know you're doing all that you can."

"Aye, we're trying. See to the lad, eh?"

Dylan rolled his eyes, but Fionvar replied, "Of course."

Watching his father stride off, Dylan breathed a loud sigh.

"He's just looking out for you, you know."

"Aye, but I'm not a child anymore. I can get to the observatory on my own."

"So it won't hurt you to show me what you're studying,

right?" Fionvar smiled. "Not as much as your father'd hurt me if he knew I'd let you go alone."

Dylan led the way down the corridors and up numerous flights of stairs, his steps seeming to grow lighter as they went. At the top, he opened the door with a key that he wore on a chain around his neck. A few others manned positions in the round chamber, mostly monks in long, dark gowns, their bald heads glinting in the late-autumn sunlight. Tubes of brass and piles of small mirrors and lenses scattered the workshop tables as they worked to create new instruments based on the latest science. Tinkers and coppersmiths in the city kept busy constructing the various stands and armatures, and etching the delicate markings needed to keep accurate records. Scraps of parchment littered the floor and decorated the walls, covered with minuscule notes and calculations. A long bookcase ran down the center, bearing all the charts and diagrams these monks had copied in various other nations.

"It's coming along more than I thought," Fionvar remarked. "I should really keep better track of this project."

"We're a long way behind," Dylan said, picking his way across the room to a ladder. "You needn't come up."

Fionvar followed. "Yes, but this tower has the best view in the kingdom."

They emerged onto the flat roof, ringed by a low wall. Dylan pulled up a stool beside one of the instruments mounted on the stone. From a chest at the base of the wall, he removed a thick sheaf of parchments and flipped through them.

While Dylan prepared his evening's work, Fionvar gazed down upon his city. The tower stood just over the roof of the new temple, and Fionvar could see the circular hole in its center. Begun during the Usurper's reign, the temple bulged out from the original wall of the city, the refugees' tents spreading like a multicolored skirt around it. Turning toward the castle, Fionvar leaned on the wall. A few stories lower than the observatory stood the King's Tower, where King Rhys had presented his new bride, Brianna, to the populace gathered in the square below, then taken a step from the rooftop and vanished. Fionvar smiled to himself; he was one of the few who knew all the secrets of that day. The same secrets that had driven away his son. He lost the smile and looked farther out, toward the haphazard arrangement of streets built up around the castle. Market squares interrupted the rabble of rooftops with open patches and colorful pavilions. Sometimes he envied Bernholt its planned capital, laid out with streets purposefully crooked and not too chaotic. Of course, the castle at Lochdale was a good two hundred years older than the palace at Bernholt. This was a fortress first, whereas King Gerrod's palace had been built during peace times, a bold and remarkable place meant to prove the glamour of the monarchs who lived there. Born a farmer and raised in the town of Gamel's Grove, Fionvar had little use for such glamour, but the wider streets and frequent wells of Bernholt City would be a big help sometimes.

Dylan cleared his throat. "I'm set here, my lord, if you want to see."

"Of course." Fionvar crossed to his side and bent to peer through the short tube. To his surprise, it had neither lens nor mirror. "But what do you see?"

"My job is to measure the moon. When it rises, when it sets, and where." He knelt near the wall and traced a slender metal staff attached to the instrument. "These markings give the height of the moon over that ridge. This scope is one of the oldest in the observatory. That means we've been watching the moon for several years, and we can predict where and when it will rise, or nearly so, anyway."

Fionvar frowned. "But if you can predict it, then why do you need to watch?"

"I—We're trying to confirm some things." Dylan hurriedly scooped up his pages. "It's only because we keep these records that we can make any predictions. We have people to watch the sun as well as the moon. These things can help us tell time a lot more accurately and anticipate seasonal changes, and we're making a map of the stars, so when someone dies, we'll be able to find that star again and again. Think about the implications for ships at sea! The charts we're working on will mean they can sail farther and longer, and always find their way."

Fionvar chuckled. "It's good to see you're so enthusiastic about your work."

Dylan reddened and looked down. "You knew all that already."

He clapped the young man's shoulder. "I'll leave you to it. Take care, Dylan."

For a moment, Dylan's eyes lingered on Fionvar's face, then he said, "He'll be back, my lord, I'm sure of it."

With a slight smile, Fionvar agreed, "We'll find him, somehow." At the top of the ladder Fionvar stopped, looking back at Wolfram's friend, perched before his instruments, already reviewing his records. Why had Dylan wanted to reassure him? Just an expression of concern, no doubt, an acknowledgment of the spot the Lord Protector was in. And if Dylan seemed a little more preoccupied than usual, he had cause to be between his injury and Wolfram's absence. They'd find him. Of course they would. To lose his son now, before he'd even claimed him—it was unthinkable.

Chapter 7

WOLFRAM RAN a nervous hand through his hair. Five months had let it grow out to a decent length by his standards, but it would be years before it was long enough to braid properly— as the Woodfolk did. He frowned, and Morra patted his cheek gently.

"Do not worry," she chided him in her own language. "The spirits have brought you, and surely they will let you stay."

"I have not smoked before," he replied, his speech hesitant as his tongue wrapped around the unnatural words. His facility with the language surprised him, but still he could understand much more than he spoke. When it would have been Finisnez—the high celebration of the Goddess in his home—he had composed a poem for Morra, as he might have done for a lady of the court. She said she liked it, but he thought the gift of a bone needle or pot of pine pitch would have been better received. Gorn and the extended family they traveled with made no pretense of liking poetry, nor understanding why he felt the need to give gifts in the dead of winter. They let him hunt with them, they cheered the tales of adventure he remembered from boyhood, they even gave blessings to the child which grew within Morra's belly, but they did not greet him as one of them, and he knew by now they never would.

Tonight, with the full moon gleaming down on the remaining patches of snow, the Woodfolk would finally admit him to the men's lodge, to smoke and drum, and call upon the spirits. Shivers came and went along his spine. If the spirits would not speak to him, he'd either be tossed out into the wilderness, or killed. Morra would not tell him honestly, but he gathered that opinions were mixed on that point. The elders weren't sure if mere banishment would be enough to appease the spirits for the heresy of adopting him. They did not like to kill him, since he was a good hand with a spear during boar hunts and had shown promise as a tracker, but they would kill him if the spirits asked it.

In his hide clothes, his skin weathered and hands cracked from the long winter, Wolfram might easily have been mistaken for one of his adopted people. He had been, in fact, one time when a hunting party from Bernholt had stumbled upon their encampment. Holding his tongue, he let them believe it, but inside he was burning with questions. What was made of his disappearance? Had they given up searching for him, or were these men not the hapless hunters they seemed to be? So even as he drank the Woodfolk's hearty ale and dined on the meat of animals he helped slay, Wolfram knew in his heart that he did not belong. The spirits might well know, too, looking into him through the ritual smoke.

Suddenly, the flap of the lodge was thrown open, his cue to

enter. Wolfram cleared his throat and turned back to Morra, his refuge from fear and anger.

She swiftly threw her arms around him and kissed him lightly. She had learned well in these few months together. Ducking her head, she slipped off the great bear claw she wore about her neck. Placing it over her lover's head, Morra said, *"Na tu Lusawe." Gifts of the spirits.*

"Na tu Lusawe," Wolfram agreed, stroking his thumb along the sharp claw. The phrase came from one of their stories, a strange and rambling tale in which the hero found his joy, and lost, and found it again. After several such cycles, depending on the mood of the storyteller, he might end with the treasure found, or the treasure lost. Either way, the moral was the same: the gifts of the spirits are precious and swift. *Na tu Lusawe shasinhe goron.* They used it as a greeting and a farewell, and for just about any purpose they deemed appropriate. Morra was telling him that he was precious to her, that her faith held true, but he had given her the child she needed, and somewhere inside, where Wolfram's long-quiet demon still lurked, he was hearing farewell.

Quickly, before he lost his nerve, Wolfram released her and strode to the lodge, ducking inside. Too quickly, it seemed, for he missed the step down inside, and stumbled in, starting a rumble of amusement among the men already gathered there. Dusting himself off, Wolfram held up his palm in greeting and crossed toward Gorn and the brothers he had traveled with. The oval lodge had a roof formed of thin, bent trees, bound in a grid and draped with deer hides. From the gridwork, various bundles of offerings hung: dried meat and fish, pouches of herbs or rare crystals, and bits of jewelry or other trade goods from the cities. Did the fur merchants know that the gold and jewels they exchanged for beaver and mink were hung as offerings to heathen spirits? From his belt, Wolfram lifted the little bundle he had assembled. Inside the carefully prepared skin of a pheasant nestled the tusk of the first boar he had slain—the one that would have slain him—and a cluster of garnets he had found by the stream. Around the pheasant's neck, he bound the chain that had once adorned his own. In this place of their spirits, he gave his formal thanks that

Morra had saved his life. Reaching up, he tied the offering to an empty crossing of branches.

Gorn, gazing up at the dangling bundle, moved over to make room for him on the ledge of earth encompassing the space.

On the dirt floor before them, a few men sat, bringing out round drums and small, stringed instruments. With the flap replaced over the doorway, the only light came from a fire at the northern end. One of the elders rose up, clattering with bits of metal and the beaks of birds. He bent over the fire, mumbling in a harsh voice. He revealed a branch with bits of herbs tied to its twigs. Lighting this, he straightened and began to make a circuit of the room, waving the smoke over their heads and down along the floor. When he had at last returned to his place, leaving Wolfram blurry-eyed from the fumes, the musicians began to play, wild, rambling music that only now and again found a rhythm.

A young man with the blood-streaked brow of a new warrior stood up then, his hands trembling and eyes intent on the pipe he held. He offered it to the spirits of earth and sky and took the first puff, breaking down in a coughing fit immediately.

The other men stamped their feet and cheered him, welcoming him into their midst. As the pipe began its circle of the room, the young man began to dance, slapping his thighs and chanting. Others joined him, their voices raised in shouts and laughter. Even before the pipe had reached the third man, someone had passed a skin full of ale. Wolfram drank deeply and wiped his mouth on his sleeve, his feet stamping the newfound rhythm. Head adrift in the scent of the herbs and the smoke of the fire, he wondered if he might suddenly find himself compelled to dance. Removed from the pressures of his father's legacy and his own curse, Wolfram felt lighter, stronger, taller even than he had been before. Laughing, he slapped Gorn on the shoulder.

The Great Hunter slapped him back, passing on another bottle.

When the pipe reached him, Wolfram took a long draw on it, taking the foreign smoke swirling into his nose and lungs. It tingled through him like inhaling starlight, and a presence touched him as surely as if a spirit stood before him. Someone took the pipe from his limp grasp, and he swayed to his feet, still stamping. Whirling in the pattern of an old-fashioned jig, Wolfram danced from his place. He whooped and hollered, leaping in the air, and many of the others fell back around him. Suddenly, he found himself face-to-face with a shaggy elder, the man's gray braids lashing Wolfram as they stopped.

"Wolfram!" The ragged man shouted on a blast of ale and smoke.

Befuddled, Wolfram cocked his head to try to make sense of the stranger.

"I knew him!" The old man thumped his own chest. "Not you!" he roared, looming closer.

"I was named for him," Wolfram shouted back, speaking his own tongue as the old man had. He searched his memory, and found the name in Fionvar's stories. "Quinan?"

Bursting with laughter, the other grabbed him in a hearty embrace and dropped him to the floor again. "Dance!" he cried. "Smoke!"

Alone on the floor, the two men danced, their arms flailing in the air, feet beating against the earth. Quinan shared his own small pipe, clenching it back between his crooked, stained teeth. Spinning like a madman, Wolfram called out the words of the song his mother had always hummed to him, and jubilantly flicked the elder's braids.

"Speak!" cried Quinan suddenly, whirling to a halt.

Caught up in the rhythm, Wolfram kept moving, but let his arms fall to his sides. The picture reached him clearly—the spirits had heard him! "I am alone in my bed." Wolfram began, speaking his own death.

From the shadows in the vision, a woman drew herself forward, he could not see her face, but knew her to be someone that he loved. "A woman I love is coming," he called out to his audience, and they murmured their approval. Buoyed up by their attention, Wolfram focused on the scene revealed to him, then he froze.

One foot hovered until his toes found the floor, but he stood poised. In his mind's eye, the woman carried a goblet. From her clothing, she drew a vial and shook it over the drink, then bent to offer it to him, to the figure in the bed he would one day be. She had poisoned him, this woman—Lyssa?—whom he loved. Even as he watched, he felt a cold dread within him. He had been murdered, yet, in his heart, he knew it was not wrong. Had he deserved this death? Was he so terrible, now and always?

Trembling, sickened, he opened his eyes and closed his mouth. He thought he could escape his place, and he was wrong.

The face of Quinan hovered in the smoke near him. "Speak."

Wolfram shook his head, trying to clear it of the vision.

Quinan frowned, drawing nearer, suddenly corporeal in the atmosphere of smoke. "Speak," he commanded.

"I saw nothing more," Wolfram blurted.

"Lie not to me, little Wolf," Quinan growled, his eyes narrow, yet gleaming.

Around them, the other men grew restless; the rhythm of their stamping faltered, then grew louder.

"Out!" a voice cried, and another took up the cry, then another until it grew into a terrible chant. "Out, out, out, out!"

The drums beat ominously beneath a hiss of voices, and Wolfram turned from the fearsome slits of Quinan's eyes. Around him in the smoke, those eyes shone from every face, wild, angry eyes. Pushing his way through the smoke, coughing, Wolfram fled.

He stumbled up the stairs and out into the brilliant clarity of the night air, and ran on, the focused glare of the Woodmen joined by the vengeful spirit of the man he had killed, howling him out into the black.

An arm shot out and caught him. Wolfram screamed, then stopped, whirled to face Morra's anxious cry. He said quickly, "I can't stay. I'm sorry."

She wailed, a crude, inhuman sound of grief. "I did not think they'd take you, not now." She pressed one hand to her belly, where their child grew.

"I'm sorry," he said again, and, touching her forehead to smooth away her coarse hair, he realized he spoke the truth. She had been kind, and asked him no questions.

She raised to her lips the bear claw she had given him, and kissed it, then kissed his lips with all the tenderness he had taught her. "Be careful," she said. She untied her belt in the darkness, and tied it about him, with its bundles of medicine, flint, and tinder.

"I will, don't worry."

"The road of your people," she said, turning him gently away and pointing through the forest.

His people. Wolfram shook his head. *"Na tu Lusawe,"* he whispered.

"Na tu Lusawe," she replied, and she stood to watch him go.

The road was quickly found, once his eyes adjusted to the darkness. Wolfram stood a moment, hesitating. Night birds called around him, and he listened to be sure it was not the Woodmen. To his left lay the mountains, and Lochalyn. To his right, Bernholt, where he had not been in years. Sighing, he realized he had no choice to make, not really. He turned right, down out of the mountains. If he struck out for the city, at least he could hear the news of Lochalyn and find out what they made of his disappearance.

Ten days' hard walking brought him there, wearing the ill-fitting clothes of a farmer who'd taken a liking to his Hurim leathers. He kept the bear claw necklace, though, hanging beneath the shirt, token of the one person who would wish him well. Trudging beneath the arch into Bernholt City, Wolfram ran a hand through his hair to comb it. Scruffy whiskers darkened his cheeks, and weariness darkened his thoughts. Still, he'd no place to stay, so he'd best find work until he decided what to do.

"Move it, boy!" a gruff voice called, and he turned to find a groaning wagon loaded with stone.

Stepping aside, Wolfram watched the blocks of marble creak past, escorted by a few apprentices. He fell in beside them to follow the stone to a mason who might give him work. Above the city, he saw the towers of the palace. He swallowed. Perhaps this idea wasn't so clever after all. Someone there might recognize him. But with this hair, these clothes? He shook off the concern. Besides, it was the best place to eavesdrop on the doings of the kingdom, this one, and his own. He moved as one of them, straight over the main bridge and down the arched tunnel until they emerged again into the sun in the royal gardens. Newly paved walkways crossed among young trees and flower beds not yet planted. He remembered a walk in the garden when he last visited the palace, some four years ago. Princess Melisande had gone on about how grand the place would be, once they had finished rebuilding. It looked nearly done, to his eyes, but he stuck with the wagon and found himself led to the back corner, where the foundations of a new chapel rose from the surrounding dirt.

The wagon creaked to a halt, and sweaty men came to unload it. Wolfram spotted the master mason standing to one side with a parchment drawing. Wolfram picked his way among the stones and stood before him.

"What?" the man barked, glowering at him.

"I, ah, was wondering if you needed an extra pair of hands, sir." He remembered to throw on the "sir" at the last moment, and the man frowned.

The master was a thick, stubby man, with huge arms. He wore a thin shirt that stuck to his broad chest, and showed the sun-baked arms and neck. His wispy gray hair did little to protect his scalp, and he winced a little when he reached up to scratch his head. "Plenty of laborers," he replied, "and you don't look near strong enough. Try the stables." He offered a crack-toothed grin.

Wolfram glowered back. A chill rippled through him. The demon, who had not awakened for these long months, stirred in its sleep, itching for a fight. "I worked five years with Mistress Lyssa, if the name means something to you."

One wiry eyebrow quirked upward. "Oh, aye? You're a carver, then?"

"I can be, if I'm needed," he replied coolly.

The mason let out a gust of laughter. "We'll see. You worked under Mistress Lyssa." A wistful look crossed the man's face, and he leaned closer. "Wouldn't you rather have worked over her?" He winked broadly.

Wolfram felt himself flush and brought his teeth down on a sharp reply.

The mason drew back, eyebrows leaping. "Or have you already?"

Wolfram took the excuse he was offered. "You've not asked why I left there, have you?"

Another gust of laughter greeted this response, and the man slapped him on the back. "Well, lad, welcome to you! What's your name?"

"Wolfram," he said before he could stop himself. Warily, he glanced to the mason.

"Aye, and isn't every lad your age. I've three Wolframs apprenticed already!" He guffawed. "Matter of fact, your mistress"—he wriggled his eyebrows for emphasis—"was here looking for that Prince Wolfram a few months back."

"She was?" Wolfram blurted.

The tone of his voice brought the man's eyes down to him. "Aye, that she was."

Wolfram wet his lips. "I'm lucky she didn't spy me on the road, then."

"I suppose you are at that." He rolled up the parchment in his meaty fists. "I'll start you at five shillings, go to seven if you're any good."

Five? How was he to find a room on so little? Why the best inns—Wolfram stopped himself, willing the demon back into its cave. He was not a prince here, just a common stonecutter, and that was a stonecutter's wage. Grimly, he nodded.

The mason nodded toward a pile of stones not far off. "'Twill be a fountain, if the Lady's willing, and the hands are strong. Foreman'll get you your tools."

Chapter 8

THE FOREMAN did more than give him tools. When he found that Wolfram had no place to stay, he offered the loft of his stables until the young man could find a better one. Wolfram gladly accepted that, plus an advance on his week's wages to buy new clothes and a bath. His nascent beard he let go, pleased to feel how thickly it grew. When he caught sight of himself in the tarnished bathhouse mirror, it took a touch of his own cheek to convince him the face was his. Tanned, with raven hair and a shaggy beard, he offered himself a grin. Even if he'd passed Lyssa, she would never have known him.

The work in the garden was hard. Even at his most ardent, lessons of statesmanship or language had always dragged him away from carving. Still, Lyssa had once claimed he had the gift, and a few days of shaping simple tiles found him lost in the element of stone. The swing of the hammer, the bounce of the chisel stretched his muscles and eased his mind. Concentrating on the work before him, he could pretend he was no more than a simple laborer too bold for his own good. Between the labor and the nights of drinking with the other lads, he could almost forget himself. If he drank enough ale to pass out, even the looming face in the darkness left him alone.

After a particularly hard night, Wolfram squinted into the glaring sun. He trudged along a path well marked by others, helping to unload great sacks of marble dust to be made into mortar. The stuff dusted the ground around him and the rough clothes he'd purchased. Plain wool made his legs itch so that his fingers twitched on the sack, dying to get at the annoyance. He'd cut back on his drinking to save money for a new pair of breeches; never having had to pay before, he had no idea that cotton cost so much. Like the others, he wore no shirt, so that the bear claw dangled on his chest, both warning and enigma to his master.

Gritting his teeth, Wolfram shifted a new sack up to his bare shoulder and turned, starting off along the new-laid marble to-ward the far end. Just then, a small party emerged from the arch not far off, and stopped, surveying the work. The three ladies, two quite young, and one older matron frowning into the glare, lifted their skirts, waving off the dust with pale hands. As they turned to retreat from the clouded sun, the man behind them stood a moment longer, hand to his brow, squinting into the middle distance. Red-brown hair touched his shoulders, and his clothes, though fine, marked him as a tradesman rather than a lord. When he lowered his hand and turned to follow, Wolfram caught sight of his face.

The heavy sack slid through Wolfram's numb fingers, bursting against the tile.

Laborers coughed and cursed around him, quick to escape the drift of whiteness that covered him, but Wolfram barely breathed. If it had not been for Lyssa's portrait, he would never have known him. The hair, the height, though at odds with legend, did not distract him from the man's face. King Rhys, his father.

Movement showed the little party approaching, and a shout heralded the master. Wolfram stood and stared, his mouth hang-ing slightly open, his itch forgotten.

King Rhys came up, frowning, waving away the dust, he began, "Are you—" then the voice—the light, strange voice—died away. Color slid from the man's face, and his trembling hand flew to his throat. He gasped, his honey-colored eyes gone wide. He stepped back, blundered into the ladies, turned and fled as if his life depended on it.

Blood roared in Wolfram's ears, and he clenched his teeth, his nails digging into his palms of their own accord. The breath he had been holding came out in a snarl. The bastard knew him, ran from him like the coward he was. All the lies washed over Wolfram in a cold torrent. If the ladies had not been barring his way—he became aware of a new sound tickling the demon within him. One of the ladies was laughing.

"What have you done to him?" the woman laughed, gesturing back the way King Rhys had run.

Wolfram moved at last, dragging a hand across his eyes, blinking fiercely to clear the dust. He swung his throbbing head to focus upon her.

Dark-haired and elegant in a gown of blue silk, the young woman burst out laughing again at the sight of his face. "You look like a ghost!" she sputtered, her green eyes twinkling. She'd let her skirts fall to the ground, heedless of the mess. "I doubt a ghost would scare him so."

"Who was that?" Wolfram demanded.

The other two women exchanged a stern glance, and their leader stifled her laughter, her brows drawing together in some consternation. She looked vaguely familiar, but he couldn't place her.

"That man who ran away, who was he?" Wolfram insisted again. Off to one side, the master mason swore under his breath.

The mirth fled her features. "Your Highness."

Wolfram's hand pressed the bear claw tight to the wild beating of his heart.

"Forgive me, Your Highness," the master said, coming up beside him.

Bury it, did everyone know him? Wolfram turned, the demon overcoming its momentary paralysis, but the master was not addressing him. With cheeks ruddy from embarrassment, the old man bowed to the ladies.

Spinning on his heel back to face them, Wolfram suddenly placed the resemblance. "Melody?" he blurted.

A heavy, stone-hardened hand smacked him so that Wolfram's shaky knees buckled, and he floundered to one side. The blow burned in his cheek even as the cold rush of fury consumed him.

Balling his hand into a fist, Wolfram slammed the man's jaw.

The lip cracked, spurting blood to dampen the whiteness of the marble.

The master staggered back, hands clasped over the injury. "I'll have your hide for this, boy!" He plunged forward again, as if to tan his workman's hide then and there.

Wolfram ducked the wild swing, bringing his own fist up smoothly to connect with the master's jaw with a crunch. The impact shivered down Wolfram's arm as he followed through, crashing his opponent to the ground. "No man lays a hand on me."

The stamp of heavy feet cut through the throbbing as guards came to the princess's aid.

"Bury it!" The eddies of Wolfram's fury whirled within him as his mind raced. When the leaders came up to one side, he dropped to his knees, then rolled.

As expected, the ladies sprang away, shrieking.

Wolfram scrambled up and ran headlong for the arch. He leapt a bed of lavender, landed hard, and sprinted for freedom. Dodging a cluster of guards by the bridge, he won through to the city, making for the main gate.

He had already reached the open market, with the wall rearing up behind, when the first sparks of reason struck through the anger. Panting, he drew up into an alley and considered his place. The master would be out for blood, but he'd also be out cold for a little while at least. As to the princess, he might have insulted her, but it was no serious offense, and he could always reveal his right to use her given name. A new chill caught his stomach. Murder, on the other hand, was a hanging offense. Even if his royalty could save him that fate, what sort of trust could he have with that deed upon him?

So he must leave, but he'd have the time to reach his loft and take away what little he owned. Wolfram set out again at a jog, winding through the progressively narrower streets toward the foreman's cottage. He let himself quietly into the barn, shushing the two horses, and climbed up into the hay that had been his home for a week. Quickly, he pulled on his shirt then found his long boar-gutting knife, and Morra's belt with its flint and steel.

Every time he used them, he thought of her, and his warmth was doubled. He fumbled in the hay to find the pouch containing his last few coppers. Then he froze.

Below him, one of the horses snorted and stamped. A shaft of light pierced the gloom from the open door and someone stepped through.

"Hello? Are you here?" A woman made her way toward the ladder. "No good hiding from me!"

Wolfram strangled the pouch with both hands. Even in his blackest rage, he had never struck a woman, not even that whore Asenith. He glanced up sharply as Princess Melody's head appeared at the top of the ladder.

"Well, hello." She grinned. "It seems I've caught you."

"Let me by," he said, "and no harm will come to you."

Her bright laughter bounced from the low ceiling. "I'll tell the captain that when he gets here; he'll not be pleased with either of us, especially since I found you first." She leaned in toward him, and whispered, "I had to steal a horse."

Wolfram slumped back on his heels, the rush seeping out of him. He shook his head. "This delay may be the death of me."

"Oh, don't be dramatic," she rejoined him sharply, then the grin slipped back. "That's what Mother's always saying to me. You should be using my title, though."

"Sorry, Your Highness." He searched the darker corners of the loft. He might have hidden, but a word from her would probably get the place torched. After four years apart, his recollections of Melody were of a tomboyish girl with capricious moods. Bright, sly, and utterly charming, alternately supporting her brother's dire proclamations about him, then wooing him back to his friendship. After the third or fourth incident when her bruise or ripped gown mysteriously became his fault, Wolfram had been banned from playing with the little princess, which he had thought just as well. But seeing her now, he could think of a few new games to play.

With a snort of laughter for his libido, Wolfram dropped his eyes from her face.

"Do I know you?" she asked suddenly.

"I work in the gardens, but not for long, only a week, I mean, Your Highness."

"Oh, no." She shook her head fiercely. "There's something about you, and there's the way Master Duncan reacted when he saw you."

"Who?" In the blackness of anger, Wolfram had almost forgotten the start of the incident. He scrambled toward her. "Who is he?"

"What's it to you?" She pulled a little back, her arms outstretched as they clung to the rails. Then, her eyes widened, and she flung herself forward again. "Wolfram! But you've dyed your hair!"

He groaned and flopped back into the hay. Doomed for certain, now.

Melody pulled herself up the last few rungs and crawled over to stare down into his face. "What're you doing here, and like this? Why are you in disguise?"

Outside, marching echoed from the buildings, and Wolfram gripped her shoulder, stopping the flow of questions. "There's no time, Melody, your men are here."

She nodded quickly, coming close. "You're in hiding," she breathed.

"Yes. They can't know who I am. It's extremely important."

"Highness?" a man shouted. "Are you here, Your Highness?"

Melody pressed a finger to Wolfram's lips and scurried to the opening. She leaned down. "After him, Captain!"

"What?"

"Didn't he pass you? He's just gone!" She stuck her arm through to point out the door. "Hurry!"

"Are you well, Your Highness?"

"I'm fine, don't bother about me! By the mount, I nearly had him." She smoothed back her hair.

Still, the man hesitated. "But—"

"Go!" She shouted down at him. "I'll just sit and catch my breath." She sat up again, turning to wink at Wolfram as the men below tramped out and scattered for the search. Crawling back over, she sat down beside him, studying him sidelong.

"Thanks," he muttered, sitting up as well, scratching his beard.

"It was fun," she replied, her teeth gleaming in the filtered light.

"I'd best be going, or they'll come back."

She caught his arm. "Don't go. I've just found you, and I want to hear it all."

Wolfram glowered at her. "Well, I'm in a hurry. We'll have to talk another time." He pushed himself toward the ladder.

Her grip tightened. "Don't go, Wolfram."

"Don't try to stop me, Melody, you have no idea what's at stake."

"I'll scream," she said simply.

Wolfram wet his lips, staring down the ladder.

"They'd come running, and they won't even bother about who you are before they hack you to bits."

"You wouldn't," he scoffed, inching forward.

She released his arm and settled back into the hay. "Try me."

Very slowly, Wolfram turned toward her. All the fun had gone out of her voice and face, her pretty lips set into a firm line. Their eyes met, and he let out a long breath. "What do you want from me, Melody?"

"Stay with me, Wolfie, a little while," she pleaded. "You have no idea how boring it is being a princess. Alyn goes off adventuring all the time, speaking the words of the Lady, glowing like starlight on earth. The only thing I have to look forward to is picking a husband from the legion of fools they keep parading by me. That fight in the garden was the most excitement I've had in years."

Wolfram grunted. "It was stupid. I wasn't thinking straight, and I blew it."

"You were magnificent," she breathed. "Great Lady, Wolfram, I've never seen anybody fight like that." She balled her smooth hands into fists, swinging at the air. "The mason must weigh three times as much, but you put him on his back like a dead fish." She smacked a fist into her palm. "I wish I could do that."

"It's not a skill I'm proud of," Wolfram growled, but he moved away from the ladder to sit beside her. He rubbed his right hand absently with his left.

Watching the gesture, Melody reached out and took his tingling hand between hers, gently chafing the numbness out. "You should be proud." She ducked her head over his battered hand.

He shook his head. "I wouldn't expect you to understand." His fingers warmed in her grasp, and he looked down at the fall of dark hair that brushed his wrist.

Their eyes met, and she smirked at him through the gloom. "You're the brother I should have had."

"What about Alyn?"

"He's off for another pilgrimage, chasing another ridiculous vision. He hears voices, Wolfram, every voice except mine." The words trailed off.

"I didn't know," he said.

"Will you let me call you 'brother'?" she asked. "And you can call me 'sister,' if you want. After all, you haven't got one."

He nodded reluctantly, though that was the last thing he wanted to call her. The scent of the hay conjured memories of other stables, other girls not half as beautiful.

"So, brother, what now?" She released his hand and shook back her hair.

"I really can't stay, Melody. It was stupid to come here in the first place."

"Why shouldn't you be here?"

"No, it's too close. It's the first place they'll—" He broke off, not wanting to reveal too much.

"They'll look for you?" she finished. "You must know Lyssa's been and left."

"I've heard." Wolfram swallowed. She probably wanted his hide even more than the master mason. Bury them both.

She cocked her head to peer up at him. "Why don't you want to be found?"

"You don't know everything. Best keep it that way."

"What did they do to you? Or was it something you did?" She drew close, so that he could feel her warm breath upon his skin. "Did you kill someone or something?"

Wolfram stiffened, looking away, but a new warmth crept up his neck.

"Oh, I see." She touched his shoulder, but he flinched away. "I won't tell anyone, Wolfie, not ever. After all, you're my brother."

"So you know why I can't be found."

Her eyes sparkled, and she whispered, "I'm running away, very soon. Come with me—think what fun it'll be."

"Wait a minute." He held up a hand to stop her. "When I saw you in the garden, who was that man, the one I frightened off?"

"Oh, Master Duncan. He's my music teacher. He has a place in the city, but he's nearly always at the palace." She brought her lips close to his ear to tell him, "I think he's in love with Mother." Melody drew back with a conspiratorial smile.

Wolfram's head reeled so that he pressed his hands to his temples. King Rhys, disguised as a teacher, in love with Princess Melisande, heir to the throne of Bernholt.

"Why did he run away from you?"

"I don't know." Wolfram turned it over, eyes narrowed as if he could see through history. After winning back his kingdom, King Rhys abandoned his throne, his wife, and his child, to live as leman to a neighboring princess. The bastard had probably already met and bedded Melisande before he ever turned his sights toward Brianna. He stopped long enough to father an heir, not to mention a legend, and ran back to his lover, after getting her husband out of the way first. Of them all, King Rhys was the biggest liar Wolfram had yet discovered. A thought jolted him, and he examined Melody's features, and what he recalled of Alyn. It was entirely possible his father was hers as well, and she had no idea. The thought sickened him, both for his own sake in the desire that still tugged at him, and for hers, her ignorance of the lies that parents tell. Whatever sordid game they were playing, Wolfram wanted none of it. He'd found his father and been left again. Twice was enough of a lesson for him.

Wolfram grabbed Melody's hands in his, drawing her toward the ladder. "Let's run away, sister, let's run as far as we possibly can."

Chapter 9

MELODY LED the way down to the stable door and peered around it. "Quick, brother!" She flashed across the yard to where a patient guard horse stood and scrambled up on its back. Wolfram mounted behind her, and she kicked the horse into a trot. Twice they caught sight of uniformed guards, still making their systematic search. The riders turned their horse, and were soon out of that quarter. The broad, paved ways of the merchant rows took over. Well-dressed pedestrians and those in carriages bowed their heads to Melody. If they were surprised by her mount, or her company, they showed no sign.

Melody brought the horse up in an alley, by a staircase that pitched sharply down to an open door. A gilded sign above read THE LADY'S TIT, and featured a leering caricature of the Goddess.

Wolfram stifled a laugh as he slid down. "How do you know a place like this?"

Melody flipped her hair in a pretty shrug. "I hear all kinds of things when I'm not supposed to listen. This place should hide you until I get back."

"Where are you going?" He frowned up at her as she gathered the reins again.

"Why, back to the palace of course. I can't run away on a moment's notice." Her bright laughter trailed after as she turned the horse and set off for home. "Back by evening!" she called over her shoulder.

The scent of roasting beef wafted from the tavern's recessed door. Wolfram's stomach loudly reminded him that he'd missed lunch, and he sighed as he ducked down the steps and into the crowded room. Elbowing himself a place at a long table, armed with a trencher of meat and a mug of ale, Wolfram set into his meal. He briefly considered leaving once he was through, letting Melody find her own adventures, but just as quickly discarded the idea. She could tell them all about him, and invent more besides—probably put a knife at her throat during the talk with the guard, or a thousand other things sure to get him to the gallows, if he lasted so long. She both threatened and charmed him, calling him "brother"; her admiration, at least, seemed genuine. For better or worse, she had bound him to her, at least for a while. Outside the city, she'd soon learn that there was little of luxury or excitement in becoming a self-made exile. After a few days of peasant's food and damp leaves for bedding, she'd be pleading to return to her palace—and he'd have plenty of time for flight.

When Melody returned, Wolfram discovered that he couldn't have been more wrong. Night had fallen outside, and the barkeep had begun to glance at him with a keenness that prickled Wolfram's beard. At last, the princess emerged into the smoky light, and Wolfram blinked a few times at the transformation.

Not only had she shed her gowns and petticoats, she wore a man's riding clothes, complete to the tall leather boots. Her raven hair had been bound into a braid down her back, and the rouge was gone from her lips. Still, when she craned her neck to spy him out, all eyes were upon her, and many a wink exchanged. Wolfram bristled at the uncouth men around him. Despite his misgivings, the title of "brother" had already taken hold, and he wanted to cuff the knaves for staring at her that way.

"There you are, brother," she greeted him. "Not too impatient, I hope?"

"A little. Let's get out of here." As they mounted the narrow steps, he added, "I hope they've not closed the gates yet."

"The gates?" She laughed. "But we're not going that way."

"What are you—" He broke off. Standing in the alley were a handful of dark-skinned Hemijrani, obviously waiting for them. He slapped his hip where his sword should have been.

"Tush." Melody trapped his wrist before he could go for the knife instead. "This is my maid, Gordiya, and her friends."

His fists clenched, and the tension crept up his neck. "Melody, I'm supposed to be in hiding, if you haven't forgotten. You can't take a bloody parade."

Laughter greeted this, and he felt the first claws of anger taking hold again. One of the short, dark men shifted forward, his hand hovering by his waist. The other two fired off a burst of rapid, high-pitched speech.

"But, Wolfie, they're taking us, don't you see?"

"No, I'm afraid I don't." His fingers rubbed at his temple.

"Well, you must have heard about the war." She goggled at him as if expecting his ignorance to be complete.

"Of course I have; Lochdale's swarming with refugees, they're driving my mother—" He stopped himself. No good following those thoughts.

Melody nodded eagerly. "Yes, yes, don't you see? My brother—my other brother—wanted to go, to preach to them, but he's been away for ages. We're sick of waiting. But look, this is our chance! You and I can find out what's behind it all." Her hands danced as she spoke, a wild cavalcade of gestures.

Wolfram tilted his head at her, frowning. The anger still throbbed but no longer seemed urgent. "You think we can end the war in Hemijrai?"

"We have to try, don't we?" she said more quietly. She laid a hand upon his arm, her face tilted to look up into his. "These people are heathens, but they are ready to listen to us. Imagine if we were to trump Alyn at his own game and convert them! If we can stop them killing each other, shouldn't we do it? Besides, when we come home—"

"I can't ever go home," he interrupted.

"When we come home," she overrode him, "you won't be a murderer, you'll be a hero!"

Wolfram flinched, ducking his head. Below him in the darkness, the light from the tavern door took on the eerie shape of an agonized face. Wolfram shuddered. Looking to the gleaming eyes in her companions' dark faces, he drummed his fingers against his hip. Something was going on with these people, with or without Melody's knowledge. "We should wait until we've had a chance to talk about it, just you and I."

Her features crumpled into a pout. "Don't you want to redeem yourself? Don't you want to be a part of something great?"

"Yes, but, these people—" He waved a hand at the little bunch.

"Don't you trust me?" she asked quietly, and her eyes seemed to glint as her eyelashes flickered.

"Does that mean I have to trust them?"

She slipped her hand into his and squeezed. "Where's the magnificent brother I saw today?" she whispered. "Don't tell me you're afraid of them."

"Why would I be afraid of them? They're just a bunch of—"

"Ah!" she said, pressing her finger to his lips for the second time that day. "They are kind, and good, and in need of us. This adventure will be the grandest possible, Wolfram. Imagine you and I saving these people." Her face lit with the vision as she slid her arm through his and drew him toward the street.

Saving you, he thought, eyeing the little company that gathered around them. His fingers itched, but he said no more. Nothing he said could change her mind, that was clear, and as to how long the plot had been hatched, or by whom, he would eventually discover whatever they were hiding. He grinned at the Hemijrani, but their dark faces showed no expression. The woman, Gordiya, took the lead, taking them with quick, silent steps down to the docks. This must have been what had taken them so long, for a small boat was waiting, with two men sitting ready to guide it. A few bundles lay heaped in the bow, and they clambered in.

Gordiya wore garments of Western cut, but made from the brighter fabrics of her home, which glinted in the light of their few lanterns. Like all of her people, she was slender, with long fingers, pink at the tips in contrast to her overall darkness. Regarding him, she did not lower her eyes. "Do not be suspicious of us, Highness Wolfram, for we are people of spirit, as are you." Gordiya joined the man at the tiller, leaving the two supposed siblings alone at the front of the boat.

"Melody, does everyone know me?" Wolfram pulled her a little closer.

She shot him an exasperated glance. "I told them you were my brother, Prince Orie's bastard by another woman," she explained, as if that illuminated anything.

"Thanks, Melody, thanks a lot."

"It was the only way they would let us room together, and I didn't want to be alone." Her breath warmed his ear.

He turned quickly to look at her, so that their noses brushed. Melody offered a slight smile. "You don't trust them either," Wolfram observed.

"I'm bored," she replied, "not stupid."

They drifted in silence for a time, the boat slipping quickly with the current, heading for the distant port and a larger, waiting ship that would carry them all over the sea, to the shores of Hemijrai. A few lights grew, then were left behind them, and, after a while, Melody began to watch these lights with interest. Finally, she leaned across him, resting her elbows on his lap to gaze enraptured at a large town on the shore. Above a wooden palisade, a hexagonal tower rose from the stone keep. Rose-tinted lights shone from the alabaster windows, and a dance tune could faintly be heard.

Melody sighed, then lowered her head to lie across his lap. A warmth prickled through the rough wool, then another, with moisture touching his skin.

Frowning, Wolfram touched her shoulder cautiously, then stroked her hair. "What's the matter, Melody?"

"That was Gamel's Grove." She shifted her arm from beneath her to wrap around his knees. "It was my father's keep before he married Mother, before he died."

"Before my father killed him," Wolfram breathed.

"It's so maddening," she sniffed, "not to know anything about him. Nobody speaks of him, except with a curse, or to make the sign of the Goddess."

Wolfram grinned ironically up at the stars. "I've had my fill of hearing about my father, Melody. That's no treat either."

"At least you know. They whisper that he wanted to kill

King Gerrod, someone even said he was mad, that he killed my uncle."

"My namesake." Wolfram frowned a little, considering this. His own knowledge of Orie, despite the legends, was not broad. Whenever the subject came up, Lord Fionvar looked a little sick, and Lyssa's beautiful face turned into one of her stones.

"I used to go 'round to old Rolf's cottage, plying him with questions. He did love to talk, and tell me stories. He even told me—" She bit off the words, her hand tightening on his knee.

"What did he tell you?" Wolfram laid his hand gently upon her head.

"That my birth was cursed," she whispered. "He said my father's lover cursed my mother to sorrow over me."

"That was a stupid thing to say, Melody, no matter how much he despised your father. Even if it's true, what power could she have?"

"She was Hemijrani."

Wolfram stiffened at this revelation, his fingers clasping Melody's silky hair. "Is that the real reason for this trip?"

"I need to go there, Wolfie," Melody continued, her hand curling into a delicate fist, beating her desperation into his leg. "I have to know if it's true. I've asked Gordiya all kinds of things— she's only been with me a few months, but I already have learned so much. The only way to find out for certain is to go there, to find people who knew her, or the teachers she studied with. Maybe there's a way to break the curse, maybe I can undo it, somehow."

"But, Melody, there's no curse to break, none but what your mind invents. You have the only power over that."

"You don't believe that," she said coldly, "I can hear it in your voice. If there is magic, if there is the Blessed Rhys, then surely there are curses just as real."

"If you want to know about cursed, someday I'll tell you everything I did the day I left Lochdale," he said bitterly. "Maybe your brother was right about me."

"Then you know that I have to find out. I'll not have this mystery hanging over me, haunting me the way that Alyn's foolishness haunts you."

For a moment, Wolfram glanced up to the mountains across the river, the boundary of Lochalyn, and the home of all the mysteries he was leaving behind. And somewhere near the dock where they had launched, his own father slept, not knowing that his secret was revealed, not knowing that his son had finally had the chance to reject him. Wolfram's face grew hard as he looked, then he turned to stare resolutely ahead.

"Beware of seeking the mysteries of your birth, Melody. You may not like the answers that you find."

Chapter 10

HER BODY immense with child, Asenith leaned against the wall, breathing hard. Fionvar turned away, allowing her this private moment to collect herself. She had trouble walking long distances, and stairs did her in every time.

"In the future, if you need something from the kitchen, have someone fetch it for you," he said mildly. This woman and her arbitrary needs had been grating to begin with, but now were a part of his daily routine. Summoned from a tedious meeting, Fionvar might even be grateful to her if she had anything other than spite for him.

"I'm not a cripple, my lord, just a pregnant lady. I'm sure you've seen one before." She gasped and was silent a moment, one hand pressed to her belly.

Fionvar remembered well the day Brianna had begun her labor. He remembered because he had not been there, because some stupid crisis or another had taken him away, and no one had thought to call the Lord Protector to the queen's bedside. Not that he would have been allowed into her room, but at least to wait nearby, to be among the first to hear the prince's voice. If there were anything in the past he could do again, he would not have ridden out that day. "I'll take you to the birth-ing room."

"You'll leave me bloody well alone!" Her body shuddered, and she beat the wall with her fist.

With a jerk of his head, Fionvar called over one of the guards who had accompanied him. "Fetch the midwife and get a mes-sage to the queen."

"Aye, sir." The man set off at a sprint.

"Come on, then." Fionvar took her arm, but she slapped him.

"Did I not just tell you to leave me alone? Can't you see I'm in pain?"

"I won't have this baby born in a hallway," Fionvar snapped, rubbing his cheek. "Your choices are walk or be dragged. Pick one."

Asenith gathered her skirt in both hands and lurched upright. "I hate you." Her beautiful face twisted with venom, showing every one of her thirty-seven years.

"That way." He gestured to the left. "Just be grateful it's on this floor."

With Asenith stopping to curse every few minutes, their prog-ress was slow. Halfway there, the guard reappeared, followed by the midwife, Lady Catherine, and Duchess Elyn.

"Is it time?" Elyn crowed. "Get me some tea and bread, I'm hoping for a long wait." She grinned, her eyes flashing. "Heir it may be, but no better than the last one, I'll wager." These past months, Elyn had taken to punctuating her remarks by rapping her cane against the floor. She did it now with a gleeful air like a child impatient for a party.

"Perhaps Your Excellency would like to wait in her own chambers," Fionvar suggested. He could feel a headache coming on.

"No, I want her there," Asenith panted. "Her time's over; she needs to know it."

"Great Lady," he muttered, as the strange parade reached its destination, a small suite of rooms reserved for birthing. The outer chamber held benches and tables for those who would wait.

Fionvar followed Asenith as far as the door of the inner chamber. Already, servants hurried to light the fireplace and bring water. A maid, carrying a load of linens that she dropped beside the birthing chair bumped into him. Curious, Fionvar leaned closer. Made of sturdy wood, the chair had a cut-out seat providing just enough support for the mother. Dark stains marked the legs of the chair, and Fionvar wondered if Brianna's blood had made them, mingling with that of generations of her ancestors.

"Two days I suffered with my son, and five hours struggling to get him out," Elyn said, inspecting the room. "Such pain, I cannot describe it. Donal swore he'd cut me open the next time, rather than hear me screaming."

Asenith, already pale, reached blindly and caught Fionvar's arm as she panted.

"Squat down, it helps some," the midwife advised. "Walk when you can."

Asenith clung a moment longer, earning Fionvar a dark look from the midwife, then she released him and stumbled around the room, her hands pressed to her back.

Leaning over to Catherine, Fionvar whispered, "Was it so for the queen?"

She nodded grimly. "Took it better, though, she did. Polite to a fault."

"Praise the Lady that I was born a man," Fionvar said, turning away.

"Oh, you've seen nothing yet, my lord. You'll be waiting?"

"I'm the Lord Protector. I lost the last heir, I won't lose this one."

Catherine lost her smile, and bobbed a curtsy.

Picking out a comfortable leather chair, Fionvar sat heavily. Wolfram had been gone so long that sometimes he suddenly sprang to mind, and Fionvar knew he had not thought of him for hours. Once, a whole day passed in some frustrating negotiations, and Fionvar realized he had not remembered his son. When it happened, he went down to the temple and lit a candle at the Cave of Life, listening to the scratching of birds on the roof and mice in the floor. Messengers and emissaries had been sent, queries unanswered. The Hemijrani refugees continued to trickle into their makeshift city by the temple, and Lyssa's letters from abroad expressed her growing frustration. She didn't know if they'd taken Wolfram, or where he was, but she was sworn to try. Sometimes, he feared his sister wouldn't return. She would find some news of Wolfram's death and, fearing to tell him, leave Fionvar waiting in vain.

Asenith cried out, and a few more maids bustled in, while the manservants fled.

Elyn hobbled over to a seat near a little table. "The prince takes too much after the wrong father, I think. Sticking it in, where he should leave it alone. King Rhys had certain advantages in that respect."

Fionvar threw his head back and laughed. "Great Lady, you say the most astounding things."

"There's nothing remarkable in what I've said." She leaned her cane against the wall as a servant approached with a tray of tea things.

Breathing in the Terresan tea, Fionvar coughed. "You and Rhys are the only people alive who could drink that foul stuff."

Sniffing, Elyn raised the mug to her withered lips and took a sip. She frowned, then took another. "I think this lot is past its peak," she complained.

"We've just got it in this morning, Your Excellency," the servant informed her.

"Be off then, and fetch me some honey." She took a long swallow of tea, and followed it with a bite of bread. "But I was saying about the prince, she must take a firm hand with him. When he was younger, I could paddle him myself, and did, but now he's just too much for any of us."

Fionvar leaned forward, resting his forearms on his knees. "You did what?"

She looked up, eyebrows raised, with a prim smile of satisfaction. "Well, so he obeyed me in keeping that secret, if nothing else. I knew if he told you, you'd coddle him like you always do."

"Sweet Lady." Fionvar knotted his hands into his hair. All the times he'd not been there when his son needed him.

"It's a good thing Rhys wasn't here," Elyn continued. "He'd've been worse than you are. I don't blame Brianna, poor thing, she has the kingdom to run. I did well raising her, I think. That boy was twelve before he could get away from me. Had some mettle, he did. Where's he got to anyhow? He should be told his bitch is whelping."

Feeling sick, Fionvar stalked to the far end of the room, planting himself on a bench with his feet up, his back pressed against the wall. When he was too young to take on the family, his own father had died, leaving him the charge of the lot of them. He'd been strict enough then to suit anyone's taste, and Orie, the next eldest after the two between had died, had taken the brunt of it. After Orie's death, Fionvar swore he wouldn't do that to his son. He would not make his own son fear him.

They passed a few hours in silence, listening to the curses and murmurs beyond the door, and picking at lunch from trays brought up to them. Needing the exercise, Fionvar walked to his chamber to retrieve Wolfram of Bernholt's journal, opening to a passage just after the prince had angered his father by claiming that Woodmen had the same needs and dreams as they did.

"*I could sit no longer and hear him saying these terrible things,*" Wolfram had written. "*I knew he'd be furious. We have never dealt well with each other, my father and I.*" Fionvar sighed, with a small ironic smile. Years after this incident, King Gerrod would cast out his son as a traitor. "*Oh, Father, there are things in my heart I would share with you, and I wonder what things you would tell me, if you could just see me as I am, and not as you would have me be.*"

Shutting the book, Fionvar slipped it into a pouch at his side. He shut his eyes and rested his head against the wall. If—no, when—he met his son again, he would ask what was in his heart and truly listen to the answer.

Dinner arrived from the kitchens, along with the queen's messenger checking for news. They had none to give him. Elyn mumbled to herself, and scribbled in a little book of her own, taking frequent trips to the privy, but always returning.

Shortly after, Dylan appeared in the open door, fingering the bump from his broken nose. "They're still in there?"

Fionvar nodded.

From the inner door came a shriek of pain, followed by cursing.

"Finistrel preserve us," Dylan gasped, turning pale. After wavering a second more, he hurried away.

Suddenly the door popped open, and Catherine stormed out, her hair in disarray and red welts rising on one cheek. "Somebody get me a rope! I can't hold the bitch any longer." She touched the scratch marks on her face and winced. "We'll tie her down."

"Tie her? But she's in childbirth," Fionvar protested.

Catherine shot him a withering look. "And it gives her strength to fight me, my lord. She's like a mad thing."

"There must be another way."

"It's been done before, my lord. If she won't let us do our work, there won't be any baby. It's got turned about somehow. Midwife needs me to assist."

"I could hold her," he volunteered, stepping forward.

"A man, in the birthing room?" She stared as if he'd grown another head.

"You can't bind her, what must the Lady think of binding a birthing mother?"

"What would the Lady think of a man's being present, that's what I say." Catherine snatched the rope from the hurrying servant and ran back inside.

Another shriek rent the air, followed by the sound of something flung against the wall. "No, you can't! I'm not in prison," Asenith yelled. "Get away from me!"

"Goddess's Tears!" someone cursed, then Catherine's voice called, "My Lord Protector, get in here!"

Fionvar entered a room of chaos, linens and spilled water making a hazard of the floor while a pair of frantic servants tried to gather the herbs from a broken pot. The midwife towered with her arms bare to the shoulders, blood on her hands. In the chair, Asenith had turned sideways, clinging to the back, kicking with all her might when someone came near. "You vixens, you want to kill my baby, I won't let you—you'd kill me if you could."

Fionvar went to Asenith's face and pushed the hair back. She raised a hand to claw at him, and he snatched her wrist. Kneeling beside her, he whispered urgently, "Nobody wants to kill that baby, do you hear me? Lady Asenith!"

She jerked her head up, her blue eyes searing into his, then the mask of fury broke, and she was weeping. "I can't do it," she whimpered. "Don't make me, I can't do it."

"You've come a long way to this moment, and you need to see it through. Don't give up. You haven't given up in almost twenty years, have you?"

Shaking her head, she buried her face in her elbow, her arm straining against him.

"Then turn around and have this baby." When she didn't move, he leaned closer and said, "Just think how Duchess Elyn will laugh if you give up now."

Her head shot up at that, and she bared her teeth. "Don't let them tie me."

"They won't, I'll hold you."

For a moment, Asenith looked uncertain, then the pain shot through her body, and she nodded desperately. Not letting go of her wrist, Fionvar lifted her arm to cross over her chest. He caught her other hand and knelt behind the chair, her head resting on his shoulder. Her body shook with release, then grew rigid with the strain.

"Push!" the midwife shouted, resuming her place on the floor, with Catherine beside her.

Forever Fionvar knelt there, until his arms were weak with the effort of holding her, and his ears numb with her screams and curses. When he thought he could take it no more, the midwife shouted in triumph.

"Praise the Lady!" Catherine called out. "It's a girl!"

Asenith collapsed against him, sobbing.

Servants rushed about, water splashed, then the baby cried. She wailed for a moment, testing her new lungs, protesting this cold, strange place she had been brought to. Then she fell silent, and Fionvar risked a glance.

A tiny pink bundle scrunched up in Catherine's arms, the baby's dark eyes could barely be seen, but she was looking. As if she knew she must understand this place, and these people, she peered about, the rest of her body still with the intensity of her looking.

Asenith raised her head, and smiled, even as tremors shook her body.

"Blankets, quickly," the midwife called, and maids draped the new mother.

Fionvar released her arms, drawing back and straightening carefully. Before he could rise, Asenith reached out and caught his shoulder, pulling him back toward her. "Thank you," she said, and kissed him.

Stunned, Fionvar jerked free, but the tenderness that had softened her for an instant was gone, and Asenith turned away, clutching the blankets.

Lady Catherine stared at him as he faced her. "I'll take this one to the nurse, my lord." She curtsied, and he nodded his leave to go.

Standing still in the busyness, Fionvar watched a group of men carry Asenith to her own bed. Even a woman like that was strong enough to bear such agony. Even she had been given the Lady's gift: to pass on life to another. Dazed, Fionvar walked out.

"A girl, eh?" Elyn said at his sleeve. "Let's hope she's more biddable than that boy of Rhys's."

"She's baseborn," he said softly, not looking at her. "There's no guarantee she'll ever be the heir, nor that it would be allowed."

"Rhys's boy," Elyn repeated, but he ignored her and walked away, to light a candle for his granddaughter.

Chapter 11

WHEN THEY finally touched the stone jetty at Khuran, the vast Hemijrani port, Wolfram knelt on his wobbly knees and gave praise to the Lady that their voyage had been uneventful. Between the unaccustomed roll of the ship and the spice of their strange foods, Wolfram's stomach had tossed quite enough without storms or swells.

"Isn't it beautiful, brother!" Melody dropped down gleefully beside him, twirling about with her arms open wide. She had traded in her man's clothing for a slim-fitting outfit of Hemijrani silk. The tunic fell past her knees, but had slits at the sides to reveal her shapely legs, ill concealed by slim breeches.

"I wish you'd wear a proper skirt." Wolfram rose unsteadily. After his predictions that she would turn back after a day of adventure, she made the best of it while he would give anything for a bed of furs and pine boughs on solid ground, and Morra's undemanding company instead of Melody's mystery and exuberance.

A blare of noise dragged his attention back toward the shore.

Along the wide stone jetty, a bizarre procession approached. It bristled with twisting goat horns and brass instruments bleating obscenities against the realm of music. Defying her name, Melody clapped as they drew nearer.

"For us, Wolfie, isn't it wonderful?"

The ranks of wild musicians parted, revealing behind them a sight even more astonishing. Wolfram gawked, his head tilted back to stare up at the six monstrosities. Each seemed the size of a small house, with gray, wrinkled hide and a huge, flexible appendage rearing and reaching out before. Flowered designs in red and blue twined up their legs and over their faces to where tiny men perched, feet behind the beasts' gigantic ears. How the riders did not come plummeting down, Wolfram could not tell.

The lead driver lifted his stick and smote his enormous mount upon the forehead, causing a retort like the explosion of lightning in a dead tree. As one, the creatures bent up their long noses, slumped back upon their hind legs and settled to the ground. Behind them marched lines of men wearing armor made from bound grasses. Every one of them held a long, curving sword and wore a patch over one eye, left or right apparently at random. Painted on each patch was a wide, unblinking eye.

Wolfram suddenly noticed that Melody had gripped his hand, and now clenched it to her chest, so he could feel the leaping of her heart. Her pale skin flushed, her mouth open, the pink tongue protruding a little as if she would taste the scene as much as look upon it. The quickening of his loins, which he had struggled to ignore every night she had lain on a nearby bunk, threatened to overcome him. "Sister, sister," he repeated under his breath. It could well be true.

"They have elephants, Wolfie. I've only dreamed of them before now."

From the tasseled enclosure on top of the lead beast, a figure emerged, assisted down by a few men taller than the rest. The woman alighted and came forward with small, swaying strides, the tassels of her own scarves twitching time with her hips. She was rounder than the others, with a full woman's shape accented by the drape of fabric in rich hues of purple. Upon her breast hung a pendant of the Sacred Pair, the joined god and goddess these heathens worshipped with who knew what rites. She wore no shoes, but rings of gold adorned her toes, and a pattern of scars decorated the tops of her feet.

When she was a short distance from them, she wiped tears from her cheek, and offered a tremulous smile. "Please, forgive me, Highnesses. I did not wish to show such emotion. It is not our way."

Embarrassed, Wolfram only gave a little shrug.

Melody moved forward to meet her, stopping a few feet short as if unsure what to do. "Please, don't cry," she said, "we've come to help you, however we can."

"I am blessed by the Two just to see you, child." The woman raised a tentative hand to her, then hesitated. "May I touch you, Highness? No harm will come to you."

"Of course, if it can give you comfort," Melody replied promptly, even taking the darker hand in hers, pressing it to her cheek.

Wolfram squinted against the sun, noting that the other woman was not so young as she had first appeared. She kept a younger woman's grace, but the tracery of lines about her eyes revealed her, as did the silvering of the hair showing beneath her veils.

"Won't you tell me what's wrong?" Melody asked.

"I knew your father, Highness. He meant much to me, and I yet grieve his loss. My name is Faedre, though I don't expect that to mean anything to you. I do not believe your mother would have spoken of me."

A sudden prickling started in Wolfram's neck, as if the demon would claw its way up his spine. Ahead of him, Melody stiffened, shifting a little back.

"Were you his—were you the one who loved him, before my mother?" she demanded, a new hardness coming into her voice.

Faedre nodded, her lips pinching together to hold back tears. "My regret was that I could never give him children. If I had, I should have wanted them to be as gracious as yourself, Highness. I see so much of him in you."

Melody's head bowed, her shoulders quaking. Wolfram clenched his fists, willed himself to stillness for the sake of the curving swords and the giant beasts around them.

"I do not mean to make you sad," Faedre went on. "It is simply that I have so longed to see you, the reminder of the man I loved. Can you forgive me that desire?"

"No need," the princess whispered, but she covered her face with her hands.

Then Faedre closed the small gap between them, taking Melody in her dark arms and pulling her close to her idol-clad chest. Melody's slender arms slid likewise around her, as if the two women had sought all their lives for this embrace.

They wept with joy in each other's arms. The Hemijrani men's painted eye patches glared on as witnesses. Only Wolfram looked full on, his neck aching, fingers clenching and flexing. Something inside him urged him to take Melody in his arms and carry her off, fleeing with her across the ocean if that's what it took.

Faedre looked up from Melody's shoulder and smiled. She beckoned to him with one hand, in a strange gesture curving up and down.

Captured by the gesture, Wolfram forgot his desire for escape. Still, he did not approach them, but felt the tugging of a smile at his own lips. If Melody had found the very person she sought, then their mission could be a brief one and, really, what harm could it do? Yet, even as he returned Faedre's smile, cold claws gripped his shoulders, kneading him with suspicion.

At last, the women drew apart, blinking at each other. Melody wiped her eyes with the back of her hand. Faedre said, "A runner from the ship came up to the castle, and I have been sent to make you welcome and bring you there. Would you go now?"

"Oh, yes." Melody nodded feverishly. "Will we get to ride the elephants?"

Faedre's laughter sparkled in the air, her eyes shining as she took Melody's hand. "Of course, Highness." She turned and led the princess back to the waiting elephant.

The prickles of anger sharpened, and Wolfram strode forward, but their assistant blocked his way. "Forgive, Highness Wolfram, this is not our way."

Faedre turned back to him. "Yes, do forgive us. It is not here as it is in your country. Men and women are mostly separate here—certainly they ride separately." She came back to him in a few quick, light steps. "I should have welcomed you more fully," she added softly, her dark eyes watching him from her lowered face. A slight smile played about her lips. "You have not had the benefit of a Hemijrani maid, Prince Wolfram. Soon, you shall become better acquainted with our customs. In the meantime, you shall rejoin your sister for refreshment when we have reached the palace." She curtsied low enough that he could see the dark opening between her breasts. Her voice had lost most of its accent, turning the words in their own tongue with evident pleasure. She rose again and turned her hand in an elegant gesture toward a different elephant.

For a moment longer, Wolfram stared at her, then glanced over to Melody. Waiting by her elephant, arms crossed, Melody glared at him, jerking her head up toward her mount. He gave a little half bow in acquiescence, and she hurried to let the man assist her up. Faedre met his gaze, and said, "You are welcome to my country."

"Thank you," he replied, his eyes flickering over her body, taking in the offer she seemed to be making.

His eyes still on her, Faedre turned and swayed off to join Melody.

Wolfram let out a whistling breath and allowed himself a smile. Perhaps Dylan had been right about the Hemijrani ladies. They were not all fragile and shy, nor was their darkness necessarily a liability. He faced his elephant, and the smile slipped, but just a little. The beast's vast flank was higher than his head. Two small men stood ready to help him up, and he gave himself into their hands, climbing up into the padded enclosure on top. Three sides of his enclosure opened to the view, with a red silk shade overhead, and a thick cushion embroidered with flowers on which to sit. He made himself comfortable and swung wildly to grab one of the wooden posts when the elephant lumbered to its feet. Its pace rocked until he thought he might be sick again. Wolfram clung to the rails with white knuckles and watched the country around him, trying to turn his mind from the mutiny of his stomach.

The stone jetty where they had landed thrust into the crystal blue water, the farthest jetty of a dozen, and by far the widest, allowing the side-by-side passage of two elephants. At the pier to his right, three large ships stood, sails lowered, their cargoes being unloaded by streams of dark-skinned natives. Some of them sported the eye patches he'd noticed on their escort. At the next dock, the crews of smaller boats heaved writhing piles of fish up onto waiting carts. The salt reek of the sea and the squirming squids and fishes threatened Wolfram's stomach. He stared toward the city, holding his breath.

It rose up in spired, balconied towers, decked with colorful laundry from the carved stone balusters. Studying the marble sills and lintels, and the decorative window ledges, Wolfram recognized their influence on the gaudy red-and-white palace at Bernholt, a sharp contrast to the rough granite of his former home. One block they passed had rows of seated merchants. Skinny arms flailed up, thin voices wailed offers he could not understand, all desperate for the commerce of a man important enough for an elephant. Behind the vendors, naked children pissed on the elegant walls, or pursued small herds of goats, which were determined to devour all the refuse. Everywhere, veiled women turned their faces from his gaze, and men wore the eye patches, their single revealed eyes staring in frank curiosity.

Reedy music wailed up from men on the corners, blowing on bulbous pipes. The height of the buildings and the density of the people roaming the dirty streets darkened his sight unrelentingly, with no patch of green common or open courtyard. As the heat began to take hold, waves of rot and the stench of humanity rose from the paving stones. Dizzy, Wolfram leaned to vomit over the side of his elephant.

They passed beneath the wall and out onto a dusty road. Here, the large flocks of goats trotted aimlessly in and out of their path, chased by jabbering herders in little more than loincloths. On both sides, as far as the eye could see, stretched fields plowed by oxen, dotted with fanciful hay mounds shaped like round huts with peaked roofs. Square cottages squatted among them, women and brown children slumping in the sunlight as they milked their goats or gathered onions into baskets carried on their backs. Rangy yellow dogs sniffed despondently at the frequent troughs. Dust from the elephants' plodding feet gave a mist to the scene around him, mile after mile of the same fields, the infrequent trees with delicate, drooping leaves. Lulled by the trundling gait, Wolfram curled onto his cushion and slept.

Chapter 12

THE JOLTING of the elephant as it maneuvered sideways awoke Wolfram. He rubbed his eyes to clear them of the darkness, then realized that night had fallen on the journey. The beast finally rubbed its wrinkled side against a high stone platform and oil lanterns showed the white-clad men waiting to assist him from its back. Once there, he stumbled down the wide steps, his right foot bursting into tingling agony. A phalanx of servants bore lanterns in a ring around them, and he spotted Melody standing with Faedre a little ways off. She sprinted over to him and threw her arms around him.

"I love elephants! I'm going to insist that my grandfather get a few to impress all those other kings." Her grin gleamed up at him. "We stopped for lunch, but you were sleeping, so we let you be."

We, he thought, *Faedre and Melody.* "I thought you and I were to have this adventure together, sister," he said, not meaning to sound so bitter.

"I'm sorry. They have such strict rules about men and women, and Faedre seemed so happy to see me . . ."

"And that's another thing. Why should she be happy to see her rival's daughter?"

"Her lover's," Melody corrected. "And she was my mother's favored lady, once. She wanted them both happy. Naturally Mother was jealous when she found out. That's probably how the story about the curse got started." The princess harrumphed. "Faedre was exiled and had to humble herself to be accepted home after that disgrace."

"She must be in good graces now," Wolfram observed.

"It's taken her years and repentance to attain her position." Melody scowled. "When you know her, you won't be so suspicious."

Across the ring, Faedre was gazing at them gently. Wolfram met her eyes a moment. A delicate smile trembled upon the lady's lips, sending a pleasant rush through Wolfram's body. Perhaps he did not want to share his adventures with Melody in any event, she who was so innocent and childlike. Even Asenith had never watched him with such interest. "After the voyage and that ride, I'm not feeling myself, that's all."

Instantly Melody's face pinched, and she stroked a finger along his cheek. "I don't seem to have any trouble with sailing. I wish I could help you feel better, though."

Wolfram turned his smile on Melody. "Your sympathy is help enough for me."

"Is that a proper thing to say to your sister?"

Reddening, Wolfram withdrew his hands. "I did not mean it so, Melody. It's just that"—he started, frowning—"it's nice to know that somebody cares how I feel."

"Surely your mother—"

He shook his head, cutting her off. "I've broken trust with her, and she always has so many other things to be worried about."

"Mistress Lyssa would not have come looking for you if you were not important. Even for murder, surely they'd rather let you vanish than try to bring you to trial."

Wolfram flinched away from her, crossing his arms against a sudden chill despite the warmth of the night. "Well, I—" he began, but suddenly Faedre was standing at his elbow, silent and submissive, and he had no idea how long she'd been there. The sickness must have skewed the senses that his time with the Woodmen had honed. He clenched his jaw. "Later, sister, we'll have more time to talk."

Faedre's smile seemed a little flat when she faced her. "Are you hungry, Highnesses? I believe there is food laid for you, if you wish to eat. Then you shall be shown to rooms for the night."

"Where are we?"

"This is the home of the Jeshan of Hemijrai. Our king, if you will." When Wolfram opened his mouth again, she held up a firm hand. "Time for more questions when your needs are seen to." She set out through the opening lines of servants.

Shrugging one shoulder, Melody put out her hand for Wolfram's. "A long day, that's all. She's probably tired, too, from preparing for us, plus her duties."

"What duties?" Wolfram led her after Faedre's swaying passage.

"She is the chief priestess, after all."

Wolfram stumbled and regained himself. "I did not know." The chill that had hold of his chest spread up with sharp claws into his neck and shoulders.

"Gordiya's been teaching me some things. It's very interesting—Faedre says they'll provide a teacher for you so you can learn about this culture."

"I'm not much of a scholar." They came up to a tall flight of stairs decked with a richly patterned rug that led them up into a colonnade surrounding a sunken courtyard. Eerie cries of birds drifted out from the dark trees gathered there like a patch of wilderness. Then something roared.

Melody jumped, clinging to Wolfram with both hands, but Faedre indulged in a throaty chuckle. She crossed to the baluster and leaned down, crooning a few words into the darkness. From below came a breathy pant. Two huge paws stretched up from the vegetation to rest upon the edge: soft, white feet each larger than Wolfram's own hand—larger than his head, he suspected, but he dared not get that close. The head of the beast emerged from the shadows, pale with black markings and large luminous eyes. Its great jaws opened in a toothy display, the thick pink tongue caressing sharp ivory teeth.

Still crooning, Faedre reached down to where the beast rose to greet her, and scratched it tenderly beneath the chin. The giant cat's eyes narrowed with pleasure, and its throat produced a purr nearly as disturbing as the previous roar had been.

Still shrinking into Wolfram's embrace, Melody hissed, "What's that?"

"Rostam is a tiger," Faedre said, "and my pet. Aren't you?" With a final rub beneath its fearsome jaw, she turned back to them.

The tiger opened his eyes fully, gazing a long moment at Wolfram, then removed its feet and sank back into the darkness.

Wolfram let out a long breath, frowning over Melody's head. "That is your pet."

"Indeed, Highness, but not one for the faint of heart." She smiled at him as his grandmother had sometimes done, lips compressed, expressing her smug superiority.

Melody straightened away as he replied, "You seem to have plenty of surprises."

"Oh? Then you must pardon me for not having prepared you. I shall endeavor to improve my performance." She nodded to him, as if bowing to his wishes, but her tongue played about her teeth as she smiled. "I did promise you food, Highnesses. This way." Faedre showed them down a series of corridors, passing many terraces and courtyards. The servants they passed as they walked turned their faces to the wall.

After a few turnings, Melody whispered to Wolfram, "I'll bet that tiger could outdo Mother's dogs. I'll bet he brings down warriors."

"I'd not like to see," Wolfram commented.

"I've heard that they use big cats in sport here, both hunting, and arena games where they fight each other." She shuddered. "They don't look safe."

"No," he agreed, eyeing a pair of smaller spotted cats led by on silver chains. The two eyed him back, licking their whiskers.

"Here we are at last," Faedre said, stepping aside with a sweeping gesture. They had come to another open-air space, partially roofed with billowing silk canopies. Fires burned in braziers dotted about the space, and unfamiliar spices mingled with the smoke in the air. Several low stone tables rose from the intricate mosaic underfoot, and one of these had cushions around it and was laden with dishes. Two dozen servants—all men with one

eye covered—waited nearby. Melody and Wolfram sat side by
side, cross-legged on the cushions. They had no personal dishes,
but could pick at will from the many platters laid out before
them: a few whole-roasted birds, their skins crackling with spices,
mounds of cut and whole fruits shaped like stars or bursting with
red seeds, steaming onions and eggplants in thick orange sauce,
and a plate of ratlike creatures fried whole, their tails sticking out
to serve as handles for dipping them into sauces. A male servant
whisked before each of them a heaping brass bowl of rice and a
smaller bowl of warm water, evidently for washing the fingers.

"Please, enjoy the meal, and I shall return for you when you
are through." Faedre bowed her head briefly, then vanished into
the courtyard.

Cautiously, Wolfram scooped up a bit of rice in his fingers and
ate it. He waited a moment for rebellion, and found instead that
the rumblings were a voracious hunger. Greedily, he reached for
the platter of fruit and selected an assortment, which he piled
up on his rice as he slurped the juice off his fingers. He used his
long knife to skewer one of the roast birds and tore off a leg, then
froze, the grease dripping along his fingers.

Melody stared at him. "Aren't you going to wait for a fork, at
least?"

Wolfram chuckled, shaking his head as he took her in, sitting
upright on a cushion, wearing strange clothing more like a man's
than a woman's, and insisting on table manners. He tore into the
meat as she tried to get the attention of one of the servants. The
servants seemed to have vanished as well, and she frowned at the
vast array of food. Wolfram pulled the last scrap of flesh from the
bone and tossed it aside.

"Barbarian," she said, but not without a smile.

Wolfram shrugged one shoulder. "Before I came to Bernholt,
I lived with the Woodmen. They have a saying, '*Na tu Lusawe,
shasinhe goron*,' which means 'the gifts of the spirits are precious
and swift.' They don't stand on ceremony and they don't wait
for silverware. If you're not quick about your dinner, somebody
else'll be eating it."

"I see," she replied gravely.

"If it makes you feel better, you can have my knife." He offered it to her, hilt first. "Pretend it's a fork with only one tine. Be glad there isn't any soup."

She hmmphed her answer and delicately started in, prodding a dish with the knife. By the end of the meal, both of them had juices of all sorts running down their hands and chins. He rinsed his fingers, then discovered bits of meat and spices decked his beard. When he glanced up at Melody, she let fly with peals of laughter. He laughed with her. With his stomach pleasantly full and the prospect of a good night's sleep, the place did not seem so dangerous. He might even begin to enjoy this adventure.

Faedre reappeared shortly, with a small man wearing an amulet similar to hers. Little scars pocked his shaved head as well as the tops of his feet, and several anklets of various metals tinkled as he walked. When he smiled, he revealed that his incisors had been elongated with gold and inset with small rubies. Wolfram winced at the sight, almost tasting the metallic tang.

"Many welcomes to you both, Your Highnesses," the man said, speaking carefully, his accent much more marked than Faedre's. "The Hemijrani are indeed most fortunate to have you here and most willingly having come to our aid."

"Thank you for hosting us so graciously and unexpectedly," Melody replied, putting on a regal air Wolfram had not known she possessed. "We are honored to come here and look forward to offering whatever assistance we may."

In the shadows behind Faedre stood the only other female he'd seen since their arrival, a nearly sexless child, slender, clad all in white, with a veil draped over her face. Only her eyes could be seen, through a narrow opening. Dozens of bronze bracelets decked her arms, clinking softly. She hung back, but the bright gaze revealed her interest. Wolfram flashed a smile, and the girl jerked, turning away. A servant stood beside her, his hand hesitating in a basket, then strewing a handful of fragrant leaves before her.

Faedre followed Wolfram's gaze to the girl, one dark eyebrow raised, but she said nothing to either of them. To Melody, she said, "I will take you to your room," gesturing off to the left with the grace of a dancer.

Wolfram, too, rose at this, but the little man let out a sharp, "Ah!" his hands held up in a placating gesture. "You must learn our customs, Highness Wolfram."

"I should like at least to be shown where my sister will be," Wolfram said, speaking slowly, one hand drawn inexorably to the growing throb in his temple. "We have come together to your country, we do not know your way, nor your language. It seems only fair that you make an effort to help us be comfortable."

"Wolfram," Melody said, pausing, "you've not been well. Go to bed, and we'll talk in the morning, yes?" She glanced to the Hemijrani man.

"Indeed, of course." He bobbed his head, flashing the golden teeth. "Come, come, and all will be spoken of in the light."

"You aren't helping, Melody," Wolfram muttered, reaching for her arm.

"Don't be an ass." She pulled away, arms crossed. "We have to live as these people do and without insulting them. Now I am going to bed."

Faedre's eyebrow notched up, one eye crinkling in a faint smile. Again, she bowed to Wolfram and swept off into the darkness, with Melody close behind. The girl in white hovered a moment, watching Wolfram, then turned and lightly hurried off, her servant frantically moving before, sprinkling the leaves for her sandaled feet.

Wolfram snatched his hand away from his face, curling it into a fist as he rounded on the man. For a moment, he breathed through clenched teeth while the other held up his palms, waving them in an attempt to placate him. If he struck the man, what could it prove? Wolfram's ignorance was complete—he had no place to run to, and he'd already soured his only ally. "Well?" he barked.

"This way, Highness, this way." He abandoned all pretext of accompaniment and trotted ahead of Wolfram down a bewildering series of corridors.

By the time they had arrived at a beaded curtain, Wolfram had regained control, though the pulse in his head still threatened to burst free.

Bowing over his hands, grinning like a fool, the man ushered him into a large courtyard with a series of doors and arches lead-ing out. "Please be welcome."

The beads trailed over Wolfram's shoulders—not unlike the way his lover's hair had done—and he took a few extra steps to leave the sensation behind. Vast bronze pots held towering trees with strange jagged bark. They had no branches except at the very top, where they spread out in pointed fingers of green. Torches thrust into the pots illuminated them from below, sput-tering green sparks and giving off a hint of spices. Seats of marble carved in the shape of elephants hunched beneath the greenery as well, occupied by a chattering troupe of dark-furred monkeys. At Wolfram's approach, they fell silent, watching him with lumi-nous eyes. They leapt for the trees, pulling themselves up easily. In a moment, small brown fruits began raining down upon him, and Wolfram covered his head, quickly dashing under the shelter of the nearest arch.

His escort shook his fists up at the trees, letting out a string of high-pitched invective. The hail of dates ceased, but the monkeys took up screeching instead. "Many pardons, Highness Wolfram. They are such filthy creatures."

"Why on earth do you keep them if that's what you think?"

"Only for holy needs." He tried a smile.

Wolfram darted a glance his way. "Sacrifice?" he asked. "It's all right. I lived with a people in my country who sacrifice for their spirits. They use birds, mostly."

"Birds?" The man brightened. "This is of interest for me! Have you done this?"

"A few times." He shrugged. "I'm better at adapting than Melody lets on."

"Yes, yes." Again the dark head bobbed. "But, many pardons, Highness. I am called Esfandiyar, and I am of the holy men here." He touched the pendant at his chest. "This is my yard, and here is a room for you. It is not near your sister." He saddened for a mo-ment, as if in sympathy, then added, "But other things are better than sisters." He made a grand gesture toward one of the arches that was draped by a curtain. Light came through the swirling pattern of the fabric, and Wolfram pushed it aside.

The chamber held little in the way of furniture. A few painted chests stood near the walls, with mirrors above to reflect the light of lanterns. Dark green silk draped the ceiling, with thick carpet on the floor softening the room. A cushion covered in striped material lay on top, with a pile of pillows and blankets of pale wool. Perched on top was a young woman, completely naked. She rose as they entered, lifting a goblet and carrying it forward, her eyes lowered. Her long, dark hair concealed her breasts and brushed along her hips as she moved.

"I thought men and women slept separately."

"Yes, yes," Esfandiyar replied, but his now-familiar fervor was tempered with warmth as he smiled at the woman. "Here is no woman, but my favored slave."

Turning back to her, Wolfram said, "I can see why."

She held out the goblet, still not looking at him.

"I think it is the hair that frightens her," Esfandiyar explained, patting a hand on his own smooth cheek.

"My beard? I'll shave it." The last of his headache whispered away, as he took the goblet. "What's this?" He sniffed its cloying sweetness.

"Rose wine. It is very special here."

While parts of him were eager to surrender to the local customs, Wolfram held himself in check and offered the goblet to Esfandiyar. "Would you care for a sip?" he asked lightly, studying the other's face.

The smile fled for a moment, and Esfandiyar made a slight bow. "Of course, Highness Wolfram." He took a swallow of the drink. "You are indeed more than Highness Melody lets on."

"It's very useful to be underestimated."

"Indeed, Highness Wolfram," Esfandiyar returned, with a glint of gold. "I shall look forward to learning more of you."

Chapter 13

WOLFRAM AWOKE in the light of a new dawn, almost sorry he had begged off the attentions of the slave girl. He felt wooed, as much as any bride by a prospective groom, and the thought made him leery of any aspect of their hospitality.

A whisper of movement made him roll over. Two slaves, both men, quietly arranged a basin and a few glinting silver trays on one of the chests by the opposite wall. Sunlight glowed red and purple through the patterned curtains, and he could hear the chatter of the monkeys in the courtyard. The two men bowed in his direction and left as silently as they had entered. A trail of steam rose from the basin, scented with oranges. Beside it lay a new set of clothes identical to those made for him on the ship. A suggestion to rise, evidently.

Wolfram slid to the edge of the bed and got up, steadying himself against a sudden wobble in his knees. He frowned, willing himself back in control. Some aftereffect of the wine, that was all. He crossed to the things laid out for him, and found the tray laden, not with food as he had hoped, but with all manner of combs and brushes, little pots of mysterious cosmetics, and a tall vial of oil. After rinsing his face and splashing his hair with the scented water, Wolfram took a few minutes to shave off his beard, a troublesome process, but with good results. The new clothes fit well, and he wondered if someone had made off with the other set during the night to use them as a pattern. He stretched and shook the sleep from his limbs, then pushed aside the curtain to see what the new day would bring him.

With a splat, a gob of something dark smacked the front of his tunic. Wolfram sprang aside from a second gob, taking cover behind a pair of pillars as the monkeys screeched out their laughter.

Esfandiyar, rising from his elephant-shaped stool, shouted high-pitched curses at the creatures. One landed lightly on the table he'd left and started rooting through the pastries of the breakfast he was evidently sharing with Faedre.

Wolfram started forward, but Faedre grabbed the monkey with one dark hand and gave it a swift shake before casting it aside into the bushes. She shook her hand as if to flick away the touch of it. She looked up to Wolfram, and her scowl eased into a slight smile as she bowed over her hands. "Good morning, Highness, I trust you slept well."

"Yes, quite." Wolfram slowed his pace to come up beside her table. A waiting servant hurried to bring over another stool. As Esfandiyar resumed his place, Wolfram realized that the monkeys had fallen silent, grouped in their treetops staring down with dark eyes. He caught the look that passed between the priest and priestess—the latter smiling a little more. The monkey she had cast aside lay at the base of a tree, unmoving.

"Will you have tea, or is there something you prefer?" Esfandiyar asked, offering a tall glass cup decorated with a filigree of silver.

The scented steam reminded Wolfram instantly of his great-grandmother, Duchess Elyn. She drank Terresan tea daily, as had his father. He wrinkled his nose. "Is this where that stuff comes from?" Wolfram eyed the breakfast laid out on the little table. One platter held stiff curls of pink and yellow—sweets, apparently—while another held fritters of shredded vegetables and the last small cakes topped with fruit. Not a piece of cheese in sight, nor any honeyed butter. Hesitantly, he took one of the cakes and took a bite. He quickly downed it and reached for another.

His companions nodded their approval, and began helping themselves again.

"How is Melody this morning?" Wolfram asked.

"I have not seen her yet, Highness." Faedre laughed lightly. "Her mother, too, liked to lie abed in the mornings."

"Is the women's quarter very far from here?"

"Not far." She sipped her tea, watching him over the rim. "You do not trust us, Prince Wolfram. Or is it simply me that you do not trust?"

"Your customs are strange to me, and it is my duty to look after my sister."

"Is it now?" She nodded and took another sip. "She is fortunate to have such a good brother." Her smile gave nothing away.

"Most of her time, of course, has been with Alyn, who is so holy and good that it disgusts both of us. So I do what I can, without becoming that overbearing." Wolfram popped a pink thing into his mouth and crunched into it.

"I have never met Prince Alyn," Faedre said, leaning forward in her interest, her breasts pressing the purple fabric of her draped gown. "I gather that he is very different from yourself and his sister."

"Quite." Wolfram cleaned his teeth with his tongue, trying to dispel the sticky sweetness of whatever he'd just eaten. "For one thing, he's pale as a star. He sees visions, speaks to the Lady, and spends his days in contemplation or study. He's always going off here or there to heed the voices, saving starving peasants or bringing the word of Finistrel to a new land, like he is now." He took a long, grateful swallow of golden liquid and found it to be a light mead. "Perhaps he should have come here."

Esfandiyar choked on a swallow of tea and sputtered as the servant fussed around him, but Faedre laughed. She stretched an arm in a long gesture encompassing all the palace and their land beyond. "For six thousand years, we have been here, cultivating this place. The oldest rooms in this palace are older than that race of savages who still run in your forests. We do not seem to be out of favor with our own gods just yet."

Wolfram's jaw tightened as he thought of Morra's face. "What about the war?" Cold claws pricked at his spine.

Her shoulders straightened, and she replied, "There is that, but we do have means to ease our suffering."

"My—" my mother, he had been about to say, but stopped

himself. "My neighbors in Lochalyn do not seem to agree with your assessment."

"It shall all be handled shortly." Her slender smile widened a touch. "In fact, I shall cross the sea to that country as a spiritual leader to our people there."

Something niggled at the back of Wolfram's memory; some part of one of Lyssa's stories touching on the subject of her brother's mistress. Lyssa had never been very forthcoming about Orie's role in the recapture of the throne of Lochalyn, and it had not struck him before as something he should know. Now, every omission in the history drew his attention. Did it conceal another lie? "Not to keep harping on the subject," he began with a smile, "but when may I be reunited with my sister?"

"I had thought we were getting to know one another, Prince Wolfram. But as you wish." She rose, resetting her pendant between her breasts.

Still silent, Esfandiyar rose as well, motioning for the servants to clear their meal. He ushered his guests before him back into the shade of the corridor. As they passed, Wolfram noticed the still form of the monkey Faedre had cast aside. A few flies buzzed around the creature's open eyes. Esfandiyar jerked his head to call the attention of one of the servants. Catching Wolfram's eyes, he grinned his golden grin, but the expression was that of a man whose breakfast had not entirely agreed with him.

Once in the halls of the vast palace, Faedre glided alongside Wolfram, leading only by subtle indications of which direction they should turn. "As a foreigner, and a man, you should be always before me."

"Not very practical for strangers, is it?" Wolfram looked around in quick glances, noting the turnings and openings around him. They passed the courtyard where Faedre's "pet" tiger lived, revealed by day as a large space of thick vines and trees. Crimson and turquoise birds flitted in the greenery, calling out to one another. The party turned along a different side of the yard, and Wolfram watched Faedre's gaze caressing the trees. She would not want to be far from her pet, so the women's quarter must open off one side of this yard. Smiling to himself, Wolfram eyed the doors across the way.

"It is one of the concessions women must make here, but living apart from men makes certain things easier." She flicked a glance up to be sure she had his attention. "Certain things, a woman would not reveal about another woman."

Wolfram felt the warm shiver of her gaze, even as she turned it demurely aside. "I would have thought your taboos would work against you, even there."

"Do not forget, Prince Wolfram, that I have lived among other people. I may not be so bound as the women who have never left the Quarter."

"Never?"

"Some girls are born in the birthing chamber and taken to nurses within the Quarter. There, they are raised among other women only. If the Jeshan should desire one of them, she would be brought to a shared chamber. Outside of such rooms, a man may not even touch his wife."

"You seem to have the run of the place."

"It is my duty now to be hostess for the Jeshan's foreign visitors because I have lived among them." She made a slight gesture to a new passage, and they turned again, climbing a long flight of steps up toward the glaring sun.

"Will we get to meet this Jeshan?"

Again, she laughed. "No, I should not think so. Even for kings, he rarely shows himself. Unless you intend to be a troublesome guest, Prince Wolfram?"

"I'll try not to be." He hoped the demon would leave him alone for a long time.

From the dazzling sunlight at the top of the stairs, a voice called out, "Wolfie! Isn't it marvelous! Is it not the most fantastic place you've ever seen?" Melody gave him a swift embrace and pulled away to study him. Today she wore loose-wrapped scarves that barely passed for clothing and made him long to forsake his fraternal vows to unwrap them.

"Well, yes, I suppose." He took her hand in his, but she pulled away.

"Oh, no. You're not to touch me, Wolfie, if we're to live as our hosts do."

"Why would I want to do that?" he griped, but trailed along after her as she ran for Faedre's side, taking her hand instead of his own.

Just as the paving in the courtyards changed with the age of the construction, so, too, the rooftops were a jumble of styles from sharply peaked to domed to low, tiled structures, all of them packed together as if someone had built a city without streets or alleys. Frequent yards punctured the uneven plain. Beyond the palace walls stretched cultivated fields, with herds of goats and plows pulled by huge oxen. More trees sprouted in the courtyards of the palace than outside it, although the hazy distance showed green mountains. He saw neither rivers nor lakes, nor any gleam of water. They must have deep wells, among the trees, perhaps. The road led back through teeming villages, and Wolfram could spy the glint of the distant ocean.

The stairs had brought them out at the base of the only tower—a slender spire rising at least ten stories into the sky. Each level was marked by a frill of decorative carving, and black letters of inlaid stone writhed upon its gleaming white surface. It blossomed into a dome, and Wolfram strained his neck trying to see the highest levels.

He had never been comfortable in high places and the thought of climbing the building made his stomach roll. Fortunately, the tower had no door that he could see, although windows pierced it occasionally after the second level. Placed at intervals around the tower, long lines of inlaid tile radiated out, punctuated by blocks decorated with strange figures.

"We have brought you, Highnesses, to our most holy place," Esfandiyar told them. "Here before you is the Tower of Ayel."

"Beneath it," Faedre said, moving up beside him, "is a cavern of equal size which is the Womb of Jonsha."

"The tower shall bring us, through His power, up into the skies."

"The womb shall bring us, through Her mystery, down into the earth."

Their two voices took on the intonation of holy office suddenly, and the two faced each other. "Only those most holy may enter here," Faedre said.

"Only those most pure may serve the Two as they would have it," Esfandiyar replied. Both leaned forward and their lips met in a brief, passionless kiss.

Drawing apart, they faced the tower in silence. Wolfram stepped a little closer to Melody. Faedre was nobody's idea of a priestess, nor of purity. Her mystery indeed.

Melody took no notice of the irony, if she saw it, but whispered instead, "Doesn't it make sense? Man and woman together creating the universe."

Almost of its own accord, Wolfram's hand made a circle before him, invoking the Goddess. "The power of creation belongs to woman, to the Lady, as it should be."

"Don't you know how to make a baby, Wolfram?"

Wolfram flushed, and Melody turned sharply away, her arms slipping to cross beneath her breasts. Shutting his eyes, Wolfram took a deep breath and let it out slow.

Wolfram sighed. He stood watching the still figures of Faedre and Esfandiyar as they performed some silent worship. "Don't be distant with me, Melody, you're all I know here."

"I'm simply not sure how much we know each other, that's all," she tossed over her shoulder.

"How will we know anything if we cannot speak freely with each other?"

She turned to peer at him. "There is that, I suppose." She stroked a palm over her forehead, and Wolfram thought for a moment that she had flamed as tellingly as he. "I do not think I could get used to this sun."

"Nor I. I prefer the shade, and plenty of trees."

"Woodman that you are," she said, stretching and turning as if facing him again were purely accidental.

As if their brief spat had loosed some unknown tension, the two figures before them suddenly relaxed, and they turned, sharing a smile.

"Forgive us," Faedre said. "This is a private worship we perform twice daily." She tilted her head to draw them forward. "Come and I shall show you a secret."

A sliver of the whiteness detached itself by the base of the tower, resolving into a small figure—the strange girl they had seen last night. A servant carrying a huge basket went before her strewing leaves that released a pungent odor when the girl's feet touched them.

Melody leaned to Wolfram's ear. "That's Deishima, Faedre's acolyte, I guess you'd say. Faedre's taught her our language, but she hardly speaks, not to the likes of me, anyhow. I think she is a daughter of the Jeshan, and thus above all the rest of us. She's only been outside the Quarter three times before we came, can you imagine?"

"That doesn't seem much of a life for a princess."

"They consider her holy, almost a living goddess. That's why her feet must never touch the ground."

The little parade approached, and the swaddled figure of Deishima presented itself before Faedre. The priestess folded her arms to bow over them, then continued, Deishima and her attendant shadowing their movements to one side.

"Are you training her for a priestess?" Wolfram asked.

Faedre glanced back, her eyes flared. "She has a very special role, Prince Wolfram. The signs of both heavens and earth have shown us that great events will happen this season. We are hopeful for the rebirth of the Two."

"Rebirth? How can that be?"

"Your Goddess walks, does she not?"

"Some have said so, and Prince Alyn claims to hear Her voice."

"Is it then so strange that my people, too, should wish for our gods among us? They might wield the power of life and death, heaven and earth in our behalf. We have been hearing the tales from your country, tales that say She is with you now, and some here have been concerned over what this may mean."

"Just stories." Wolfram shrugged. "Not every story means something."

"But are not our very legends of the gods, simple stories? And yet their meaning carries a people through ages. Who is to say which story is the fire and which smoke?"

"It's like these stories the refugees tell us," Melody observed. "They claim that terrible things are happening, and yet I've seen no evidence here."

"So you see."

A prickling touched Wolfram's neck, and he glanced about sharply. On her trail of leaves, Deishima's veiled face turned toward them, then flicked away again. "Then, if there's no war, our work here is done, right, Melody?"

"Of course there's a war," Melody scoffed. "Just not here and now, and not as atrocious as those people would have us think."

The little group gathered at the opposite side of the tower. Here, the twining of black letters led the eye to a panel of stone a little smoother than the rest. "Welcome to the place of Her mystery. You cannot come in, of course, but I shall let you see."

With a careful push of one hand, Faedre released the delicate balance of the stone. It swung down with only a gentle sigh, showing a dark and twisted stair. Deishima's veil fluttered with her own sigh as Melody gasped, leaning in close.

"Very few men, Prince Wolfram," Faedre murmured, her eyes on his, "very few have known Her mystery." Her clove-scented breath caressed his face and that now-familiar shiver reached deep inside him.

He'd always enjoyed a mystery.

Chapter 14

APPARENTLY GRATIFIED by their reactions, Faedre rose. "There are a few things we must do, if you would not mind waiting here. It will not be long." She smiled graciously. "A servant will bring you drinks to wait with."

Melody continued staring into the hole a moment longer. "Your goddess is of the earth," she breathed, "not the stars."

"Indeed, Melody. Here, the male aspect is of the sky, the female is deeper. Between the tower and the womb a small chamber, round, like one of your temples, joins the two aspects. It is there that Esfandiyar and I meet for our rituals."

Wolfram eyed the tower, imagining that the priest had already gone in through some way even more secret than this.

"Please." Faedre gestured away toward the stairs they had taken. At the top, a small group of servants had erected a temporary shade over a carpet with a few chairs. Wolfram offered his arm to Melody, and, after a moment's hesitation, she accepted it, lightly resting her fingers by his elbow with none of her former intimacy. The cold claws prickled the back of Wolfram's neck as he led her toward the shade and placed her in the central seat. Cool fruit juice had been supplied, and they sipped gratefully.

The servant sprinkling leaves before Deishima led his charge over to them as well, and she stepped delicately upon the carpet. Two others rushed over to drape her seat with a golden cloth, and she perched, taking no refreshment but looking back toward the tower. In the small gap where her eyes were revealed, Wolfram saw twin vertical lines of consternation. Perhaps she wondered why she had not been invited to this ritual, whatever it might be.

"I hope your room is as comfortable as mine," Melody said. "It's right near the garden and the outer wall, so the birds come in. They have the most remarkable flowers."

"We don't have flowers," Wolfram said, "we have monkeys. They're noisy and messy, and I'm rather glad they're to be sacrificed."

"What a frightful thing to say!" She glared at him. "Really, Wolfram, I think you spent far too long with those Woodmen."

"Maybe so, but I'm not the one doing the sacrificing, your precious Faedre is. She killed one of them this morning."

The veils over Deishima's mouth rippled with a sudden breath, but Melody had turned to face Wolfram, her cheeks flushed. "Finding Faedre is halfway to finding my father, it's like having a second mother, and a kinder one than mine ever was. Maybe you don't like her, but you haven't even given her a chance."

As if it had been waiting for this, the demon sprang to life. Wolfram's head throbbed with sudden agony as his muscles tightened for the fight, one hand raised to his temple. "Look around you, Melody! Something's wrong here. Faedre shouldn't love you, she should hate you because your mother took Orie away. And why did your maid bring us here? Did she know who would meet us at the dock, Melody? You're so busy with your second mother that you're not paying attention to what's going on."

"Why shouldn't Faedre love me, for all the reasons she said?" Melody snapped back, slamming down her glass. "Of course something's wrong, Wolfram, there's a war on! That's where all the tension is, and the attention as well."

"Where's the bloody war, Melody? I don't see it." He spread his arms to take in the countryside. "Where is it?"

"Well, how should I know? I don't live here; I'm trying to be a civilized guest. I'm sure we'll understand everything if you just give it time."

He leapt up to stare at Deishima. "Where's the bloody war, Princess?"

She jerked back, white showing around her dark eyes. "South," she murmured, a ruffling of the veil. "Far to the south. Many of our men have gone."

"See?" crowed Melody.

He continued staring, meeting the faceless eyes, his head pounding. "I'll believe it when I do," he said at last, and flopped back into his chair. He grabbed his glass and finished it, shaking it at a servant until it was refilled to be emptied again. For the rest of the time, they sat in silence, Deishima staring at her hands, Melody glancing around as if curious about all she could see, and Wolfram searching the far horizon, wondering how he'd gotten to this place. He examined the rooftops around them, noting the rhythm of courtyards and domes, catching the scent of horses on the slight breeze. Behind and toward the front of the palace he found the small yard with the ragged trees and monkeys, some of which perched upon the roof's edge: Esfandiyar's quarters. Off at the far corner of this uneven plain stood a squat, round structure, with stone gates set about and dark slits of windows. Wolfram puzzled over the thing—high enough to be a guard tower, but the windows would hardly allow a good view—then let his gaze move on.

By the time the priestly couple returned, the shadow of the tower had aligned itself with one of the dark lines of tile, then separated from it again and moved on. Wolfram sprang from his chair as they approached, glad of an excuse to rise again. "Esfandiyar, I want to ride out to see your country today, will you arrange it?"

Faedre froze a moment and glanced to her partner. Esfandiyar gave a wavering golden grin, his eyes flicking to her, and back to Wolfram, and back again. His face seemed to have gained a few more lines since he had entered the tower. "I do not know, Highness, if such a thing can be arranged like so?"

"Yes, I believe you do know. Or am I a prisoner, not allowed beyond these walls?" The pulse throbbed in his temple, but he forced his hands away and felt them curling into fists.

"Of course we're not prisoners, but surely you'd like to see the palace first," Melody said someplace behind him.

"Ah!" Esfandiyar said brightly, the gold gleaming in his mouth. "Indeed, we have arranged a visit to the finest rooms!"

"Is that what I asked for?" Wolfram replied coldly.

The priest wilted under his fierce stare. "Perhaps, something can be done, yes?"

Faedre stepped nearer, her shoulder brushing Esfandiyar out of the way of Wolfram's fury. "There may be an elephant available for a short trip, Prince Wolfram." Her voice had lost all its honeyed tones.

"I would prefer a horse." He folded his arms across his chest.

"I have no doubt that this is true," she said, smiling now, "but I do not believe—"

"You people do an awful lot of believing." Wolfram pointed to a courtyard near the outer wall. "That is a stable, is it not? And there appear to be plenty of horses."

"They are reserved for the guards and messengers," Esfandiyar piped up, earning a black look from Faedre.

"Well, naturally, we will inquire on your behalf," she purred, shifting her stance so that her breasts pushed a little forward. "Why not take a tour of the palace, and we will tell you if arrangements can be made?"

"I have a better idea," Wolfram said, his hands herding them into motion, "let's go now and ask." Without a backward glance, he took the steps two at a time and turned into the darkness of the corridor. A quick patter of feet told him they were following.

"I must apologize for my brother's moods," Melody said loudly. "I've no idea what's gotten into him."

"Orie had such tempers at times. It required all of my skill to settle him," Faedre told her. "I have heard that such things may be passed within a family."

"Then Wolfram must have gotten a double dose from someplace."

Wolfram kept an ear out for their dialogue but paid more attention to his route. He had been tracing the rhythm of rooftops and courtyards, and now swept along the passages they had concealed with little pause for consideration. His only fear was to find one of the rooftops had hidden a forbidden temple or women's area that he could not take into account. For a time, Faedre's and Melody's voices were brazen, rife with mocking. No one stepped up to lead him, and all evidently expected him to become lost in the palace maze.

Doggedly, he kept on, until he came to a covered pool, surrounded by vegetation. The far wall had no walkway, so he must choose here which direction they would need on the other side. Wolfram paused, and the little group behind him caught their breath. He could almost hear Faedre smile. His eyes narrowed. Instinct told him he could not be far away now—instinct honed by his months of tracking with the Woodmen. He shut his eyes and willed his heartbeat to silence in his ears. A slight breeze touched his cheek on the left, accompanied by the merest whiff of horses. Wolfram allowed himself a grin. He turned left and, in a few more turns, had brought them to the balcony overlooking a grassy courtyard where the horses pricked their ears at the newcomers.

Wolfram leaned against the rail. "Where do we inquire about borrowing these fine animals?"

"How did you do that?" Melody came up beside him, her irritation swept away. "That was amazing! All those corners; I had no idea where we were going."

Still smiling, he turned to look at her. "A little too long with those Woodmen, I suppose. The skill is useful, though."

Expecting to hear a sting in his words, she slowly returned his smile. Behind them, Faedre spoke a few words to Esfandiyar, who went pattering off and emerged onto the green below, where he entered into a conversation with a nodding groom.

With a rustle of silks, Faedre, too, came to lean on Wolfram's other side. "Indeed, a most informative display. I shall be sure not to hide things from you, Prince Wolfram; you seem able to track your prey even in the darkness of ignorance." Her eyes slid to caress his face, then slid away, her profile serene.

"I try never to let ignorance stand in my way."

Down on the green, Esfandiyar was waving his arms to them, and Wolfram straightened, pleased to see the groom leading a few horses. "Coming, Melody?"

Hesitating, she looked to Faedre. "I think I would prefer to stay here. There is much to be learned."

"Indeed, Melody, I shall be happy to continue our conversations." Faedre took her arm. "We shall allow the men to take this adventure."

Wolfram paused, considering the pair of them. "Then I guess I'll see you later."

"Yes, brother." Both bowed their heads to him, and they turned to go together, even the sway in their strides seeming to grow more alike.

Watching them go, Wolfram felt a twinge of doubt, but he shook it off. Melody would take care of herself, and Faedre was very affectionate toward her. She'd be sharing stories of her father, no doubt—and wasn't that what she really wanted? He spun on his heel and found the stairs going down.

The Hemijrani horses were small and light-boned, tossing their delicate necks. They looked ready to run, taking the tight-est of curves with no loss of speed. Wolfram had not ridden for over six months, but his head stopped throbbing at the sight of the horses; here was a chance for speed, for a small measure of freedom. He'd soon find out if Esfandiyar and his guards could keep up.

Once in the saddle, they were led to a large, arched gate that gave way onto a road following the wall of the palace. "What is it you would wish to see?" Esfandiyar asked, his voice resigned, his round face showing his distaste for this mode of transport.

"One of your villages." Then he thought of something else. "And that river where we stopped yesterday—I slept through it, and I understand it was quite lovely."

"This way, then." Esfandiyar relayed his instructions to the two men with them, one of whom trotted up to take the lead.

"Down the main road, eh?"

"No, no over here—" He drew breath for more, but Wolfram turned his horse's head for the main road and leaned down over its blood-bay neck. He tested his boots in the strangely shaped stirrups. Esfandiyar seemed to sense what he was about and cried out a warning, but Wolfram set his heels to the horse's flanks and called wordless encouragement to its pricked ears. It did not need to be asked twice. With a few strides, they'd overtaken the leader, and flew along in the shadow of the wall, the dark mane flicking his face, wind rushing over his body. Wolfram whooped with laughter.

One of the guards came up alongside, riding hard, his face intent on Wolfram's. With a nod, Wolfram grinned, and nudged his horse a little harder. He saw the answering grin for the briefest moment as his mount sprang away.

Reveling in the bunch and stretch of the animal beneath him, Wolfram led the way. Occasionally the young guard took the lead, but the blood-bay horse wouldn't let him have it long. The horse's mane lashed tears from Wolfram's eyes, so that he finally pulled up as they plunged down the slope at the front of the palace. They'd burst into a stream of wagons headed up from the fields, startling the stolid oxen and eliciting shouts from the nearly naked peasants who led them. Wolfram and his companion trotted a while to settle the horses and drew up in the shade of a tall clump of spiky trees to wait for the distant figure of Esfandiyar, bouncing awkwardly on his mount.

The guard, only a few years older than Wolfram, grinned again, panting with the joy of the race. He gestured at Wolfram and spoke a few words. Wolfram shrugged his incomprehension, and the other man nodded amiably. From one of the brass knobs that decorated his saddle, the guard pulled up a leather bottle on a thong. He popped the cork and offered it to Wolfram, first taking a tiny sip himself and smiling.

Wolfram accepted the flask and took a swallow of something sweet and strongly alcoholic. He shook his head as the stuff hit him, then returned the smile, and took another swig. From the guard's excited chatter, Wolfram gathered that he had trained the horses they rode and was proud of their performance.

When at last Esfandiyar joined them, Wolfram had learned the guard's name—Dawsiir—and half the vocabulary he'd require to get a job at the stables. The priest's face bent into a frown, and he started in on a lecture to Dawsiir, who immediately dropped his face and gaze from Wolfram, losing all trace of his excitement.

"It's not his fault, you know, I started it. He was just trying to keep up with me."

"No, Highness Wolfram, among our duties is to keep you safe, and this race might have broken your neck." Esfandiyar glowered at him. "That would be to place me in a most uncomfortable position."

"Forgive me, Esfandiyar, I had not considered your position," Wolfram replied with all the grace he could muster—a good deal, from the changing expression on the priest's puzzled face. "Perhaps you and your man should set the pace." He offered them the lead, and Esfandiyar accepted, turning their horses out onto the road.

Pretending to adjust his horse's reins, Wolfram hesitated. When Dawsiir pulled closer to see what the trouble was, Wolfram clapped him on the shoulder, and flashed a wicked grin. He caught the thong of the flask, and uncorked it for a final swallow. The pair rode on in silent companionship behind their proper elders, on the path that Wolfram had chosen.

The road teemed with people. Most went on foot, toting baskets with the straps across their foreheads, or pairs of jugs balanced on sticks. Several of the oxcarts were loaded down with a dozen or more people packed together, some hanging on to the sides. These mostly wound their slow way down toward the seaport. On the wagons heading for the palace, many of the men wore the eye patches Wolfram had noted earlier, though most of these were simple scraps of cloth with no painted decoration. He called out the question to Esfandiyar, who straightened in his saddle.

"For the royal women, Highness Wolfram, a sign of respect that they shall not look fully upon them." The words came haltingly, and Wolfram dismissed them immediately but made note of the deception.

Turning to Dawsiir, he placed a hand over one eye, and made as if to ask him.

Dawsiir immediately shuddered, and replied, "Ashwadi." He made a strange gesture, and frowned, before letting loose a stream of words that made no sense. At last he shrugged and pulled something from his shirt, passing it over.

The guard's eye patch was leather, with a well-painted eye on the outside, and Wolfram examined it, but there was no hint of what its purpose could be. He offered it back, but Dawsiir shook his head, patting his shirt to indicate that he had another. Shooing gestures convinced Wolfram that the man meant him to keep it. He nodded his thanks and tucked it away.

Smaller dirt roads twined off among the brown fields in both directions, leading toward distant clumps of trees, or small, tilted buildings surrounded by dark-skinned children. Oxen carts laden with huge barrels headed toward these dwellings, greeted by shouts and running women. Wolfram's suspicions grew.

At last, they came to a halt near a band of trees and dismounted. The older guard followed a path through the trees while Esfandiyar hung back, fussing over his saddle. The area was trampled by large, flat feet—elephants, he assumed. Wolfram and Dawsiir shared a look, and even the young guard seemed suddenly apprehensive. The man returned, shaking his head and waving his arms. Esfandiyar snapped at him, then broke off to grin at Wolfram.

"We will rest a moment. Would you care for drink?" He offered a flask of water, and Wolfram drank deeply.

"What was the man looking for?"

The eyes flickered away. "Just seeing to natural needs, yes?"

Wolfram nodded slowly. Then he announced, "Me, too," and set off for the path.

"Highness Wolfram, please! There are stinging plants." Esfandiyar hurried after him, plucking his sleeve, but lacking the courage to lay hands upon him. "There are snakes, and insects!"

Shrugging him off, Wolfram took longer strides, and immediately came through the trees to a narrow strip of grass beyond. A riverbed wound its way among the trees. At the bottom, a puddle of muddy water stood, the last of whatever river there had been.

Esfandiyar stood beside him, looking down at the puddle. He called something back over his shoulder, and the guards shortly appeared, leading the horses to drink. Wolfram walked a little ways along the bank, following its curve until he was out of sight of Esfandiyar's bleak gaze. Just around the bend, he found a dam of mud and stones. Several huge barrels rested on their sides, bung holes empty and dry. He turned and walked in the other direction, past the silent priest, and found a similar dam there as well. Slowly, he returned to where he had stood, arms folded.

"There is no river, is there?" he asked gently.

Shoulders stooped, Esfandiyar shook his head.

Together, they watched the horses quench their thirst. "It is the dry season. There has been river, and there shall be," Esfandiyar said.

"Why have you pretended there was one? Someone wasted all of those barrels here, just to convince us." No answer was forthcoming, and Wolfram remarked, "Faedre must have been awfully disappointed that I slept through the display."

"We wish for you to see the bounty of our country, Highness Wolfram. It is misfortune, only, you come when the season is so dry. When we have rains, the road even here is flooded. Some people must live on boats, with their cattles." He waved his arms, indicated a field of water. A measure of life had returned to his voice.

Wolfram nodded again. "That would be something to see."

"Perhaps you are staying so long, yes?" Esfandiyar turned with his familiar grin.

"We'll see. This would be a lovely place, when the river is high." He studied the trees opposite; no telltale bundles of grass hung in their branches, nothing to indicate that a flood had been here for many years.

"Indeed, yes, Highness Wolfram. Shall we ride?"

"Let's do that." Wolfram accepted his reins, and followed them along the path, not looking back to the dead river they left behind.

Chapter 15

DARKNESS HAD fallen before they returned to the palace, and Dawsiir bowed to Wolfram with a twinkle in his eye as he led the horses away.

All afternoon, Wolfram had been on his best behavior, allowing himself to be led here and there, shown the finest houses, and wells in the valleys where he could draw up good water. Now, he turned to his guide. "Thank you, Esfandiyar, I enjoyed that immensely. I think I just needed to stretch my legs a while."

"You are most welcome, of course, and I hope that you feel better now?"

"Yes, much—in fact, I'm starved!" They had taken a simple luncheon at one of the fine houses, but that was a long time ago.

"Then we shall find again our quarters and food shall be brought there." Esfandiyar brought him to the stairs, then raised his plucked eyebrows. "Unless you would care to lead?"

Wolfram chuckled. "No, I couldn't manage that one. I have no idea where we really started out. I only found this place because of the smell."

"Ah," said the priest. "I had wondered that. Do not fear that I shall reveal your secret." He wriggled his little eyebrows and took the lead.

Following his slow pace—Esfandiyar clearly was unused to such a long ride—Wolfram contented himself with confirming the way he had suspected they would follow. He had already tipped his hand to an alarming degree that morning, but Esfandiyar seemed content with the explanation. The priest's rooms were nearly at the opposite side of the palace and quite a hike from the stables, which were in an older or less fashionable area. Somewhere between the two lay the forbidden women's quarter, and he was beginning to put together the clues as to where. *Good work for one day*, he thought.

As they arrived, Esfandiyar asked carefully, "Would you wish to see your sister tonight, or has the day tired you, as I know it has done for me, Highness Wolfram?"

Wolfram yawned broadly, and sighed. "I would like to see her, but I think I can wait until the morning. Besides, don't you still have your evening ritual to perform? Faedre mustn't be too happy having to wait for you."

Bobbing his head, Esfandiyar said, "You speak truly, Highness. But I shall see to your supper before I must go."

They ate a quick meal together, and, after Wolfram declined the services of the favored slave, Esfandiyar took his leave. One of the ever-present servants coaxed a monkey down from the trees and tucked it into a bag, which he handed off to the priest. Esfandiyar wrinkled his nose, and Wolfram offered an understanding smile. Carrying the squirming, shrieking sacrifice, the priest vanished out the door.

Wolfram lingered over his mead a little while, then retired to his chamber, quickly snuffing the lamps and pulling off his boots. He listened to the shuffling of the servants outside as they cleared the remains of the meal, and took advantage of an argument that rose between them to slip through the curtain of beads, their clinking hidden by the other sounds. The door to the outside stood remarkably unguarded—Esfandiyar was more the fool than he seemed. Wolfram moved through the ill-lit corridors with the air of royalty and purpose, nodding as the servants turned their faces to the wall for his passage. When he found himself at the tiger's yard, he strode confidently along the side and disappeared into the shadows at the far corner, where he quickly doubled back and crouched, peering through the darkness.

Three burly guards lurked around the larger central door, armed with spears and swords. No chance for a frontal assault. Melody had said that her room was near a garden on the outside wall. If he could scale it—but that would be just as absurd. The roof stairs were not far away, and he wouldn't have to pass too near the tower where Faedre's ritual was taking place. He won free to the rooftops, letting his eyes adjust to the glow of the moon before he set out as softly as he could. Keeping to the stone roofs less likely to carry his sound to those below, he returned to the tiger's yard, and from there made a beeline for the outer wall. When he found it, he saw that the garden was quite large, and had many shrubs and paths, and even vines that swarmed over the wall toward the outside. A fountain gleamed at the garden's center, with a main pathway leading toward the shadowy entrance of the chambers within. If there were guards, he couldn't see them from here. He'd have to take his chances on the ground.

As he climbed down a sturdy vine, he wondered why other men hadn't made use of this to visit the ladies. Or perhaps they did it all the time. He quashed a chuckle as he let himself down. Now, all he had to do was find Melody's room and entice her out here for a private and serious talk.

Soft grass grew in the paths, coddling his bare feet, and he let the sensation relax the tension his secrecy compelled. The flowers Melody had mentioned perfumed the air though he could not make them out in the darkness. Somewhere ahead lay the fountain he had glimpsed from above, which must mark the center of the garden and his best hope for checking the status of any guards at the doors. Most of the way there, a slight movement arrested him. Not far off, he caught an unexpected gleam of white in the darkness. He took a stealthy creep forward and came to a little opening.

At its center, a figure leaned back upon her hands, her head flung up to face the moon. She wore only a light chemise that revealed far more of her than it concealed. Her small breasts pointed skyward, trembling a little with her breathing. Again, she shook her head a little—the motion that had caught his eye—and resettled her hair upon the grass around her. The gleaming black hair flowed in waves over her shoulders and trickled toward the flowers. When she had moved, a tendril of it fell so close Wolfram could see the near-violet twist of one curl resting by his finger. If she were to stand, the hair must reach below her knees, nearly to her ankles, even.

She was an image of peace and perfection—a kind of peace that Wolfram had never known. Wolfram caught his breath, imagining, just for a moment, the feel of that silken hair trailing over his chest, stroking away the demon that haunted him. Almost without thinking, he inched his fingers closer and allowed himself to draw one trembling finger over the vulnerable curl.

He let it twine around his rough finger, the fine hairs catching on his tiny scars and dry skin. His mouth, too, felt dry. Shaking with the impulse, he raised the lock ever so carefully to his face and breathed in her scent—sweet, and strangely familiar. He breathed in the serenity that she possessed and shut his eyes to hold it deep within his chest.

Silently, he kissed the curl, letting it slide back from his unwilling fingers.

She arched her back, then raised her head, her shoulders straightening.

Just for a moment, the hair caught over his hand, and she turned to free it.

The scream sent him jolting to his feet.

She, too, jumped up, flinging the treasure of her hair behind her to face him—all the way to her bare ankles, some tiny part of him saw. The scream went on and on, her eyes white with terror, her flimsy dress catching on the bushes behind her as she backed away.

"No, it's all right, I didn't mean anything." He took a half step forward, and the scream seemed to choke off. She flung up her hands to ward him off.

Her slender arms waved before him, cutting a pattern into the sky, and he was suddenly as frozen as if he had forgotten how to move. His mouth hung open dumbly, his eyes still fixed upon her. He could hear shouting behind him, catch glimpses of light as guards entered the garden, but he couldn't turn, couldn't bolt for the wall and the safety of the rooftops. What had she done?

The woman took a careful step forward, and he saw her eyes reflecting the moonlight—Deishima's eyes, he was sure of it. Great Goddess, but he'd dropped himself in it now.

Her tongue darted out at the corners of her mouth and she hugged herself as if she could be cold in this boiling night. Suddenly, she shot out a hand and made a grabbing gesture, pulling her fist away.

The paralysis lifted, and Wolfram stumbled forward, the way he had been leaning. She sprang away from him, but he hadn't the slightest intention of staying. He spun and ran for the vines, cursing under his breath.

The movement caught the guards' attention, and they crashed after him. One of them caught his leg, even as he was nearly above their heads. Strong hands jerked him down, tumbling to earth with leaves clutched in his skinned hands.

Wolfram rolled and dove for an opening, back for the door or the far wall.

Tripping, he smashed headlong into a spiky bush, the fragrance of roses filling his senses as if to mock him.

Hands laid hold of him again, pulling him free. He struggled desperately, all the strength of the demon wild within him, his head roaring, his throat sore from cursing.

He'd shaken off a few, but one man had hold of his wrist and yanked him off-balance, then flung him into the wall.

Dazed, Wolfram let the stone support him, his fingers scrabbling for purchase in the vines.

The guard loomed up again, gripping the front of Wolfram's

shirt. He pulled his prisoner toward him, then smacked his head and shoulders back against the wall. As the moonlight faded from sight, Wolfram thought that might have been the blow to finally release the demon and set him free. In place of the moon, he saw Erik's pale face, the mouth flapping at him, shouting blood.

Chapter 16

WOLFRAM WAS searched and prodded, and shoved into some dark place to wait for the dawn. When he sat up straight, his head touched the ceiling of his cell, and he could not stretch out on the floor. From the moans and prayers in the air outside, he knew that his cell was one of many, guarded by a dozen men who roamed listlessly across the courtyard between them. Like the rest of the cell, the door was stone, but had a series of openings pierced into it through which the sounds and the breeze of a passing guard could reach him. One corner of the cell had a hole bored through the floor that revealed its purpose by the lingering odor. Wolfram sat close to the door, his head turned to catch whatever air he could.

His head throbbed, but the damage was not as bad as he had feared. The blood had finally dried to a sticky patch on the back of his head. His shoulders ached, as did his palms. With little else to occupy him, he rolled the scene over and over in his mind. Her gestures had been some sort of magic, no doubt about that. The bracelets and the eye patches must all be related somehow; respect for the royal women indeed. Wolfram laughed aloud, but he did not like the sound of the echoes.

The growing dawn brought visitors for several of the other half doors, mostly poorly dressed women trying to push bits of food through the vents. When his own visitors arrived, Wolfram's heart rose. Surely, as a foreigner and a prince, they'd not allow him to languish here like these other sorry souls.

Faedre and Esfandiyar knelt outside, while Melody hung back, waiting her turn.

Her eyes ringed with even darker circles, Faedre gazed at him a long moment before she spoke. "Highness, I am afraid you will see the Jeshan as you asked, and under such circumstances as I had feared."

At these words, and the vanishing from her countenance of all her grace, Wolfram's heart lurched. He glanced to Esfandiyar, but the other would not meet his eyes.

"All night, we have been pleading in your behalf, you must believe me."

He swallowed hard. "Tell me straight, Faedre. Is it prison? How long?"

Her eyes welled with sudden compassion, yet they seemed unfocused, as if she saw through him to something else beyond.

Esfandiyar took a breath. "Not prison."

"Death," Faedre breathed.

"For touching her hair?" he shouted, pressing his face to the openings. "It was a mistake! It was a bloody stupid accident! Great Goddess." Esfandiyar flinched. "I wanted to see Melody, privately. Look, I don't even belong here; surely there's something you can do?"

"Ignorance has stood in your way, then, Prince Wolfram," Faedre said, some answering flare rising in her own face, "because the Jeshan does not listen to reason when his daughter has been defiled."

Wolfram flung himself back from the view, letting his bruised shoulders strike the wall as if the pain could jar him from this nightmare. He had fled a murder in his own country, only to die for touching a woman's hair. How many other crimes he might be held accountable for, yet this stupid impulse he had followed would be the death of him. Great Goddess indeed.

Faedre rose with a subdued rustle of silk and turned away.

Hovering a moment longer, Esfandiyar said, "I wish that you had told me, Highness Wolfram, and there should have been another way." Wolfram glanced up briefly as Esfandiyar's weary figure rose and retreated.

At last, Melody came, settling herself near his door and leaning into it, pressing her fingers into the openings. Redness haunted her eyes, and her lips trembled. "What was so important, Wolfie? Why couldn't you wait for me?"

He reached out a hesitant finger and stroked her fingertips, pale and warm against the cold stone. "Could I ever wait if now seemed like the time?" She bent her head to lay her cheek on the stone. "It's not your fault."

"How could you leave me like this? I was just getting used to having you around." She sobbed on the other side of the wall.

He rested his hot forehead on the stone that separated them. "I haven't been the brother to you that I should have been. For that, I am sorry."

"You wanted to protect me, Wolfie. I should have protected you."

"You tried. All of you tried, Melody, I know that."

They sat in silence a long while, their fingers brushing, before Wolfram got the courage to ask, "Do you know how I'm to be—"

"Don't ask that," she wailed, pulling free her fingers. "I can't tell you." Her face buried in her hands, Melody fled into Faedre's comforting arms. "What can we do? There must be something we've not tried."

Faedre glanced back to Wolfram's hole with a calculating stare. "We have another ally, if she can be reached in time, and I am sure the Two will not allow this travesty." She drew Melody close to her side, and the trio left his limited range of vision.

Lying back on stone, Wolfram let his mind wander over all the terrible tortures he could imagine. What did they have in store for him? He recalled that Faedre said he might see the Jeshan. Could he plead his case then, or would the king simply witness his execution, whatever hideous form it might take? Lost in such musings, he almost missed the tap at his door. Rolling over, he propped his head on his hand and looked out. Instantly, he scrambled up and hunched in front of the vent.

On the other side, dressed in her full robes and wrappings, knelt Deishima. A servant hovered nearby with his basket of leaves, looking nervous.

Could she be the ally Faedre had spoken of? But she already knew; she knew it all. "You're about the last person I expected to see here, after getting me killed."

"I have got you killed, Your Highness?" Her voice was light and lovely as the accent curled around his language with consummate skill. "It was not I who broke so many laws."

"If you hadn't screamed like that, if you hadn't frozen me with your bloody hands—bury it, there's a thousand things you could have done, starting by listening to my explanation, or would that be another defilement?"

Two little lines appeared between Deishima's brows. "It was night, and I was alone, or so I thought. Would any of your ladies have done any differently?"

"What about that magic, then? What did you do to me?"

"Ashwadi," she replied. "It is a skill of the royal women of my people."

"It's why all the men wear eye patches, isn't it?"

She inclined her head briefly.

Wolfram patted his shirt, and fished out the eye patch Dawsiir had given him. He slipped it on, and turned back to Deishima with an ironic smile. "I guess I'm safe now." Another part of his world had gone dark with the gesture, and what remained lacked depth and feature.

The arch of her brows crinkled, and he thought for a moment she might weep. "You will not wish to be wearing that soon."

"Why not?"

"Have you not been told the sentence?"

"Why tell me, it's only the last day of my life." The pulse started in his temple, and he felt the impotent rage building up behind his eyes. He shut the one concealed from her, pressing the lids tight to squeeze out the pain.

"It is to be leopards," Deishima replied. "You will fight the leopards."

"A fight? So I have a chance."

"There will be eight leopards."

"Can't you just stab me now? Or poison, maybe? Bury it, no wonder Melody wouldn't say. Goddess's Tears, what have you done to me?"

"As I told you," she said calmly, "this is what you have brought upon yourself." She paused and frowned again. "Why did you touch me?"

"Who knows? Because I'm an idiot who lets his cock lead him to the slaughter every time." And yet it was not his lust that lured him last night, but something deeper, a longing he dared not articulate. He pressed his palm to his forehead. The pain had never struck so hard before; perhaps the blow to his head angered the demon more than ever.

"Forgive me," Deishima breathed, her face close to the opening.

"What?" he snapped.

"I have said too much and angered you." Her quiet words reached through the stone as if they were the breeze.

He eyed her sidelong. She had apologized before he spoke, as if she could see the demon swelling within him. "Why did you come here?" he asked more quietly.

"What you say is true, there are things I could have done and did not. Forgive me for my part in this, Highness Wolfram."

Her words utterly disarmed him. He wanted more than anything to hurt something, to break or tear or rage, the way he always had, and yet he couldn't focus that rage upon her, though she sat so close he could smell the spice of her breath. He flipped the eye patch up and let his eyes flash over her before smothering them with the heels of his hands. "Go away," he moaned. "Please go away."

"I am sorry," she said again, then rose and left as silently as she had come.

He did not have long to wait; it seemed the Jeshan would not postpone his entertainment. A rattling of chains signaled the guards' arrival, and they hauled him out of the darkness into unbearably strong sunlight. He stumbled between them, trying to see. They paused to fiddle with a gate that allowed exit from the prison block, and someone grabbed his hand.

Wolfram turned sharply. Over the top of the wall, a dark, anxious face regarded him. Dawsiir whispered urgently, but to no avail. He made a vertical sliding motion with his hand, and closed Wolfram's fingers over a handful of stout, stubby bits of wood. Neither the action nor the gift meant anything to him, but the groom's desperation was clear, so Wolfram flashed him a grin, as if all were understood.

Dawsiir nodded firmly, and disappeared to the other side of the wall as the guards pulled Wolfram into motion again. He clutched the sticks with all his strength. If he were a good shot, he might blind a leopard with them before he had his arms ripped off.

He didn't bother to keep track of the turns and yards on this journey; one way or another, he wouldn't be returning to his cell.

At last they reached a large octagonal courtyard with benches and seats stepped up on all sides near the edge of a pit. Men filled all the seats—guards and courtiers of the palace, and a few who might have been merchants and tradesmen. Off to the left, a large balcony shaded by purple showed where the Jeshan watched. From below, it was hard to see more than the bulk of the man and the gold that twinkled in his turban wrappings. A tall figure stood near, hand dangerously near a sword, as sharp voices reached Wolfram's ears. Unconcerned, the Jeshan merely gestured below, toward the gate where Wolfram had appeared.

A short sword was thrust into his hand, then the men grabbed him and heaved him forward.

One foot—still bare—struck the edge of the pit, and he curled up as he fell, absorbing the impact on his left hip and shoulder. He rolled, and stood immediately, though swaying, turning quickly to see where they'd thrown him.

About twelve feet deep, the pit was scattered with a few bones, mostly animal from his brief inventory. Each of the eight walls had a gate centered in it, with a grate at its center and a chain allowing it to be drawn up along grooves in the wall. Dawsiir's gesture returned to him, and Wolfram sprang for the nearest gate. Fumbling, he shoved one of the blunt sticks into the slight gap between gate and groove.

Even as he ran for the next, the chains groaned, and the gates began their ponderous rise. He jammed the next gate with a gap at the bottom—two fewer leopards. Not much better odds, but a start.

A roar rose above him, and he whirled, his back to the wall.

Across the brown-stained marble leapt the first of the cats, a sleek, spotted devil, its ribs showing its hunger, and powerful jaws issuing a terrible snarl.

Darting to the floor, Wolfram abandoned his sticks and grabbed the largest bone he could, smacking aside the overeager cat as he rose. Already, the others were on him. Claws ripped at his leg, barely deterred by a swift strike of his sword.

He slammed aside another with his bone club, sending it reeling into its fellows. Hissing, two of them tackled the fallen one, leaving Wolfram the time to thrust sharply through the neck of a third.

Shaking off the corpse unbalanced him, and he slid along the wall. The trapped leopards yowled, and one paw shot beneath its stuck gate to tear into his shoulder.

He ducked below the lashing claws, letting them swipe at the furious spotted shape that flung itself at his head. Blood slicked his sword, his own and the cats'. Wolfram tightened his grip and hacked at a leg. He tried to force his legs to support him and gained the wall again on the far side of his caged attacker.

The tenor of the roar in his ears suddenly changed, rising in a shriek of surprise. The leopard nearest kept coming, but a blur of motion behind showed the others changing course.

A feline cry of agony split the bloody air as a shape from above tackled it, jabbing and tearing with a gleaming blade. "On your feet, Wolfram!" a familiar voice cried, and he did not question the command.

Hope surging within him, Wolfram pushed himself up and threw aside his enemy, smashing the knob of bone down on its skull even as his blade swept its chest.

In seconds, his ally had fought her way near, her hammer breaking the jaw of a flying cat as a determined grin spread over her face. Hunting him across the continents, Lyssa had found him here. Her blade joined his, and her voice cried aloud to the Lady.

The Lady indeed had come to him at last. With renewed strength, Wolfram thrust through a leopard aiming at Lyssa's back, then left the wall to defend her. Back to back, they finished the last two cats, and she stepped aside for him to skewer the one still yowling blood from its ruined face.

Shaking, he left the sword in the soggy fur and turned back to her. He wiped sweat from his eyes, replacing it with blood, and laughed at himself for doing it. "Great Goddess, Lyssa, you're here!"

She slipped her sword back to its loop, and the hammer joined it. In a long stride, she reached him, her strong arm catching him to her chest before his legs could give out again. "Wolfram, you little fool, don't you ever do that to me again, you hear? So help me, I'll kill you myself," she muttered into his hair. Turning her face skyward, she bellowed, "Get us out of here, you bastards!"

Chapter 17

In LYSSA'S chamber alongside the women's quarter, servants slathered Wolfram's wounds with a concoction made from honey and herbs that seemed to dull the sting of the claw marks. In some far corner of the palace, they were discussing whether his punishment would be considered complete, or if Lyssa's intervention violated some part of their archaic law. For the moment, Wolfram didn't care. He lay at last on a comfortable bed, his wounds tended, his dry throat soothed by some of Esfandiyar's special rose wine. Lyssa paced not far off, overseeing all that was done for him, snapping at the servants if he so much as flinched. His Lyssa, brought like an avenger from nowhere to save him. How could he have forgotten how beautiful she was. A thousand questions buzzed inside him, waiting for her undivided attention.

Lyssa spoke Hemijrani adequately well, so he surmised that she had been here for some time. Her bare scalp was deeply tanned, accented by the vine tattoo over her eye. She must have been the ally Faedre spoke of, called back from whatever adventure she'd been on. Faedre's part in it was another, larger question, but one he put aside for the time being. If Lyssa would go through all of this, she must be after more than vengeance. Had she come for his mother's sake or his own? Drifting in a haze of wine and herbs, Wolfram let himself be lulled to sleep by the patient hands. Lyssa would be there later; she would always be there.

When he awoke, he took a moment just to breathe, quiet and safe. The light had changed from sun streaming from an open door to lanterns set about on the chests. This room was much like his own, save for the swaths of cloth draped over the bed. One of the two doors opened into the ladies' quarter, so the cloth was probably an attempt at atmosphere for the lovers who would meet here. Lyssa herself sat on a stool by his side, her sword resting across a polishing cloth on her lap, though she made no move to touch it. Instead, her eyes lingered over his bare chest, flickering up to his throat, and away again, a frown twisting the corners of her mouth.

"Lyssa, what are you doing here?" he asked, the first and easiest question that came to mind.

Lyssa started, the sword clattering to the floor. She retrieved it with a scowl and slapped it down on a table. "Looking for you."

"Then Bernholt must know where we've gone."

"What's Bernholt got to do with anything?" She placed an elbow on her knee and leaned her chin on her hand, studying him. "I've been here for ages, negotiating for your return."

He laughed. "But I've only just gotten here. Three days ago, I think."

She made a sound like a growl. "Where've they been keeping you, then?"

"Nobody's been keeping me anywhere. Look, do I have a concussion, or is this conversation not making any sense?"

"Fine then, you first. Tell me all."

"Well . . ." He hesitated. "Actually, I haven't eaten since yesterday. Why don't you get us some food, then you can talk while I eat. I'll fill in whatever you don't know." He plucked at the light wool blanket.

Lyssa maintained her stare a moment longer. "I'll hold you to it." She rose and called to someone in the hall. Moments later, a half dozen servants appeared, toting trays and bowls, which were spread on a chest by his head. Wolfram collected enough pillows to prop himself up and took a greedy swallow of mead before starting in on a roasted leg of something.

Filling her own cup, Lyssa took a sip, then described the scene at the castle when they'd realized he was gone. "Your mother was frantic, and they were sure you'd been kidnapped by these refugees, maybe to be exchanged for our aid in this war they're fighting. Gwythym found Erik dead in the streets, and Dylan injured—I understand he's recovered now," she added, in response to Wolfram's flash of concern. "I thought you'd run away," she continued, describing her fruitless journey to Bernholt.

While she spoke, Wolfram tried to piece together the events of that night. Erik must have gone for Dylan at the observatory when he discovered Wolfram had left. Asenith would have admitted that much, anyhow. Dylan would have known he'd go to the west gate to try for a horse, it was what they'd always talked about if they wanted to leave town in a hurry. The corner of his mouth betrayed a smile as he recalled hiding out when they were twelve, planning secret escapes and adventures. Whatever had happened in the confusion, he was glad Dylan was all right.

"So I left Bernholt and came here on some awful little boat. The Jeshan accepted me as a royal emissary and set about confusing me with kindness. Every sort of gift and honor they could give me. I had to flee my ambassador's quarters for this place just to leave all the men they kept sending. I tried explaining the Lady's way, but they'd have none of it." She snorted, the sound so characteristic that it broadened Wolfram's smile. "I thought it might be language getting in the way, so I learned what I could of that, but still they admitted nothing. They denied nothing,

either, but they did it all in such a way that I was convinced
they had you someplace. It was like bargaining in a marketplace.
I couldn't tell if they wanted to draw us into this war or try to
get us to stop it. Three days ago, the Jeshan's men said they'd take
me to see 'something worthwhile.' You—I thought. We wound
up at an ancient temple complex, hundreds of these towers and
wombs; have you seen the one here? That's where the messenger
found me last night. I think I rode the legs off my horse to get
back here." She took a long swallow and regarded him sternly.
"Now you."

Licking his fingers and wiping them carefully, Wolfram considered what to tell her, and what to leave out. Finally, he began,
"Someone tried to kill me that night I left. Thief, maybe, or one
of the refugees, I don't know."

"Great Lady!" She sighed, reaching out a hand to the scar at
his throat. Her touch sent shivers through him, as it always had.

"I was running away, Lyssa, you were right about that. After I
broke free, I just ran. I wasn't thinking clearly. You know me." He
threw in a chuckle and ran a hand through his hair. "Anyhow,
I wound up in the woods, and fell down a cliff or something.
I woke up in a Woodmen's camp. They took care of me, and I
moved on with them." *Them,* he thought, *not her, not Morra.* He
felt a twinge of guilt at leaving her out, but neither could he
explain what they had done for each other—not to Lyssa. Suddenly, he touched his throat and cursed. "Where's my bear claw?
Did those guards get it?"

"No, it's right here." Lyssa produced it, blood-soaked leather
thong and all, and handed it over. "I guess they didn't think it
could do much harm."

He closed it in his fist, feeling the reassuring jab of the tip.
"The Woodmen gave it to me. It's all I have of that time. Well,
not quite all." Cleaned of blood and grime, his skin revealed the
tracery of scars from boar hunting and spear play, and one not
far from his heart where a rival had struck a glancing blow for
Morra's sake. He hoped the man had gotten her; she deserved a
dependable mate. "I learned a good deal of tracking and hiding
in the five months I was with them."

"Five months! All that time I was trying to deal with these people, you were playing in the woods?"

"I didn't think you'd care," he said. "Why should any of you, for all I'd done?"

She leaned in close to him, frowning to make out his soft words. "Why should we? You're the heir to a kingdom, in case you've forgotten. And the only one, aside from the bastard child you left us with."

"Ouch. Why not just let the baby have it? Finistrel knows I'm not fit."

"That's just what Duchess Elyn says," Lyssa growled. "The last letter Fionvar wrote he told me Elyn went so far as to suggest Brianna should remarry, and get a new heir or a few, rather than have you or your baby." Lyssa looked away from him, and he suddenly wondered if she might be keeping as much from him as he kept from her.

"And leave the memory of the Blessed Rhys? I think she'd rather die."

"You don't know what you're talking about, Wolfram," Lyssa snapped. "So maybe you should shut up until you do."

In the face of her sudden outburst, Wolfram shrank back from her. "Ouch."

"That's right, Wolf, and maybe you should remember that you're not the only one who's hurting."

"So I've wounded all of you, you think I don't know that? Goddess's Tears, Lyssa, why'd you think I ran away? It seems like no matter how far I go, I'm still hurting you. I should've died with the leopards and had it over with." He turned away from her, arms crossed, throat aching.

From behind him came the last sound he expected: Lyssa's laughter. It was not a sound of humor, but a strangled little cry of pain. "Yes, Wolfram, yes, the farther you go, the more I hurt. Great Lady, Wolfram, if you want to stop hurting me, you've got to stay close. Oh, by all the stars and spirits, couldn't you figure that out?"

In the silence that followed her words, Wolfram shut his eyes tight, holding back the hope for what her words might mean. He covered his face with his hands, trembling, but she reached out and gently drew them back again, into her own.

"It's wrong," he whispered, "what I feel for you. It's all wrong."

Again, she made that queer laugh. "Oh, you don't know the half of it, you really don't."

The pain, the exhaustion, the longing stormed inside him, and he did not speak, not knowing what part of his divided soul would answer. Then, she stroked her powerful hands down his chest, over his scars, just as he had always dreamed she would, and Wolfram gave a cry, almost a sob. He wanted this so badly, more than anything he had ever wanted before.

She took his cry for his surrender, and the strength of her embrace took his breath away. Then her lips caressed the scar at his throat, and his fingers traced the blue vine as it trailed behind her ear, and down her neck, half-unwilling. The claw marks on his hip and shoulder ached. The fire within him blasted the demons and the wounds, and he took his hand from her naked scalp to grasp her buttock, to forget what she was, what he was. Wasn't this what he always wanted—and yet the demon haunted him still, taunting him with Alyn's long-ago curses. Evil, he was, in the arms of a priestess. Tears burned his eyes, but he would not let himself weep.

Gripping him with arms honed by years of swords and stone, she moaned into his ear. Her hot breath steamed his cheek as she murmured incoherently. He caught her prayers, he caught his name—and not his name.

Wolfram's eyes snapped open. He broke the embrace, pushing himself away to stare into her face.

Breathing hard, she opened her own eyes, their vivid green sparkling in the lamplight. "What's wrong? Wolfram?"

"That isn't what you said a minute ago."

"What?" She frowned, raised a hand to her brow, and lowered it again. "I said a lot of things; I always have."

"Orie?" he asked sharply. "Did you say that?"

"I may have." She matched his tone. "Meeting Faedre again has brought him to mind. What of it?" Red heat rose in her cheeks even as she spoke.

"Nothing," he said. "It's nothing." He rolled off of her to the outside and sat up, sucking in a breath at the twinge of pain from his wounds.

"He was my brother, Wolfram, that's all. What are you thinking?" Her voice grew almost wild to regain his attention, but he had already risen.

"I'm going to the garden. I trust they're not going to kill me again for that offense." Casting his gaze around, he spotted a long robe like the ones Esfandiyar wore and pulled it on despite the protest of his stiffening shoulders, ashamed of the lust that still enflamed his body.

"Oh, Wolfie, what have we done?" she said from somewhere behind him, in a voice that sounded like a sob.

Wolfram's throat ached, and for a moment he wanted to turn back and take her in his arms, but that broken sound left him gutted. He swallowed hard and shut the door behind him as he left.

Wolfram struggled to regain his bravado as he stood in the hall of the women's quarter. Unfulfilled lust knotted his belly and loins, the dream of Lyssa turning sour as it slipped away. He still had too many questions, questions the garden air would only lull into complacence again. One, at least, he could get answered readily enough.

A young woman coming up the hall spotted him and gasped, turning away. He marched straight up as if he would touch her and demanded, "Where's Faedre?" She whimpered, pressing close to the wall. "Faedre?" he repeated more loudly.

One arm thrust out, pointing toward a grandly carved door not far from Lyssa's.

Wolfram crossed to it. He rapped sharply, waited, rapped again.

A voice called out in Hemijrani, soft and feminine.

"It's Wolfram," he answered.

A moment later, the swish of fabric announced her coming, and the door opened.

Beyond her, the hall was brightly lit with lanterns of pierced silver, backlighting her so that he could see all her curves through the sheer fabric of her robe. Faedre smiled up at him. "I had hoped you would come to me one day, but this is an unexpected pleasure. Won't you step inside?"

The thought of Lyssa suddenly emerging from her room pulled him over the threshold, barely waiting for Faedre to shut the door before demanding, "I look like Orie, don't I? I'm the image of him."

Faedre searched his eyes, then nodded. "You are so alike, you could be his twin, in more ways than one."

"Bury it," he muttered, leaning against the arch.

"Are you his son, in truth?" she asked, stepping nearer.

"I don't know."

"Mmm," she murmured, drawing a finger down his cheek and across his collarbone. "It seems unlikely," she said, letting her finger drift down his arm, back up his chest, "that I wouldn't have known."

"If you say so." He rested his head back against the wall, not moving away, not caring why. The secret love he held for so long crumbled, and he did not know which of them was to blame.

"Do you know," she breathed against the naked flesh at his throat, "how much I longed for one more night with him."

Wolfram's body wanted her, wanted someone—anyone—to take away the pain, but he recalled the moment in the garden and the longing that slipped beneath his defenses. Would a moment of passion fix the broken dream or answer that longing he had never known he felt?

"Or have you had enough pleasure for one night?" She kissed the open neckline of the robe, her breasts brushing against him.

He could feel his body responding to hers. "Is there ever enough?" The question rang hollow within him, echoing through his memory. One after another, every pleasure he sought turned to bitterness and left him only angrier and more alone than ever.

Faedre delicately danced her fingers over the cloth of his bandage. "Do not worry over your injuries, Prince Wolfram, I can be very gentle," she whispered, "infinitely patient. There are pleasures you have not even imagined."

She stood so close that he could breathe her in, even as he knew it was not Faedre he wanted, and it was not her scent that stirred the longing in his soul. The longing felt like a gap in his armor, a chink just waiting for a well-placed blade. He was Prince Wolfram, invincible, untouchable, defended by the sword of fury. There must be no softness in his heart.

Faedre watched him under heavy eyelids, a secretive smile curling her lips. Asenith used to smile at him just so, as if they shared a secret no other could know. His body begged for release, urged him to accept the smile—just a smile, just a woman's willing flesh—even if he did not know the price.

Wolfram's wounds stung as deeply as his heart and he said, "No."

Chapter 18

WHEN WOLFRAM emerged, Melody sprang up from a seat against the far wall and took two quick steps forward, then stopped, a wrap clutched to her shoulders despite the warmth of the evening. She did not look up at him but studied the pattern of the floor. "Lyssa said you'd gone to the garden."

"I didn't." She looked very young and innocent, but his desire did not answer as once it might. "Shouldn't you be in bed?" he said, more gently.

Crimson flared in her cheeks, and Melody stared pointedly at the doors before her.

Realizing in an instant what she must think, Wolfram cursed himself, crossing quickly to stand in front of her. "All I mean is that you've had a hard time these few days. You need rest." He reached out to put his hands upon her shoulders, but she slipped away.

"As do you, Prince Wolfram."

"You're right," he replied, almost laughing at the understatement. "But I don't know if I can sleep."

"We might talk, since that's what got you in trouble, wanting to talk." Her shrug slid the shawl down on her arm, revealing only a narrow strap of ribbon. "To me, I mean."

Distracted, he nodded. "Yes, of course." He came to stand beside her, facing the open arch at the end of the hall. "Is the garden empty?"

"Yes, I suppose. It's awfully dark, though." Melody glanced that way, then up toward him.

"Your room, then?"

"Yes, all right." Offering a tremulous smile, she led the way.

Her chamber was small, but richly carpeted, and lit with sparkling silver lamps like Faedre's. Melody quickly took the only stool, leaving the soft bed to Wolfram, who sat awkwardly, favoring the wounded hip. He really did need to get some rest if the wounds were ever to close properly. By the time he was Lyssa's age, he wouldn't have an inch of unscarred flesh remaining.

"Would you like a drink? I don't have much to offer, I'm afraid." She rose abruptly and fussed over a decanter and two little metal cups, one of which she brought to him.

Tossing back her drink, Melody smiled into its emptiness. Her eyes glittered unnaturally bright, and Wolfram wondered if it weren't her first that evening. He sipped his own drink more carefully, beginning to feel the return of sobriety even as the liquor passed his lips. "Was there something special you wanted to talk about?"

"I wanted to say"—she took a breath, still toying with the cup—"how glad I am that you're alive. When I saw you in that prison, I realized how much I would miss you. I'm glad, now, that I don't have to."

"Thank you," he said sincerely. "It means a lot to hear you say that."

"In spite of your impulses, you are still the best—" Her breath caught at her throat.

"The best brother?" he finished for her, unsure where this was leading.

"Do you think of me as your sister, truly?" She met his eyes for the first time, straightening her shoulders. The wrap slipped a little more, and she made no move to adjust it, to draw it back up over her creamy shoulders, bare except for the thin ribbon straps of a chemise. He flashed for a moment to Faedre's dusky skin, to the hardness of Lyssa's unyielding body . . . to the exquisite touch of a single lock of hair.

Wolfram drained his cup, trying to remember when his feelings for Melody had changed so sharply, his desire converted to protectiveness, conspiracy to mere affection. "We might as well be. Faedre tells me I'm the image of your father, and then—"

"Then what?" she asked, a sharper edge coming into her voice.

"There is my father," he finished. "He's not dead."

She dropped her cup on the floor. "So? I don't think my parentage is in question."

"Part of the reason I went to Bernholt was to find him, and I did. He's your music teacher, Master Duncan. You told me yourself he's in love with your mother. Don't ask me how he's managed—" Melody's laughter interrupted him, drowning out his words in a torrent of giggles.

"Oh, Wolfie, then there's nothing to it!" She dropped the shawl and crept up beside him on the bed, her feet tucked beneath her delicate shift like a child's. "There's no blood between us, don't worry." She reached out to tuck a lock of hair back behind his ear.

"No, listen, Melody." He caught her hand and held it firmly. "He is my father, I recognized him from the portraits and the bust Lyssa was carving. He's changed his hair, and he doesn't look like a king, of course, he's in hiding. He's probably been in Bernholt ever since he was supposedly taken to the stars. He must've gone there to be with your mother, don't you see?"

"Of course I do." All the laughter had left her, to be replaced by an avid smile. "But you don't know all. I've seen him naked, getting out of the bath once when I arrived early for lessons. He didn't see me, thank the Lady!" She made the circle sign of the Goddess.

"So what?" Something pricked the back of Wolfram's neck, and he was not at all sure he wanted to hear what came next.

"He's a eunuch, Wolfram, he can't be anybody's father."

"That can't be true!" His grip tightened on her hand until she jerked it free.

"I've seen it!" she snapped back at him, edging away. "And even if you're right, if he was King Rhys, then it fits. Don't you know your own history? There were always stories that Rhys had been castrated. Thorgir was supposed to have done it, precisely to stop him having children."

"Of course I've heard that." He had, but he was the man's son; the rumors were lies, maybe the first of the lies surrounding him. He slowly massaged his temple, his fingers pulsing with heat.

"Look, he may've been my mother's lover all these years—he probably killed my father, or some such thing; but he is not my father, Wolfram, and I am not your sister." She pounded her fist against her own chest, between her breasts. "Are you even listening to me? I am not your sister." Holding back her wild dark hair with one hand, Melody glared at him. "Answer me, won't you? Don't I deserve something from you?"

"Bury it, Melody, so you're not my sister! I'm listening, I've heard every cursed word you said, but have you?"

Cringing, she scooted away from him, but he pursued her on hands and knees, confronting her with her back against the wall.

"Don't you hear what you're saying? He's not your father, he's not mine either! Who is? Goddess's Tears, Melody, who am I? Isn't there something about me that's not a lie?" His pulse roared, and the cold wash of fury welled up within him.

Sucking in a ragged breath, she said, "I don't care who your father is, why should I? Or who you look like, or what—"

He uttered a cry almost like a howl as the truth worked its way free at last, and he slammed his fist into the wall by her head. Wolfram rocked back to his heels, and Melody whispered, "Are you hurt?"

"I've been such an idiot," he said to the ceiling. "How could I be so stupid?" Lost in a daze of throbbing veins and a flood of remembering, he slid off the bed onto the floor and turned away.

Lyssa herself had told him, years ago, that her elder brothers might have passed for twins. How long had he railed against his absent father only to realize now that his father had been there all along. The scene in his mother's chambers replayed itself before him, every word, every fleeting expression crossing Fionvar's face. "*Adulterous bastard,*" he had called him; no wonder, now, that the Lord Protector had looked so close to laughing. "*You're not my father!*" Suddenly, Fionvar's forbearance in not laughing louder struck Wolfram as extraordinary self-control.

A thousand miles away Melody called his name, not for the first time. Her hands caught at his arm, but he shook her away. "I'm sorry," he murmured, then he pushed through her door out into the hall, turning for the garden.

Shaky legs carried him to the farthest corner, a patch of soft grass half-hidden by roses. Wolfram flung himself down, wrapping his knees with both arms, back to the wall. His mind skimmed backward through his life, looking for his father, and finding him at last. Fionvar gave him his first pony and the leg up to ride it. Fionvar learned that his favorite snack was honeyed chestnuts, something his mother never recalled when she was trying to bribe his fleeting good humors. When the queen sat at court, and a weeping six-year-old was unwelcome, Fionvar had gathered him up to hear the whole tale. Wolfram could almost feel those arms embracing him. Everywhere in his childhood, he found Fionvar's presence, much as he had tried to push him away.

Later though, when he'd started outgrowing boots faster than the cobbler could make them, Fionvar vanished. Suddenly he stood on the far side of the aisle, or the far side of the room. He didn't come to archery practice, or Wolfram's bouts with Lyssa, or even to the unveiling of the prince's first finished sculpture. Wolfram discovered girls, then women; he haunted the dark alleys of his city, and the tempers of his boyhood grew into the demon that haunted him. He shivered with recollection. The two events—Fionvar's distance, his own growing rage—existed unconnected in his memory, or he thought they had. After twice being abandoned by King Rhys, Wolfram now discovered a third, more subtle retreat. What had come first? Why had his father, secret though he must be, withdrawn from his life?

And how could Wolfram ever look on him again, without that storm of memories overwhelming him? If he faced his father again, how could he not be consumed by the demon rage?

The ache of his bruised fist began to seep through to him, and Wolfram opened his eyes to the night. He jerked back, striking his head painfully on the wall.

Not three feet away, seated by the roses, Deishima regarded him steadily. If it had not been for the moonlight glinting on her hair and in her eyes, he might not have seen her at all.

"Bury it," muttered Wolfram, rubbing the back of his head, his fingers slowly working their way back to his throbbing temple. "Can't you just leave me alone?"

Deishima made a tiny gesture with her hand, clinking the bracelets she wore with her embroidered robe. "You are safe, Highness Wolfram. With these, I can do nothing to you."

Jolted a second time, he realized he hadn't even thought of her magic. "I'm not safe if your blasted guards can sneak up on me like that." He shrank a little farther into the wall.

"They cannot," she told him. "And I will not call them."

"I have no intention of touching you. I can't imagine why I ever did." The lie burned his throat, but the chink in his armor lay all too open if she chose to place her blade.

She ducked her head, turning the bracelets slowly about her wrist.

"Have I spoiled your garden?" He started to rise, gritting his teeth against the pain. "I'm sorry, I'll go."

She held up her hands, palms toward him. "No," she said. "No, it is I who have disturbed you." He paused, eyeing her, and she continued, "It is I who should beg forgiveness. Again."

Sighing, Wolfram slumped down again, momentarily grateful not to have to go; he'd no idea where he would have gone in any case.

"Are you well, Highness Wolfram?" She pronounced his name as if the vowels were both the same, deep and hollow.

"Aside from being ripped up by your leopards, I'm fine." Both elbows rested on his knees, both hands gripped into his hair. Not her fault, not really, he told himself over and over.

"I do not think it was they who wounded you so deeply, but if I am mistaken, then I am also sorry." She edged around the bush to get a better look at him.

"Didn't I just say I'm fine?"

A frown flitted between her brows. "When I believe that it is so, I will be most pleased to leave you."

He shut his eyes again, pushing his back against the stone. "So I'm wounded, it's nothing to do with you."

"I would not wish to think I had done such a thing after so brief an acquaintance."

He hoped the hitch in his breath did not reveal him as he answered, "I would hate to think you could."

"So we have ruled out that I have done it. Who remains? There is my mistress, whom you have lately seen; and the foreign lady, the ambassador whom I believe you have known. Your sister-princess, from whose room you came—"

"Have you been following me?" He leaned forward to glare at her.

"There is the scent of my mistress upon you," she explained, her pulse jumping in her throat though she did not pull away from him. "The ambassador has come a long way to find you. And to the last, I sat in my circle when you entered the garden; I saw where you came from, though you did not notice me."

Slowly, Wolfram drew back to his wall. He wanted to be left alone, and yet, he did not want for her to go. "I haven't got the strength to play this game tonight."

"Then I shall tell you a story instead." Deishima shifted her position, crossing her legs and bending over them to touch her forehead briefly to the earth. "The Two sat in their palace at the center of the world, when they heard outside a terrible shouting. They came into the sunlight and found that one of their warriors had fallen from the wall where he was to march. He was not injured, but angry, and so he beat upon the wall and cursed it.

"The Two approached, and asked of him, 'Why do you rail against this wall, which thought only to support you?'

"'It has allowed me to fall, and so it should be punished,' he told them, and again struck the wall.

"The Two laughed together, and he bowed to Them and asked what was the cause of Their humor. 'You punish this wall,' They replied, 'and yet it is yourself who feels the pain.' "

Again, she touched her forehead to the earth, a strand of her hair nearly brushing his toes as she raised her head.

"That was a stupid story," Wolfram muttered, letting his hands fall from his face. He plucked at a shoot of the vine reaching to start its ascent.

"Why do you rail against this wall?" she murmured.

Shutting his eyes, he buried his face in his folded arms. In the moments of her silence, the night grew cold. He heard her moving, turning away. Wolfram couldn't stop shaking: the demon had retreated, but it had left that hollow feeling behind, an empty place in his chest. He swallowed again and again, yet his throat stayed sore. The shivering chafed his bandages and his scraped palms. He wanted to scream or to die. Then something whispered in the air around him.

A tingling warmth began to grow in his toes and slowly crept up his ankles.

Barely breathing, Wolfram looked up.

A little ways off, Deishima lay on her back, her face to the moonlit sky. With that whispering toss of her head, she had blanketed his bare feet with the richness of her hair.

Chapter 19

SUNLIGHT TOOK a long time to reach Wolfram's little corner, but he awoke on the instant as a callused hand reached for his shoulder. He jerked upright, relaxing only a little as he found Lyssa staring down at him.

"Great Lady, Wolfram, have you been here all night?"

He shrugged, trying to gauge her mood from the shortness of the question. "Most." A light blanket of wool so fine it was nearly transparent covered him. Slipping it from his shoulders, he stroked the material between his hands. A cup of tea, long since cold, sat beside him as well, and he took a sip of it as if he'd been expecting it. The sharp flavor perked his senses, rolling in a complex blend of spices down his throat. He had never bothered to try it before, and now he could see the appeal. Draining the cup, he rose, wincing at the stiffness of his wounds.

Lyssa stared, arms folded. "You're lucky the guards didn't find you here; I guess the bushes hid you well enough." Her voice crackled with an energy concealed in her hooded eyes.

"Or they weren't looking very hard."

One shoulder shrugged. "You'd best wait the morning in my chambers, Your Highness. I have to go before the Jeshan and beg him to exile you instead of lopping off your head. If you get in any more trouble today, I doubt I can manage that."

"I appreciate the favor, but I can't leave." He started to brush past her, but she caught him in a grip of stone.

"What does that mean? Haven't you had enough of antagonizing the heathens?"

Wolfram met her eyes—she still had an inch over him. "Something's going on here, Lyssa, something serious, and I'm not leaving until I understand it."

"I've never known you to be so driven before, not where it didn't concern your own skin." She sucked in her breath once she'd said it, as if taking back the regret he could read in her eyes.

"You're right, Lyssa. I happen to think my skin is involved somehow; and I'm sure that Lochalyn is."

Her fingers dug a little deeper. "Tell me."

"I don't think there's a war; I don't think there ever was. Not that it would surprise me—there's not an acre of unplowed ground in this county, people everywhere, and no water."

"Oh, be serious." She dropped his arm and snorted. "I've seen the battlefields to the south, and I've been to the river as far as that's concerned. Where do you get these ideas?"

"What river? The one not far off, there's a handy little oxbow in the trees where the elephants wait while you go down to drink?"

Her eyes narrowed. "That's the one."

"I've been there, too, only the water was gone. I found the barrels that river sprang from, and the dams to hold it in for a few hours—for a few foreign guests. Tell me about the battlefields."

"Bodies, torn-up ground, scorched fields, broken weapons—it was a war."

He frowned, considering that.

"And they like to cut one eye out of their prisoners, surely you've noticed, most of the guards here—"

Wolfram laughed. "That one, I know. The eye patches? Most of the men wear them, none of the women. It's not a war wound, it's a defense against magic: women's magic." He waved his arms around in an imitation of Deishima's gestures. "Royal women can do things with their hands, and they only work if you can see the gesture with both eyes. That's how Deishima caught me here before. Ashwadi, they call it."

Again, Lyssa snorted, but there seemed less certainty in the sound.

With a chill, Wolfram recalled the moment of their arrival, his suspicions of Faedre being allayed by a smile and a few movements of her hands. "Talk to Faedre; see if she lies to you." He started walking, and she fell in beside him.

"She must've gone to a lot of trouble not to meet me these past few months. Of course, in this place, it isn't difficult to hide."

Distracted a moment by Melody's door, Wolfram nodded vaguely. He wondered where his erstwhile sister had gone, what she had done after he'd left her. He didn't know how he would ever apologize to her.

"Hey!" Lyssa snapped, regaining his gaze. "You don't have to respect me, Wolfram, but I would appreciate a little of your attention."

"It's not that," he said. "Really, I just wondered where Melody was."

She stared at him with hard eyes, her lips expressionless.

Flustered, he stumbled on. "We convinced them we were brother and sister. Well, we look it, anyway. I hurt her feelings last night."

"That sounds familiar."

The cold claws began flexing in his spine, and he gritted his teeth. "You know what a wreck I am, you've always known, so don't put this on me. We almost made a terrible mistake; it won't happen again."

"Did you make a mistake with Melody, too?" Her eyes flinched shut a moment as the words left her lips.

"Not that kind."

Lyssa shook herself and crossed her arms. "They went to the tower at dawn or thereabouts—Faedre and Melody both. I'm supposed to pick up the priestess for this meeting with the Jeshan."

"Good. Then I'll come along and find Melody. We'll both be happy."

"You shouldn't—" she began, but he was already walking. In two long strides, she passed him. "Do as you will, Your Highness. If I keep you from death, it'll be for his sake."

Wolfram didn't have to ask whom she meant as they cut a path to the tower, matching each other in anger and purpose, ignoring the hapless servants who dodged out of their way.

Out of the shady garden and the stone walls of the palace, the day had already grown hot. Wolfram waited, arms crossed, in the sun, despite the headache throbbing his temples. Ever watchful of her naked scalp, Lyssa stood in the long shadow of the tower. Restless, Wolfram started pacing, following the path marked by the decorative tiles inset in the floor. Each one had a different picture, frequently showing the sky, with the sun or moon partially visible and strange creatures writhing among the stars. Letters in black stone, like those on the tower itself, formed a border around each panel.

"Highness Wolfram!" Esfandiyar bleated, emerging from behind the tower. "Here you should not be, for the Jeshan's anger is yet terrible." He hurried forward. Faedre and Melody appeared behind him, with Deishima and her leaf-strewing servant following.

Wolfram went quickly to meet them, darting a glance to Lyssa as she approached. "Melody, I need to speak to you, please."

Melody raised her head, her shoulders back. All of her clothing was richly embroidered with a pattern of stars and the moon and sun centered over her breasts. About her neck hung a figurine of Ayel and Jonsha. "I no longer wish to hear you."

"I'm sorry about last night, if you could just let me explain—"

"Have I not said that I've heard enough?" Her hands clenched into fists at her sides, and Wolfram let his own hand fall.

He hung his head and sighed. At the hem of her wrapped skirts, Melody's feet poked out. Twining symbols in dark red traced their way over her toes, and he snapped his eyes back to her face.

Melody looked sharply away. "Holy One, I am not feeling well."

"I understand, my daughter, and you may go," Faedre answered her, her voice dripping with sympathy.

Gathering her skirts, Melody fled down the stairs, with Wolfram left in her wake.

"She has elected to take the Two into herself, Wolfram," Faedre's gentle voice told him. "Perhaps later she will discuss her choice."

Lyssa and Faedre brushed past him toward the stairs. The servant scattering his leaves followed more slowly, with Deishima upon her path. She did not look his way, but flicked the fingers of her left hand, making the bracelets chime, as she passed.

"Highness Wolfram," Esfandiyar said. "It is not wise, truly, to be standing in the sun so long."

Wolfram looked back at him at last. "When have I ever been accused of wisdom?"

Embarrassed, Esfandiyar gazed into the distance, his bare toes crossing each other and uncrossing as he stood.

Faedre and Melody stood at the center of whatever plan they were building, but Esfandiyar could not be too far away himself. Wolfram found a smile. "Why don't you show me your palace? If you're with me, I can't get in any more trouble, right?"

"Yes, yes!" Esfandiyar brightened immediately. "What would the highness wish to see?"

Taking in the palace rooftops in a slow circle, Wolfram fixed on the strange dome he had noticed before. He pointed, and said, "What's over there?"

Some of the brightness quickly faded. "It is my holy office, Highness Wolfram."

"You don't seem very pleased about that."

"I am simply uncertain if this is the right place to be showing you at the present moment." He gazed at the dome, a smile flitting about his lips.

Suddenly sure of his plan, Wolfram inquired, "What harm could it do? Is it near the Jeshan or his daughters?"

"Indeed, no." Esfandiyar clasped his hands behind him, regarding Wolfram from his dark almond eyes. "Then we shall see it. I think there is not any harm in it for you." He puffed out his chest and showed his golden teeth. "Coming as you do from a—less settled place, surely this will be a sight for you."

Esfandiyar gestured for Wolfram to walk beside him, and they set out across the roofs. A narrow path paved with stone tiles picked its way ahead of them, curving between sharper roofs, and draping itself over those more shallow, skirting the sudden openings of courtyards. Each yard gave a little glimpse of the life of the palace as servants brushed away insignificant dirt or rearranged the stone stools and low tables. Several sprouted lush gardens, tended by yet a legion more of servants. A few held cracked tiles populated by lizards and little else, evidently unused for many years. These occurred with greater frequency as they approached the dome. The roofs themselves had plain tiles and little ornament compared to other sections, and their pale, weathered color showed their age.

At last, the dome rose up before them, a perfect hemisphere, and yet quite as old at the rooftops they had passed. Here and there cracks traced the stone structure, and patches showed darker on the surface. Great bands of metal clutched the dome, etched with lettering and strange symbols similar to the tiles surrounding the tower. Interspersed around the structure, small windows pierced the dome, even cutting into the metal to let in tiny bits of sunlight.

Esfandiyar led the way around to one side and into a narrow stair, the treads so cupped by many feet that Wolfram had to press both hands to the walls to steady himself. Not that this was difficult—his shoulders barely had room in any event. Descending from the sunlight, he squinted into the darkness ahead, only to be confronted with a wall.

The priest clasped small metal protrusions, performing a series of twists, then lifting a section of the wall out before him. Though grunting under the weight, he urged Wolfram past, and replaced the door behind them. It slid smoothly into place, and the sequence of motions was repeated to lock it.

Inside, except for the apparently random piercings of the dome, all was black.

"How about a light?" Wolfram said, putting forward a cautious foot.

"Ah! Indeed no!" Esfandiyar clutched his shoulder, holding him still. "Many pardons, but it is essential not to walk until your eyes are used to darkness."

He released Wolfram, and they waited. Gradually, Wolfram could make out other features of the space in the intermittent light. He looked first to where he stood and took a sharp breath. They stood on a narrow walkway not even as wide as the stairs behind. Both sides fell off precipitously to the corresponding half of the sphere below. Wolfram shot a glance back to Esfandiyar and caught the tiny glint of his golden smile.

"Many pardons, Highness Wolfram, I should have been warning you not to step astray here."

"Yes, you should." As he studied the points of light in the dim space, they began to seem less random. Some of the openings were round, some square, with a very few octagonal. The lights they cast were distorted upon the round walls, stretching into strange shapes picking out the edges of elaborate paintings. Here and there, a face showed, obliquely illuminated in vivid colors. More often, he made out patterns of marks and letters. The only one of the lights close to perfectly round illuminated such a patch. The characters upon it looked familiar, and Wolfram dared a few steps along the narrow way to draw up across from it. It was the same as one of the tiles he had lately examined around the perimeter of the tower.

Suddenly, he laughed, turning back to Esfandiyar. "You keep the hours here—and at the tower as well! These round holes mark the hours." He gestured up to the dome, then frowned. "Some of them do, anyhow."

"Aha!" Esfandiyar agreed, coming surefootedly to join him. He pointed to the round spot on the wall. "We should soon be eating."

Wolfram turned a slow circle, studying the walls. He had been in Dylan's observatory in Lochdale: it did not look much like this, but if he accounted for the distortion of the sphere, the flat markings they used back home would bear a similar pattern. Of course, their observatory was only a few years old, with many measurements yet to be taken, while this one must have stood for centuries. Paintings dimly seen and little blocks of letters encrusted the walls. The path he stood on bisected another, and he could make out one even narrower going around the edge of the dome. From what he could see, the markings continued on the floor below, interrupted by the pathways above, and he imagined generations of priests like Esfandiyar crawling about with paintbrushes or balancing on ladders to mark the various chips of light that held such great significance for them.

"It's extraordinary," he breathed, wishing Dylan could see what the Hemijrani had accomplished. Dylan was one of the moon-watchers, just beginning to trace the path of the night sky. One set of holes—perhaps the squares—would mark the moon's pale light. Knowing the effort his friend put into complicated measurements and records, Wolfram stood in awe of the room he now witnessed, with the full pattern of the sky arranged around him. "You tend this place?"

"Indeed. It is the wonder of our people."

Wolfram smiled at the pride in the other man's voice. "Indeed. You must have rooms devoted to records and charts."

"We could fill another palace with such things, Highness Wolfram."

"We're just building an observatory back home to mark the locations of the stars." He hesitated. "What do you know of our Lady Finistrel?"

"But little, Highness. Indeed I should like to hear more."

"Among my people, we believe that we are made from stardust and earth. When we die, our bodies are burned, to return the dust to the stars. The first star seen through the smoke of the fire is the star where we were born." He looked at the priest, gratified by the interest in his face. "For us, to mark the paths of the stars is to know where our ancestors are and who is watching over us."

"Ah," Esfandiyar replied. "For us as well, this is a holy place. Our God watches through the eye of the sun, and his Lady through the eye of the moon. The stars are as their many words to us. Each hour and turn of the sky holds great meaning. Some such meanings are inscribed here, and marked by these lights as you have seen. Not only do we read their ideas for us by this, but also shall we know what they hold for us in the future."

"That's more than our wizards can do," Wolfram said, aware

of the skepticism creeping into his voice. For all her months here, he doubted Lyssa would have seen this place and wondered what she'd make of it—a monument to the heresies these people practiced. Now Esfandiyar claimed to tell the future with his observations, even as the Woodsmen saw doom in a flight of birds or the cracking of ice on a river. Wolfram chuckled. The stars of his ancestors hid no such secrets.

"Indeed, Highness, and when you have studied a thousand years and more, and devoted your spirit to the power of the Two, such knowledge may be plain to you as well."

"I don't mean anything by it, Esfandiyar," Wolfram said, "but, these paintings are the past. The skies you're watching don't change except with the seasons. You must make the same predictions over and over. That's no great knowledge."

"Do not affront the Two with your ignorance, Highness Wolfram," Esfandiyar said. In his Holy Office, the assurance he lacked outside suddenly rang in his voice and posture. "Come!" He hurried Wolfram before him down the crossing path and out to the wall. With the dome arching high over them, Wolfram crouched slightly to avoid brushing the decorations—that would probably be another death-offense, knowing these people. "Here!" Esfandiyar's arm jabbed upward past Wolfram's ear. "Do you see the Two?"

Not far above, he saw the edge of an elaborate painting a little off from the path marked by the current round circle. The figures of the holy couple could be made out, but were very small in relation to an encompassing circle of darkness ringed again by flames rendered in gold.

"The darkness, the light, the sun and moon, Ayel and Jonsha—this is the birth of the Two. And they have promised us they will be reborn! When this place again is marked, then the Two shall return among us and all of their blessings be upon us. Every man shall know their power, and our every enemy they shall smite from the world."

Wolfram studied the painting, and the intersection of the line of images that contained it with the arc the sun traced as it reached for the next round circle. "Then I don't see what you're on about—the sun isn't anywhere near it. No wonder you're having so much trouble, if you're waiting for that mark to bless you."

"Then you are stupid and wrong! All the skies move, all are changing. When you have watched for two thousand years, then you can know how it is they will change. You can look for the signs, and you shall know the rebirth, as I do, even if the motion shows—" Suddenly he broke off, his face red, beads of sweat forming on his forehead in the stuffy space.

"What?" Wolfram asked eagerly. "What does the motion show?"

Patting his face with a bit of cloth, Esfandiyar backed away, trying to bow despite their awkward positions. "Many pardons," he said, breathless. "Many, many pardons I must beg of you, Highness Wolfram. I have spoken overmuch, and given offense. Please, you will pardon me. Please."

Wolfram cursed himself under his breath. Whatever the priest had been about to reveal was gone. All of their mysteries must tie together somehow—this anticipated rebirth and the rumor of war. His head throbbed, but he pressed his fist against the pulse and forced himself to regret instead of anger—anger that would earn him no more favor from this man. "No, the fault is mine. You know better than I what messages the Two have placed in the sky. I was foolish to laugh at you, and at them."

"No, indeed, Highness Wolfram. Always I am insulting you, and yet I do not intend so. Many pardons I must beg of you."

Wolfram rolled his eyes in the shadows and took a few careful steps toward the crossway where Esfandiyar waited. "I guess we should both admit our ignorance about each other and leave it at that."

Stilling the patting motion of his hand, Esfandiyar peered at him, then nodded, and gave a little bow. "Indeed, Highness Wolfram, there is wisdom in you for all that you deny it so."

"Thank you, Esfandiyar. That's more than I deserve."

They watched one another a little longer, then Wolfram glanced up to the wall, where a new mark approached the circular. "Didn't you say something about eating, not long ago?"

"Yes, indeed, we shall." He stepped lightly across the path. "Do use caution, Highness Wolfram. Even for those who know it, this is a difficult place."

"I can see that it would be," Wolfram agreed, grateful when they had again found their way out of the darkness.

Chapter 20

WOLFRAM FOLLOWED Esfandiyar through a workshop full of busy servants, most of whom were packing strange devices into sturdy crates. Eyeing them, Wolfram noted that some of the brass contraptions resembled those that Dylan used in the new observatory. Parchment scrolls and bark tablets, some of them dark and crumbling, were placed carefully into cases of their own and sealed with wax. The writing on some of the pages even resembled Dylan's, and Wolfram smiled to think of the same notations used by sky-watchers the world over.

"Are you moving, then?" Wolfram inquired.

"No indeed. I believe that Faedre has mentioned her mission to your country to entreat our countrymen to return. At that time, I shall go as well, to make observations with these instruments."

"One of my friends works at the new observatory in Lochdale, with instruments a little like these."

"Ah," said Esfandiyar, looking over the shoulder of one of the workers.

Sidling around a large crate on the floor, Wolfram felt a twinge across his side and winced. The reminder brought to mind his narrow escape, and he paused. Dawsiir, the guard who had given him twigs to block the doors, deserved some reward of him, and yet there was little to offer. Frowning, Wolfram considered a moment. "Do you have a spare bit of parchment?"

"Indeed, of course." Esfandiyar procured a square, and a pen carved from a slender bone. "Will you write now?"

"At lunch will be fine." Wolfram's stomach growled, and he laughed. "Better than fine, I think."

While they waited for their meal in a colonnaded balcony overlooking a fountain, Wolfram scratched out a few lines on the page, blowing on them gently to dry the ink. Warm food arrived quickly, and Wolfram observed, "You must have kitchens all over this place."

"Of working hearths, Highness Wolfram, they number seventeen. A few of these are reserved for the Jeshan or his ladies."

"Seventeen kitchens! I could get to like that." He helped himself to a breast of fowl, sticky with honey.

"Indeed, I hope that you one day have that opportunity." Esfandiyar ate neatly and sparingly, dipping his fingers into scented water after every morsel.

Wolfram slurped juices from his own hands and washed them with a sigh when he could devour no more.

"We shall continue our tour, Highness Wolfram?"

"Of course, as long as we visit the stables at some point."

Esfandiyar's eyes shone suddenly white in his dark face. "You do not wish to ride again?"

"No, not today," Wolfram said, grinning at Esfandiyar's obvious relief. "I just wanted to talk to one of the men we met there. He has done me a favor I should repay."

"As you will, Highness."

Wolfram swore they saw at least a dozen of the kitchens by the time they came to the stables again. Esfandiyar seemed to hope he would forget, but Wolfram's own sense of direction steered them inevitably the right way despite the priest's diversions. Dawsiir was brought out, looking a little apprehensive himself at whatever the summoner had told him. He bowed immediately, and kept his eyes upon the ground, though they flickered often to Esfandiyar's naked feet.

"Will you translate?" Wolfram elicited a reluctant nod. "First tell him he can meet my eyes."

Hesitantly, the young man did so, and Wolfram smiled, nodding encouragement.

"You have done me a service so great that no treasure may repay it," he told Dawsiir, through Esfandiyar's voice. "So I guess it's a good thing I haven't got any treasure anyhow."

Esfandiyar stumbled through this, and Dawsiir flashed a tiny smile. Evidently, he understood.

Wolfram slipped the rolled parchment from his sleeve. "I am a prince in my own country, for what it's worth, so I can give you this." He held out the page, and Dawsiir accepted, glancing briefly at the strange script, then back up, questioning. "If ever you come across the sea, this will tell anyone who reads it that you are my friend, and should be allowed free passage, at least to my own home." His brow furrowed as he considered what to say. "Some refugees from Hemijrai are not treated well; certainly they aren't trusted. This writing gives you my protection."

He waited for the translation, watching Dawsiir's intent expression, regretting that these few words were all he could offer to a man who had probably saved his life. "I'm sorry I don't have anything more, not here."

Dawsiir shook his head quickly, clutching the parchment in both hands, and bowed over it. Raising his head again, he beamed, and Wolfram returned it.

Quickly, Esfandiyar said a few more words, and the guard who had found Dawsiir jerked his head back to the stable. Dawsiir said a few words and bowed again before being hurried off to his work.

"He thanks you, and honors you for your gift," Esfandiyar translated, warily watching them leave.

"For what it's worth," Wolfram murmured.

The sky above them showed the orange flare of sunset, and Esfandiyar examined it a moment. "I have said that we shall rejoin your ambassador and our priestesses for the meal, and to see what shall be done, yes?"

"Lead on."

Back in the courtyard where Wolfram had eaten his first meal in Hemijrai, they found the women waiting. Faedre and Melody sat side by side upon a marble bench while Lyssa paced furiously in front of them. Off to one side, nearly in darkness, Deishima stood in her veils while a servant meticulously folded a length of silk and laid it upon the stool and the ground before it so that she might step from her path of leaves. At their appearance, Lyssa stopped short, waiting to pounce until Wolfram had taken a seat not far from Melody.

Lyssa stalked over and planted herself before him. "Tell me you haven't gotten in any more trouble, please."

"If I had, the whole palace would know it by now. I never do anything halfway."

"Good, because I've gotten you safely exiled, leaving on the ship tomorrow."

"What? But that's not long enough," Wolfram protested, claws beginning to prickle at his neck. He dropped his voice to a hiss, forcing her to bend toward him. "Haven't you heard what I've been saying?"

"So what evidence did you find today? Is the priest running a whorehouse inside the Quarter?"

"Lyssa, please," he began, but she straightened away from him.

To his side, Melody turned away quickly, refusing to witness their scene.

"Prince Wolfram, you will be awakened early to ride an elephant back to the docks, like the royalty you are supposed to be. If you're still here after dawn, they'll kill you."

"I can't just leave." He pressed a fist to his temple, staring up at her. He itched to grab her and shake her until she understood.

"If you can't, then other means will be tried."

He narrowed his eyes. "What are the options?"

She set her teeth in a feral grin. "One, you leave of your own accord. Two, I make you."

"Oh you will?" he spat back at her, feeling ready to take her on despite the nagging sting of leopard clawmarks.

"Don't make me drag you home in chains, Wolfram," she murmured, her breath steaming against his face. "Don't think I wouldn't do it." Her uneven breaths caught in her throat, and she turned away, vanishing into the darkness in the direction of her quarters.

Wolfram felt limp, and he did not doubt her. He took a deep breath, afraid to turn back to Melody and Faedre on their bench. Across the table and a little distant, Deishima's still figure leaned toward him slightly. She held her braceleted hands palm up upon her lap. Her shoulders rose and fell with slow, deliberate breaths. Strange, how he could see so little of her, could not even see her eyes from here, and yet he found her so compelling. Almost he suspected her Ashwadi, despite her claim that the bracelets would prevent it. He became aware of the hushed steps of servants, the slide of platters onto the low table, then of his own breathing, matching Deishima's rhythm.

Wolfram shook himself, and Deishima leaned back as a goblet was placed beside her. Settling upon his stool, Wolfram allowed himself to look to Melody and Faedre. The priestess sent her slender, sensuous smile his way, flickering her eyes to Melody with a tiny roll of her shoulder as if to suggest he should forget her. The princess herself stared rigidly ahead, the hard line of her neck and backbone pinning her in place, her hands clenched together, the pendant of Ayel and Jonsha swaying slightly with her careful breaths.

They ate in silence—Deishima only sipping from her goblet— and rose uneasily at the meal's end. Esfandiyar, turning with Faedre in the direction of their evening ritual, assigned a servant to escort Wolfram back to his room. Wolfram went willingly enough, vowing somehow to wake before Lyssa's messenger could find him—assuming he slept at all, for dread of the voyage ahead of him. He couldn't decide which would be worse: to face his mother again, after all he had done; to see his father again, for the first time; or just the days of agony on board ship, wishing he could drown rather than roll belowdecks in his wretchedness. He might rather have faced the leopards after all.

❦

TRUE TO his fears, Wolfram spent most of the night tossing more than he might even on board the ship. There seemed to be an endless pattering of servant feet outside, and Esfandiyar did not return until very late to chastise the servants for their furtive movements. At last, Wolfram stripped the cover from the bed and piled it on the floor, curling into the mound and imagining the furs of his place among the Woodmen. He pictured Morra's round, pleasing face and could almost hear her voice in the murmur of healing song. He finally slept and dreamed of hunting a ghostly boar through the wild, lush trees of Hemijrai.

Even so, his eyes popped open early, and he found his old clothes, neatly laundered, with the rips and worn patches carefully repaired. He dressed and slipped through the curtain of beads into the silent courtyard. Stars hovered in the lightening sky, and the strange trees were shaggy silhouettes. Wolfram searched the ragged leaves—not a single monkey. Curious now, he prowled the perimeter of the yard, looking for where they might sleep, and found no sign of them. He returned to the entrance as the door moved open to admit a bowing servant, who beckoned him along.

The silence persisted until they reached the elephant yard, which teemed with activity. Horses and carts filled the spaces between the huge gray beasts, busily loaded by legions of dark servants. One cart contained the crates full of Esfandiyar's instruments. Sure enough, the priest himself was overseeing the final strapping of the load. Spotting Wolfram above the crowd, he bowed and grinned, gold gleaming in the early light.

The servant brought him to a pair of elephants, where Lyssa was snapping commands at people who barely understood her. In a wagon not far off stood a tall cage of metal bars, with Faedre's pet tiger pacing inside. Scenting the wind, it turned its malevolent gaze toward him, opening the great jaws in an eager pant, ears laid back. Wolfram tore his eyes from it and came to stand by Lyssa. "I didn't realize we were part of a caravan."

"Nor I. Faedre claims you knew about this plan of hers."

"I knew she planned to come over someday, when the war was done, she said, to convince her people to come home, but I didn't expect all this." He swept a hand over the busy court.

"Gifts for the royal family and wonders of Hemijrai." Lyssa

snorted. "It's turned into a parade. Wagons have been going to port all night long."

As their elephants were led to the mounting platform, Wolfram searched the crowd to no avail. "Is Melody coming?"

"Do you jest? She's Faedre's new acolyte. I am very glad she's not my problem; I can't imagine what Melisande will say."

"Probably that she's got too much of her father in her." Wolfram crossed his arms, watching the elephants sidle up to the stone platform. "I think they're ready for us." He led the way, and soon was mounted on a cushioned platform swaying high above the ground. From this vantage, as his driver prodded the beast into motion, Wolfram caught sight of Dawsiir among a small herd of nervous horses. By their delicate bearing and fine color, Wolfram knew these must be royal gifts rather than cart animals. He called down and waved as they passed. He might accept his rightful place again if one of those horses were meant for him. But then he recalled his mother, her consort, and the mistress he had left behind with child. The babe must be born by now. Wolfram shuddered and forced these thoughts aside. Time enough to deal with that. He kept busy watching the countryside, counting the number of children who gathered before their huts to watch the elephants pass, and keeping an eye out for the glint of water or the hint of war.

Lunch this time was packed in a little chest at his side, and he nibbled on the chilled offerings as they rode. A large ship—the same he and Melody had crossed over on—tugged at its moorings and rubbed the stone jetty. Slender and long, the ship boasted four masts banded with iron for strength. The sails now loose upon them were nearly triangular, stiffened by narrow strips of wood and strung about with more ropes than a lady's tapestry had threads. Hundreds of men swarmed around it, loading the contents of the wagons and settling the finicky livestock. The color and variety of birds in cages astounded Wolfram until he recalled the delicate wire aviaries in the gardens at Bernholt. Perhaps these were Faedre's attempt to appease her former mistress. The brightness and exuberance of all involved, far from convincing Wolfram of the riches of their country, left him wondering if it was a vast smoke screen for another plan entirely. This could be the circus meant to engage their attention while darker things moved behind the scenes.

Lyssa, on the other hand, was almost smiling now, especially as she saw the horses herded up a wide plank. She nearly stopped breathing for a moment after that, as a large team of workers struggled to haul a huge block of stone up the same plank. Lyssa approached with caution, gazing up at the pinkish surface, its shady side slightly luminous with the sunlight.

Glowering, Wolfram waited his turn for the passenger's way. Whatever instinct Lyssa might have had for danger was dulled first by their own argument, and now by the gifts reserved for her. A sailor showed him to a small berth at the stern, more cramped and sloping than the one he'd had before. Wolfram's body swayed with the roll of the ship, and his stomach began to question the wisdom of having eaten at all. The sailor bowed and strode away, easily matching his walk to the motion. The round window above the bunk alternately showed sea and sky, and Wolfram eyed it before he swallowed his pride and went in search of a bucket to keep him company for the long voyage ahead.

Lyssa, Faedre and her acolytes, and Esfandiyar were soon installed in the few nearby berths—displacing the captain and first officer—passing his door nearest the ladder as he lay on his bunk, hoping to adjust. When Melody went by, her glance fell upon him, and he fancied he saw a hint of compassion there, but contempt easily overwhelmed it. Deishima's leaf-strewing slave couldn't be always with her here, so she wore sandals with thick leather heels. Each step released the scent of the same leaves, pressed someplace beneath her soles.

At last, the sailors above began calling out to one another, and the great ship set into motion. Lyssa and the others must have gone above to watch, but Wolfram's rebellious stomach kept him still. To see the dockside slip away would only bring to mind the growing distance between himself and dry land.

A rustle at the door announced the visitor, even before her quiet knock.

Wolfram raised his head to find Deishima's shrouded form regarding him from the tilted doorway. "What is it?" She did not answer, and he let his head sink back to the pillow. "Well, come in if you want. I can't promise I'll be good company."

She entered, hesitated, then slid the door shut behind her before lifting the veil over her face. For a time, she looked anywhere but at him, glancing in particular back toward the door.

"What is it?" he repeated.

"I am not to allow men to see my face, and yet you have already seen me, so I think this is no harm." She took a step nearer. "And yet I am unsure."

"As you say, I've already seen you—touched you, even—and you seem to be fine." He attempted a grin and let it go.

Coming closer, Deishima glanced to the window over his head, nodding once, very slightly, her hands pressed together. "I am not to wear my bracelets here, Prince Wolfram, in case I should need to defend myself. If this frightens you, I may go."

He fumbled under the bed and found the handle of the drawer there, pulling it open. Inside were the few things he brought with him, including the painted eye patch Dawsiir had given him. Wolfram studied the wide-open eye depicted on it.

"Yes, you should wear that, Highness Wolfram."

He flickered a glance toward her again, fingering the leather patch as he studied her downturned head. The veil revealed the top of a row of dark braids lying flat to her head. She looked more like a penitent child than a sorceress of any form, and he lay the patch upon his chest. "You can't make me worse off than I am."

Again the slight nod. "We two are like leopards stalking, each afraid of the other." She raised her head then, her hands still pressed tightly together to convince him of her faith. "I have not come to make you worse, Highness Wolfram, but better, if I am able and you will allow it."

He slipped the patch into his shirt in case he needed it later. "How?"

"In order to learn the Ashwadi, it is necessary to first learn to be still and to know your limbs and organs. I think this may be of help to you."

"You're going to teach me Ashwadi?"

Quickly she shook her head. "The Ashwadi is reserved to women only, but I think there is not harm if you learn the stillness. If you are willing."

"I know how to sit still, and I know my own body already."

"If you already know such control, Prince Wolfram, then you have no need." She raised her chin a little more but did not quite meet his eyes.

"Control?" He laughed derisively. "I think you know better than that."

"Is it your wish that I should teach you?"

"I should warn you that I'm a notoriously bad student."

Something that might have been the beginning of a smile touched her face. She settled herself alongside the bunk, full robes rippling out all around her, a dark braid tip peeping out from beneath. "It may be helpful if you can sit, as I do."

Wolfram sat up, arranging himself cross-legged as she had done. He waited a moment for his protesting stomach to accept the new position. "Now?"

"Now we shall breathe."

Wolfram laughed, then shook himself. "Sorry. Yes, we'll breathe." He took a deep breath and let it out loudly, then another, watching her face.

Deishima did not change her expression, her own breathing deep, but nearly imperceptible. It was the rhythm she had been using last night. Her dark eyes focused on a spot someplace beyond his navel, beyond the ship itself it seemed. Wolfram stifled his urge to wave a hand before her face and instead, let himself try to match her breathing. As he had last night, he found the rhythm. It was long, almost like sleep itself. After a few minutes, he thought he could feel each breath coming and going, reaching out from his chest into his shoulders and hips, down into his legs and feet, and all the way out to his hands. When it reached into his head, the slight throbbing at his temples eased into the same rhythm, quiet and calm, approaching the serenity he had witnessed in her.

The ship groaned as it began tacking on the long escape from the bay, turning toward Lochalyn, and Deishima's gaze grew suddenly focused. She looked to the window, then flicked the veil over her face. "I am to be going; they will soon return."

Startled, Wolfram let out a last long breath, and stammered, "Sure, yes."

Deishima rose smoothly, fluttering her white garments back into place. "When you feel that your body is not in control, breathe this way." She took quick steps for the door, then her covered head turned back to him. "I will return to teach you again, if you wish it, Highness Wolfram."

"It does give me something to do."

"Very well." The door whispered back into the wall, and she was gone.

The corridor had been lit with glass-enclosed candles, and the little window showed stars now, with a fading orange glow. Something gnawed at Wolfram's innards, and he frowned, rubbing an absent hand against his belly. Then he laughed. Unbelievably, he felt hungry.

Chapter 21

THE NIGHT before they reached port, Wolfram felt well enough to prowl the decks and empty his own bucket. Deishima's breathing techniques had made definite improvement, but he had not yet mastered control the way she claimed was possible. Still, he was on his feet, and had managed to keep some food down over the trip. Thank the Lady they would be on land again the next night. Although the length and breadth of the ship made it by far the largest Wolfram had ever heard tell of, the deck was crowded with crates heaped between the masts. Bundled-up sailors and servants slept there as well, tucked up against the rails, while their fellows on night duty listened for the navigator's whistled commands. A grate of wood showed the dimly lit hold below and the cages of birds with the horses beyond, nickering and stamping from their long captivity. He could only imagine what the tiger must be feeling, and it brought a chill to his spine. The horses reminded him that Dawsiir was aboard someplace. Now that Wolfram could hold his own against his stomach, he decided to go looking.

Leaving the bucket by the ladder to his berth, Wolfram picked his way around the ropes and sleeping men and found another ladder down. He'd just ducked into the hold when a hand caught him, a hushed Hemijrani voice urging him back up the rungs. Catching a glimpse of Dawsiir's agitated face, Wolfram did as he was bid, then rounded on the man. "I was just coming to see you." He pointed to himself, then Dawsiir.

Shaking his head furiously and gesturing, Dawsiir immediately began a long narrative in his own tongue. Wolfram gathered he had heard something, something vital about himself, but couldn't get farther than that. Sighing, he waved Dawsiir to silence and thought.

"You heard something?" He cupped his ear with a hand to indicate listening, and was rewarded with a vigorous nod.

Dawsiir began to speak again, then stopped, taking a breath to steady himself. He pointed to Wolfram, then held up both hands, crossed at the wrists as if bound.

Frowning, Wolfram repeated the gesture. "Someone wants to bind me? To imprison me?"

Another nod, the paired wrists shaken emphatically.

"Where did you hear this? From whom?" Getting ahead of himself, Wolfram gritted his teeth and broke the question down. "Where?" He pointed to one end of the ship, then the other, shrugging his confusion.

Dawsiir indicated the bow, and down. He held his two cupped hands together, raising them to the sky, then bringing them down as if toward the ground.

Wolfram grinned his understanding. Back on the first day aboard, Faedre and Esfandiyar created a makeshift temple someplace in the bow. Since then, they had held their rituals, dawn and night, with Melody and Deishima in attendance. He turned and started in that direction, but Dawsiir caught him again, and as quickly let go, shaking his head, and murmuring fiercely.

"They're still down there?" The reply made no sense, except to establish that he shouldn't go. "If so, all the better." He set out again firmly, and Dawsiir followed.

Descending into the darkness, Wolfram took a moment to let his eyes adjust and moved, his back bent to avoid bumping his head, toward the bow. They descended again at Dawsiir's reluctant direction, then the Hemijrani grabbed Wolfram's shoulder and immediately released him. At the end of the narrow corridor a thin, flickering light showed beneath a door. They crept a few feet closer, and crouched to listen.

From within, hushed voices argued in Hemijrani for a moment before an exasperated Melody burst in, "You know I can't understand you!"

"Many pardons," Esfandiyar said immediately. "I become excited and cannot recall manners."

"We are merely reiterating our points, Melody." Faedre's lilting voice entered the conversation.

"Do you never give up?" Melody asked. "Find somebody else!"

"Indeed, Highness, we would surely wish to comply," Esfandiyar said—and Wolfram could picture his ingratiating smile—"but it is not for us to determine the needs of the Two, and if your brother will not submit himself—"

"My brother's in Drynnlynd, and you know it."

"Indeed, yes, and therefore we are forced to accept a lesser tie to yourself, and his birth stars are most auspicious."

"He's a bastard, in every possible sense of the word. Nor is he worthy of the Two."

Wolfram winced and swallowed hard. Dawsiir, not comprehending anything, peered at him in the dark, and did not return the grin intended to reassure him.

"Of course you are correct, Melody," Faedre purred, "and if it should come to his complete refusal, then we will find a substitute, and pray that the Two will accept a man not of your blood."

"I do not think, Holy Mother," Esfandiyar began, even more

hesitantly, "that any sacrifice could serve to make such a substitution palatable to the Two, in particular not to Ayel, in whose
service I humbly make my offerings."

"You are a literalist, Holy Father," Faedre replied, gently
mocking.

"I am not knowing that word you employ."

"It means you take everything too seriously," Melody cut in.
"It means you can't understand that some of your stories are just
stories."

A strained silence ensued, and Faedre let out a tiny sigh.

"I—" Melody began, then went on peevishly, "Forgive me,
Holy Father, you know that I am new to the teachings of the
Two. It's hard for me to accept everything you say, especially to
believe what will happen to me."

"I understand, of course," he said quickly.

"I am glad the two of you are beginning to understand each
other," Faedre said. "Naturally, we all hope that this goes smoothly
and that no substitution is necessary."

"I wish we could have stayed in Hemijrai a little longer," Melody complained.

"Sometimes, the Two require us to undergo difficulties in
their service," Esfandiyar said. "They know that this has forced us
to change and hurry, and it will be truly a mark of our worthi-
ness should we succeed in spite of these difficulties."

"Indeed," Melody replied, and Wolfram hid a snicker beneath
his breath. Converted she might be, but unchanged.

"It may not be so difficult as you think," Faedre offered. "Tell
them, Deishima."

Another pause, then a high rush of words: "He has been very
receptive to my teaching, Holy Ones, though this has been a first
step only, and a small one. His mind is truly quite clear if it can be
reached, and I believe that these lessons have begun to do so."

Wolfram jerked away, knocking his head against the wall, as
the claws of anger snatched hold of him.

The gathering inside the room fell silent, and Dawsiir,
crouched beside him, stiffened, shifting his weight ever so carefully to make ready to run.

"I hate ships," Melody said suddenly. "They're so noisy."

"We will be on ground again tomorrow," Faedre reassured her.

"Thank the Lady!" she blurted, then giggled. "I mean, thank the Two! Sorry, I'm just getting tired."

"All this talk has taken far too long, Melody, you must be exhausted. Soon will come the day that you feel nothing but power. In the meantime, we should conclude the service." Faedre began speaking in Hemijrani again, with Melody's voice carefully repeating the words.

Tapping Wolfram's arm, Dawsiir pointed back the way they had come. Reluctantly, Wolfram nodded, and followed him back down the dark corridors to the deck covered with slumbering forms. The pair hunkered down beside a wrapped mound of crates while Wolfram considered his next move. They were planning to use him somehow; it sounded like a sacrifice—one that Deishima's compassionate teaching was preparing him for—but why would Melody go along with it? She didn't have a death wish; if anything, she was longing for some exploit to boost her own fame past her brother's. Maybe she thought this would be it.

The ship rolled with a series of waves, and nausea touched Wolfram's stomach. He grimaced, then shut his eyes, preparing his mind the way Deishima had taught him. Abruptly, his eyes popped open again, and a prickling began at the back of his skull. *Deishima.* He should have known she'd never teach him this skill without some devious thing in mind.

The ship rolled again, and Wolfram considered what harm there could be in using what he had been taught. He gave in, and started the special breathing she had taught him; he needed to be well for whatever lay ahead. Melody at the least would know he had no intention of heading home, so before they went ashore, these conspirators must try to get him in their power. Lyssa would no doubt hover nearby, if she guessed what was in his mind. He needed a plan to lose them all, and a way to put some distance between himself and Lyssa. Beside him in the darkness, Dawsiir made an inquiring noise, and Wolfram's plan began to form.

"You and me," he said, pointing to each in turn, then held up two fingers close together, "we're friends, we can look out for each other."

The gesture made sense to Dawsiir if the words did not, and he nodded sharply.

"Will you escape with me?" Again, the gesture of togetherness, coupled with the extension of his hand to imply the distance.

Dawsiir hesitated, glancing to his countrymen about him, then back to Wolfram. He nodded more slowly this time, adding a few words in Hemijrani.

Reaching out, Wolfram took from Dawsiir's belt the roll of parchment with his note of free passage. He led the way down to his own berth, and found a pen and a bit of ink nearly dried. On the back of the parchment, he sketched a map, drawing a crude picture of the ship at dock so Dawsiir could follow him. In gestures and symbols, he showed a route to a Woodman's circle where they might meet, just far enough from town that they might arrive unnoticed. Last, he drew a pair of horses, and a man with them—pointing to Dawsiir.

The Hemijrani watched this process, nodding his comprehension of the map, then exclaiming softly at the sketch of the horses. His brow furrowed, and he conveyed his apprehension.

Wolfram nodded, and smiled reassuringly. "I'll distract them, so you can take the horses." He pointed to himself and mimed a group of people looking dismayed and angry. "While they're watching me, you take the horses and go quietly."

Wolfram put out his hand and clasped the other's darker one. They shared a grin as Dawsiir tucked the map back into his belt, then ducked silently out the door back to his place. Wolfram had no idea what the Hemijrani might be thinking of this enterprise, but they'd have time enough to learn each other's language on whatever adventure came next. Shutting his eyes, Wolfram imagined the pair of them becoming notorious highwaymen or hiring out to guard caravans crossing the southern desert. These visions accompanied him to sleep.

WOLFRAM ATE a light dinner in his room as the ship was made fast to the dock. He'd only just finished when a strong knock sounded on his door. Lyssa pushed her way in without waiting and frowned. "You're well, I trust?"

"I suppose so—after all, I'm nearly home, right?" Wolfram pulled open the drawer beneath his berth and stuck his few possessions into a sack—pen and ink, spare clothing, scraps of parchment with bits of verse Deishima had dictated to focus his thoughts. The boar-hunting knife he had somehow managed to keep was thrust beneath his belt, while the bear claw necklace hung upon his chest.

She regarded him sourly, arms crossed. "I know they'll be happy to have you back—that's the only thing that keeps me going. I didn't even have time to send off a letter to my brother, so it'll be a nice surprise for him."

"Perfect," Wolfram replied. He followed her up the ladder, where the planks were already being placed to meet the wooden dock below. If the tide had been out, this large a ship would have had to anchor off and send them all ashore in smaller boats. Wolfram thanked the Lady that he needn't endure that, anyhow.

Shouldering a waiting pack, Lyssa struck out for the nearest plank, her sword slapping at her hip. "Come on, we've four days of travel to get home."

Wolfram, spotting the livestock being unloaded farther along, followed more slowly, considering what he could do to create some confusion, covering his own escape as well as Dawsiir's. The plank they were approaching was the nearest to town—very handy for his purposes. If he could stall a little while, the animals would already be onshore.

"Highness Wolfram!" Esfandiyar hurried up from the bow. "Indeed you will accompany us to your city, yes?" The gold teeth flashed in a nervous smile.

Behind the priest, the rest of the holy party gathered, Deishima covered head to toe once again, while Melody wore veils that framed the antipathy on her face. Beneath the veils, she wore a new gown of local style. Wondering if she had reconsidered her conversion, Wolfram offered her a smile, and saw her eyes and lips narrow in response, though she met his gaze.

"I think Mistress Lyssa planned for us to travel alone."

Servants carrying some of Esfandiyar's crates appeared, blocking the plank as they struggled with the heavy load. Beyond them lay the dock and the dirty port town, so unlike what they'd left behind. Esfandiyar said something else, but Wolfram focused again on the two men. The crate they carried should have been taken over the side by block and tackle, or down one of the wider planks. Faedre, too, was in his path now, smiling her most seductive. She raised her hands, and Wolfram instinctively looked away. He felt for the eye patch he still carried in his shirt.

"We don't have time for this," Lyssa snapped, her arm falling just short of pushing them out of the way. "There are many people in Lochdale awaiting our return."

"Indeed, Ambassador, indeed I am sure that there are." He rubbed his hands together, looking to Faedre for assistance.

"Wouldn't you rather ride home upon the finest steeds, and at the head of such a parade as we can provide?" she purred. "Your people would stand in awe of you, would they not?"

Wolfram's gaze fell upon Melody and Deishima. His—cousin, was the right word, though it still did not come easily—stood with her fists clenched at her sides, a sullen participant in whatever they wanted from him. Beside her, Deishima's tiny figure seemed to waver, her dark eyes searching the deck, braceleted hands clinking beneath her drapery. She darted a glance up to him and quickly looked away.

"Perhaps if you rode on ahead, Ambassador, and prepared the welcome your prince deserves, he might spend a few more days with us?" Faedre was suggesting.

The back of Wolfram's neck began to tingle, and his temples throbbed. To both sides, a good number of guards and deckhands stood idle, except for the few moving carefully to block his way. He did not know what they wanted, or what they would do to him, but he knew he must not let it happen. He rubbed absently at his forehead, and heard the jingle of bracelets as Deishima flinched for some reason. Their eyes met briefly, then he lunged for her.

In two quick motions, his arm went about her middle, while his off hand slipped the knife free. Lifting her effortlessly, Wolfram pressed her to his chest, holding his knife at the ready. "Get out of my way, or this deck will run with her blood."

Thunderstruck, Esfandiyar stood with his mouth hanging open, caught in a sick half grin, the rubies of his teeth winking in the evening light. Lyssa and Faedre, in midargument, both stared, then Faedre pulled back, her eyes flaring even as Lyssa leapt forward, pushing into the men at the plank. "Let us by or the girl dies!" she shouted.

This was not at all what Wolfram wanted, but Lyssa had thrust herself into it, and her powerful presence encouraged the men to swift obedience rather than defiance. Letting go their curved swords, they jabbered at her as they backed away.

Shaking his head clear of Deishima's veils, Wolfram hurried after, passing Lyssa on the dock as she drew her sword, watching his back. With his captive flung upon his shoulder, Wolfram ran. Once clear of the Hemijrani dockworkers and animal handlers, he sheathed his knife and struck out for the eastern road, the one he'd mapped out for Dawsiir. Somehow, he hoped, he'd lose Lyssa and still make the rendezvous.

"What's going on, Wolfram?" Lyssa's strident voice demanded as she easily kept pace with him. "Were they trying to stop us leaving?" They cut through the fish market and up into town, brushing past disgruntled merchants and startled wives.

"I told you they were up to something, but you wouldn't listen!" he called back, tightening his grip on Deishima, though she had not struggled. He spotted the gate and sprinted into the courtyard, then stopped and set down his captive.

"What are you doing?"

"Letting her go—I have to disappear."

Lyssa shot out her hand and grabbed the girl's robe. "You can't do that—we have to know what's going on."

"Oh, now you're interested? Great Lady!" Wolfram heard the sound of running feet from the streets behind, with voices calling out in Hemijrani. "Goddess's Tears, Lyssa, let's get out of here—if we leave her, they won't follow."

"Whatever it is, she's got to know!" Lyssa swept Deishima onto her own shoulder.

"Lyssa—" Wolfram broke off, catching sight of Deishima's eyes squeezed shut behind her off-kilter veil. She had betrayed him, hadn't she? "Holy Mother," he muttered, and they took off at a run.

Chapter 22

THEY SLOWED their pace after some time, and Wolfram began looking for the turning to the place Dawsiir would meet him. Lyssa marched on in grim silence, with Deishima a muffled form draped over her shoulder.

"Oh, Great Lady!" Lyssa cried suddenly, stopping short.

Wolfram spun back, his hand already on his boar knife. "What is it?"

"I've got Fenervon stabled outside of town—he's been there since I left."

"He's a horse," Wolfram replied, relaxing. "He'll wait."

She glared, and said, "We'll take forever to get anyplace this way. If we can get mounts, we'll be home in a couple of days. The stable's not far from here, if we can find a place for you and the girl to hide."

Wolfram drummed his fingers on the hilt of his knife, then sighed. "I know a Woodman's clearing a little farther on."

"Is that why we're on this road, rather than the direct route?" Lyssa asked, closing the distance between them. Lyssa's strong arm encircled her captive, and Deishima's thick-soled sandals dangled limp, as if the girl had given up hope.

"The direct route, need I point out, is also the expected route, and the one that whole caravan will be following anyhow."

Her wide green eyes searched him out, then she snorted her

disgust. "I hate being lied to, Wolfram, but we'll play this your way for now. We'll talk about it when I get back with the horses."

Claws of tension kneaded the back of Wolfram's neck as he returned her stare. "I can hardly wait." He started out again, watching the underbrush.

Shortly after, they crossed the brook he'd been expecting and found the subtle signs of the Woodmen's path. Dark was already falling among the trees, but Wolfram followed the path like a tracking dog. They ducked under branches and weaved among the trees, accompanied by quiet protests from Deishima as her veils or trailing braids snagged on the grasping trees. At each stifled cry, Wolfram flinched, and Lyssa growled but they did not speak.

The clearing itself was ringed with tall and ancient trees, their thick roots forming deep crevices as they reached toward the brook bounding one side. A shallow pit at its center was the only sign of its frequent occupation. The last of the evening light filled the place like a temple in the woods, and even Lyssa gaped upward at the enormous trees. After a moment, she shook herself and deposited Deishima between two upthrust roots at the base of the tallest tree.

Dirt marked the girl's white robes, along with little dots of blood where twigs had scratched her. Torn veils and ragged braids covered her face, and she made no move to clear them away but huddled against the tree with her shrouded knees drawn up and her arms around them. Wolfram felt a twinge of regret for the mess made of her glorious hair. He squeezed his eyes shut and popped them open again with a start. Kneeling, he pulled free one of Deishima's small, dark hands. "Where are the bracelets? Bury it, Lyssa, what happened to her bracelets?"

"What does it matter?"

The girl's arm was rigid in his grip, even as she pressed herself closer to the tree.

"What have you done with them?" Wolfram leaned in to her, stroking the veils and braids from her face.

The whites of her eyes flashed, and she turned her head sharply, a tiny gasp escaping her. "On the trail," she whispered.

"Every so often, I dropped one." Her chin rose a little as she said it, her eyes darting to glance at him, and away again.

"Holy Mother—she's marked the trail." He drew her up by her arm, but Lyssa stopped him.

"I'm going back that way, Wolfram, I'll find them. Maybe I'll make her eat the bloody things when we reach Lochdale."

"Give me something to tie her hands." He dropped her to the earth again.

"What'll she do to you? Look at her—she's scared out of her mind."

"She's magic, didn't I tell you?"

"There's only my sword belt, and I'm not leaving that." Lyssa glanced around the clearing, then back to the prisoner. She grabbed a handful of veils and braids, and drew out a sharp knife.

"No!" Wolfram said, in spite of himself. He sorted a long scarf from the tatters of fabric and set about tying Deishima's arms.

"I wasn't going to hurt her, Wolfram."

He straightened up, looking down on the dark braids. "What would the Lady think if you cut her hair?"

"What would She think of your snatching the girl to begin with? Maybe you should have thought of that sooner."

"I said we should let her go—she got us off the boat, that's all I wanted."

"So now you're regretting this?" Lyssa shook her head. "You're the most hypocritical person I know."

"Just because she's our prisoner doesn't give us the right to abuse her."

"I never held a knife to her throat, Wolfram. And you're the one who wants her bound."

"Of course, you're right. Aren't you always right?" He met her gaze, pressing his fingers into his temple to drive out the headache building there.

Lyssa grunted her reply. "I'm off then, if you can handle the scary sorceress. There's always your knife if she gets too rowdy."

"Go then." Wolfram crossed his arms and turned sharply away, listening to the crunch of Lyssa's retreating footsteps. Why had he stopped her? Whatever the Hemijrani had planned, this girl stood in the thick of it, her patient teaching merely a way to prepare him. And the tension between himself and Lyssa was nearly unbearable. After years of wanting her attention, he couldn't tell whether turning her down had been strength or weakness. He couldn't tell whom she despised more—him for the desire that nearly swayed her or herself for giving in.

Wolfram stood in the clearing feeling like a fool, the demon tearing through his insides with no way to vent his simmering anger. When the chill began to reach him, he cursed himself for having neither cloak nor blanket, and turned to Deishima once more.

She lay huddled in the notch of roots, her bound hands pulled close to her, her breath beginning to show misty puffs in the moonlight.

The sight of her twisted his insides and nearly drove away the demon. He'd be lucky if she survived the trip to Lochdale, or wherever Lyssa would take her after Dawsiir brought him a horse. Watching her shiver, Wolfram longed to run again, off into the woods to hide his shame. For all that he had done wrong in the past, he wasn't sure he had truly felt ashamed before. He should have, he knew, but this act of tearing the sheltered princess from her life, dragging her into a foreign land—this was surely the most unforgivable thing he had ever done. If she had been frightened by the touch of his hand upon her hair, what must she be feeling now?

He cleared his throat, but she only curled farther into herself. "I'll make a fire," he said, his own voice sounding harsh and hollow.

Slipping into the woods by the trail, Wolfram foraged for deadfall. As he snapped a branch, something froze him, sending the prickles of the demon back along his spine. He listened and heard nothing. Still tense, he snapped another branch, and moved to add it to his load, but found himself listening again. Was it a breath he heard from the darkness? He laughed to himself. His own breath, or a sob from Deishima, perhaps.

The stillness of the dark oppressed him, weighing down already dark thoughts, and he began to move a little faster. The tension building in his shoulders became an agony.

Again he stopped, rolling his head side to side to try to relieve the taut muscles. Again he listened.

Something shifted softly in the pine needles down the path.

"Lyssa?" he asked, his voice coming out as a whisper. He cleared his throat, and called again, "Lyssa?"

Twigs crackled, feet scuffed on the path. Something large approached him in the darkness, leaving a rank new odor in the still air.

Every nerve in his body seemed to quiver. His heart pounded. Some small animal part of him urged him to run far away, or at least scramble up a tree or hide in the brush praying to be saved. Whatever it was passed him by with no hesitation. Slivers from the branch stung his hands, and he ran: straight for the clearing.

Deishima shrieked even as he came.

In the moonlight, a huge shape crouched. Breathy growls issued from its throat, and its hindquarters tensed, bunching for the leap as the long, striped tail lashed.

Wolfram yelled, striking the tiger with the branch he still clutched. He threw himself between it and the hollow where Deishima struggled to rise.

The tiger surged forward, its breathing rising into a snarl, spreading its whiskers back from wicked white teeth.

It knocked Wolfram hard against the tree, his stumbling feet catching in Deishima's robes.

He smacked the branch across its furry cheek, breaking the feeble weapon, his off hand searching his belt.

Pulling back, the tiger struck out with an enormous paw.

For an instant, he felt the grit of its pads, the brush of the fur—then the terrible claws tore into his face, flinging him aside.

As he fell, he wondered if the demon had been torn from him at last. He struck hard against the tree, bouncing back to the ground, the breath knocked clean out of him. Gulping desperately for air, he waited the killing blow.

Dimly, through the blood, he saw the creature turn. The unnatural hunter didn't stop to finish him. The boar knife slid into his hand, and he forced himself to move. Getting a leg under him, he launched himself against the soft flank.

Deishima was shrieking—had she begun again or never stopped?

His knife bit into striped fur to the flesh beneath, and the tiger snarled, twisting to meet him.

Wolfram fell aside, his heels scraping the dirt to push him away.

This time, the tiger came after him with terrible, deliberate grace. Such a weak sting was hardly worth its notice.

Still struggling for breath, Wolfram faced the monster. He slashed at its upraised paw, causing a flinch, and—it seemed to him—a toothy grin. Blood streamed down the right side of his face, but there was no pain, not yet.

The tiger pounced, Wolfram rolled, barely dodging its forelegs.

Even as he did so, the tiger turned its head and lunged.

Moist breath steamed Wolfram's side. A drop of saliva burned his skin as the teeth tore into him, sinking through muscle, scraping the bone of his hip.

A scream ripped through him. Again and again he slashed the tiger's face and neck until their blood mingled in a red stream.

Darkness passed over him in waves as he began to shiver. He thanked the Lady for the hot bulk of the tiger pressed against him, keeping him warm. He wanted to sob, but his raw throat would admit no sound, so he was left gasping, his blood-streaked hand still clenched around the knife. His other hand buried itself in the thick fur, hanging on.

A ghostly figure hovered, weeping and wailing like an animal.

The forest crashed around him, then a sweaty man replaced the ghost, gibbering at him.

One of his eyes didn't work. He blinked over and over, confused by the ringing in his ears. He clung to the pelt of the dead animal. "My kill," he told the sweaty man in Hurim—the language of Woodmen. "This is my kill," he repeated, the words emerging on a stream of blood.

Strong dark fingers gripped his hand, tugging at the pelt, and

Wolfram slashed at them. The man yelped, catching his fist and prying free the knife. He bent over Wolfram's face and spoke carefully, fiercely.

Wolfram whimpered as the first claws of pain worked their way through. He shook so hard that his fingers worked free of the fur and would not obey him. Pain racked his body, and seared at his face. Blood from his torn cheek seeped to the back of his throat, and Wolfram gagged. With what little strength he had, he prayed for darkness. But darkness brought a howling face—pale and wide, the mouth flapping with terrible laughter.

Chapter 23

LYSSA SLOWED Fenervon to a canter as they approached the little brook. The bundle of bracelets at her waist clinked together. Frowning, she eyed the ground, then the once-concealed entrance to the path. The branches they'd ducked around were bent and broken, the ground disturbed by hoofprints. Lyssa twitched the horse to a standstill and listened, making out a murmur of Hemijrani voices. Bury it—they'd been found somehow. Might as well see—then she noticed the stream, and caught her breath. The water ran dark.

A nudge of her knees sent the huge dappled horse plunging into the woods while Lyssa clung low over his neck, feeling a growing panic.

Fenervon's ears pressed back, and he snorted his own concern, barely soothed by her hand upon his neck.

They burst into the clearing, the horse sliding to a halt, and Lyssa already off his back, sword in hand. A Hemijrani bent over a bloody form on the ground, while Deishima stood nearby, unwrapping her layers of silken scarves. The man rose, a knife in his hand, turning toward Lyssa even as she sprang to the offensive.

She caught his throat with one hand and spun him, pinning him against the nearest tree.

"What have you done?" she shouted. "Where's Wolfram?"

Choking, the man pulled a parchment from his belt, sputtering something unintelligible. Lyssa grabbed the page with two fingers of her sword hand, flicking her gaze over it. Hesitating, she read it again more slowly: it was a note of safe passage written in Wolfram's own hand. On the back, the same hand had drawn a map to this very place.

"Bury it!" Lyssa dropped him and swung back to the clearing. Wolfram lay, barely recognizable, pressed against the belly of a huge dead cat. White silk bound his face, leaving only his nose and chin visible. "Holy Mother protect us," she breathed, sheathing the sword.

The Hemijrani man crossed to the stream and cut a handful of grasses there. Blood from his hands and arms colored the stream as he worked. He returned to kneel beside Wolfram.

"Is he alive?" Lyssa knelt as well, feeling the prince's throat.

Deishima retreated a few steps. "He is, Ambassador, but only just."

"Who's this?" she asked, then switched to Hemijrani, catching the man's hands as he reached out with his bundle of grasses. "What are you doing?"

"These stop the blood," he said, not looking at her, his arm straining against her grip. He dropped the knife to take a length of cloth from Deishima. Although blood spattered the cloth, the girl herself appeared unharmed.

"We have to do something!" Lyssa muttered, annoyed at the man's deliberate movements. "Get that thing away from him, at least." She rose to push at the tiger's body, but the man stopped her with a quick gesture.

"It is warm," he said. "The Highness is not. Have you another sash, Holiest of Royal Ladies?" He kept his head bowed as he spoke, holding out a hand. "Will you raise him, Ambassador?"

Confused, Lyssa looked from one to the other. The touch of Wolfram's chilly flesh jolted her at last from her bewilderment as she put her arms around him, raising his chest to allow the first of many wrappings. Lyssa recalled too well their last embrace, with the mingled shame and humiliation. She held him, praying he would not die—praying the Goddess could not sense the mixed emotions that tangled her thoughts.

When Deishima had no more to offer, she stood trembling in a tiny chemise that barely concealed her childlike body. Still, she looked somehow older, with the tracks of tears still streaking her cheeks and blood on her bedraggled braids.

Somehow both reluctant and relieved, Lyssa lowered Wolfram's torso, nudging him closer to the cooling tiger.

The Hemijrani man crossed over the brook to a pair of fine-boned horses tethered on the other side. From one, he untied a bundle and shook it out to reveal a light cloak. This he brought back with him, and, head lowered, offered to the shivering princess.

Lyssa reached out to snatch it before the girl could respond. "Don't you think Wolfram should have whatever help we can give?" She looked from the man's dark head to the slender girl, and the flare of her anger died away. Wearing only her chemise and one thick sandal, her breath coming in puffs of white, Deishima had no power to deny her anything. A fresh course of tears began upon her cheeks, and Lyssa wordlessly handed over the garment, Wolfram's voice ringing in her ears. *We have no right to abuse her.* "This thing came hunting him, and he killed it with that stupid little knife."

Deishima clutched the cloak to her chest, hunching over it as she shook.

"At least put it on," Lyssa snapped, and turned back to the man. "Who are you?"

"I am a groom of horses, Ambassador," he told her. "Dawsiir is my name, and the Highness is my friend."

"Dawsiir, fine. How bad is it?"

He swallowed, and his eyes traced the form of the huge cat and the dwarfed figure of Wolfram lying beside it.

"Goddess's Tears," Lyssa sighed, her own eyes burning. How would they ever forgive her, to have brought him so far, only to leave him alone when he needed her most? She searched the stars. If ever she needed guidance, now was the time. By every-thing holy, there had to be a way. Suddenly, she grinned. "Get your horses, Dawsiir—I know a healer, but we'll have to ride fast."

"I cannot ride," Deishima whispered.

"He'll help you." Lyssa turned to Fenervon, rearranging her gear so that the saddle could take two.

"I cannot touch her, Ambassador."

"Don't be an—" She had no word for it in their language. "This is more important than your stupid taboos."

Shaking his head violently, Dawsiir retreated a few steps, his voice pleading. "I cannot touch her—there is no way upon this earth that I am worthy to do so."

"Get the horses," she snapped, and he jumped to obey her, bringing the skittish animals across the stream. "Princess," she said, turning to Deishima, who now huddled in her blanket. "You sit here—" she slapped the cloth saddle—"and you hang on to the horse's hair." She put out her hands, and Deishima backed away. Grinning again, Lyssa grabbed the girl's waist and swung her easily into the saddle, forcing her to get hold of the horse's mane while Dawsiir held its reins.

"I cannot do this, Ambassador, please believe—"

"Don't fall off, because I'm not stopping for you. Dawsiir"—she swung herself up into the saddle—"lift him up to me."

Gathering the fallen prince, Dawsiir carefully passed him up to Lyssa.

She stared down from the great height of Fenervon's back, eyeing the small, light horses, and the terrified girl clinging to one of them. They'd never keep up. She sighed, then pointed toward the road. "Follow me if you will, Dawsiir. Right on the road, then left over the river. If not, tell your masters that I'll be coming for them." She turned the horse's head for the road and set out, one hand on the reins and Wolfram's body slumped against her.

When she had won free of the trees, she kicked Fenervon to a gallop, and aimed his head for Bernholt. She had no idea how far it was to Gamel's Grove—at least half a day, it must be—but they must get there or die trying: the oath she had made deserved no less. She had not gotten far when more hoofbeats joined hers, and she glanced aside to find the two delicate Hemijrani steeds easily keeping pace with her warhorse. Dawsiir nodded acknowledgment, then returned his focus to his companion.

Deishima lay forward on the horse's neck, both arms wrapped around it. Her lips moved fervently, and the occasional word of desperate prayer reached Lyssa's ears.

She hardened her mind against this pathetic act. She'd found the bracelets, yes, but the tiger had still found Wolfram. Why had the girl bothered with such a gambit if she knew the tiger was coming anyhow? Of course, she had to get rid of Lyssa somehow, couldn't have her showing up again in the nick of time, sword in hand. Lyssa growled over Fenervon's neck, and he snorted in recognition of her mood. No wonder Deishima looked so scared—she was probably waiting for her rescuers to retrieve her when Wolfram's friend had arrived. Now she was forced to ride with them, farther and farther from her protectors. When they got to Gamel's Grove, Lyssa would show her something to fear.

Dawn's light grew before them as they rode, turning to full day by the time the octagonal tower of the keep rose up against it. The little village of Earl Orie's time had grown into a thriving town with its own stone wall instead of a wooden palisade. Banners flew from the ramparts—a pair of crossed swords in a field of nine stars—symbol of the keep's new masters. In the last decade, the town had become known as haven for wizards. Despite King Gerrod's antipathy for magic, he dared not confront the Wizard of Nine Stars, who ruled here, the one who had once brought him so low with sickness that he thought he must die. Nor would he anger her companion, Jordan, the legendary Liren-sha, the Wizard's Bane. Lyssa used to wonder why wizards would choose to settle in the shadow of the one man whose presence prevented their magic from working, but Nine Stars had explained how relaxing it could be to feel free from the magic for a while, to feel that they could live like normal men. Of course, after she had healed the Liren-sha those many years ago, his power had ceased to have any effect on her own magic, or, apparently, that of her children. And that's what Lyssa was counting on.

She laughed with relief when they drew close enough to see the banner on the topmost tower—the banner that showed that the lady was home. Nine Stars had once brought Jordan back from the brink of death. Surely she could do it again; she had to.

Guards upon the gate made ready to call out to the approaching party, but they waved them on instead, recognizing the dappled horse and the lady who rode it, one arm wrapped around a bloody form. Lyssa rode hard all the way to the side court where the stables stood. When the grooms came up for her reins, she instead handed down Wolfram into their arms. "Find the Countess—now!" She sprang down and accompanied them into the hall, not bothering to aid the pair who followed her.

They laid Wolfram on a table in a room not far away, hurrying to find their lady, as well as water and blankets. Lyssa pressed her fingers to his cheek, crouching level to watch the weak, uneven rise of his chest. "Hurry!" she yelled to no one. Casting her gaze to the ceiling, she murmured, "Dear Lady, let him live—if ever you have heard me, hear me now."

"What's happened?" Alswytha, the Wizard of Nine Stars, barked with her usual forthrightness. She brushed past into the room, flinging off her embroidered surcoat. The wizard no longer bothered with magical disguises, instead allowing herself to be seen for the plain, blanched woman that she was. True to form, she wore a ragged gown beneath the surcoat, and pushed the sleeves up as she came. "Holy Mother! This is the prince?" She picked up one limp wrist.

"He was attacked by a tiger." Lyssa paced at the head of the table.

"A what?" Alswytha started stripping away his bandages and remaining clothing as a few others joined them.

"A tiger—like a catamount, but bigger."

"He's lost a lot of blood already," the wizard commented to one of the newcomers. "We don't have tigers here, Lyssa, what's going on?"

"I don't know!" She stopped her pacing as Deishima came to the door. "Get her out! Out!"

Flustered, the girl froze, her eyes wide. "Ambassador, I have been—"

"I don't care." She crossed the floor and towered over the girl. "Get out—get away from my prince."

Alswytha looked from one to the other. "You'd better go, or I can't restrain her," she advised Deishima, who gave a distracted nod and backed away, with Lyssa still menacing her from the doorway.

"Bites or claws?" a new voice asked, and Lyssa faced the wizard's daughter, Soren, a girl of fourteen with her mother's yellow eyes and her father's dark hair.

"Claws, I think. His side may be a bite."

"Were you there? Was anyone?" Soren continued.

"Only the little bitch who betrayed him."

A quick nod.

"Too much blood," Alswytha muttered. "Soren, we need to wake him up."

Lyssa returned in a flash. "What?"

The wizard gave her queer little smile. "Unless he asks me a question, I can't do anything for him, remember?"

"You healed Jordan when he was worse off than this."

"True—he was already dead. So—choice one, I wake up Wolfram, and he asks me a question. Choice two, I wait until he dies. Pick one."

Lyssa howled her frustration. "Do it," she said. "Just do it."

"Maybe you should go." Alswytha straightened and met her eyes.

"No, I can't leave him, that's why this happened in the first place!" She shook her head vehemently.

For a moment, the wizard's eyes cut to the side, over Lyssa's shoulder, then she turned back to her patient.

A gentle touch on her shoulder made Lyssa jump and spin. Jordan stood before her, his crippled right hand outstretched. "Lyssa, come away."

Eighteen years had passed since she made her decision, turning away from this man to the path of the Lady. Eighteen years had redrawn his hairline and added creases to the corners of his sapphire eyes, but it had not dimmed their sparkle. Lyssa hesitated, then nodded, accepting his arm about her shoulders as he drew her away from the room.

"To the chapel?" he asked, already leading her that way.

They passed Deishima in the hall, and she turned her face to the wall, pressing herself against it.

"Odd girl, that one," Jordan remarked. "I said hello to her, and she nearly died."

"Good."

"I'm sensing she's no friend of yours?"

The warmth of his touch on her shoulder guided her up the broad staircase. Several flights up they had restored the rooftop chapel where Lyssa's mother used to pray and later had jumped to her death. These thoughts flitted across Lyssa's consciousness, but she brushed them aside. Any place where the Lady might hear her would be a good place right now. If the Lady would ever hear her again. She shook herself and looked up at Jordan. "The girl's a Hemijrani princess. We took her hostage to get free of the Hemijrani caravan back in Freeport. Somehow she led the tiger to us. She betrayed him once before and nearly got him killed then. Leopards." A snort of laughter. "Wolfram's got bad luck with cats these days—maybe it's his name."

"As I recall, Wolfram's had bad luck with lots of things. It wasn't so long ago you passed through to look for him."

They entered the round sanctuary. It was only a little larger than the family chapel Lyssa was building in Lochdale, just room enough for a single rounded row of benches and the shallow niches to the four directions. Jordan gently pushed her west toward the Cave of Life and lit a small fire there. They settled onto the bench nearest, gazing up through the hole in the chapel ceiling. It seemed strange to see sunlight pouring down rather than the twinkle of stars.

"I swore an oath to take him home or die trying," Lyssa said to the sky.

Jordan observed, "You've gotten him this far."

She shot him a withering look. "I don't want to take him home on a funeral litter, Jordan."

He sighed, shaking his head. "That's not what I meant." He turned his face to the sky, fingering a scar that ran ragged across his neck. "Alswytha brought me back from a lot farther. If he can be saved, you've brought him to the person who can do it."

"And if he's lost," she murmured, "then he's not the only one."

Chapter 24

A SHARP pain yanked Wolfram from the edge of darkness. He opened his eyes, causing the pain to flare, but he saw nothing.

"Your Highness, can you hear me?" a woman's voice asked.

"Yes—I think," he mumbled through the blood and pain.

"I'm the Wizard of Nine Stars. I can heal you, but I need the question."

"Yes," he said again, then a wave of agony twisted his insides and he sobbed. The image of Erik's face swam before him in the misty whiteness, and the stony face of the sculpture he had ruined, and the ironic smile of the man he now knew as his father. Even the fear in his false father's eyes. The humiliation in Melody's form as he rejected her, the fury that he and Lyssa both wielded to cover their shame. The small and terrified figure of Deishima, bound by his own hand. Suddenly he wanted nothing more than to never see again. "Let me die," he moaned.

"Bury it!" A fist smacked the table near his ear. "I can't do that, Wolfram! Ask me a bloody question."

"He wants to die?" another voice asked.

The wizard's voice retreated. "No, he doesn't. He's in pain, delirious, probably."

"I'm not," he gasped, or tried to. Every word stabbed into his skull somehow. "Pain, yes," he hissed, "mad, no."

"Great Lady, Wolfram. I don't want to argue with a dead man. Ask me a question."

He tried to shake his head, but it hurt more than speaking, and the wetness of tears seeped into the dried blood. "No," he whimpered. "Leave me be."

"If you die, so help me, I'll haul you back from the stars and beyond."

He laughed without sound, and the hand slapped the table again—trying, he now realized, to keep him focused.

"Wolfram." The voice said his name as three syllables, soft and foreign.

"What's she doing here?" A sudden cacophony of voices and denials. "You have to get out."

"Wolfram!" Deishima called again, her voice more distant. "Please breathe! Please!"

A door slammed loudly.

"Holy Mother, why me?" the wizard wondered aloud. "It's good advice, Wolfram, keep breathing, blast you."

Wolfram tried to breathe, but every breath was a fire within him. Every inhalation cracked like a whip. He sent his awareness out into his body, past the wrenching agony of his belly, and found to his horror that he couldn't feel his leg on one side, that all he felt was a growing cold. *Is this what it's like to die?* he wondered. What a waste of days his life had been. Why had she told him to breathe? Why had she said "please"? He ran his tongue over his lips. Someone leaned closer, shading the white of his vision. "Where is she?" he whispered.

"Got you, you bastard!" the wizard shouted

Another voice—Soren's, he remembered—said, "She's upstairs, Your Highness, she's fine. Just waiting for you."

"Start here," the wizard instructed.

"What about his face?"

"I need you here," she snapped. "Just there!"

He felt a slight pressure, and growing warmth. The awareness he had spread within him did not retreat, nor did the darkness return as the two women worked.

"Give me a knife." Then, a few minutes later, "Not too deep,

Soren, you won't have much strength left to heal yourself when we're done."

A sudden heat flooded up from his side, and a shifting tide of energy washed over him as the wizards spilled their blood to mingle with his. Their voices sank lower as they began a chant in some mystic tongue. The breathing pattern they adopted was so like the Ashwadi that he thought of telling them so, but not just now. It seemed more important to keep to himself, to dwell within this body rather than reaching out. Shivers of pain stretched along his side, but they lessened as time wore on. He fancied he could feel the layers of muscle brought together, knitting up again as nerves joined one another.

Hours must have passed before the skin itself fused along the ragged lines, and the warmth withdrew, leaving him calm. He had all but forgotten the ache of his temple and cheek and the blinding whiteness that shielded his eyes.

"Bit of a rush job," the wizard remarked, her first words in the common tongue for a long time.

"He'll live, though," Soren pointed out. "The face?"

"Yes—mainly cosmetic, I expect. Great Lady, but I'm exhausted. I'm getting too old for this stuff."

Soren giggled.

A cool strip of metal slid along his cheek, then drew upward, slicing the layers of silk stiff with his blood. Wet cloths descended, and a splash of water that struck him rigid with pain.

Two breaths drew inward sharply, then blew out, and he could picture the women, side by side.

"Oh, for the love of the Lady." Alswytha sighed.

"We can't do it, can we?" Soren asked, her voice trembling.

Alswytha gently tilted his head to the left and sighed again. "We'll do what we can, Finistrel help him." The heat of her fingers hovered, then touched him, and the pain shot him back into darkness.

SITTING AT Asenith's bedside, Fionvar cut slivers of chicken from a roasted bird. He passed them toward her mouth and watched as she carefully chewed and swallowed, her eyes never leaving his.

"You brought this?" she asked again.

"In my own two hands." He offered another sliver, watching her thin, pale face. Her hair, limp and ragged, was tied back under a kerchief. On good days, she could sit up and handle her own utensils. On days like this, the room was kept in shadows with only a pair of candles for light, and servant after servant found him at her request, until he brought a meal and fed her as much as she would take—probably less than her baby was getting from the wet nurse. Most of the time, she seemed lucid if listless, and their conversation ranged over the same ground. Had he brought the food himself? Was he sure no one had touched it? Had anyone been around her door? She was sure she had heard something.

"They'll get me," she whispered. "They're doing it now."

"My lady," he said, returning the meat to the platter, "there are times I can't come to you—like today, you waited hours to eat." He was careful to turn away when he inhaled, lest the scent of her sickness sicken him as well.

"They're poisoning me, I know it," she rasped.

Sighing, Fionvar bowed his head. "It was a difficult birth— I was there. It's just that you need to eat more to keep your strength up. Whatever ails you can't be helped by your staying abed for so long."

"How is my daughter?"

"She's fine." Relieved by the change in topic, Fionvar offered her a slice of turnip, which she ignored. "She's growing so fast, you would be amazed, and I think she's got your eyes."

"All their eyes are blue at first," Asenith breathed, turning away.

Fionvar put aside the tray and leaned on the bed. "Look, isn't there someone else you trust? Someone from the city, perhaps, who could come to stay with you?"

Her head moved very slightly. A nod?

"Talk to me, my Lady, I'm trying to help you."

When she faced him, her eyes glistened, and her voice sounded a little stronger. "Wolfram had a friend, a redhead."

"Dylan? Dylan DuGwythym?"

Definitely a nod this time. "Met him some times, always together."

"That would be Dylan. Do you want me to see if he'll visit with you?"

Another nod, with her eyes shut. "How's Elyn?" she breathed.

Better than you, he wanted to say, though not by much. "She's old," he told her. "It's surprising she does as well as she does."

A near-silent laugh escaped her. "Her bile keeps her alive."

"You may be right." Fionvar smiled, but her eyes remained closed, and the smile slipped away.

Her lips parted a little to allow her shallow breaths to deepen.

When he was sure she slept, Fionvar rose, taking the dinner tray with him. He let himself quietly out and handed the tray off to one of the waiting servants. Standing in the hall, he took a deep breath and let it out slowly, rolling his head from side to side. He remembered hating her, not so long ago; now, there was only pity and worry. She had quickly deteriorated, her muscles shaking, her stomach weakening, until she lay in bed all day and refused even the best food they could think to bring her. Sitting there, Fionvar believed that she was dying. He did not know how or why; perhaps someone was poisoning her. If so, it was a very stealthy someone, for neither Fionvar nor the healers could find any evidence.

"This is the last place I expected to find you, visiting an ailing whore." Queen Brianna stood at the corner, her arms crossed.

"What's come over you?" Fionvar met her in a few long strides and took her elbow, but she shook him off.

"You've been awfully thick with her since the birth, haven't you?"

"I helped her when she needed it, nothing more." He reached out again.

"Nothing?" She laughed, a bitter sound that echoed in the hall.

Fionvar stepped forward until he was nearly on top of her. "There's no need to yell at me outside her door."

"Do you call kissing her nothing?" Gathering a handful of her satin skirts, Brianna spun and headed back the way she had come.

"She kissed me!" he protested, catching up to walk alongside her.

Brianna hmmphed. "And when were you going to tell me?"

"I didn't think of it."

"No, you didn't think of me. Catherine had to tell me. I've been waiting for your explanation, but it didn't come, then I find you visiting her, over and over. Tell me what to think, Fionvar!"

Even in her anger, she did not forget herself completely but took him to a private chamber, where he shut the door behind them.

"She needed help, and I was there. I didn't tell you about the kiss because there was nothing to it—she had a terrible time and was grateful the whole thing was over. Weren't you?"

"What were you even doing there?"

"I'm the Lord Protector, and my job is to look out for the crown. She gave birth to a potential heir, the only one we have at the moment, and I think that warrants some consideration on our part." He flopped into a leather seat and stared up at her.

"There are better ways to get an heir," she replied.

"Nothing springs readily to mind, unless—" Breaking off, he drew in a breath and his chest ached. Fionvar slowly rose, coming to stand before her. For a moment he stood, wanting to be sure his suddenly weak knees would support him. "Unless you are thinking of marriage," Fionvar finished softly.

Brianna tilted her head to meet his eyes. "No kingdom can truly be secure with only one heir. As Lord Protector, you must know that better than anyone."

Fionvar reached out to her crossed arms and touched the golden marriage bracelet she wore. King Rhys had given it to her on their wedding day, the day he vanished. The three of them and a well-paid goldsmith were the only ones who knew the band was hollow. Hidden inside for all these years rested a bundle of hairs from a violin bow: the marriage band Fionvar had given when he had nothing else to give, long before she wed the king. "You're married twice already, or had you forgotten?"

"I'm the queen, Fionvar, queens make choices for many reasons, and love is only one of them." Her voice faltered, though her gaze did not.

"Do you want me to fight with you, to make the choice easy on you, Your Majesty?" He struggled to keep the hurt from his voice and turned his back to her, his fingers encircling his own bare wrist.

"You know what I'm saying, Fionvar," she pleaded. "You know it would be easier on all of us if she died, if the baby died, if we could just forget this ever happened."

Fionvar pressed a hand to his mouth and shut his eyes a moment. "Do I know? Can you forget that this is our grandchild, that, if Wolfram never comes home, this baby is all we have of him?"

She did not answer for a long time, and Fionvar was not sure he breathed again until she spoke. "It is my duty to think of this kingdom, whatever my personal feelings might be," said Brianna evenly. "If you consider more deeply, I think you'll find that it's your duty as well; it's why Rhys chose you for my protector."

"No, no, no." Vehemently, Fionvar rounded on her. "He chose me because he made me a promise. He swore to keep you safe for me, to find a way for us to be together. He chose me to be here for my own son—in which I've failed—and for you. I don't think he considered how much the crown would change you, Brianna."

"Well, it has. One of the first things I loved about you was your dedication to this crown, to restoring the true line upon the throne. Don't you even care about keeping it that way?"

"I've changed, too, Brianna," he said. "I've learned that there's more to the world than a crown."

She faced him down, finding the fear behind his words. "You just won't admit that Wolfram's never coming home. It's been six months without a word. When are you going to give up?"

Reeling, Fionvar whispered, "I will not give up on my son."

Brianna uncrossed her arms, hesitated, then crossed them again. "Well, then perhaps you can see why the crown must go forward—without you, if need be." Her brows pinched together, and her hands seemed to be holding her steady.

"Have we grown so apart, Brianna, or did I never truly see you until now?"

Swallowing, she turned her face from him.

Fionvar nodded slowly, and pulled open the door, nearly colliding with a breathless servant. "What is it, man?"

"Is the queen about, my lord?"

"There she is." He gestured the man inside, pivoting on his heel to pay attention.

The man flung himself into a shaky bow. "I have news from Gamel's Grove, Your Majesty. It's the prince—he's alive!"

"Oh, thank the Lady!" Fionvar shouted, slapping the doorframe, a ridiculous grin overtaking his face.

Over the head of the messenger, Brianna raised her eyes and stared at him, her face drawn and her mouth set. "Perhaps you should hear this, my lord," she said carefully.

He returned the stare, his relief fading as he studied her. "I've heard all I need to, Your Majesty."

Chapter 25

DARKNESS. THE scent of Lyssa hovering over him—she had a scent, he discovered, though he must have always known it. He'd simply been too overwhelmed by the sight of her to notice. Other people came and went quietly, and he felt the softness of cloth and down beneath him rather than the wood of the table. Cloth draped him as well. His fingers traced the wrinkles splaying out about him, followed them up to his chest, to the bear claw necklace that still hung there. A new knot held the thong, so someone had found it and brought it to him. He caught a whiff of the tiger and felt a rush of fear, but soothed himself with the memory of its death.

His door opened again and ushered in light this time.

"Is it all right, the candle?" Lyssa asked, her voice subdued.

"Should be," Alswytha said. "He'll take some recovery, after what he's been through. He's lucky we put him back together in one piece." A pause, then she added, "Well, almost."

"Almost?"

"They didn't tell you? No, I guess they wouldn't." The wizard sounded weary, and yawned. "The right eye. We didn't know it was so bad. There wasn't anything we could do by the time we looked."

"Why didn't you look sooner? I thought I could trust you."

"You didn't tell us what the damage was. It was probably too far gone even before he got here."

"You're telling me he's blind." The anger cracked in Lyssa's voice.

"Just the one eye—the other's fine."

"Great Lady, will that be a comfort to him? Or to his parents?"

"Next time, my Lady, ride faster." A rustle of fabric accompanied the wizard's departure.

"Goddess's Tears," Lyssa murmured. She came closer and set down the candle on a table nearby.

Wolfram left his eye shut, trying to absorb what they'd said. He wasn't ready to be awake just yet.

A whiff of familiar leaves entered the room, and Lyssa snapped, "What are you doing here?"

"I came," Deishima began, then cut herself off. "No. I am sorry."

"I thought I sent you home days ago. I can't believe you're still here."

"Please, Ambassador—"

She crossed the creaking floor. "Not anymore; I wouldn't go back to your country for a thousand horses. Get out of here."

"Where have I to go, my Lady?" she whispered. Wolfram squinted with his good eye and turned his head a little to look toward the door. Deishima, clad in a long robe of local make, was trembling in Lyssa's shadow, her head bowed beneath a scarf of wool.

"Home, or back to Faedre's parade—What do I care?"

"My Lady, I am no longer able to go home, or to return to the Holy Mother's gathering. I have spent a night with a man not my husband. As far as my father or my Holy Mother will believe, I am already dead."

"Don't be ridiculous! You were barely alone a few hours, and nothing happened"—she let out a snort of laughter—"so far as I know. But then, knowing Wolfram . . ." Lyssa trailed off. Her shoulders tilted back. "So you're an outcast now? No longer a princess, no longer a holy whatever?"

"I am nothing."

"Then go to a whorehouse, I'm sure they'll find room for you."

"If I have done any harm, this has not been my intention, my Lady." Deishima glanced up for a moment only, toward the bed where he lay, then looked again to the ground. "Neither was it my intention, nor my wish that any harm should befall him, or anyone." She broke on the last words and fled the room with the resounding slam of the door behind her.

Lyssa stood there a moment longer, arms crossed as if she would throw the girl out all over again, then she turned back to the bed and froze, jaw working, her eyes meeting his. "You're awake."

His lips twitched into a tiny smile. "I could hardly help that," he whispered.

Coming nearer, she bent over him, studying his face. She couldn't conceal the wince that crossed her fine features, and he reached up toward his cheek. Lyssa caught his hand. "Don't."

"It's my face, Lyssa, I have to know the worst." Again, he slipped that tiny smile. "And I don't suppose you brought a mirror."

"Very well." She released him and flopped onto a chair.

Steeling himself, he reached up and found the narrow, parallel scars of the claws upon his face—a nice match for the ones the leopards had left him. He carefully followed them upward to the rim of his eye. Above the edge of bone, he found smooth skin, stretched flat—the wizards' solution. Beyond that empty plain, the scars continued all the way to his scalp. He slid his fingers back down, lingering on the absence where his eye had been. "At least the beggars won't bother me; they'll be frightened."

"How can you joke about this?"

"It's not your fault, Lyssa."

"Not mine, that heathen witch. You even told me she was magic."

He let his hand drop back to the bedclothes. "Not hers either. She didn't summon the tiger. It came for her. Walked by me to get her."

"Then how did you get in the way, Wolfram? Great Lady!"

Wolfram looked away. "You know how."

She leaned on the bed, trying to recapture his gaze. "What were you thinking? She threw you to the leopards, or had you forgotten?"

"I could not let her die."

"Better her than you."

"Better for who?"

Lyssa flung her hands in the air. "Oh, for pity's sake, Wolfram, suddenly you had to be a hero?"

He laughed soundlessly. "After all this time. Amazing, isn't it?" He studied the table beside him and pushed himself up to pour a mug of water from the waiting pitcher. His side ached dully, the new skin protesting his movement. Taking a swallow, he looked back to her. Everything looked flattened and dull, even this woman he had been so in love with. "Could you have done it? Let the tiger pass you by?"

"To kill my enemy?"

"To kill anyone."

Their eyes met again, and Lyssa shifted in her seat, then looked away.

"The Goddess abhors violent death without cause, you've told me that yourself, often enough."

Lyssa rounded on him, eyes flashing. "You've been telling me that they want us in a war, that they're after you. I think the Goddess would see just cause in the death of a heathen and a traitor to one of Her own."

Dizziness sneaking up on him, Wolfram clumsily set down

the mug. "Is this about me and the tiger, or about you and your brother?" he rasped, mustering the last of his energy. "You trying to figure out how to explain what happened when we get home?"

Bitterly, she shook her head. "Not when we get home, Wolfram, when he gets here. He'll be here in three days."

WHEN DARKNESS fell, Fionvar forced himself to dismount and rest. His heart urged him onward, toward this meeting he had been preparing for these last six months, but he knew he needed to rest. He needed time to consider what happened next, how he would tell his son all that he had kept secret for so long. His son. After eighteen years of calling him "Your Highness," Fionvar finally let himself speak the truth, if only in his own mind. That last encounter with Brianna still weighed heavily upon him. Would he now have to think of her as "Your Majesty?" They had grown apart these last few years, of course they had with the pressure of maintaining their roles alongside that of maintaining the kingdom, aside from trying not to tip their hand to the few courtiers who did not suspect their relationship. Ironic to think they had done better in the early years, when King Rhys was fresh in everyone's minds and Brianna was his proclaimed successor. Back then, Fionvar's closeness was only a facet of his devotion to the role. Of course he cared for the young prince: King Rhys had told him to.

When Wolfram began to run wild, when Fionvar was told to keep his distance for fear their growing resemblance would create the scandal they had tried so hard to avoid; that was when the rift between Fionvar and Brianna had begun as well. He wondered if Duchess Elyn had been whispering to her all the years since then that if she married again, the kingdom could have a new heir, one not sired by a peasant, one more biddable. Elyn obsessed over what would happen on her death, when Brianna had no advisor and might go astray. If Elyn and Asenith didn't hate each other so much, he might suspect them of conspiring to put a child of Asenith's on the throne. Fionvar laughed. How had he found himself surrounded by all these women? He pulled a blanket roll from the horse's back and stretched out beneath a tree. He was on the nearside of the mountains now, and one day more would bring him to Wolfram's side—all of this could wait at least until morning.

From the woods beyond a strange bird called, and Fionvar sat up, frowning.

The call came again. Fionvar shrugged out of his blanket and rose, whistling a response.

Out of the darkness, a Woodman emerged, the antlers of a stag decking his head while a cloak of wolf skin draped his shoulders. Pushing down a mask of feathers, Quinan came up and pressed his palm to Fionvar's forehead. When the gesture had been returned, they settled on the ground and Quinan untied a thong at his neck, lowering his headdress to the his lap.

"How do you fare, Quinan? Has the hunt served you well?"

"Many stags, many birds." The Woodman plucked a pipe from his belt.

Rooting in his saddlebag, Fionvar came up with flint and steel and struck a spark to the fragrant herbs. "It's been a long time, Quinan; tell me the news of your people."

At this Quinan lowered his pipe and did not offer it to Fionvar. "You will not smoke with me," he said, his voice rough on the strange language.

"What?" Fionvar frowned, holding out his hand for the pipe. "Of course I'll smoke with you, why wouldn't I?"

"Wolfram," Quinan replied simply, watching for Fionvar's reaction.

Fionvar withdrew his hand and cocked his head. "The first, or the second?"

"Yours, your Wolfram. Two full moons pass, I saw him."

Confused, Fionvar gritted his teeth. "I've never known you to be coy. Tell me what you know. Why did you see Wolfram?"

"Sister's daughter, called Morra, she sees him. No man for her, two winters, and no babies." Quinan growled deep in his throat and spat on the ground. "Spirits bring this man for her, she say." Quinan picked at a bit of moss on the antler of his headpiece.

"He lived with this woman, Morra?" Fionvar began to feel cold and drew the blanket up about his shoulders. The blanket did nothing for him.

"Five moons. Brother Gorn say he come to lodge, he speak death, he smoke, maybe she right about spirits?" Quinan shrugged, tossing his broad, rough hands.

Fionvar's stomach turned. He dreaded the truth, and yet he demanded, "Tell me."

Quinan put up a restraining hand, nodding resignedly. "He no speak. He see, this I know." He rested a fingertip on his forehead, indicating the place of the knowledge he received from the Spirits. "He see, but he no speak."

"What does that mean?"

Fiddling with the antlers, Quinan grunted. "He break faith— no speak." He flipped his hand in a negligent gesture and made a quick noise to indicate that Wolfram had been thrown out.

So one part of a mystery had been laid to rest, only to give life to a few more. "Prince Wolfram was with your people for five months? Why didn't I hear of this? You might've whistled—I would have come." He scowled at the man he thought a friend.

Pressing his finger to his forehead again, Quinan muttered something in his own tongue. "My people—not my tribe, not me. Me, I only see two moons pass. Moving camp, finding food, talking spirits . . ." Again he shrugged to indicate all that they must do to keep the tribe alive and out of the way of huntsmen and rowdies who refused to grant the Woodman their due. "Why you don't ask?"

Hanging his head, Fionvar rubbed his own forehead in consternation. "I know, I haven't been out to see you. Since the prince vanished, there's been so much to do, and we have all these refugees, foreigners—there's always some problem or another."

Grunting, Quinan took a puff and blew out wild smoke rings.

"He was with you, you didn't tell me." Fionvar shrugged in his turn. "Snow on the fire, now, Quinan. I'll still smoke with you."

Shaking his head, Quinan handed over the pipe, and said, "You tell prince his woman have a son."

Fionvar coughed on the drifting smoke, and waved it away. "What?" he wheezed. "Great Lady, not another one!"

At this, Quinan burst out with a great guffaw and took several minutes to stop laughing and rocking back and forth. "But two?" When he had overcome his mirth, Quinan grew serious again. "This prince, he break faith. With tribe, with woman—she happy," he allowed. "—not speak death. This prince, he should have different name."

Lowering the pipe, Fionvar studied his friend. "He should have a different name?" he repeated softly.

"I know Wolfram, I know him!" Quinan thumped his chest fiercely. "This prince, he need different name."

When Wolfram of Bernholt was killed and Fionvar left to hold vigil with the body, Quinan had come to him. Quinan, the longtime friend of the dead prince, had accepted Fionvar as his last, best friend, and taken him to the tribe to speak his own death. The Woodman had shown him a secret route back to Bernholt City and all that happened there. Eighteen years now, they had met in the woods, exchanging tidings and weather predictions. This man thought Wolfram was not worthy of his name.

Toying with the pipe in his hand, Fionvar examined the carved bowl with wild beasts and magic signs. "You know that he is my son, this prince."

Quinan's face fell. "I think this may be so," he agreed.

Their eyes met as Fionvar hesitated. He could almost feel his life dissolving around him, his queen telling him she might remarry, now his friend delivering this gentle, unforgivable insult. "You think my son is unfit to bear his own name."

Quinan picked up his antlered headpiece and nodded before placing it on his head.

Quietly, Fionvar passed the pipe back. "I hope to prove you wrong."

"My hope also." He took the pipe, still trailing a bluish stream of smoke, and stared down into it, then stood. Reaching up to a hollow in the tree, Quinan thrust the pipe inside, out of sight. "When we smoke again, you come. I find you."

Fionvar, too, rose. "It has been good to smoke with you, Quinan. My son is not yet lost, and we will prove you wrong."

Drawing the skins about his shoulders, Quinan made no answer as he vanished into the forest.

Chapter 26

WOLFRAM JERKED awake, the scent of the tiger strong in his nostrils. Immediately he stilled himself and listened. He thought the door had opened and softly shut, but there was no sound of breathing aside from his own. No stealthy footsteps stalked his bed. No moist breath touched his skin, nor did he sense the heat of the beast.

Cautiously, Wolfram raised his head, shifting toward his back, and feeling the twinge of the new scars on his side. He edged himself up on the pillows, turning bit by bit until he was propped up on his back.

A spasm jolted through him, smacking his head against the wall as he scrambled back.

Warmth dampened the bed where he sat, and he muttered, "Goddess's Tears," willing himself to relax.

Alternating stripes of fire and darkness, with the whiteness of its belly showing, the tiger lay at the foot of the bed. Or rather, the tiger skin. Some kind soul had thought to go back for it. Somebody—Lyssa?—had prepared it while he slept, and brought it as a surprise. He would kill her. He would throttle her with his bare hands once his heartbeat had gotten back under control. Not to mention his bladder.

Wolfram bowed his head, releasing his grip on the blankets

and tensing, then relaxing his fingers. He took a deep, if shaky, breath, and followed it with one more steady. He'd just gotten the nerve up to shove the tiger off onto the floor when the door banged open, and he hit his head all over again.

"Jumpy?" asked the newcomer in a jovial tone. He offered that gleaming smile that made Wolfram first want to kiss his feet, then smack the teeth out of his head: Alyn.

Who else but Prince Alyn of Bernholt could show up out of nowhere, unexpected, and manage to catch Wolfram terrified and sitting in a puddle of his own piss?

"Please tell me you brought that thing so I have an excuse to take your head off." Wolfram straightened the covers quickly, with a flick to indicate the tiger skin.

"What, don't you want the trophy of your kill?" Alyn's rich tenor voice made the whole room seem brighter, and he drew the curtains to enhance the effect, turning back to Wolfram with that same smile.

Sunlight lent a halo to the tight golden curls and the velvet of his mantle. "I cannot claim the reward for that gift, however, as I believe it was Mistress Lyssa who brought it. I greeted her on the stairs." He stripped off his riding gloves, dropping them and his mantle onto one of the chairs, then pulling the other one closer to the bedside. "It's a fine skin—I don't believe I have ever seen its like!" He dropped into the chair and swung his legs up to rest his boots on the tiger's back. When he crossed his ankles, a little cloud of traveling dust rose up into the beam of light and settled down on the fur. "So you slew the monster with your bare hands and a boar knife. Do tell!"

Wolfram rubbed his temple with two fingers as he tried to meet Alyn's gaze; one eye to two. As if Alyn needed another advantage.

Still smiling, Alyn let his bright eyes travel the whole of Wolfram's face. He let out a little sigh and shook his head. "Hard to handle a bow now, wouldn't you say?"

"What are you doing here?" Wolfram managed.

"The Lady let me know that you were in trouble, and Melody, of course. Where is she, by the way?" He tilted his chin up with a false lightheartedness.

Head pounding, Wolfram allowed himself a sneer. "What, the Lady didn't reveal her to you? Didn't show you a vision of Melody in some Hemijrani soldier's bed?"

Unfazed, Alyn replied, "She's still a virgin. I would know."

"Divine knowledge, or direct?"

Alyn lost his smile. He let his feet drop back to the floor and leaned forward. "Do not you accuse me of incest, Prince Wolfram."

Wolfram felt cold down to his toes. How much did the Lady let Alyn know, and how much did he guess? Wolfram could never be sure.

A knock sounded at the door, and Alyn called, "Come in!" in his most mellifluous tone.

When Soren entered, she was already smiling. "Alyn! We'd no idea you were coming." They embraced as old friends.

"I'm so sorry I did not send word; it seemed best under the circumstances to come as quickly as possible." He shot a sympathetic look toward the bed.

"Oh, of course." She released Alyn and walked over to lay a hand on Wolfram's brow, without bothering to look at him. "But weren't you in Drynnlynd? You must've left before this ever happened."

Alyn lowered his head. "I had a feeling I would be needed."

Soren made the sign of the Goddess. "She truly watches over us, doesn't She?"

"With or without Alyn's help," Wolfram growled.

"The Lady shares her love with all, except for the unbelievers. For them"—Alyn met Wolfram's single eye—"there is only pity."

"What about for the sanctimonious, self-righteous bastards?"

"Wolfram!" Soren protested.

Alyn stilled her with a gentle touch. "He's had a difficult time, Soren. He doesn't know what he's saying. It's a good thing you came in." Alyn leaned over, and whispered, "I think he needs his bedsheets changed."

Soren rolled her eyes. "I'll find someone to help lift him."

"I can do it," Alyn said, over Wolfram's "I don't need help."

"Oh, no. I couldn't ask you to do this. Can you really heal with your hands alone? Is it like magic?"

Alyn's laughter echoed in the spacious chamber. "No, that's a ridiculous rumor. It takes someone like you, a trained wizard. I'm just a voice for the Lady, not the hands to do Her work."

Inching to the side of the bed as they spoke, Wolfram sat up. He gritted his teeth against the complaints of his muscles, tugging his nightshirt down as best he could. Sliding his feet to the floor, Wolfram stood braced against the bed, trembling with weakness.

"Here, let me help you." Instantly, Alyn jumped to his side, taking his arm in a firm grip. "You shouldn't be doing this, not in your condition." He smiled at first, then wrinkled his nose. "Do you think he's up to a bath, Soren? He's starting to smell as bad as his girlfriend."

Startled, Soren stopped gathering the sheets. "What girlfriend?"

"You know, that Hemijrani heathen child—the one who's living in your stable."

"Oh, her. I thought you were serious." She tossed her braid over her shoulder and went back to work.

"Deishima, you mean? You've seen her?" Wolfram demanded, pulling his arm out of Alyn's grasp.

"Briefly, when I brought my horse in. She asked about you, and I assumed she was another of your whores."

Wolfram pulled back and made a fist, but Alyn caught his hand. "Don't strain yourself; everyone knows about your women now." He chuckled as he let Wolfram go. "Most people are pretty impressed, actually. Carrying on for so long under the queen's nose."

"Get away from me," Wolfram spat, struggling to master his muscles. He couldn't have hit Alyn any harder than a feather. "Why is Deishima in the stables? Where's Dawsiir?"

Soren shrugged. "Lyssa told everyone not to let them in. I guess that's where he felt most comfortable, so he took her along. That's all I know."

"Goddess's Tears, she's a princess and an acolyte of their high priestess—Didn't Lyssa tell you any of that?"

"Lyssa did tell me that what's-her-name was dispossessed and wouldn't be allowed near the priestess anyhow. Maybe this is what these people do, how should I know?"

Alyn patted his shoulder. "We'll find them a hut someplace, or a loft or something. Maybe I should try to convert them," he mused.

Wolfram slapped the hand away and stumbled toward the door. Catching himself on the handle, he popped it open.

"What are you doing? You shouldn't even be out of bed so soon!" Arms full of sheets, Soren pursued him into the hall, with Alyn on her heels. "Talk sense to him, would you?"

Alyn laughed. "He doesn't understand sense."

Maintaining his momentum, Wolfram plunged down the stairs, hanging on to the rail to control his descent. They tilted crazily in all directions, nearer or farther than he expected, as if he'd forgotten how to walk. He stubbed his toes and smacked his feet down hard, panting with the exertion. Even when he'd been falling-down drunk it had never been this difficult. Alyn stayed one step behind, calling out advice but not touching him again.

When they reached level ground again, Wolfram fell against the wall, gasping, hiding his ruined face. The demon tore at his neck and shoulders, urging him onward. A few servants came up, but Wolfram shook his head violently, and they stayed back, staring and whispering.

Alyn gave his eloquent shrug. "I think he's headed for the stables. Has anyone seen Lyssa? Perhaps you could send her along."

"Why don't you fetch her, Alyn? You're so good at finding people." Jordan, the Liren-sha and lord of the manor stepped up, briefly gripping Alyn's hand, then gently pushing him on his way. When Alyn hesitated, Jordan assured him, "Go on; I'll stay with Wolfram."

Briskly, Alyn nodded and set off with long strides.

Coming to Wolfram's side, Jordan murmured, "I would offer you my hand, but I don't think you'd take it."

For a moment, Wolfram's pride stiffened his spine. He mastered his breathing then looked up, shaking the ragged hair back from his eye.

Jordan slipped off the glove he always wore and held out his right hand. Crippled fingers bent together, the knuckles bulbous, the bones at odd angles. During King Rhys's war, a torturer had broken each bone with hammer and chisel—the tools of the stone carver Lyssa had became. The wizard had healed the flesh but could not make the bones straight again or make the fingers bend. This was the hand he now offered. Jordan met Wolfram's gaze. "It'll be harder for you because they'll want to look you in the eye without seeming to stare. At least I have my gloves."

Licking his lips, Wolfram studied the hand, then looked back to Jordan's face. The demon's claws pricked a little less, and Wolfram reached out for Jordan's arm.

Slowly, they made their way down the hall and out into the sunlit courtyard. Servants who parted before them bowed their heads to duck their master's warning gaze.

The stables formed one wall of the small courtyard with open stalls at one end and a building enclosing a few more stalls at the other. The two delicate Hemijrani horses shared one stall, and a dark man paused in the act of refilling their water trough. He dropped the bucket and hurried over, placing his arms together and bowing. A white grin split his face, followed quickly by a frown. Dawsiir bowed again and kept his head lowered, darting glances upward as if unsure what to do next.

"Dawsiir! Thank the Lady. Where's Deishima?" Wolfram reached out and touched the man's arm, surprised at his own relief.

Dawsiir let off a stream of Hemijrani, then sprinted ahead of them toward the building. Still leaning on Jordan's arm, Wolfram followed. The stench of the stable struck him first, and the heat rising from the half dozen horses who munched their hay. It took a moment for his eye to adjust to the dim interior as Dawsiir led them toward the far corner. A narrow stall stood open though the gate had been draped by an old blanket. Dawsiir spoke urgently over his joined hands and, after a moment, Deishima answered him.

Slowly, she came to the doorway, head bowed and concealed

by the shawl she had worn yesterday. She huddled close to the wall, her dark fingers pressed against it, the nails ragged and dirty. One bare foot on top of the other, Deishima stood waiting, one dark eye visible from the folds of the shawl. A few strands of lusterless hair straggled beneath its hem.

A shudder passed through Wolfram from his scarred face to his own naked feet. "Oh, sweet Lady," Wolfram murmured, releasing Jordan's arm to prop himself against Deishima's wall, his face three feet from hers. She seemed to him as a wraith, a desolate spirit still among the living by no choice of its own.

"Wolfram!" Lyssa shouted from the doorway. "What are you doing out of bed?"

"He would not listen to me, of course," Alyn was saying as he followed her down the aisle.

"She was—" Wolfram said, not turning. "No, she *is* our responsibility."

"She brought the cursed tiger down on you, or had you forgotten? Whether it came for her or you, the fact of the matter is you're a cripple because of her!" Lyssa jabbed her finger toward Deishima, who shrank back into the stall.

"So arrest her, lock her in a dungeon as a royal prisoner— she'd be a lot better off than she is now!"

Cutting in front of Jordan, Lyssa crossed her arms. "It's not your concern, not in your condition. We need to get you back to bed."

"I can't leave until I know she's being taken care of."

Lyssa growled, "I'll take care of her—I'll pitch her into the street."

"She saved my life," he said, kneading the pain in his temples, trying to ignore the ache in his side.

"What? When? You didn't tell me that."

"In the surgery, she told me to breathe." He rubbed the empty eye socket, feeling dizzy.

The concern that had quickened in Lyssa's face vanished into chill. "Don't be an idiot. It was Alswytha and her daughter who saved you."

Shivering, Wolfram tried to shake his head. "You don't understand. I don't have much time," he mumbled, waves of nausea spreading through him. "Dawsiir."

The groom appeared before him, by Deishima, but not so close that he could touch her, even by accident.

"Sell the horses—get clothing, food, find a room." Wolfram managed to summon up the Hemijrani word for horse. "Buy her some shoes." From Deishima's wrappings, a tiny voice emerged, translating.

Dawsiir babbled for a moment, looking from one to the other.

"Didn't you even learn their language?" Alyn chimed in.

Wolfram picked out the tall, handsome prince leaning casually on an open gate, looking clean and elegant even in these surroundings. Wolfram's own garb consisted of the thin nightshirt someone had loaned him, stained and stinking. He could barely keep himself upright, never mind strike a nonchalant pose. "You know, Alyn, I don't really need your help to look ridiculous right now."

"Highness Wolfram," Deishima whispered. "He says he has sold all that he could, his knife and belt, other things. He brought me these clothes and some food. He says he has tried to sell the horses, but these people cannot speak with him and do not trust that these horses are his to sell." She looked up suddenly. "The Ambassador is right; you need rest and to heal yourself. Do not worry over me; I am no longer worth the concern of another."

"See?" Lyssa crowed, setting her hand on Wolfram's arm.

It was Jordan who removed the hand, holding her back by the wrist, with something akin to fury growing on his face. "Don't sell the horses, not yet. I will give you a room, and all the food you can eat. Clothing, too—my youngest is about your size."

"She's a heathen, and a sorceress, Jordan; haven't you been listening to me?" Lyssa pulled against his grasp, but could not break it.

"I don't think I have, no. Let's find someplace to talk." He jerked her off-balance and towed her out to the courtyard.

"Well, well." Alyn sauntered closer. "You do know how to stir up trouble."

"I'm not up to this right now, Alyn," Wolfram said, as evenly as he could with the demon pounding inside his skull. He tried to remember the lessons Deishima had taught him, but they were swept away by waves of nausea.

"Oh, you're always up to something, Wolfie, just never anything good." Alyn stared at Deishima. "Is that what passes for a princess in Hemijrai? A bundle of rags and refuse."

Wolfram rolled his shoulders so his back was to the wall. His temples throbbed, twitching the new scars unmercifully. With one hand, he held the hair out of his face. "I will not warn you again, Your Highness."

Alyn paused a moment, then let his smile return, with that sickening edge of pity. "Why waste what little strength you have on such chattel as this? Even you generally show better taste."

"Get out!" Wolfram bellowed. "Get out now before I rip your throat open with my bare hands!" He lunged forward, but Alyn was already dancing out of reach, retreating from the stable with more than a little white to his eyes.

For a moment, Wolfram stood, the power of his fury supporting him, then his knees buckled, and he pitched forward. Before Dawsiir's arms caught him, and lowered him to the ground, he saw movement from the corner of his eye.

Deishima dropped to her knees, her arms outstretched, her hands shaking as if they resisted what she tried to do. She could not have caught him from there; she couldn't even reach him, but the warmth of her offered palms touched him even so.

Chapter 27

WOLFRAM'S NEW room was on the ground floor—no more treacherous stairs if he felt the need to go gallivanting, or so Countess Alswytha had told him. She bent over him now, examining the scars on his side, prodding to see if he still felt pain. Since the healing, he felt a strange sort of kinship for the wizard—a factor of having her blood in his veins. Since he had blacked out in the stables the day before, one wizard or another stood guard over him. They needn't have bothered; the bed suited him just fine as long as Alyn was banned from his room. Jordan had given Deishima a room just along the hall from this one, looking out onto the courtyard garden.

The wizard finished her examination and grunted, dropping into the room's single chair. "Please tell me you're done with running about the place, Your Highness."

"Can I walk?"

"If you feel ready. You'll be weak for a while yet. If that bite had been a bit higher, he'd've taken out your liver; a bit lower, and you'd be missing a leg. As it is, your pelvis stopped him from tearing a chunk out of you. It's the intestines I worry about," she grumbled, running a hand through limp gray hair. "I haven't done much internal work like that—we'll have to see how it holds up."

Wolfram rearranged his blankets. "Does that mean I get more than broth today?"

She laughed. "Not much more." She regarded him with a

steady, pale gaze. "I'm sorry about the eye. We were too spent to do more than we did."

Looking away, Wolfram trailed his fingers down his cheek. "I know."

Alswytha sat a moment longer, silent, then rose and stretched her back. "Look, we're pretty sick of watching over you. Can I trust you not to be an idiot?"

This made him smile, a little off kilter given the scars on his cheek. "Probably not."

"Figures. No matter what tiff you two have had, Lyssa will have my hide if you leave any more injured than you came in, so try to keep the damage to a minimum."

"You're starting to talk like Jordan, you know that?"

Shrugging, the plain woman said, "You're not the first to notice. Just wait'll you find a bride." She headed for the door, then turned to add, "Jordan wanted me to tell you this is the room King Rhys stayed in when Orie was the earl here. He thought you'd be amused."

King Rhys, not "your father." Wolfram called, "Wait!" and the wizard turned back again, looking wary. "You had something to do with it, didn't you? How King Rhys disappeared that day?"

She shut the door. "It's not my place to speak of that, Your Highness, as I think you know."

"Was it a disguise? Some sort of illusion?"

"I'm sure there's someone better to tell you what happened."

"But who will? Next month is my eighteenth birthday: if they haven't told me now, why should I think they ever will?" His empty socket twitched as if trying to blink, and he pressed it with his finger to make it stop.

The wizard bowed her head for a moment, massaging her neck with one hand. "How much do you know?"

"Plenty," Wolfram replied, a little too quickly.

"Hah! That's what I thought. You'll not find out more from me, oh, no." She shook her head, with a little smile. "Ask me something I'm at leave to answer, and I'll do it, but this is a story for another."

Wolfram wet his lips, then said, "I need to know if you can disguise me."

Alswytha regarded him steadily, her eyes the color of old parchment. "I could hide your face as it is, Highness, but an illusion lacks expression and doesn't age. The people who matter would know in an instant that you were hiding something—you'd be better to get used to it."

Slowly, Wolfram shook his head. "That's not what I meant. Other men have scars worse than this and have to live with them." He gave a slight shrug. "It's just my hair." He pulled at the dark mop, clean but still unkempt. "You probably know they've been bleaching it all these years."

She nodded, watching him closely.

"So I can't go back like this, or the lovely secrets you've all been keeping will start popping out, won't they? Can you change my hair?"

Relaxing, she came back to his bedside. "Is that all? I could do that in my sleep."

"Well, then, Wizard of Nine Stars, will you give me hair the color of my legendary father's?"

Her long lips quirked into a smile. "Interesting phrasing, Prince Wolfram." Laying a hand on his head, Alswytha mumbled a few words, then withdrew. His scalp tingled. "It suits you."

Wolfram found the mirror he had cajoled Soren into bringing him and studied his reflection. His hair was a tawny gold—not unlike Alyn's, as he thought about it, a thought that made him wrinkle his nose. He drew his fingers again along the parallel scars, traced the rim where his eye had been. While he lay not sleeping for the aches that assailed him, Wolfram had struck upon a plan that might redeem him, at least in small measure, if his face didn't ruin it. He frowned at himself. For once, he had not searched for a resemblance to King Rhys, nor recognized a resemblance to the man he knew had sired him. He fingered his nose and smoothed the blond hair back from his forehead. Studying the terrible wound, Wolfram tried his new, strange smile. For the first time, his face was his own.

Alswytha cleared her throat. "Are you satisfied?"

"Quite. Thank you." He replaced the mirror on his side table. "I dread the day you call in all the debts I owe you."

She laughed, turning at last to go.

"Leave the door open, would you? There's a nice breeze."

Still chuckling, the wizard swung the door wide. "Don't go far, Your Highness, I haven't the strength yet to save you again."

Wolfram lay back on his pillows for a moment, running his fingers through his hair. That bitch Asenith had been right, dyed hair was much stiffer than the real thing.

He rose carefully, standing a long while before he left the bedside. In a small chest, Wolfram found linen trews and a tunic with a touch of embroidery awaiting his recovery. Slowly, he dressed, leaving his nightshirt where it fell. Winded, he leaned back upon the bed for a moment. A few other items lay at the bottom of the chest, and Wolfram let himself down to kneel beside it. A new leather belt coiled there around the hilt of his familiar boar knife. Gently, he picked them out, drawing the blade. Someone had cleaned and polished it, honing the edge sharper than it had ever been. Lyssa, again, trying to defend her prince from the tigers. When he shut his eye, he could still catch her scent upon it, mingling with the oil. Stone dust, and sweat, and something vaguely animal and infinitely enticing.

Wolfram took a deep breath and let it out in a sigh. He would go home, but it would never be the same.

Strapping on the belt about his tunic, Wolfram reached back for the last item: the painted eye patch Dawsiir had given him a long time ago. He slipped it over his face, fluffing his hair over the band. For a moment, he let himself believe that the darkness was due to that alone and he could toss it away as easily as pitching the thing across the room. Shaking himself, Wolfram let the image go. Someday, he would adjust. This would be simply a part of himself, unremarkable. Maybe he could forget that his vision had ever been true. Rising unsteadily, he misjudged the distance to the bedpost and stumbled.

"Goddess's Tears," he whispered, "how am I ever to get through this?" He took a deep breath and felt the rise of his chest, the subtle drying of air over his lips. With the second breath, he drew his awareness deeper, past the scars upon his skin, past the torn and mended muscles, into the coursing of his blood and the white strength of his bones. Ashwadi, the Spirit's Wind. He walked with purposeful strides out the door to Deishima's room.

From a bench before the door, Dawsiir sprang up and made his customary bow, letting his grin tell all that needed saying. He wore new clothes a little awkward for their local style but clean and untorn. Deishima's self-appointed guardian rapped softly at her door. Wolfram heard her cross the floor and whisper.

Dawsiir's words were encouraging, and the door opened a crack, letting a sliver of sunlight illuminate Deishima's feet, clad now in soft suede. The gown above hung loose over her slender frame and was topped with a new shawl, a ragged opening revealing her eyes.

"It is good of you to inquire after my well-being, Highness Wolfram."

"Are you well, then?" He advanced a little, but stopped when she stiffened. Skittish as a fawn, she hovered just inside, with no place to run.

"I am, Highness. There is no need for you to concern yourself." She glanced to Dawsiir and back, quick movements rippling the white shawl. "It is your own well-being you should see to." Her dark eyes roved over him.

Self-consciously, Wolfram straightened his stance, trying not to let the twist of scars lean him to the right, nor to let the weariness show.

Two little lines appeared between her eyes, and he knew she was not fooled. "I should return to bed, Highness. I have not become used to your days here."

"Then you should come out, into the sun. It's the only way," he added, flustered for no reason by those little lines of her concern.

She darted glances left and right, looking for enemies, or for the safety of the women's quarter she had lived in all her life.

Suddenly dry-mouthed, Wolfram blurted, "You should at least see the grove, Your Highness. Will you walk with me?" He held out his hand, then knew his mistake and quickly took it back.

She vanished into the darkness of the room, but the door did not shut.

Bury it, he had to be more careful. This girl had nearly gotten him killed for touching her hair; she wouldn't take his hand in a million years.

Stepping up, Dawsiir called something inside and listened to the answer. He gestured toward Wolfram and repeated his inquiry. He wanted to know what had been said, Wolfram realized, recognizing a few words he had heard before.

Moving up beside Dawsiir, Wolfram pointed toward the room, then himself, then the door at the end of the cloister, leading out to the grounds and the woods beyond. "I want her to come out. To go walking. Not far, I can't go far," he assured them.

Studying him, Dawsiir nodded, then touched the door with careful fingers and pushed it a little farther.

Startled, Deishima flinched from the stripe of light upon her floor. From the safety of her veil and her little room, she stared at Wolfram.

This was not her world, not any part of it, this place where men and women mingled freely, where even a stranger might take her arm. Before she met him, she had never walked upon the dirt, and now she had been forced to live in it. In that light, the very act of opening the door seemed like a daring display. Wolfram fought his impatience and felt the growing strain in his right side. If she was the skittish fawn, he must be a more cautious hunter. "Very well, if you won't come out, would you mind if I sit down? I'm awfully tired."

She nodded quickly, and he took Dawsiir's place on the bench facing her door. "I think you would like the grove, Your Highness—is that what I should call you? Do you have another title?"

Beneath her veil, Deishima's eyes frowned at him.

"It'll have to do. Anyway, the grove is a lot like your garden. There's a pond in the middle with tiny silver fish and a few lily pads. I think it's a bit warm for the frogs to be out, but they make a bloody racket at the right time of day. Someone's built a couple of benches, and the moss on them is so thick you think you're sitting on furs. The grass is better for sitting, or lying down. I remember you liked to go barefoot in your own garden." He was babbling, conjuring up images he didn't even know he had remembered. If she stayed in her room, she might never come out again. He took a calming breath, but, before he could go on, Deishima stood on the threshold.

"What is it that you wish, Highness Wolfram?"

"I wish for you to walk with me out that gate, down to the grove. I want to see if everything is as I remember." And to get away from anyone who might listen, but he did not tell her that.

Again, she looked to Dawsiir, her countryman and only supporter. He offered a smile and a shrug, spreading his hands to take in the brightness of the day as he spoke.

Deishima's head rose, and she stepped outside the door. "I will walk for a small distance with you, until you have tired, Highness."

As he carefully rose, she examined him from behind her shawl. Fearful, he did not look at her but spent a moment adjusting the fall of his tunic. He wore the belt loose over his hips rather than at the waist where it might rub.

"They have changed your hair also, Highness Wolfram."

He sighed. "It's a long story, and I don't even know most of it myself. Someday, I hope, I'll be able to explain."

"This way, is it?" She waited for him to precede her with Dawsiir coming behind.

No matter how Wolfram tried, there was a slight hitch to his stride, which served him ill in combination with his strange new vision. He hoped the path was level and clear.

They emerged from the gate onto a strip of lawn surrounding the keep, crossing the grass toward a footpath leading into a gleaming birch wood. The white trees and their fresh, green leaves looked cool and inviting. Warblers and sparrows flitted among them, maintaining a constant chatter. When he glanced back to her, Wolfram found Deishima looking all around her, eyes intent on this tree, then that bird. All the things he took for granted must be so new to her. These birds were drab and dull compared to the ones in her home, and the trees were stunted compared to the jungles he had seen there. On the other hand, Bernholt had no tigers, and no catamounts had been seen in these parts for decades while the wolves stuck to the deeper mountains of Lochalyn.

Deishima suddenly said, "There is no such healing in my country, Highness Wolfram. I am . . . surprised by your recovery. I would not have expected that you should be so well as to walk a matter of days after such an attack."

"You thought I would die." He turned to face her.

Ducking her head, she replied, "I did."

"Then why did you come to me in the surgery?"

"In my country, you would not have survived. In your own country, I hoped otherwise."

Tilting his head to see her better, Wolfram waited a moment, but she said no more, and he led them onward, carefully negotiating the way over roots and stones.

By the time they had covered the short distance to Gamel's Grove, Wolfram was ready to sit still for a long while. The hitch had become a limp, and his breathing came too hard. With a negligent hand, he offered Deishima the nearest bench, and sprawled in the grass a little more roughly than he had intended. Taking deep breaths, he admired the golden glints upon the pond, shaken by tiny ripples as the fish came up to kiss the air. A newer stone slab thick enough to serve as a bench crossed one edge of the clearing, by the path, which led onward to a chapel in the deeper woods. Hemlock trees shaded that side, home to a trio of chattering squirrels that chased each other up and down, performing acrobatic feats from one tree to the next. When he had been a Woodman, Wolfram had spent long hours like this, waiting while the beaters chased a deer or boar toward him, and he concentrated on being a part of the wilderness, invisible and harmless. He drew himself up to sit and found Deishima watching him.

Her shawl twitched as she turned away.

"It's all right to stare," he said. "Everyone will, I have to get used to it."

She turned back to him, sitting slender and straight, her tiny hands in her lap. "It is a beautiful place, this grove."

"I've always thought so. This is the place where Strel Gamel prayed to our Lady, and She granted his heart's desire."

"It is a holy place?" She shifted on her seat.

"No, the chapel is farther on. This," he told her, considering how to word it, "this is a quiet place. A place where all are welcome."

Nodding, she seemed to relax.

Wolfram plucked at the grasses, then steeled his nerve and began, "I have to ask you about something I heard, on the ship."

Instantly, she stiffened. "What is it that you heard, Highness Wolfram?"

"You, Faedre, Esfandiyar, and Melody were talking, about me, I think. You said you were preparing me for something. I need to know what you meant."

Her eyes glinted white then dark in the shadow of her shawl. "There was a ritual we desired to perform. It would also require your participation, but it cannot be, not now that I am defiled."

"How are you defiled?"

"I have been too long away, in unclean places. I am no longer pure."

Twisting the grasses about in his fingers, Wolfram pondered this. "So their plans, this ritual can no longer happen?"

"Not in the way in which they intended it. I do not know what they shall plan now." Her shoulders drooped, and her hands slipped in beneath the veil. For a moment, they covered her eyes.

"Then it's true that you can never return to them; you can never take back your place," he said softly.

Deishima shook her head just once, as if she had lost the energy to do more.

"What about your father? I can send you home."

"I would be punished most severely for the time I have been apart from my guardians."

"But you would still be a princess."

Very softly she replied, "I would be dead."

"He would kill you for that? But it wasn't even your fault, you have done nothing!"

Framed by folds of cloth, her dark eyes met his. "There is so little you understand about my people. To be a woman in my country, it is very different than your women here. The Jeshan would have only my word that I am still innocent, and my word would not be enough. In order to avoid the dishonor, he must execute me for my defilement."

"That's barbaric! It was my fault; whatever happened, I brought it on you." Claws pricked inside his temples.

"The honorable thing would have been for me to die rather than to be taken by you, Highness Wolfram."

"You're right, I don't understand." He swallowed hard and forced his hands to stillness, tossing down the blades of grass he had been mutilating. "What if you were married?"

"The penalty for a married woman to be in the woods with an abductor would be the same."

Shaking his head, Wolfram rephrased the question. "What if you were married to me?"

"But I am not." She shook her head as well, then paused. "I am not, we are . . ." Deishima braced her hands on the bench, leaning forward. "What is it that you are saying, Highness Wolfram?"

He rose to one knee and met her gaze. "I am asking you to marry me."

Chapter 28

FOR A long time, Deishima stared.

Wolfram let out a nervous laugh. "I wish I could see your face right now."

At last she lifted the edge of her veil, drawing it up to drape down her back. Her fine, dark features showed no expression, her lips lightly held together as if she would speak but did not know what to say. She replaced her hands at her sides, resting on the mossy bench. Her toes brushed the grass underneath, her heels not quite able to reach the ground. Breathing carefully, she watched him, searching for something.

Wolfram traced her features, studied the black sheen of her hair peeking out from the fold across her forehead, then back to her eyes. At last, he looked away, sitting back on his heels, letting his hands fall to his lap. Hovering near the pond, Dawsiir caught his eye for a moment, raising his hands in a gesture of confusion, then found something to occupy himself with on the far side of the clearing.

"I cannot marry you," she said, clearly and carefully.

"I know I'm not much—not much to look at, not likely to be good company for someone like you, I have no honor . . ." Wolfram trailed off and shrugged. "I want to undo some of the damage I've done. I've ruined your life, and all that I can offer you is a new one in return. A different life. I am the crown prince of Lochalyn. If you marry me, someday, you would be queen, your children will be queens." Children, he thought as he said it, he should not have mentioned children.

Silence fell again between them, and he studied the grass, examined the sunlight falling through the trees, tried to identify birds by their songs. High above, a squirrel sprang to a new bough, barely hanging on with a flip of its tail. Wolfram tracked its progress limb to limb as it nibbled off the buds of flowers yet to come. One of the silver fishes flashed briefly into the air and back with a splash. The little pond smelled of decay and fertility.

"Highness Wolfram," Deishima began, and the two little lines marked her brow. "Perhaps I should have said that you cannot marry me. I am the Jeshan's seventeenth daughter. I am not meant for marriage to anyone. I am sure that the queen of your country has more in mind for you than that you should wed such a one as I. Perhaps as a fourth or fifth wife, I might do."

With that nervous laugh bubbling up again in his throat, Wolfram shook his head. "In my country, there is only one wife, and it is up to the woman to choose—within reason. Wait—" he urged as she opened her mouth to object again. "If you would not have me—and Finistrel knows I can understand that—then think of your country and mine. Your father has been seeking to draw us into this war of yours. If we were to marry, our two countries would be allies. The spices and the cloth of Hemijrai are in great demand here, we can never get enough. Our mountains are rich with iron and copper. This could be a boon for both our nations."

"You have spent much time thinking on this, Highness Wolfram," she observed. Her breathing seemed strangely uneven, as if he had shaken her somehow, found a way around her careful composure.

"I had all night." He plucked a blade of grass and nipped off tiny bits between his ragged fingernails.

"Even though these reasons sound compelling, you cannot marry me," she repeated. "I am defiled."

"Bury it, Deishima, if you're defiled, then I'm the one who defiled you!"

With a quick breath, she withdrew to the far end of the bench, and Dawsiir was beside her in an instant, his face set into a wary mask.

"Oh, sweet Lady, I'm such an idiot. I shouldn't use your name, I don't even know what to call you. I'm sorry." He turned from her, dropping his face to his hands, shaking. "I knew I'd never get this right," he mumbled. His temples throbbed, and he wanted to pull himself up and run deep into the woods, yelling and daring the Woodmen to come and take their vengeance upon him. The ache in his side told him he'd never make it.

Whispers of Hemijrani reached his ears as Dawsiir demanded some explanation. The tone of his voice had lost some of its reverence for the sacred princess, and Wolfram wondered whose side he would be on if Deishima told him all that they had said. His head pounded like a mason at work, and he lay down in the moss, ripping off the eye patch to press his ruined face close to the cool earth. He breathed in the scents of dirt and moisture. Knowing he must look like even more of an idiot, Wolfram didn't care. She could walk more easily than he—let her escape and pretend that nothing had happened. He had lost his dignity sometime ago, but enough of it lingered that he did not want to rise and limp like a dog from her sight.

Behind him, she rose with a soft rustle of skirts and scuffing of shoes into the grass. "Highness Wolfram?" she ventured. "Are you well?"

He could think of nothing to reply. He listened to her breathing, and almost missed the stealthy tread that joined them.

"Yes, Highness Wolfram, are you well?" Alyn's voice called. He crossed quickly and his feet filled Wolfram's limited view. "You really need to get more sleep."

"I thought I told them to keep you away."

"From your room, yes. From the grove, no. And I have to talk to you. You could at least sit up and act like a man."

The demon swelled and howled, tearing at his insides, but Wolfram felt powerless to rise. "Why do you do this to me? Why do you strike at me every time we meet? You've been doing this since we were five years old, Alyn; what did I ever do to you?" Spent, he tilted his chin up and tried to breathe.

Alyn's answer was a long time coming. Finally, he said, "To me? Nothing—not yet." He took a breath and puffed it out. "But there is evil all around you, bad things hovering like vultures."

Already exhausted and caught once again humiliating himself, Wolfram curled up on the ground, clenching his teeth to keep them from chattering. Alyn, the Voice of the Lady, saw evil around him. Of course Deishima couldn't marry him, she must see it, too. Could she see the terrible face of the murdered man who haunted Wolfram's dreams, or the demon that ripped at his neck, or the thousand little wounds that Wolfram had delivered every day? Wolfram whimpered, feeling the tiger's teeth.

Then Deishima spoke. "But this is not true, sir. I do not know who you are, but I wish to know why you should lie in such a terrible manner. By what right would you say such a thing?"

"By the right the Lady saw fit to give me. Not that I would expect a heathen to understand, but it is Her voice I hear, Her visions I see. And he"—Alyn thrust his finger toward Wolfram— "is a vision of the blackest kind." From the narrow view afforded him, Alyn towered upward, his accusing finger reaching down from the very stars.

"Then I am glad that I am not myself sworn to such a blind Lady as yours must be." The moment she said it, Deishima gasped and backed away, pulling the veil down over her face.

His lips forming an unaccustomed grimace, Alyn raised a shaking fist as if to strike her.

Wolfram scrambled to his hands and knees.

Alyn let his hand drop. "I thought your kind were supposed to be retiring, not even speaking without a man's permission. I guess I shouldn't be surprised that Wolfram managed to find the shit among the roses." He glared down at Wolfram. "Please tell me you weren't trying to seduce her, not here—or do you bother with persuasion these days?"

Grabbing a clod of dirt, Wolfram flung it straight at Alyn's face, where it landed with a satisfying splat. As Alyn wiped the dirt from his eye, Wolfram tried to rise, but the muscles of his right side gave a fierce spasm, dropping him back to the dirt to curse.

Even with grass on his face, Alyn laughed. "It's a good thing I'm not like you physical types, or I might have to redress that blow. But it seems you don't need my help to hit the dirt. Why would my sister go anywhere with you?"

"She didn't go with me, I went with her, it was her idea," he mumbled through the pain, beaten by a man who had not even touched him. "I think her Hemijrani maid had been working on her for a long time to make the trip."

"Where is she now? What's happened to her?"

"How should I know? You're the one who's so good at finding people."

Alyn crouched down, tilting his head to stare at Wolfram. "I can't feel her anymore. I lost her a few weeks ago, that's why I left Drynnlynd, that's why I'm here—not to help my dear friend recover from his own absurdity. She's my twin, and I can't feel her."

"I don't know, Alyn, I swear I don't. Maybe with Faedre on her way to Lochdale." Summoning the last strength of his anger, Wolfram managed to raise his head. "Please leave me alone, Alyn, I am begging you."

"I don't believe you've begged for anything in your entire life!" Alyn grinned. "Say it again."

"Please, Alyn, I beg you to go." His voice cracked, and he lowered his head.

Without any comment, Alyn walked away.

Lying on his left side, his good eye shut against the grass, Wolfram fought the shaking that had overtaken him. The cramp in his side eased slightly, but tremors of weakness tugged at the scars, and he felt his insides knotting. He hunched into his crossed arms, praying for some deliverance. Tiny, gulping breaths rasped in his throat.

Even the birds had fallen silent in the wake of the confrontation. Dawsiir was muttering in Hemijrani—cursing himself, or so it seemed.

Why wouldn't they go? Wolfram had to give them some sign, but he could not speak, knowing that his pain and frustration would be what they heard. He opened his eye, tilting his head to focus on the sharp, green blades. A tiny hemlock cone snuggled in among them. Patiently a beetle climbed up the nearest blade, its antennae quivering as it tried to determine the nature of the obstruction that Wolfram had become.

In a few steps, Deishima was before him, her borrowed skirt held up to reveal the toes of her new slippers. She stood there, the rest of her unseeable above him, then sank down to her knees a few feet away from his face. Her lips trembled, and her eyes glistened with unshed tears. For a moment, she pressed her fingers to her mouth, trying to master her breath as her shoulders shook. When she bent forward, hiding her face, her veil slipped and fell over her. One quick dark hand grabbed a handful of fabric and yanked it off, flinging it aside with a glittering trail of hairpins. Her midnight hair shone in the sunlight, tumbling all about her, making a black cloak over her shoulders and forming a pool around her on the grass.

Wolfram relaxed his arms. He reached a cautious finger to stroke a dark ribbon of hair. "Please," he whispered, not sure if he wanted to be heard, "please don't cry. I'm no good with tears."

Shaking her head, Deishima peered at him over her hands.

Her small and shaky voice said, "Jeshnam is my title of birth, Highness. You may call me Jeshnam."

He slipped his fist beneath his cheek, and repeated, "Jeshnam."

Deishima nodded. "That man is Highness Melody's brother."

"Her twin, yes." They spoke in tones so hushed that Wolfram could hear the muffled thumping of his own heart.

"And he hears the voice of your Holy Lady, is this true?"

"Yes."

She raised her chin a little and propped it on her joined hands. "I hope that She is not so harsh in Her judgments as Her messenger would appear to be."

"Me, too." Wolfram felt another gripping pain in his guts and winced. "He has no right to talk that way to you, Jeshnam."

"Nor to you, Highness," she said so softly he could barely hear her.

"You don't know me," he told her. "You don't know the things I have done. I should never have asked you . . ." He gazed at her through the screen of grass, with her face revealed to him in the sunlight, framed by the rivers of her hair.

"By the Two and Their every glory, Highness Wolfram, you have given me a thousand reasons why I should wish to marry you." She tucked the creeping tendrils of hair back behind her ears. "What I do not understand is why you should wish to marry me."

"I need your compassion." He smoothed out the grass before him to see her clearly. "Your grace and your serenity. And your wisdom. I have learned so much from you already." He thought to leave it there, but he knew this was not all, was not even the start. "I don't know why I'm so affected by you. When he told me you were in the stables, I went mad. I had to find you, to see that you were all right. From the first moment I touched your hair, Jeshnam, there has been a fire in me." Two little lines pinched between her brows, and she looked quickly away from him. All of his fury, his misery, and his folly had been laid out before her—there was nothing he could offer in his own defense. He let his head sink back to the earth. His eye shut on the unfamiliar burn of tears.

One small and gentle finger stroked down his cheek so lightly he could almost have imagined it. Her fingers traced the scars like rays of the sun. Her thumb ran along the jagged line of his eyebrow, down by the smooth new skin to the edge of his jaw, and lingered there. "Why should you battle a tiger for me, Highness Wolfram?" she breathed. "Why should you anger your people? Why should you suffer the ridicule of your enemy on my behalf?"

He dared not move for fear of breaking the tenuous warmth of her touch. "Because I love you."

She drew back, but he reached out and caught her hand, holding it as he might hold a wounded bird. Wolfram pushed himself up on his hand and searched her face. "I have had women before. I have lusted after so many, and I have been so low in my pursuit of pleasure that I'm not even sure I will be welcomed home. I thought I had everything I could ever want, and now I can see that it was nothing." He opened his fingers so that her delicate hand rested lightly on his palm. He let her go, but she did not run. "If the leopards had torn me to pieces, it would have been worth it to have that single touch of you."

Her dark eyes met his, the twin lines between them smoothing, then returning as she regarded him. Her warm hand trembled upon his own, her smooth dark skin a sharp contrast to his pale, callused palm.

At last, her lips parted. "You are like no one I have ever heard of, Highness Wolfram. Not even in the chronicles of time."

"Jeshnam, Deishima, will you marry me?"

For the first time, she smiled, spreading a radiance over her face brighter than the sun to his eyes. "Yes, Highness Wolfram, I will."

Chapter 29

THE NEXT day, standing as straight as he could before the mirror, Wolfram critically eyed his new haircut and the satin doublet he'd borrowed from Earl Jordan. It fell a little long for him since Jordan was a good six inches taller, but the russet set off the blond hair nicely. Still, he had to adjust to seeing himself as a prince again. He had been a hunter, a tracker, a tradesman, a fugitive these last six months. How he would ever fit back in at court he had no idea—to the extent that he had ever fit in there. He slipped the eye patch down and stared at his face. No, best to get it over with. Pulling the patch back off, he tucked it into the doublet. The missing eye made him look like the veteran of a harrowing war.

A knock came on the door.

"Enter," he said, trying on his princely ways. They no longer fit as well as once they had.

A servant came in and bowed briefly. "The Lord Protector of Lochalyn has arrived, Your Highness. He is requesting an audience."

"Requesting, is that what he said?" Wolfram's eyebrows rose.

"Aye, Your Highness."

"Where?"

"If you'll follow me, Your Highness." The servant bowed him out of the room and brought him past the little garden courtyard. He looked for Deishima, but did not find her there. Since she had accepted him, he had not seen her. They had walked slowly back from the grove, and he had fallen gratefully into his bed, waking only for a light supper. This morning had been taken up with fretting over Lord Fionvar's approach. He had so much to say, so much he wanted to ask, and yet he did not know if he would be treated as a prince or a criminal. "Requested" seemed like a good sign.

They reached the open door of one of the countess's better chambers, not far from the keep's famous dance hall. Dismissing the servant before he was announced, Wolfram leaned a moment on the door.

Inside, Fionvar stood with his back to him.

Lyssa, at her brother's side as he poured a goblet of wine, was saying, "Well, I heard from the guards that you'd entered the city, I was just surprised you didn't come straight here, that's all."

"Avoidance, maybe," Fionvar answered, then took out a parchment packet. "And these." He studied the packet and shrugged. "I wanted—" Following Lyssa's stare toward the door he broke off.

Instantly, Wolfram straightened, resisting the tug toward his right, sorry he had not heard what Fionvar wanted. Taking a deep breath, Wolfram stepped inside, and bowed. "My lord Protector, we are well met." Several paces separated them, but he could not miss the shock that crossed the other man's face, the way his jaw stayed slack a moment too long.

"Wolfram!" Lyssa protested. "Should you be out of bed?"

He had fended off her visits the last two days, and she had not seen the new hair. At the concern in her voice, Wolfram felt the claws of anger at his shoulders. He wasn't a child, nor was he an invalid, not really. He gave her a brief but pointed stare, and Lyssa hesitated, withdrawing her outstretched hand.

With a glance at his sister, Fionvar stayed in his place, carefully replacing the goblet on the table. As Fionvar bowed, Wolfram caught his eyes shutting, the tremor of unknown emotion making his hands shiver. He straightened and smiled broadly at first, then less so as he took in Wolfram's bearing. As Wolfram watched, the smile vanished completely, replaced by a sort of uncertainty Wolfram had never seen there before. Now that he studied him,

Wolfram could see his own face there as well, in the shape of his nose, the set of his lips, the darkness of his eyes.

For a long time, the two men stood staring at each other across the room, and Lyssa kept out of their way.

Wolfram's own perusal gave Fionvar permission to stare, and he did, taking in the scarred face, even the tracery at Wolfram's throat. Under his father's eyes, Wolfram scarcely dared to breathe lest something give away his weakness, his own uncertainty, or the fury that lingered in the taut muscles of his shoulders; the demon begged its due, as he had known it would.

With a turn of the hand, Fionvar gestured to the large table and cushioned chairs. "I've had a hard journey, Your Highness. If you don't mind, I'd like to sit."

"Please," Wolfram stammered, as if he were a host who had forgotten his manners.

Placing the packet he'd been holding in the center, Fionvar lowered himself into a chair toward the middle, and Lyssa took one opposite him, still silent.

Wolfram crossed the distance too quickly, taking the end chair for himself.

"Can I pour you some wine, Your Highness?" Fionvar asked, a slight tremor in his voice.

"Please," Wolfram said again, then scowled at himself. He had already let Fionvar get the upper hand, getting him to sit down before he fell down.

Turning away to pour the wine, Fionvar began, "To say that we've been worried would be something of an understatement, Your Highness, as I'm sure Lyssa has told you. Of course I want to hear your story, but the queen takes precedence, and I'm sure you'd rather not tell it twice."

Wolfram had expected many things from this meeting, but this game of diplomacy was not one of them. "How does the queen?" he asked lightly.

Fionvar set the jug down abruptly, splashing a bit of wine on the table. "She's well, aside from your absence." He offered Wolfram a goblet and sat back when it was accepted. "She's worried about Duchess Elyn, as well, Your Highness, who has not been doing well of late."

Lyssa frowned. "I was sure she'd outlive us all. What's the trouble?"

With a glance to Wolfram, Fionvar said, "She's old, of course, but there's a new shakiness and some difficulty walking. Fearsome as ever, though." When his gaze returned to the prince, he seemed afraid to meet his eye.

Lyssa grunted, crossing her arms as she, too, turned to Wolfram. "I thought you'd let your hair go dark," she commented, narrowing her eyes.

"I am—" he started softly, then louder, "I am not who I was when I left Lochdale." He directed this toward Fionvar. "I know I made a mess of things the day I left," he told Lyssa, "so I asked the wizard to change my hair."

"Is that an apology?"

"No," he said, "it's a peace offering."

Fionvar's head rose at that, his fingers playing with the chain of office he always wore. The question formed on his face before he voiced it, but he leaned forward and asked carefully, "Why do you need to make an offering to us, Your Highness?"

Wolfram brought his fingers together, phrasing his response. "I have not been the prince I should have been, but I am striving to be better."

Leaning her arms on the table, Lyssa said, "You're making me nervous, Highness. What have you done?"

"Must you always assume the worst of me?" he snapped back, the fury rushing through his tense muscles as a howling force. "Great Lady, I am doing the best that I can, and you don't even know the half of it."

"What should I assume from your past behavior? That you're suddenly transformed into this responsible, thoughtful, obedient prince, or that you're about to spread another pile of lies?"

"Lyssa," Fionvar said, with an undertone of warning.

Grinning fiercely, Wolfram said, "Do not speak to me of lies, Lyssa—sometimes even you prefer them."

Lyssa leapt to her feet, shooting her brother a startled look, then slammed her arms across her chest and turned away.

His palms up in a bid for peace, Fionvar glanced between them. Wolfram stared at him, transferring his rage, praying that Fionvar misinterpret their words and their anger. Fionvar slowly swallowed, and said, "I know you had a thousand questions when you left, Your Highness, questions that should have been answered years ago."

Breathing carefully, Wolfram nodded, not letting his relief show.

"I am ready to tell you everything you wish, Your Highness." He gazed steadily, his face intent, his hands open.

Nodding once more, Wolfram spotted the forgotten parchment packet. He could smell something sweet and vaguely familiar. "What's in there?"

Fionvar blinked, then laughed, flopping back in his chair as if all the tension had gone out of him with that one question. With a quirk of a smile, Fionvar prodded the package closer to Wolfram. "I found them in town. My peace offering."

Turning back, Lyssa came a little nearer the table as Wolfram unfolded the end and released a whiff of sweet steam into the still room. Staring into the bag, Wolfram's mouth went dry, and something stung behind his missing eye. Honeyed chestnuts. After all these years, Fionvar remembered.

With a quick movement, Wolfram bundled them back up. "Thank you," he mumbled, then paused. "I'm not ready to know everything, not yet."

Fionvar regarded him for a moment, then said, "I am here, Your Highness, when you're ready."

The words carried an unexpected weight, and Wolfram turned the packet of chestnuts on the table, not wanting to acknowledge what had been said, not daring to find out if there were other meanings left unspoken. Uncomfortable under Fionvar's eyes, Wolfram said, "There is something I must tell you, my lord." He took a deep breath and glanced at Lyssa. "The princess Deishima of Hemijrai has agreed to marry me."

Mouth dropping open, Fionvar twitched as if he had been struck.

Lyssa pounced forward, slapping her palms on the table. "What? She agreed? What are you talking about?"

"I have asked Jeshnam Deishima to be my wife, and she accepted," he said carefully, drawing himself up. "There's nothing difficult about that."

"Difficult? Holy Mother, Wolfram, what were you thinking? Don't you think you've had your revenge already?" She slammed a fist against the table, and the goblets jumped, sending a spray of red wine across the wood.

"This princess—what did you call her, Jeshnam?—is the one you took hostage to get off the ship?" Fionvar cut in.

"She's the sorceress, the one who had him thrown to the leopards," Lyssa supplied, "and led the tiger to them. Great Goddess, Wolfram, what did she do to you? Or is this some perverse joke?"

Wolfram's temples pounded. "She didn't do anything, Lyssa. I asked her, or did you miss that part?"

"Don't be ridiculous." To Fionvar she said, "You see? You see what he's been like? I should have left him in the leopard pit or taken him home, let Elyn whip some sense into him—"

"Lyssa, shut up!" Fionvar rose, leaning on the table, glaring at his sister. "Will you just for a moment, please, shut up."

"Bury you both!" In two strides she reached the door and burst into the hallway, slamming it behind her.

Kneading his temple, Wolfram watched a dribble of wine snaking toward him. The demon snarled inside him, and he struggled to keep it in check, not to give these people another reason to dismiss him.

"Tell me about this marriage, Your Highness," Fionvar said quietly, seating himself again. His fingers interlaced on the table, gripping each other.

"What we did was wrong," Wolfram burst out. "In taking her from her people, we destroyed her life—they would have killed me for touching her hair, yes, but for her to be in the woods with no chaperone, for that they would kill her." His head jerked up as he added, "Nothing happened, there was nothing between us, even when Lyssa left."

Fionvar nodded, looking grave.

"While I was—recovering—Lyssa banned them from the keep; Deishima and my man Dawsiir were living in the stables with no money, and no place to go. There she was, abandoned in this strange country, terrified. She couldn't go home even if she found a way, and I did this to her." A wash of shame crept up his neck, and Wolfram pulled his hands together in his lap. "I did this."

Picking up his neglected goblet, Fionvar took a slow drink and set it gently down again. His every movement was methodical, and Wolfram wondered what must be going on inside, if Fionvar had his own demons.

"So you would marry this princess to repair the damage you think you have done?"

Squirming, Wolfram pointed out, "Look at the trade possibilities, the kind of luxury goods they can offer us, not to mention the skilled craftsmen—the fabric alone would be worth an alliance."

Fionvar raised his eyebrows. "You would marry her to bring our nations closer together?"

Wolfram's temper flared and he shoved the chestnuts out of the way. "I would marry her because she taught me how to breathe, because she tore up her veils to bind my wounds. She showed me compassion when she had nothing to gain but misery. She is the best thing that ever happened to me, can you understand that?"

With the slightest of smiles, Fionvar said, "I would like to try, Your Highness. Will you introduce us?"

"Come on." He flung himself away from the table, jerking open the door to startle Lyssa standing on the threshold. With a growl, he swept by her, feeling the heat in his cheeks, longing to take back all that he had said, everything he had never meant to reveal.

"Where are we going?" Lyssa asked, striding at her brother's side.

"To meet the prince's betrothed."

"You're not going to let him go through with this!"

"It's not my place to deny him."

"How can you say that, my Lord Protector of the Crown?" she demanded. "You must see that this is some scheme—"

How Fionvar shut her up again, Wolfram did not know, but the rest of the walk was in silence. He swung automatically into his long, accustomed stride, and the ache in his side intensified with every step. Refusing to show any weakness, he took them past the garden. He slowed a little as they turned the corner, trying to breathe more deeply, to get himself back under control before he made this introduction—perhaps the most important of his life.

Dawsiir's bench opposite the door was unoccupied, and Wolfram frowned. Turning to the door itself, he found it open. The room stood empty, and all traces of Deishima were gone.

Chapter 30

FIONVAR AND Lyssa exchanged a look. "This is the princess's room?" Fionvar asked.

"Of course it is, bury it!" Wolfram hovered in the doorway, then stepped inside, turning at the center of the little room.

"Perhaps she's gone for a walk, Your Highness," Fionvar suggested.

"She wouldn't," he snapped. "I practically had to drag her out last time."

"What makes you so sure she was willing to marry you?" Lyssa asked brightly, her arms tucked behind her, feet apart in a stance like a waiting warrior.

"She said yes." His head and hands throbbed, and the bare patch of skin twitched wildly. He fumbled the eye patch loose from his doublet and slipped it on.

"It wouldn't be the first time a girl says yes to appease an unwanted suitor, then ran away—the gate's right there, she and her man could've slipped out anytime."

"Why are you doing this, Lyssa?"

"Isn't it better this way? You only asked her out of some misguided obligation, now you don't have to go through with it, and we don't have to figure a way out of it." She glanced to Fionvar in expectation of his support, but he kept his eyes on Wolfram.

"It may be," Fionvar said carefully, "that she had second thoughts."

"She wouldn't leave like this; you don't know her."

"Do you?" Lyssa shot back.

A spasm of pain shuddered through him, and Wolfram reeled. He sagged onto the bed, holding his head in both hands. "She said yes," he mumbled.

"Look, maybe she really has gone for a walk, she has your friend with her, right?" Fionvar said.

Wolfram gasped in a breath and let it out, then another. Bit by bit, he fought back the demon, ignoring whatever was said around him. He took a deep breath, let it out slow. On the next inhalation, he held his breath a moment and frowned. Drawing back his hands, he raised his head and sniffed. There it was again! Deishima's cool, herbal scent still lingered, and with it hung a whiff of animal, something wild and grubby. Monkeys.

Wolfram's eye popped open. "She didn't just leave, she's been kidnapped."

"What?" said Lyssa and Fionvar together, their quizzical faces showing the family likeness.

"She was kidnapped," Wolfram repeated as he rose to shaky legs. "Can't you smell the monkeys?"

Frowning, Lyssa said slowly, "She was kidnapped . . . by monkeys?"

He jabbed a finger into her face. "Don't mock me."

"I'm just trying to understand what you're talking about, Your Highness."

"Great Lady, Lyssa, can you let him explain?" Fionvar asked wearily. "What do you think happened?"

"I can smell monkeys in here. The only person who deals

with the monkeys is Esfandiyar, he's a chief priest who came over on the ship. He must've come here and taken her away."

"She's been here a week, why wait so long?" Lyssa challenged.

"How would they know where we were?"

"So how did they figure it out now?"

"Maybe they have a spy."

"They do—Deishima!" she countered. "The girl figured she had to get out of here now that you were after her in more ways than one."

His face burned as he glared at her. "Stop it, Lyssa, just stop it." To Fionvar he said, "Can't you smell it?"

Sniffing, Fionvar shook his head. "There's no blood, no sign of struggle."

"She's so small I could pick her up with one arm—"

"And you did," Lyssa cut in, "holding a knife in the other. For love of the Lady, Wolfram, of course she agreed to marry you—she was probably terrified."

"You weren't there—"

"Who was?"

"Dawsiir saw the whole thing."

"He doesn't even speak the language; but you produce him, and I'll ask what he thinks." She spread her arms magnanimously.

"You were there when we left the boat," he said, a pleading note slipping into his voice. "They tried to stop us. There's something they don't want us to find out about, and she could have told us. You said so yourself."

"Is this true?" Fionvar asked.

"I thought so, at the time." She shrugged. "Now? Who knows. All I remember is some men who seemed to block the way. Maybe they were just unloading baggage."

In his mind, Wolfram went back to the ship. It wasn't just baggage, they were up to something; they had to be. "What about the tiger?"

Lyssa smoothed a hand over her bald head, her expression almost sad. "You kidnapped their princess, Wolfram, I guess they ran out of leopards."

"No, it wanted her; it would have killed her if I hadn't gotten in the way, she knew that, too. There is some ritual they want to perform, but she said they couldn't do it without her. Now they have her."

"She also said she was no good to anyone now that she'd been ruined. By you."

"Bury it, Lyssa, that's why I was going to marry her!" He shoved past her out the door and collapsed onto the sunlit bench, one fist digging into his side, trying to ease the spasm. His whole body quivered, and he wanted to hit someone or break something.

Tense whispers emerged from the room, and Lyssa stalked out, with Fionvar following more slowly, looking thoughtful. Wolfram leaned his forehead on the pillar at the end of the bench. He winced with pain. Deishima was gone—where? why? He had smelled the monkeys, hadn't he? His mind whirled as he fended off unconsciousness.

"Perhaps you should rest, and we can go talk to the city guard, surely they would have seen something," Fionvar said. "Your Highness?"

Wolfram nodded, rubbing his head on the stone of the pillar; cool and rough, it helped him focus. "The guards, of course." He rose unsteadily, and Fionvar caught his elbow as he staggered. He wanted to pull away, but could not manage it.

"You're not coming," Fionvar told him firmly.

"I have to know," Wolfram gasped, hunched over his right side, his eye squeezed shut.

Steering him toward his own room, Fionvar said, "Look at it this way. You're no good to anyone if you fall apart—least of all to her, if you're right."

The bastard was right, again and again. Wolfram's head must be more muddled than he thought. "Bury you," he muttered, falling full length on the bed. "If you're not back to tell me what you know, I'll be gone, I'm warning you." He cradled his head in both arms and wondered how he would ever follow through on that threat.

SHUTTING THE door behind him, Fionvar turned to Lyssa. "Find someone to guard the door, I'll wait."

She gave a half bow and hurried off, returning in a moment with a strapping manservant. Giving explicit instructions that the prince was not to leave his room, they left in the direction of the stables.

"Dawsiir brought the horses," Lyssa explained as they walked. "They had some plan about meeting up in the glen where I left Wolfram and the girl. I guess Wolfram never intended coming home."

"Mmm." Fionvar frowned. "He did look awfully relieved when I said he could wait on telling the tale."

"He probably needs more time to make up a good one," Lyssa remarked. Then, "Sorry."

"Granted, he's made mistakes—indeed, many of them—but this is hard enough without your pouncing on him every time he opens his mouth."

Lyssa reddened and glanced away. "I know. I'm sorry."

"What has he done that's gotten you so upset?"

Shrugging, she tossed her head as if taming the wild red hair that used to curl over her shoulders. "He makes everything so difficult."

"Especially loving him," Fionvar murmured, glancing up sharply as Lyssa stumbled. He narrowed his eyes at her. Something had happened, something more than Wolfram's usual chaos. "It's Melody, isn't it? She and Wolfram?"

Giving him a keen stare, Lyssa replied, "I suspect them, nothing more. I haven't any evidence, but, knowing him . . ."

"Did he really ask that girl to marry him?"

"Probably. He's been acting queer in different ways lately. He went mad when he found out they were staying in the stables, kept talking about our duty to her. Honestly, I don't know what he sees in her that gets him going like that. I can't imagine he'd really marry her just to save her honor."

Considering this, Fionvar rounded the corner to the stable yard and stopped as his heart seemed to pinch within his chest, and he knew the answer, the one thing nobody else had offered Wolfram in a very long time, himself included. It was not the compassion Wolfram claimed, but something more precious: trust. Fionvar and Lyssa and Brianna and all the rest could make hours of conversation from things they only suspected Wolfram had done, not to mention the fiasco of his mistress being the Usurper's daughter. Yet this girl, who had as little cause as any of them to believe anything the prince told her, this girl had apparently agreed to marry him. She had offered him a gift more wondrous than she even knew. If it were true, then Fionvar would do all in his power to let this betrothal stand. And if that girl had lied and run away, then she was all that Lyssa thought and more.

"What is it?"

Fionvar shook his head. "Just thinking."

"You think too much, you always have."

"Maybe you don't think enough," he said lightly, but she sprang once again into motion and let him catch up at the stable.

Most of the outside stalls held the large, leggy horses favored by messengers, but one held a small, fine-boned horse of deep brown gleaming to red when she tossed her head. "That's one of the Hemijrani horses," Lyssa said. "There were two, one for each of them."

"Makes sense, if they ran off, that they would have taken both horses, don't you think?" He reached a hand out to the beautiful, delicate animal which snuffled him, then dismissed him. "This horse kept up with Fenervon?"

"He's heavy," she growled, affronted. "I don't know if they'd take both horses. Dawsiir seemed to consider that one of them belong to Wolfram. I thought he was on the level. He'd done Wolfram some service and gotten a right of passage in return."

"I wondered why the prince referred to him as his man. So that means the guards would have no reason to detain them."

"Let's go find out."

They walked the dusty street as far as the main gate, the only one typically open to free passage, and Lyssa's call brought down a mail-clad sergeant.

"Well, we had a group of them darkies in last evening, my man said. Left again this morning they did, early like."

"Did they have a girl with them; she might have been covered head to toe?"

"Aye, riding double—if it was a girl, hard to tell with the shawls and what."

"That's true," Lyssa said. "She would have been very small."

"Aye, sounds right."

"Were they in a hurry?" Fionvar asked. "Could you tell if there was any coercion?"

"The girl, you mean? No, didn't seem like it. They went pretty leisurely, turning for the Lochalyn road. Seemed like they was coddling her, I'd say, taking it slow cause she had to hang on."

"You saw her hands, then?" Fionvar inquired, wondering what else they could glean.

The man nodded. "All them bracelets, hard to miss with the sun glinting, and especially the jingling."

"Thanks, you've been a big help."

Brother and sister turned back toward the keep, Fionvar standing with his arms crossed, head bowed.

Lyssa touched his arm. "I know you want to believe him, and support him, Fion, but look at his record. We're supposed to believe that the smell of monkeys means she's been kidnapped? Maybe she just put him off until her rescuers could get here. It certainly sounds like she left willingly."

"You're right as far as that goes." He let himself be soothed into motion again.

"And he's been through a major trauma, he's probably smelling all sorts of things. Alyn told me Wolfram panicked when he had the tiger skin in his room. A near-death experience changes a person. On the other hand, this paranoia of his about the Hemijrani started long ago, but it seems to be getting worse."

"Well, he'll be better off back home, in his old haunts. Great Lady, I haven't even told him about Asenith and the baby."

"I don't think he's up for that yet, not 'til he's gotten over this nonsense about asking that wench to marry him." She laughed. "He must have been out of his head."

"Not as far out as you think, Lyssa. Go easy on him, would you?"

She gave a noncommittal grunt.

The manservant gave a quick bow as they approached Wolfram's room. "No sound, my lord."

"Good. Wait here, would you? We may still need someone on duty." Fionvar knocked quietly and heard a mumble in return. "I left so quickly, I didn't know what had happened to him," he whispered. "It's killing me just to look at him."

Bowing her head, she said, "I'm sorry, I should have been there."

"You got him here, Lyssa, thank the Lady for that." He pushed the door open.

The only light came through the arrow slit in the opposite wall, making a streak of golden sun on the sheepskin rug. Wolfram lay curled on his side in the patch of sun, like a cat seeking warmth, or a child afraid of demons. Gazing at the ceiling, Fionvar took a deep breath. So much time had gone by since he had held that child in his arms that he had forgotten how; and Wolfram now would only push him away, only hate him even more than he already did. "Your Highness."

Lyssa crouched down. "Are you well? I'll fetch the wizards."

"No," he croaked, pushing himself to sit up. "I'm fine. I can't get used to beds is all." He clasped his arms loosely around his knees, keeping his face down. "What did you find? Not her, I gather."

"She left with a party of Hemijrani early this morning, willingly from what we can tell." Wolfram was already shaking his head, but Fionvar went on, "They came in last night on horseback and left that way this morning, with the addition of your friend and the girl. No sign of coercion."

"Where did they go?"

"The Lochalyn road. Makes sense, if Faedre and that lot came to talk the refugees back home."

Getting to his knees, then all the way up, Wolfram raised his head at last, and his eye was bright. "Then it must be time to go home."

"You can't ride," Lyssa said, standing between him and the door. "Not in your condition. The countess said at least a month in recovery, taking it slow."

Still shaking his head, Wolfram said, "There's no time; they came now, they came for a reason."

"Your Highness, you can't just—"

"Get me a horse, get me a carriage, get me an elephant, just get me on that road."

Fionvar moved to his sister's side. "I can't let you do this, Your Highness, I'm charged with your protection, even from yourself."

"Will you arrest me?" Wolfram challenged, taking one step closer to stand eye to eye with Fionvar. "Will you throw me in the dungeon in chains, my lord?" There was a wicked twist to his lips as he added the title.

"I hope that's not necessary." This close to, Fionvar could not avoid the staring painted eye that concealed the maiming of his son, and the sight turned his stomach.

"I am past the age of majority, my lord, do you know what that means?"

For a moment, they were silent, barely breathing, the prince a hairsbreadth taller, his shoulders broad with working muscle, his scarred face deadly serious.

"You no longer command me."

Fionvar's chin edged upward; he squared his shoulders and could not think of a response. His mind had gone empty at those words, a swirl of mixed emotions from fury to despair as he knew that it was true; he held no power over this hard and angry man. He did not even know him, and he was not sure he ever had.

"Get me a horse," Wolfram repeated slowly. "Get me a carriage, get me what you will, but we will leave tonight and make haste for Lochdale. Have I made myself clear?"

"Yes, Your Highness," Fionvar answered, and the words left a foul taste in his mouth as he bowed out of the presence of royalty.

Chapter 31

WHEN THE door closed, Wolfram sank back to the rug. The rush of power that had overcome him left him dazed, unsure if he could celebrate. It was no victory, but only the latest skirmish with this strange enemy who was his father. Whatever they might be to each other, Wolfram was still the crown prince, and this man was his sworn servant. The thrill of euphoria hovered in the air with Fionvar's parting bow. Long ago in Deishima's garden he had envisioned hitting his father, cracking his skull as he had broken that false father Lyssa had carved. He was used to being carried off by his fury, but this new power shook him. He did not need to be polite to this man, he did not need his help, his peace offerings, or anything else he had to offer.

He had been a fool to try to bargain with them when this path lay open to him, especially now that Deishima had vanished. What he needed was to get her back, to get the truth from her at the very least. Even Deishima, slight as she was, could have put up some struggle. Even she had a voice to scream or her Ashwadi to ward them off. Esfandiyar had been here, he had taken her away with him—willingly or otherwise—and Wolfram would find out. Fionvar might have been of some use to him had he put aside his suspicions for a moment, but Lyssa clearly had her brother's ear already, so it was up to Wolfram alone.

When he left behind his castle and his place, Wolfram had left as well the air of royalty. He had just discovered how to put it on again, draping himself with his birthright as if he already wore the crown.

Fingering the thick wool of the sheepskin, Wolfram remembered the simple beauty of Deishima's hair, and royalty fell from him like the sham he knew it was. It was a tool, nothing more, a chisel to carve his own way or a blade to cut through the games the Lord Protector sought to play, and he would use any tool at his disposal to find her. She had not left him willingly, he must be sure of that. The demon growled, and there was no breath to stop its roar.

THE CARRIAGE they gave him was small and scarcely more comfortable than riding, or so Wolfram thought. The Hemijrani horse tethered to the back pranced along as easily the fourth day as it had on the first, and Wolfram enjoyed watching it, imagining the day he would ride it again. Somewhere among the baggage strapped over his head the tiger skin rested, wrapped and hidden from his view. The shifting wind would bring a whiff of it and a shiver to his spine though, thankfully, not so strong a reaction as the first time. They stopped each night by the roadside, and Wolfram got a chance to walk and work the kinks out of his aching body. On the first such stop, he had caught a scent of a Woodman's pipe, and made some remark about it. A strange look passed over Fionvar's face, but he said nothing, and the Woodman never appeared.

The guards who accompanied them from Gamel's Grove turned back when they met an official entourage from Lochdale, surprised to find the prince already on the move only the day after the Lord Protector had arrived. With a broken axle, it took them seven days to reach Lochdale, and Wolfram was more than ready to escape his confinement. People in the streets acted as if there were no carriage as it approached, then hurried to point and whisper as it drew away. The air of mystery surrounding his return must have enthralled more than any ordinary homecoming would have, and Wolfram spent the trip from the gates to the castle peering out between the curtains suddenly thinking it had all been a very bad idea.

Returning from her advance mission to the castle, Lyssa slowed Fenervon to walk beside the carriage. She leaned down to the window and tapped for Wolfram to draw back the curtain. "Thought you should know she's here. Living in the guest quarters with the Hemijrani embassy."

"Have you seen her? Has anyone?" Wolfram's head was already aching from the taunting tone of Lyssa's voice.

"Everyone has; she follows Faedre everywhere like a proper little acolyte." She gave a little smile. "You should be glad to be shut of her, Your Highness."

"It can't be—she wouldn't just go like that."

Lyssa straightened up. "Suit yourself, Your Highness, you'll see soon enough."

The carriage pulled up before the grand stairs where a gathering awaited him. From behind the curtain, Wolfram eyed his mother and Duchess Elyn, side by side, both looking drawn and worried, their faces grown more alike in the time he had been gone. A step down from them, at ease in his finery, Prince Alyn of Bernholt chatted with one of the ladies, sunlight glinting from his golden curls as he spoke. He must have come straight to the capital after their last encounter. Then the prince glanced up to the carriage and Wolfram got a clear view of his companion: Princess Melody. Dressed in a gown of local make, with her hair done in ringlets, she turned expectantly with the others.

Rubbing his temple, Wolfram squinted to glower at her. He'd hardly recognized her out of the Hemijrani garb she had adopted, with her feet concealed, talking with her brother as if they'd always been close. The prickling began at the back of his neck, and he smoothed out his rumpled traveling clothes.

Setting a hand upon the door, Wolfram started forward when it popped open from the outside, and he nearly tumbled out.

The footman bowed and apologized, but Wolfram caught the glint of a smile on Alyn's lips, the frown deepening upon his mother's.

With as much dignity as he could still muster, Wolfram descended and walked up the steps to meet the queen.

Brianna held out her hand to him. "Welcome home, my

prince. I trust this last part of your journey was not so trouble-some as what went before."

Bowing over her hand, Wolfram said, "I am glad to see you well, Mother."

"And I, you," she replied.

He looked up to meet her gaze, and her cheeks paled be-neath their hint of rouge. Her eyes danced about his face, then shifted away. "Would you dine with us, or would you prefer to rest after your trip?" She returned her gaze to his with a little more grace.

"I could eat," he said warily.

"Excellent." She smiled timidly, but warmly enough for that.

On the step beside him, Fionvar shifted forward, ready to offer his arm as was their custom, but the queen slipped her hand around Wolfram's elbow, turning them both away and drawing him up the stairs.

Following behind, the group seemed awfully quiet—full of murmurs, with an absence of cheers or laughter. Wolfram felt on edge, surrounded by a new and denser web of lies—suggested by the expression on his mother's face, the way she had turned aside from her lover—it should have been a sign of her welcome that she had taken her son's arm, instead it felt like an insult to some-body else. Melody's laughter rang out briefly, and the shushing of Alyn's unmistakable voice. Everything around him had become an elaborate farce, everyone trying to put on their show and he the only one who did not know his part.

The queen led him to the greater of her private dining cham-bers, seating him at her right hand, while Alyn, as visiting royalty, took the left with his sister beside him. As they came to the door, Fionvar and Lyssa exchanged a furtive look; one of them should take the place beside him, and neither was eager for the honor. Both stepped forward, bumping each other, and Lyssa let out a harsh laugh as she yielded to her brother. A few other courtiers filled in, with Duchess Elyn at the foot of the table.

When everyone had taken a place, Brianna rang a bell, and the servants' door flew wide to admit the first of many trays laden with all manner of foods. After the time on the ship and the months of unseasoned roast meat with the Woodmen, the scents of this meal seemed as strange as those of Hemijrai. Baked apples surrounded a roast piglet, while a mound of turnips made a nest for lamb encrusted with savory herbs. They had gone to the trouble of a small feast for his return, and it made him feel unsettled, even more out of place.

As the guest of honor, he was offered each dish first. The stewed meat and bread he had eaten the last week could not rival this fare, but he couldn't be sure he was ready for all of this. He smiled often to prove his delight, but moved the food around his plate more than he ate it.

Queen Brianna looked to him with a nod. "Tell us about your adventures then, or what you might?"

Fear quickened his heart as he stared back at her. "I thought you wanted to be the first, Mother."

"Well, Princess Melody has told us of the palace at Hemijrai." She inclined her head to their royal visitors. "But Lyssa tells us you spent time with the Woodmen in our own mountains. Why not tell us about that?"

"I'm no good at stories," he said under his breath.

She leaned toward him, still smiling. "We have to tell them something, Wolfram, something to take back to the streets before the rumors start."

With a slight nod, Wolfram sat back and took a long swallow of ale. "I couldn't get enough adventure here, as you all know," he began, allowing himself a smile. "So I went to the forest to learn the ways of the Hurim. They were unsure about me, but let me stay to prove myself. We hunted boars together, using long spears rather than bow and arrow." Glancing at his mother, he untied the cuff of one sleeve and rolled it past the elbow, displaying a curving scar that ran the length of his forearm. "To prove my worth, I had to kill the boar with a knife—before he killed me. I won, but not by much."

"The same knife you used on the tiger, was it?" Alyn asked brightly, leaning over to admire the scar.

Wolfram slipped back his arm and tied the sleeve. "That's the one." He drew the knife from his belt and held it up.

"You've brought the skin, haven't you? We should have it out so everyone can see how brave you've been."

Clasping her hands together, Melody gave him her most beautiful smile. "Oh, yes, brother. Can't we see?"

A general murmur rounded the table, and the queen made a shooing motion with her hand to send a servant out.

Wolfram's palms grew clammy and his eye socket twitched. He laid the knife on the table in front of him. "I was not brave," he said, "but desperate."

"Don't be so modest," Melody said, bringing his eye back to her face.

"I'm glad you have forgiven me," he murmured across the table.

For a moment, her face lost its expression. "So much has changed, Wolfram, you'd be amazed."

"We can talk later?" A touch of hope soothed the pulse at his temples.

Leaning away, she sipped her goblet and eyed him. "Later," she said, as the doors were flung open with a flourish.

Three servants paraded in with the tiger skin stretched between them. One brought the fearsome head up level with the queen so that the striped hide took the length of the table and a bit more to display. The courtiers gasped, and even Duchess Elyn's eyebrows rose.

Taking a long drink, Wolfram mastered the shudder that ran through him, shutting his eye until he could breathe again. He opened it to see Melody watching him with a curious, calculating stare. With one hand, she stroked the soft white fur of the creature's belly.

Turning aside, he found himself confronted by Fionvar's profile.

"Holy Mother," Fionvar whispered, setting down his knife. He shot a quick glance to Wolfram, then bowed his head. "I hadn't seen it before."

"I've seen it too much," Wolfram replied. He took another drink and waved to have the mug refilled. It had been much too long since he was stinking drunk.

"So here's the beast that laid you low," Alyn remarked. "Amazing to think it was raised as a lady's pet. Gentle as a pussycat, she says."

In answer, Wolfram flipped back the eye patch and stared Alyn full in the face, gratified by the way he blanched at the sight. "Have you ever faced down death, Alyn?" He retrieved the knife and pulled it from its leather sheath. "I'll get you a tiger of your own, Alyn. I'll even loan you my knife."

"Put that away, Wolfram," the queen murmured through a pleasant smile.

He jammed it back into the sheath and flipped the eye patch back into place.

"I'm sorry you feel it necessary to resort to juvenile behavior, Wolfram," Alyn said. "I do not believe there's any need for me to prove myself against you, is there?"

"Let's step outside, and I'll show you some truly juvenile behavior."

Under the table, the queen kicked him, hard. "Now, boys," she said lightly. "Let's not have any of that. Perhaps Alyn should tell us about his trip to Drynnlynd."

Sliding the knife back into his belt, Wolfram seethed as Alyn began some anecdote about a distant monastery where they had begun to worship the moon. "Where's Dylan?" Wolfram asked suddenly. "Is he well?"

"Visiting your whore, most like," Elyn's voice cut through the admiring chatter of the nobles so that all turned a little pink or pale and studied their plates.

"Oh, sweet Lady, I should have told you more," Fionvar muttered. "You have a daughter, unnamed, and Asenith is not well."

"You didn't tell him?" Brianna asked sharply.

"Don't judge me until I've given my report," he replied. "Your Majesty."

"It seems, Your Highness, that the Lord Protector has been remiss in his duties. Yes, a daughter was born to this woman. She claims the child is yours. Of course, it's hard to say, isn't it? She has been living by her wiles these last years." The queen's gaze was cool and pointed, urging some action upon him.

Asenith. He had not thought of what to do about her or the child she bore. Trying to look noncommittal, he replied, "I guess I'll have to hear her story."

"She's on the threshold of the Lady," Elyn chimed in. "Won't matter a dram before too long." Grinning, she drained a cup of her ubiquitous tea and set into a coughing fit.

Wolfram rose too quickly, leaning his fingertips on the table. "I'd like to go to my chambers for that rest after all. Sorry, Mother."

"I understand, of course. I'll walk with you." She, too, rose and held out her hand. "Please, everyone, finish your meal."

The assembly rose as well, and the servants holding up the tiger skin gathered it up into a mound of fiery fur. They prepared to follow, but Wolfram turned. "No! Don't bring that to my rooms—I don't care what you do, I don't want it."

"Aye, Your Highness." The man bowed, looking befuddled.

"Put it in the trophy hall," the queen advised, "where all can see it."

The servant hurried away, and the door shut them off from the gathered nobles.

Queen Brianna drew him on, setting a slow pace. "Much has changed here, Wolfram, since you left."

"I guess so."

"We thought you were kidnapped, you know that, but there was no proof. Now I found you were larking about with the Woodmen. Did you think of us then, Wolfram?"

His face burned. "I made mistakes that day, I know—"

"Mistakes? You have entangled this castle with the Usurper's daughter. You have left us a pile of scandals that we are just beginning to sort out. Now you return, a grand adventurer, to pick up where you left off."

"Things have changed for me, too."

"Yes. You got mauled by a tiger and became even less presentable than you were."

He tried to free his elbow, but she clung on. Not facing her, Wolfram pushed back the burn in his eye, scrubbing his face with his free hand.

"I hope you've changed, Wolfram. I hope that cat slapped some sense into you." She broke her grip abruptly, presenting his own door. "Rest well, because I have a thousand questions for you. I'll hear Fionvar's report and Lyssa's. I've already heard from Princess Melody and the Hemijrani delegation, and I've even heard from that poor girl you kidnapped to cover another escape."

Although she was much shorter than he, the points on the crown gleamed aggressively, and her posture echoed her authority. "You'd better get some sleep, Your Highness, and get your story straight. I'll send for you in the morning. Oh—and there will be a guard on your door tonight." She backed off one step and stared at his face as she let out a sigh, her arms crossed. "You should know that I am considering remarriage. I'm not so old yet that I cannot get another heir." With that, she turned and left him, shaken, at his old front door.

Chapter 32

SHORTLY AFTER a dinner tray had been brought to him, another knock sounded at his door. "Wolfram?" called a tentative voice.

Wolfram leapt to answer it, grinning. "Dylan! Sweet Lady, but it's good to see you!" He pulled his friend in and shut the door.

"I was on my way to the observatory, but I had to stop by." Dylan turned about to look at him, and caught his breath. "Oh, I didn't know it was that bad!" He went pale, dropping into a chair by the hearth, his case of pens and a bundle of scrolls in his lap.

Slipping his eye patch back on, Wolfram sat more slowly. "It's pretty bad," he agreed. "Some days I think there's nothing left of me but scars." He tried another smile, but it was not returned and he looked for his mug instead. "Tell me all; I'd heard you were injured." He wanted to search his friend's face but couldn't bring himself to do it.

Clearing his throat, Dylan said, "Aye—not bad, though. I was out for two days."

"Two days? And that's not bad?"

"It was the night you left. We—I went to check on you, then down to the gate." He let out a strangled laugh. "I remember we always said we'd go that way, if we ran away. There was the fight."

Wolfram risked a glance, and found Dylan's face averted. "I'm sorry, I—" He broke off. "I don't know what to say. I should've talked to you."

"Aye, you should," Dylan murmured, fingering the pen case.

The silence hung awkwardly, then Wolfram asked, "How's your work?" The observatory was the one thing that could always get Dylan talking.

Dylan flinched. "Fine, very well. This project I've been working on is nearly up. We'll get to see how well I've done." His voice petered out.

"You never did tell me the specifics," Wolfram prompted, wondering how bad the injury really was if it had made Dylan go all quiet like this.

"Just some calculations, predictions, you know."

"No, I don't, and it seems unlikely you'll tell me. What's come over you?"

Again, Dylan jerked, shrinking back into his seat. "Don't be angry, Wolfram. It's the long nights. Hard to sleep by day, and I've got my other lessons and all. I've not been doing too well on that." He eyed Wolfram sidelong. "I saw your tiger."

"My tiger." Wolfram snorted, shaking his head. "Ask me about anything but that. Have you ever done something stupid and risky and thought it was all right because some woman would thank you for it?"

Dylan's pen case tumbled to the floor, and he scrambled to collect the spilled nibs and wooden tools. "For a woman? Sure, you know me." He cackled a little, then gave it up, muttering something under his breath.

Wolfram's head throbbed and he rubbed his temple. "What did you say?"

"What? Nothing. I have to get the latch fixed on this thing." He fiddled with it as he got to his feet. "I have to go, Wolfram, I'm sorry." Then he looked up. "I'm sorry."

"They've got me under house arrest; any visit's better than none at all."

Popping open the door, Dylan said, "I'll be back, tomorrow, or sometime. Sorry."

"Do that," Wolfram said into Dylan's wake. He stood a moment at the door, watching his friend's retreating back. Maybe Dylan, too, had heard something or been warned away from him. The two armed men in the hall watched him intently after perfunctory salutes. Sighing, he shut the door.

Wolfram hardly slept that night, after trying the bed and the floor in both rooms. His mother had spoken to everyone else by now—everyone but him—and had all the stories. What would they tell her? What was left for him to say? A long time ago he had been a golden child, son of a blessed king who had saved his country from the Usurper, but Wolfram had destroyed all that the legend meant. He had been glad to escape his father's shadow, only to find himself unprotected and alone. He would like to be able to blame Alyn's precocious curse, but it was he who had lived up to the prophecy.

He lay on the floor of his sitting room, staring at the window. From youthful adventures, he already knew it was too high to reach the ground without a rope. Might as well make a move, do something so bad that she'd cast him out on his ear and get herself a new heir or a few. Suddenly he realized that Fionvar must know. The Lord Protector had acted so strangely, especially when the queen's name came up; he must know the threat of marriage hung over them both. And just a week before, Wolfram had been so cocky in his royal attitude, playing with the airs that princes have and ordering the man around like a common servant. The man who was his father, though Wolfram could not bring himself to use the word.

A scent reached him, and Wolfram sat bolt upright, the demon springing to life in an instant. Wild, raw, hot and feline—the scent of the tiger drifted through his room.

Wildly, he spun around. It must be the skin; someone had brought it up. But no, he hadn't left his room all day, and no one could have snuck past him.

Then came the sound, a low huffing breath.

Wolfram froze, his skin cold, his heart beating madly.

Trembling, he willed himself to calm. There was no tiger. There was no tiger, for he had killed it with his own hands.

In the space his fear had filled, the rage quickly followed. In a few strides, he jerked open the door. "Where is he?"

The two guards sprang to alert, swords drawn. "Who, Your Highness?"

"Prince Alyn, or whoever he got to haul that tiger skin up here." Wolfram grinned with triumph. It was a wicked joke, but he'd figured it out.

The two men shared a look. "There's no one here, Your Highness."

"Not now, of course, but a few minutes ago."

Shaking his head slowly, the man replied, "There's been no one since the maid picked up your tray, Your Highness."

"Did he pay you to keep your tongues, or is it his glowing praise you're after?"

Bristling, the man said, "We don't take bribes, if that's what you're about." The look of disgust his partner gave made Wolfram want to strike the haughty expression from his face.

"All I want is to know who brought up the tiger skin and to make sure it doesn't happen again."

"It's in the trophy room for all I know, Your Highness. Nobody's been by."

The other relaxed, sliding home his sword. "You've had it rough, Your Highness. Get some rest and let us do the looking out, eh?"

Glaring, Wolfram said, "You'll have it rough when I find out what's going on." He went back in and slammed the door.

Inside, arms folded, Wolfram went over it in his mind, the unmistakable scent, the sound of the tiger's voice. Even had someone brought the tiger skin up to surprise him, that sound was another matter.

Crossing to the window, he pushed open the latch and leaned out. Barely wide enough for his shoulders, the window afforded a narrow view down into the city. His chambers were on the side opposite the temple, so he looked out to the plains beyond instead of the forest. Searching the wide street below and both sides gave him no insight. He even twisted about to look upward, to see if there was a way that someone had lowered the skin past his window. Nothing.

Pulling himself back in, Wolfram put his back to the wall. His side twinged, but not so much that it brought him down. Granted that he might have imagined the sound, would he conjure the scent as well? Scent was a tricky thing, as his days as a Hurim tracker had shown. Perhaps he'd put Dylan's mention of the tiger together with his lack of sleep and imagined the whole thing.

Wolfram settled back onto the rug, staring at the ash in his fireplace. He sat with his legs crossed and practiced breathing. In, out. In, out. After a moment, he tried to recall one of the poems Deishima had given him as a focus.

> *Coming together, the sun, the moon*
> *Coming together, Ayel, Jonsha*
> *Bringing their peace, the earth, the sky*
> *Bringing their glory, the darkness, the light.*

IN HIS mind, he chanted the lines over and over, and let his awareness seep into his body until the room was gone, taking with it the hardness of the floor, the chill of the air, the memory of the tiger.

Wolfram sat until the sun rose, and, for a time, he was at peace.

MOST OF the clothes in his closet no longer fit since his shoulders had filled out, so Wolfram settled on a loose-fitting silk shirt and his best hose. He toyed with the boar knife, unsure if it would be welcome in his mother's court, and slipped it on. Let her tell him to leave it behind; it had saved his life before. The bear claw necklace he set aside on his bed stand, then took that as well. *Na tu Lusawe shasinhe goron.* If the Gifts of the Spirits were revoked from him today, at least he would remember that he had known them.

As he sat over the last of his bread and cheese, someone knocked on the door. Rising, dusting off the crumbs, Wolfram went to the door.

On the other side stood Fionvar, the Lord Protector, in velvet and with a sword at his side. They regarded each other quietly.

"The queen sends for you, Your Highness," said Fionvar, stepping aside.

Flustered, Wolfram blurted, "She sent you?"

After they'd gone a few paces, Fionvar murmured, "I waylaid the messenger."

Wolfram grunted his acknowledgment.

"The second shift of guards reported all quiet, except that you asked them about the tiger."

"It was nothing. I must have been dreaming." Their strides matched in length and rhythm, and Wolfram hesitated a half step to break the match.

Fionvar flicked him a glance, then looked toward the audience chamber. "I put it away, Your Highness. I wanted to tell you." Again, he stepped aside and bowed, gesturing Wolfram into the room ahead.

Wolfram looked down at the man's dark head, silvering at the temples, bowed before him. "You put it away?"

From his sleeve, Fionvar produced a small key and dropped it into Wolfram's hand. "In a chest. That's the only key."

Staring at the key, Wolfram slowly closed his fingers.

"I'll burn it, if you wish," Fionvar said softly. "Your Highness."

A sound from the room caught his attention a moment, and the paralysis was over as Fionvar told him, "You'd best go in."

Tapestries of wool decorated the walls of the small room, punctuated by two doors. At least one more door stood concealed by the hanging to the queen's left, depicting a fanciful group of wild animals dancing. The queen's throne commanded the center of the back wall, flanked by two lower seats. Lady Catherine, with a tablet of parchment on her lap, occupied one of these and, with a low bow, Fionvar crossed to take the other. Duchess Elyn had her accustomed chair in the corner. A lower half-round chair was placed opposite the throne, and two guards stood at the ready beside it.

Wolfram's fingers felt warm, his shoulders tight as he made his own bow. His own smaller throne had been moved to one side, awaiting the queen's decision. The layout was for an inter-rogation or a sentencing; the chair given in case the defendant should collapse at hearing the verdict of the queen. She seemed set against him already, everything arranged for her foregone conclusion: that her own son was a criminal.

He held the little key in his grip, focusing his strength on that rather than unleash the demon. Then he glanced to the Lord Protector and to the queen.

Ignoring the chair, he walked slowly to the center of the room and stood before her. Despite the protest of his injury, he sank down to one knee and gripped his fingers together on top. Bowing his head, Wolfram said, "Queen Brianna, fair and merci-ful, I ask your pardon."

In a careful voice, she said, "Go on."

"Six months ago, I fled your anger, thinking to leave behind all that I had done. I have learned that these things cannot be undone so easily. I didn't want to come back here, knowing this, but I have reason to fear that Lochalyn is in danger."

"What danger?" Then, a little louder, she said, "Look at me, Prince Wolfram. What danger do you speak of?"

Raising his head, Wolfram felt an edge of fear. "There is no war in Hemijrai. They have no water there and too many people. These people you've been sheltering are no refugees. If anything, they are colonists."

"The war is over. That's why the Jeshan sent his delegation, to gather his people to go home. We are not in danger from these people." His mother leaned back in her throne, overcoming the surprise of his kneeling as a penitent. "And in any event, that's not why we're here. After ransacking my rooms and insulting myself and the Lord Protector, you fled the castle. Furthermore, the Usurper's daughter came before me to reveal that she would bear your child, which she has done—unless you can deny that you've been with her?"

Swallowing, Wolfram said, "I cannot deny it."

"So," she continued, "you ran away, leaving me your lover and your bastard to deal with. You fled to the forest. What then?" Before he could answer, she went on, "Ah, yes, you went to Bernholt, in the guise of a stonemason. There you met the Princess Melody and convinced her to join you in flight."

"No," he protested, kneading his temple. "She had a plan, a Hemijrani maid. I told her to stay home, not to get mixed up with me."

"And did she stay home?"

"No, but—"

"I've put up with quite enough from you already," she snapped. Regaining her composure, she took a sip of wine and continued, "Next, you fled to Hemijrai, rode some elephants, were welcomed by the High Priestess, and started breaking *their* laws."

Wolfram slipped his knee down and sat back on his heels, staring at her in disbelief. "I did not know their laws; I went to the women's quarter looking for Melody, to make sure she was all right."

"And assaulted a princess of their realm for the first time."

"I didn't assault her, I touched her hair! It was stupid, I know that."

The queen made a beckoning gesture, and Wolfram turned.

Faedre and a few other Hemijrani entered the room, with Deishima in their midst. She walked up to Faedre's side and gazed at the queen.

"Deishima," Wolfram breathed. "Jeshnam, I did not expect you."

From the opening in her veil, her eyes flicked to his and away, blinking quickly.

"If you knew it was stupid to touch her, Wolfram, why did you do it again? Why did you put a knife to her throat?"

"They wanted to stop me from leaving the ship." He stared at Deishima, willing her to look at him, to give him a sign.

"What did they tell you they wanted?"

At this, Wolfram frowned, looking back to his mother, and he remembered.

"Well?"

"They wanted to provide me with an escort to return home," he mumbled.

"They wanted to provide you an escort," the queen repeated, "to come home. Are you starting to understand why I am angry with you, Your Highness? They were taking you home, and you were so eager to get away that you took a knife to a defenseless girl."

Not exactly defenseless, Wolfram thought. "That's not how it happened."

"What have I missed?"

Rubbing his temple, Wolfram slowly got to his feet and turned to face her. "You said I would tell my story, you said you would listen to me."

"What have I missed, Wolfram? Tell me now." She stared him down from her throne. "I would like to believe it was different, but they have a dozen witnesses. One of them is Lyssa, who has no reason to be against you."

"How did the tiger get loose? Why did it come after us?" The fury swirled within.

"It was a tracker, Wolfram, like you are. It found the princess, and you killed it." She raised a hand to recognize the obvious objection. "It's understandable that you felt you had to defend yourself; how were you to know the beast was trained? Faedre has demonstrated with some of her other pets."

"Then it could have been trained to kill, did you not think of that? Jeshnam?" He sought her out, but the Hemijrani party stood close together.

"Perhaps we should be going, Your Majesty." Faedre ducked her head sadly when she glanced at Wolfram. "We do not wish to interfere in a family matter."

"You believe her"—Wolfram pointed at Faedre—"and not me. I'm your son, doesn't that mean anything?"

Queen Brianna clasped her hands in her lap. "When have you ever given me cause to trust you, Wolfram?"

"I'm trying to change; I tried to put it right by asking her to marry me! Bury it!" He whirled back to the veiled women. They were filing out the door and he lunged toward them. "No! Deishima, help me!"

The guards caught him firmly by both arms, pulling him away from the door as her slight figure, nearly hidden among the others, ran through.

Wolfram struggled to break free, the demon rage howling in his throat.

When they dragged him around to face her again, the queen was weeping. "Look at you, Wolfram. How can I trust you when you get like this? I don't know what happened to you, maybe it was my fault—"

"They're lying, can't you see that? Can't you see what's going on?"

"I am supposed to believe that everyone's lying except for you, Wolfram. Why? Because you are my son? I'm sorry, but that's not good enough."

His arms pinioned, the fury draining away, Wolfram hung his head. The little key dropped from his grasp to wink upon the floor.

Chapter 33

WATCHING THE proceedings from his chair by the throne, Fionvar found himself assailed by doubts. Now, seeing the queen's face change from grief to disdain, he could keep silent no longer. He recalled another throne room, where King Rhys held court in exile, and another Wolfram was brought before him, held captive. Rhys had not seen an enemy but a friend, abused and mistrusted, and he had not hesitated for an instant.

"Brianna." Fionvar was on his feet, placing himself before her.

She bristled at this interruption. "What is it?"

"If you cannot listen to him, then listen to me." His voice held a calm he did not feel as he spoke. "Wolfram has just come home; tracker or no, that tiger nearly killed him, and he has not even had a day of rest. Don't make a decision now, based on what's happening here. Give it a fortnight. The Hemijrani will have their meeting and go home. The prince will have fourteen days to prove he can control himself. It's been eighteen years; isn't it worth a few more days to be sure? Give him a chance, Brianna."

Even as he urged patience, he knew it was not for Wolfram alone that he argued, but for himself. If she exiled her only heir, she would need another, and soon.

The queen transferred her imperious gaze to him. "Why give him another opportunity to dishonor me, and the memory of his father?"

Her words, so coldly spoken, struck a dart of pain straight through him, pain that quickly turned to anger. Fionvar's hands balled into fists. "Clear the room," he said.

"I beg your pardon?"

"Clear the room, Brianna, or I will not be responsible for what I am about to say." He linked his fingers about his wrist, their sign for the secrets they held between them.

"I will be happy to speak with you at another time, my lord—"

Their eyes locked, and an anger he had not known he could contain swelled within him. "The time is now, Your Majesty."

"Very well, but I will be speaking to you about your behavior lately. Go on, Catherine." With a wave of her hand, she dismissed Duchess Elyn, who grumbled out the door with Lady Catherine.

The guards released their hold on Wolfram, but hesitated. "We're concerned for your safety, Majesty."

"I am the Lord Protector, and I will not let anything happen to her, understood?"

Unhappy, the two men bowed and left, shutting the door behind them. On his knees, Wolfram kept his head bowed, bringing his hands together before him. Trancelike, he reached out for the key and slipped it into his sleeve.

"Your Highness," Fionvar said. The blond head shot up, the still-unfamiliar face closed and wary. "Please, take a seat."

Carefully, Wolfram rose, with a slight bend to his right side and limped to the chair that had been left for him.

"Enough preliminaries, Fionvar, you've made me look like a fool."

"No, Brianna, you did that to yourself, shouting your questions, calling your witnesses, without even giving him a voice. What did you expect him to do? What would anyone have done in that position?"

"It doesn't take provocation, Fionvar; you saw him at lunch yesterday, threatening Prince Alyn, unless I'm very much mistaken."

"He has a temper, we've always known that—if I didn't know better, I would think you're trying to make him do something reckless to justify your own conscience."

"How dare you say that!" She rose and stared him down. "I've done the best that I can for him. Maybe if Rhys were here—"

Thrusting his finger at her, Fionvar said, "If I ever hear you saying he dishonors his father, ever again, I will march to the market square and tell the world who his father really is, do you understand me?"

She froze, her eyes wide, then snorted. "Oh, for pity's sake, Fionvar, you know what I mean. He's a prince, he has a legacy to live up to regardless of his parentage."

"Your King Rhys is a lie and a sham, and I am sick of it." Fionvar folded his arms, feeling as if a great weight had been lifted. He heard a little sound of dismay behind him, and turned to Wolfram. "You know some of the truth, Your Highness, and I know you didn't feel ready for more, but I've been waiting eighteen years, and I can't take another minute, if you'll excuse me."

Looking dazed, Wolfram nodded, settling back in his chair.

"I know we've had to keep up the charade in public, Brianna, of course we have, but lately you've been denying me to my own face."

"If this is a personal discussion, then let us retire someplace and chat, Fionvar. If not, get to the point." She folded her arms as well, sinking back on the throne.

"Every time Wolfram makes a mistake, you're there with this legend looming over you, waiting to pounce because he doesn't live up to it. Only two people in the world ever expected that from him; you're one of them, and Wolfram is the other. Stop trying to make him something he's not; you'll both be a lot better off."

She waited a moment, then arched an eyebrow. "Is that all?"

"Not quite, no. A long time ago, I was an advocate for Rhys when he was afraid to speak for himself." Fionvar stood between the prince and the queen, staring at the woman he loved. "I am asking you now, you brought him in here and set him up to explode; do you intend to listen to what the prince has to say?"

"I don't know what more you expect—"

"Do you," Fionvar repeated coldly, "intend to listen?"

Brianna unfolded her arms and toyed with the bracelet about her wrist, then glanced toward her son. "If he can talk in a civilized fashion, I will hear him."

STUNNED BY what was unfolding before him, it took Wolfram a moment to realize that his turn had come. He had never been struck dumb before; the demon had always been ready to roar. Now he needed the demon's silence, for this might be his only chance. Carefully, Wolfram rose, and Fionvar ceded the floor, going to sit in Elyn's place.

"If repentance is possible, Mother, then I have repented. I rushed headlong to accept my disasters and never thought to avoid them. My Lord Protector will have told you about my hair"—he waited for her nod—"and the proposal I made to Deishima. I am trying very hard to change. I can't promise that I will succeed."

"If you assaulted her, why should she agree to marry you?" Brianna asked.

"Lady be my witness the only time I acted violently toward

her was when I took her from the ship. If you spoke to Lyssa, then you know I also tried to set her free."

"She also told me that you thought the girl had been kidnapped."

"I did believe that, and I still do. Deishima would not have left without telling me."

"Then how do you account for her presence here, with the freedom of the castle? It doesn't make any sense, Wolfram."

"I can't explain it, not yet. If you give me time . . ." He gasped as the ache in his side cut into his breath. As he schooled his breathing, pushing away the pain, he thought of the veils, and Deishima's eyes. "Have you heard her speak? Is she truly at liberty?"

"She goes about with Faedre—"

"A woman not to be trusted," Fionvar muttered, earning a black look from the queen.

"But I have seen and heard her. She spoke in defense of the men condemned in Erik's death."

"What?" The words were a blow. He ran to escape his own crime; it had not occurred to him that that might make it someone else's.

"Erik was murdered the night you left, in the fight at the gates. A few refugees died as well, but we captured five. We were awaiting the results of Lyssa's embassy to Hemijrai before executing them."

"But they're innocent," he blurted.

Queen Brianna studied him gravely. "Tell me what you know, Wolfram."

Tugging free the ties at his throat, he pulled away the collar of his shirt to show the scar. "That night, someone tried to kill me. I heard someone call my name, and I turned. He dropped a chain around my neck."

Flinching, Brianna turned aside to look at Fionvar, who kept to the edge of his seat, listening and watching.

"It seemed halfhearted; if he'd been more serious, he would have succeeded."

Brianna frowned. "It was Erik who tried to kill you?"

"I thought so at the time; it was dark, confusing. I thought he was coming at me." He squinted remembering, crouching slightly as if anticipating the attack. He leaned back, turned, touched his throat, and recalled looking up to see Erik's shouting face. As if on command, the knife was in his hand.

The queen gasped, but Wolfram let out a rush of breath and straightened up, looking down at the knife, not the dagger he had used that night, but just as sharp. He might have sliced himself a piece of the silence that filled the room.

"You killed Erik," Fionvar murmured. "It was you."

Wolfram met his gaze. "Yes." He should have argued, repeated the threat against himself, but he looked at his father, and his throat constricted.

Shoulders sagging, Fionvar's head fell to his hands, and he let out a sound like a moan or a sob.

Swallowing, Wolfram felt a new pain growing into the hollow places. Quietly, he laid his knife at the queen's feet and gave himself to the guards outside.

THE ROOM remained silent a long while, then Brianna slowly walked toward Fionvar, still crumpled in his chair. She hesitated, then placed her hand on his shoulder.

"Sweet Lady, Brie, what happens now?" he murmured, shifting one of his hands up to cover the warmth of hers. It seemed an age since they had touched.

"Oh, Fionvar, my love, you have to let go."

Raising his head, he let his other hand drop to his lap. "I don't understand."

Setting aside her crown, Brianna knelt before him, her warm eyes roving over his face. She stroked his cheek, and he leaned into her touch. "You say that I demand too much, wanting him to live up to the legend of Rhys." She blinked, and he caught a teardrop on his fingertip. "Have you never thought your own expectations too high for him?"

"I want him to succeed, to find a way to live within himself, not have to lash out all the time, that's all I want," he whispered.

"What if it's too much? He will never be the son I want, Fion, I've let go of that in the time he's been gone. What if he cannot be the son you want either? Not only unworthy of the crown but unworthy even of his freedom?"

Before she'd even finished, he was shaking his head, catching her fingers in his grasp to take them away from his face. "No, Brianna, I cannot believe that."

"He killed his own servant, a man who had no harm in him at all, Fionvar."

Fiercely, he replied, "He was under attack; he didn't know whom to trust."

"He never does. He wounds indiscriminately; you, me, Lyssa— there is not a member of this household who has not been hurt by him. You are his father, you cling to this hope that he will someday, somehow be better than he is." She sighed, ducking her head. "I'm his mother, Fionvar. I used to share that hope."

"But no more?" he asked, stroking her hair.

Brianna moved closer, laying her cheek upon his knees. "I am also the queen, Fionvar. I cannot hold on to hope when it may lead to the ruin of this country. Even for my son, I can't do that. I had to let go." She lay silent a moment, her breath a moist heat upon his thigh, stirring him even now. "And so do you."

Fionvar leaned his head back against the wall and sat, cradling her head, stroking her hair, feeling all the heat and life of her. Shutting his eyes, he saw her twenty years younger, wandering into Gamel's Grove, following the sound of his fiddle and smiling at him. In the grove that brings the Heart's Desire, they had found each other. Last week, his son had walked there. His reckless, brash, and uncouth son had coaxed a lady from her room to walk with him in that same grove. For a moment, Fionvar could picture Wolfram kneeling before this foreign princess—hiding the pain it still caused him to move—and asking her to be his wife.

For a moment longer, Fionvar held his love, then he spoke. "No," he told her on a sigh, "I cannot let go."

A new moisture seeped to his skin, and her shoulders quivered.

"If there is a chance for him, even if it takes a miracle, Brianna, then I will not let go."

"He's a murderer, a liar, a scoundrel by every account, Fionvar, including his own." A pleading quality had crept into her voice, but Fionvar slowly shook his head.

"You may have"—his voice cracked, but he went on—"another husband, other children—other chances, Brianna, but he is my last, my only, do you understand that?"

She pulled away from him, her hair draping over her face. "Is this about Orie, about how you think you failed with him?"

"No," he said too quickly, then, "I don't know. I don't know if I can trust him or even like him sometimes, but if I am the only person who still has hope for him, then how can I take that away?"

Shaking back her hair, Brianna met his gaze, and her eyes flared. "And if he never changes, Fionvar? If he never grows up or learns to stop himself before he kills again, where will you be Fionvar? Where?"

Slowly, Fionvar rose. "Where I should have always been, Your Majesty, beside him." He slipped from his neck the chain of office and let it fall.

Chapter 34

FOR THREE days, Wolfram feared to leave his room. He sat expecting any moment the knock on his door, the chains to haul him to the dungeon. What more had passed between Fionvar and the queen he did not know. On the second day, there were no guards outside his door and by the third he started to think they would not arrest him; indeed, that none but the three who had been in that room knew that he had killed his servant. It did not absolve him, but it gave him a reprieve, a time to remember how to breathe without anger. Wolfram slept on the floor, missing his boar knife when the tiger's growl awoke him late at night. The darkest hours he spent with his back to the wall and his heart racing, the tiger's scent and sound surrounding him—and nothing was there. With a tiny file, he sharpened the bear claw he wore at his throat. He read a little, wrote a few verses, and spent a long time just sitting still, gathering himself.

On the fourth day, the knock came, and Wolfram bolted from his chair, spilling his ink in a black pool upon the stone.

"Enter!" he called.

The door popped open, and Melody stood on his threshold, dressed in an elaborate gown with two sets of false sleeves and a dizzying pattern of vines on the bodice. Her face fell at the sight of him, and she gathered her skirts and bustled in. "But Wolfram, you're not even dressed!"

Glancing down at his long tunic, loosely belted, Wolfram frowned. "I haven't been asked back to court, Melody, what else would I wear?"

"My party, silly! Didn't you hear?"

"Apparently not."

Melody flopped into a chair, as unprincesslike as ever despite the gown. "It's our Naming Day, Wolfram. I specifically told him to invite you."

Warily, Wolfram sat back down, nudging the ink bottle with his toe. "If it was Alyn you told, then I'm not surprised he forgot me."

"If I can learn how to get on with my brother, Wolfram, then so can you."

Picking at his ragged fingernails, Wolfram said, "He thinks I'm evil, Melody. It's hard to forgive someone for that, you know?"

"He's always spouting warnings of doom. Since we met again, he's been practically following me around—I had to shake him off to come see you. I've not even seen you since you got back!"

"You know where I've been."

"Hiding in your room, I believe." She reached out and touched his knee, drawing him to face her. "You've got fourteen

days, Wolfram, surely you can control yourself for fourteen days."
Melody gave him her secret smile.

"Ten." The touch sent veins of fire straight to his loins, and he
wasn't sure he could even control himself for the next few minutes, the desire to lose himself burned through his self-control.

Staring at him, Melody whispered, "Can I see your eye,
brother?"

The fire chilled in an instant. "I've only got the one," he answered, trying to sound cocky.

Pulling back her hand, she said, "You know what I mean."

He fingered the patch of leather, tracing the thick paint, then
eased the strap up and over his head, letting it dangle from his
hands in his lap. Slowly, he took a breath, and faced her.

Gasping, Melody drew back. Still, she studied the empty place.
Her hand rose as if of its own accord, the fingers bent to form
claws, imagining the strike of the tiger's paw. "What's it like?" she
murmured. "Does it hurt?"

"It aches, sometimes, or itches. Sometimes I think I'll take off
the patch and be able to see again."

"Even after that, you still managed to kill Rostam."

Wolfram paused in pulling on the patch. "Who?"

"The tiger," she explained. "I can't stay long, or I'll be missed
at my own party."

"Shouldn't you be doing this at home, with your own court?"

"Should be, but Faedre will be leaving after their gathering, and I want to see her off. Alyn didn't like that, let me tell
you." She rolled her eyes. Somewhere a bell tolled, and Melody
grabbed her skirts again, making for the door. "You are coming,
aren't you?"

Rising to see her out, he said, "I don't think it's a good idea
for me to be anyplace where Alyn is."

"So you're never going to leave your room again? That's not
what I expect from you, brother."

The pulse started at his temple, and Wolfram growled, "I'll
come—but I'll change first; will that be acceptable?"

"Wonderful!" She grinned and swirled off into the hall with
a whisper of satin.

Another turn in Melody's mercurial heart. She had apparently forgiven him his rejection that night. Perhaps he could ignore her charming self and simply be her friend again as he once had been, now that she had come home and put off the insanity of heathen religion. Poking through his wardrobe, Wolfram found a suitable tabard, forgoing the royal colors in favor of dusky blue velvet. He even discovered a forgotten pair of dancing slippers—not that he would dance, but it was her Name Day, so he could not refuse her politely. The last dance he had done had been at winter camp with his Hurim family, dancing around the fire to celebrate their hunt. At Melody's party, there would be no drums. Almost as an afterthought, he picked up the golden circlet that had been waiting in its chest these long months. Even before, he had rarely worn it. Now, setting it on his head, it sent a shiver down his spine. How much longer would he be allowed to wear the symbol of his position?

The image of Deishima in the garden with her hair down flitted through his mind, and he pushed it aside, trying to quell the ache that lodged in his throat. She had forsaken him, denying her acceptance, and Melody had returned, embracing him again. The princess was his cousin, to be sure, but beautiful and exciting, a woman nearly as unpredictable as himself. At the door, he paused and wondered why she had not yet taken suitors. He had heard nothing about it despite their close ties to Bernholt. The matter of his own betrothal had been brought up a few times in the past, always with a sort of tension he did not understand. Now, it made him think they might have delayed offering his hand lest they be stuck with him, or with his heir. Wolfram went into the hall, slamming the door behind him.

Wolfram followed a back staircase that would bring him out near the servants' quarters and their more private way into the Great Hall. This path would shield him from most of the guests and enable him to sneak in without Alyn's notice. The long hallway was lit by only a few torches and had no windows to the outside. As he walked, his footfalls echoed and his passing flickered the torch flames.

Behind him came a soft, leathery tread.

Wolfram glanced back, over his right shoulder, and cursed. The blind eye afforded no view, and he looked the other way.

A servant came from one of the doors, and disappeared through another.

The torches guttered with the wind of the closing door.

Standing in the hall, Wolfram rubbed at his temple with one fingertip. He started to turn back and heard the sound again—the pad of a soft yet heavy foot.

His heart beat a little faster as he peered into the gloom. Nothing was there.

Resolutely, he faced the Great Hall and went on.

The footsteps came a little faster.

Breathing shallow, Wolfram said aloud, "There is no tiger. It's just my mind—there's no bloody tiger."

A puff of hot, moist air touched his neck, setting his heart pounding.

Deliberately, he kept his pace slow. "There is no tiger," he repeated. "I killed it. There is no tiger."

Then, a low growl eddied around him.

Wolfram ran. The bear claw, his only weapon, bounced on his chest.

Bursting through the wide door, Wolfram tried to stop. The dance shoes slipped, sending him headlong across the polished floor, his circlet rolling madly to one side. Fetching up hard against a table leg, Wolfram lay still, panting. His scraped chin ached. The table leg bruised his shoulder, and he shut his eye.

Dimly, he heard the gathering crowd and pushed himself up. "I'm fine," he gasped. "Fine." Still, his head hung, and his hands trembled.

"You do know how to make an entrance, Wolfram," Alyn said, drawing laughter from his guests. "Let me help you up."

"Leave me be," Wolfram snapped back, looking up.

In finery to match his sister's, Alyn stood offering his hand. Slowly, still smiling, he withdrew it. "Have it your way. I know you haven't been out much lately, so I'm glad you could make it."

Wolfram grunted, getting his feet under him and rising unsteadily. "I'm not used to these shoes."

"I'm sure!" Alyn grinned. "Hopefully you can keep them under you long enough to do some dancing."

Clearing a way in the crowd, Melody appeared at his elbow and held out her hands. "Come on, you'll like this one."

Having broken off at Wolfram's unexpected appearance, the musicians started up a lively tune and, fortunately for Wolfram, an easy one to pick up. Melody danced him around the floor with a spirit that lifted him. By the third repeat, he'd nearly forgotten his fear, and the next dance found him smiling. He was not the best dancer by far, but it didn't seem to matter to Melody. In fact, when she was called away, another lady stood ready to take her place, and another after that. On the walls of the Great Hall hung banners showing the green leaves of Lochalyn and the three hills of Bernholt, the colors picked up again in swaths of fabric on the tables laden with food and drink. During a break, Wolfram fetched a mug of ale and found himself the object of numerous glances and whispered asides. By that time, his side had begun to ache, and he wandered over to a chair not far from Melody and Alyn, waiting to catch her attention.

"But Alyn," she was saying, "it's just for an hour or so, and it'll encourage them so much—they'll be ready to go home after that."

For the first time ever, Alyn looked awkward as he regarded his sister. "You're asking me to impersonate a foreign—no, a heathen deity, Melody, and I don't believe the Lady would be as forgiving as you think, even for an hour."

"Please, Alyn, it means so much to me."

"I think you've grown unnaturally attached to that woman, that's the trouble." He turned away to adjust the lacing on his doublet.

"She's only here for a few more days, then I'll never see her again, Alyn." Melody leaned closer, placing her hand on his shoulder. "Can't you see your way clear to help me out?"

Wolfram, enjoying the moment, suddenly put in, "Give him a chance to preach to the refugees, and he'd likely do anything."

Startled, Melody shot him a glance, but Alyn said eagerly, "I've already spoken to them, in their encampment. They are a heathen people, not as civilized as ourselves, of course, but I think the Lady might accept them as her servants."

"You find them uncivilized?" Wolfram asked.

"Well, of course. Look at how they treat their women. The women are segregated, and only the priestesses have any education. Their religion amounts to worship of the sun and moon, and any transgression results in severe punishments. I've even heard that they make sacrifices on these holy days."

"They won't on this one," Melody cut in, but the two men ignored her.

"I guess you would have to be convinced of Finistrel's reign in order to talk the way you do, Alyn, but you haven't looked deep enough. They do worship the moon as their goddess, yes, but she also resides in the earth—not so different from the story of the Second Walking, when Finistrel took the starstuff from the dirt and made all of us."

"I wouldn't go that far," Alyn said slowly. "And there is still that sun-god."

"A god and a goddess creating together?" Wolfram grinned. "Doesn't sound too far-fetched to me."

Alyn turned scarlet and took a quick drink of his wine as Melody giggled. She nudged Wolfram and gave him a wink. Taking a sip of the ale, Wolfram marveled over the brief conversation. Talk to him about religion, and Alyn suddenly paid attention, acting as if he wanted to know what Wolfram thought. After the constant bickering of their childhood, it had never occurred to him before to talk to Alyn about what he held most dear. In return, Alyn eyed him warily, holding his tongue, even though Wolfram had delivered the parting shot.

"It's a wonderful party, Melody. I'm glad I came."

"So am I," she returned, her face lighting up with her smile.

Alyn went back to fiddling with his laces, then jumped up. "Must be time for another dance, Mel, won't you join me?"

Still gazing at Wolfram, she accepted the offered hand and rejoined her guests.

Warmed by that smile, Wolfram sat sipping his ale. Deishima's betrayal seemed a long time ago, despite the tenderness that lingered when he thought of her. Lyssa might have been right all along, and he couldn't really blame Deishima for not wanting to marry him, of all people. He had been a fool to ever hope otherwise. The dance was slow and stately, with plenty of bowing and posturing. Melody and Alyn, well tutored by their dancing-mad mother, made an elegant couple. At each parting, Melody struck careful poses, adding a few graceful gestures as she did.

Setting down his mug, Wolfram leaned forward, elbows on knees, staring intently. Another break, another gesture, and Wolfram's head began to pound. The more they danced, the more Alyn seemed pleased by whatever Melody was saying to him when they came together again. Ashwadi—Melody had not forsaken the foreign ways she'd become so enchanted with in Hemijrai, oh, no.

Wolfram leapt up and threaded his way among the dancers. When Alyn turned out at one point, Wolfram stepped in, bowing at the appropriate moment to Melody's astonished face.

"You can't do that, Wolfram!" Alyn protested, hovering nearby.

Taking Melody's hand, Wolfram said, "It's done." He had not meant to snap, but Alyn flinched a little at the words.

Still, he smiled to his guests and left the floor, ceding his partner.

"What are you trying to do?" Wolfram murmured.

Recovering, Melody said, "I'm trying to dance, Wolfram. How about you?"

They split to stand across from one another while each performed the series of little steps and postures. Melody's hands fluttered and Wolfram laughed. Catching her hands, he said, "Didn't they teach you yet? It takes two eyes."

Her cheeks slightly rosy, Melody said, "I don't know what you mean."

"Oh yes, you do." They were the head couple of the line, and Wolfram suddenly broke away, taking her with him to a place by the wall. "I can't stand Alyn, you know that, but I also won't stand for him being manipulated that way."

"What way?"

Wolfram pulled her closer. "Stop playing innocent with me,

Melody. You've learned Ashwadi, and you're trying to get Alyn to go along with something."

"So what if it's true? What's that to do with you?"

"Tell me what you want," Wolfram said, "and I'll leave you alone." He stared down into her face.

For a moment, she froze, uncertain, testing the strength of his grasp. With a smile, Melody pressed a little closer. Her breath warmed his chest, and she replied, "What do you think I want, Wolfie?"

The stirring of his blood turned to ice, and he pushed her away to hold her at arm's length. "Don't taunt me like that; you don't care about me."

"How do you know what I care about, Wolfram?" she returned, the color in her cheeks heightening her beauty. "You just play with your women, you court some foreign hussy, then you think I'll forgive you and welcome you home. Did you really think I wanted to be your sister?" Her lips twisted, and her eyes gleamed. "Surprise, Wolfie," she said with a bitter edge.

Stunned, Wolfram released her and let the wall support him. He had thought her flirtation in Hemijrai no more than the false intimacy of close companions, certainly not an infatuation she carried with her—for how long? She brought her arms close, biting her lip as she watched him.

"Of course Alyn doesn't want you here—he had a vision, he saw me swoon in your embrace, Wolfie, but you won't embrace me, will you?"

Wiping sweat from beneath the eye patch, Wolfram protested, "You're the one who called me brother."

Crossing her arms, Melody spat, "Oh, you're such an idiot!"

"I didn't know, Melody, how could I know?" His head swam with mixed emotions.

Shrugging one shoulder, she scrubbed away a tear. "It doesn't matter now, does it? You've shown me what you really think about me. I should have known better after the last time."

Wolfram put a hand on her bare shoulder, but she shook him off. "I'm sorry," he said. "I didn't know I was hurting you. I didn't think—"

Melody spun so quickly Wolfram found his back against the wall. "That's right. You ask that little hussy to marry you, and now you claim you're sorry?" The grin she gave had none of her earlier charm. "Watch your back, Wolfram, when my power comes."

Chilled, he said, "But you won't be queen for years."

Melody laughed. "And chances are good you won't ever be king, little Wolf. But that's not the only way to take command—and there are powers much higher than a crown."

"What has Faedre promised you? What does she have in mind, Melody?"

"Oh, this and that."

"I'll stop it, whatever it is—they'll never carry it off."

"Go on and try, Wolfie. I'll tell your mother that you hit me. I'll tell her you raped me—remember that day in the stables in Bernholt? I'll tell her every wicked thing I can think of."

"I never laid a hand on you, Melody," he whispered.

"No one will accept your word, Wolfram," she said, stepping away. "No one will believe a thing you say."

Wolfram turned his face to the wall, clinging with his fingertips while the demon roared. He must not turn; if he so much as called her name, he was a dead man. She could take him down with a word, and he had no defense against her. Melody's laughter rang in his ears as she started another dance.

Fleeing the party, his head pounding, Wolfram ran down the hall. His slippers skidded a bit, but the stone here had been left rough, and he managed to keep his footing. He reached a pair of peaked doors and flung them open, emerging onto a balcony that overlooked the small courtyard by the temple. Here, he sank to the stone, resting his head on the balustrade, his chest heaving. After a while, he leaned back and cupped his hands together. Carefully, he took a breath and let it out slow, willing himself to relax. Just as he thought he was banishing his headache and the demon along with it, he saw a party enter the courtyard below. Walking slowly and talking, Faedre and a Hemijrani priest led the way, followed by a little group of their companions. At the end came the slight figure that must be Deishima.

Inside, the fury was unleashed and Wolfram sprang to his feet. The foreign hussy, as Melody had called her, had turned him down. Was there not a soul under the stars who wouldn't lie to him? Now she walked freely about his castle, where he had to watch his every move. They would be heading for the guest quarters, and he knew a back way. Dashing through the doors, Wolfram paused a moment to snatch off his slippers and toss them away.

Barefoot and fleet, he made for the back stairs.

He moved quietly, dodging startled servants, like a wolf who'd found the scent he was after. The side twinged, but he ignored it, pushing himself to get there first.

With one hand, he caught the last corner and swung around it, catching sight of Faedre passing at the opposite end.

Creeping now, Wolfram moved up the dim hall, pressing himself against the wall and waiting. The group seemed to dawdle, but at last, they passed by, with Deishima still at the end.

He pounced, snatching her from behind and spinning her against the wall. "You heathen bitch, couldn't you even tell me no?"

The hidden figure let out a tiny whimper, dark eyes gleaming, the whites showing.

Grabbing the veil, he flung it back and froze.

Chapter 35

BENEATH THE veil, a scarlet band of silk wrapped Deishima's mouth, cutting into the corners, catching the tears that now spilled from her eyes.

His own mouth fell open even as his anger fell away. Aghast, he couldn't think, couldn't even breathe for a moment as he searched her face.

Her eyes darted toward the hall and back, her eyebrows pinched together.

"Sweet Lady," he gasped at last, then quickly flipped the veil in place again. The lines between her eyes smoothed as she tried to blink away the tears.

Brushing his lips to her concealed ear, Wolfram whispered, "Your hands are bound, too?"

He felt a single nod against his cheek.

"I'm sorry, I'm so sorry." Cupping her face in his hands, Wolfram kissed her through the layers of fabric, feeling the heat of her beneath the silk. "I love you," he murmured, starting a fresh stream of tears.

Pulling away, Wolfram crossed his arms. "Don't I deserve an answer?" he shouted, even as three dark men hurried up, with Faedre close behind them.

He lunged forward as if he would rip off her veil, but the lead man grabbed her and dragged her backward.

"You've been rescued this time," Wolfram yelled, "but you just wait. I'll be coming for you!" Holding her frightened gaze, he started after her.

Faedre stepped before him. "This is hardly the way to speak to a holy person, Prince Wolfram."

As Deishima disappeared around the corner, Wolfram turned his eye to Faedre. "She claimed to be defiled, she claimed you'd never have her back—she's a worse liar than I am."

With a pretty frown, Faedre explained, "Of course this was not so, Highness. She had forgotten the ritual cleansing which we can perform. Naturally, she must undergo penance."

"I'll give her penance!" He stepped forward again, but Faedre did not move, so that he brushed against her breasts. The medallion of the Two grazed his chest. Distracted, he met her gaze.

"Ah, Your Highness, I can, of course, understand your frustration. Part of her penance has been to sever her earthly ties. Since there is no women's quarter here, she must not speak to men, nor, indeed to anyone outside of our rooms." Faedre's voice became a purr as he did not move away.

Turning his scowl into a sly grin, Wolfram lifted a hand to toy with a strand of her hair. "How can you understand my frustration?" he asked, forcing back his anger.

"It was not even allowed for her to say farewell, or to tell you why she must go. Naturally she regrets this, although she is pleased to be able to serve again." She smelled of cinnamon and musk and let her fingers brush against his thigh.

"That's all she's fit for—I tried to do her a favor," he grumbled.

"And a very great favor indeed," Faedre murmured. "One wasted on the mere seventeenth daughter of a distant tyrant, Your Highness."

At last, Wolfram turned away. "Tell her I hope she dies as a shriveled old virgin," he tossed over his shoulder.

After a throaty chuckle, Faedre called to him, "I am sorry about your eye, Prince Wolfram. I wish that my pet had been more gentle with you—and you with him."

Wolfram cast back a glance to see her teasing smile. "Maybe someday I'll show you how gentle I can be," he replied, keeping the chill from his voice.

She turned toward her room but looked back coyly over one shoulder. "I hope you do, Highness." Swaying her hips so that the tassels on her veil twitched, she moved off down the hall.

Almost her flirting could distract him, but Wolfram shook off the trance and hurried away. On the ground floor now, he found his way to the smaller courtyard he had overlooked earlier and wrapped his arms around a carved-stone pillar. Pressing his cheek to the cool, rough surface, Wolfram let the jitters overwhelm him. He could not have spoken even one word more without screaming. His side ached, and his empty eye twitched as the rush slowly began to fade.

Shutting his eye, he calmed himself, then grinned with a terrible glee. He was right! Deishima, bound and gagged, hadn't left him of her own will—she had been carried off, abused and threatened, and the Lady knew what else. Kidnapped. Horror and anger quickly drove out his surge of satisfaction.

Faedre and the rest held her prisoner, parading her around to prove what a fool he was, to try to convince even him that he was wrong. Deishima must be terrified—had she even under-stood what he tried to tell her, or had his own fury only scared her more?

Suddenly, he wished he had fled without speaking once he knew the truth. Then again, he couldn't leave her there as she had left him, without hope. No, she would remember his words tonight, in whatever dark hole they kept her. She would know that he would come for her.

Madly, Wolfram laughed. For a long time, he couldn't stop, the false mirth bubbling over. Imagine someone being comforted by the thought of him. Imagine himself being the savior—it was almost more than he could bear. He was reckless at best, evil at worst: a murderer, a liar, and a bastard. Reformed, maybe, but would she know? Besides that, to free her would take the kind of stupid secretive stunts that had gotten him in so much trouble to begin with. If he succeeded, his mother would disown him. If he rescued Deishima, he wouldn't have even his position to offer her.

The manic laughter died away, leaving him drained and slumped against the pillar as he turned it in his mind. They would not believe him, Melody was right about that. And she was still tight with Faedre. If he told what he knew, even if he had Deishima to back him, Melody would make good on her threat. Along with his true crimes, the rumor of rape would be enough to hang him, prince or no.

Letting go of the pillar, Wolfram began to walk off the ner-vous energy that had possessed him. To free her meant exile, to tell anyone meant death, and to pretend he had not seen . . . ? What might it cost him to let her go, to pretend he didn't know the truth? If he were no longer a prince, she would blame herself. She would refuse to marry him all over again. He could keep his own counsel, stay quiet and out of the way. In a few weeks, they would have this celebration they were planning and go home. She would return to whatever her life had been, undergoing this forced penance and forget about him, given time.

He stalked the hallways and stairs, making first one choice then another, trying them on to see what fit. After a while, he found himself staring at his dull reflection in a highly polished rosewood table. The whorls of the wood brought to mind Deishima's eyes, dark and gleaming. If all they wanted was to get her away from him, to bring her home, if that was all, why was she terrified?

Suddenly something that Alyn had said echoed up from his memory, "*I've even heard that they make sacrifices on these holy days.*" Monkeys, Wolfram had thought at the time, but what if the day were especially sacred, a ritual that required years of preparation—even to the point of raising someone so pure she was not allowed to tread the ground outside of her own garden? It could no longer happen, she'd told him, now that she was defiled. "*I am not meant for marriage to anyone.*"

Wolfram reeled, his skin gone cold, and braced his hands on the tabletop. He had little evidence, but he knew with a terrible certainty. Whatever the Hemijrani planned, Deishima would die.

She had known all along. She had been raised for this and accepted it as her sacred place—until the unthinkable happened. Taken hostage, carried off into the woods, defiled by the touch, by the mere presence of a man. But Wolfram had turned her world around again by asking for her hand.

"Can I help you?" a voice behind him asked.

Rubbing his arms to get some life back into them, Wolfram turned.

The door across the hall stood open, and Fionvar stood there with an armload of books. "Oh. I didn't—I'm sorry, Your Highness." He briefly bowed his head.

Wolfram touched the table behind him. He should have recognized it right off, and probably would have, if his mind had not been elsewhere. Somehow his wanderings had brought him to the door of the Lord Protector's study.

Shifting the books a little, Fionvar asked, "Were you looking for me?"

Numbly, Wolfram shook his head.

Fionvar nodded a little. "Well, you've found me anyhow, Your Highness. Is there something I can do for you?"

"I need," Wolfram rasped, brought into his body again, "I need to sit down."

Hesitating a moment longer, Fionvar nodded again. "Come in." He led the way and dropped the books in a heap on his desk. "Can I pour you some wine?"

"Thank you." Wolfram sat gingerly on the sweeping curved bench facing the desk and the tall stained-glass windows. The room had seven sides, and a peaked roof with highly carved beams. The little table in the hall, carved in the same style, had been moved out to make room for Fionvar's desk.

Holding out the goblet, Fionvar said, "It took a special court and consensus among the barons for me to get permission to use this room after King Rhys left it." He swung one leg up to perch on the edge of the desk and sighed, studying the ceiling, his hands clasped in his lap.

Something in his tone drew Wolfram's attention from the welcome drink. Fionvar no longer wore the chain of his office. The familiar tabard with the royal arms had been replaced by a simple black tunic. Looking back to Fionvar's face, Wolfram thought he looked older than he had that day, the first day Wolfram had ever seen him angry. "Where's your chain, my lord?"

"I've resigned my office, Your Highness. I'm sorry, I thought someone would have told you."

Wolfram laughed weakly. "Who would even talk to me these days?"

Shoulders slumping, Fionvar shut his eyes. "Again, I am sorry."

Wolfram let himself lean back into the cushions. Now that he had come to sit down, he discovered every ache in his bruised body, plus the stinging scrape on his chin.

Abruptly, Fionvar rose and rounded his desk to pull a few more books off the shelf and add them to the pile. Then he took down something else and held it, his back to Wolfram. "I don't know how to talk to you anymore," he murmured.

"What?"

Fionvar turned and placed what he held on the leather surface of the desk. About a foot tall, carved of rough marble, stood the figure of a woman, the folds of her cloak just beginning to be roughed out. Fionvar touched it gently with one finger, tracing the shoulders, tapping the stump of a neck where the head had broken off. "You were twelve—"

"I remember," said Wolfram hoarsely. The chisel slipped, the marble cracked, and the figure he had been working on was ruined. Throwing down his tools, the young prince had fled, requiring days of coaxing from Lyssa before he would try again. "Why did you resign?"

"She wanted me to make a decision I could not accept, not yet." Fionvar stared at him with dark and tired eyes.

"You chose—" But Wolfram could not complete the thought aloud, not after all the years of anger that lay between them. He clutched the goblet with both hands.

As he settled into his leather chair, Fionvar's frown returned. "Are you well, Your Highness?"

Shaking his head, Wolfram drained the goblet and held it out for more. "I thought the day I left was the worst day of my life," he said. "Maybe I was wrong. Back then, I had the option of running away."

"Don't you still?" Fionvar asked lightly, raising an eyebrow.

Meeting his gaze, Wolfram answered, "Not if I am ever to be worthy of the crown."

"That reminds me." Reaching into a bottom drawer, Fionvar revealed Wolfram's coronet. He held it out across the desk. "One of the ladies brought this by. They found it in the Great Hall after you left the party."

Tentatively, Wolfram took it but did not replace it on his head.

"She told me how you lost it, Your Highness," Fionvar said gently. "What happened?"

Wolfram gave a little laugh. "It doesn't matter."

"What you told us in the audience chamber," Fionvar began, knotting his fingers together and untangling them again. "It was a terrible thing."

Nodding, Wolfram waited.

"But you need not have told us. No one but you knew the

truth before that moment. If you had kept silent, who would have been the wiser?"

"Five men would have died."

"Strangers," Fionvar supplied. "Hemijrani."

Feeling the prickle of demon claws, Wolfram said, "Innocent men."

Suddenly Fionvar smiled, and Wolfram almost thought there were tears in his eyes. "Yes," he agreed. "That took courage," he said softly, "and compassion. And something else." The smile grew a little more broad. "Honor. Every man does things that he regrets, but few are willing to own their deeds unless they are compelled to."

Again, Wolfram gave his offhand shrug.

The smile slipped away, and Fionvar asked, "Do you want to tell me what happened?"

Wolfram laughed, shaking his head. "Yes, more than anything." He laughed again because he suddenly realized that it was true.

Raising his eyebrows, Fionvar waited.

Wolfram took a deep breath and sighed. "I can't." He slipped up the patch and rubbed at the scarred skin. "Oh, Sweet Lady, how I wish I could."

"Try me." Fionvar folded his hands, leaning over the desktop. "Tell me one thing I couldn't possibly believe."

"One thing," Wolfram repeated faintly. He searched the revelations of the last few hours and started shaking his head. Any one of them would only make things worse.

Wetting his lips, Fionvar said, "Please."

Well, there was one thing that would damage only Wolfram's reputation and he could see no point in defending that. "I fell into the party because I was convinced the tiger was chasing me. I could hear it, I could smell it, I could feel its breath on my neck. I was scared out of my mind when I took that fall." He clutched his elbows with his hands, the remembered fear shivering through him.

Silence hung for a moment, then he heard Fionvar rise and walk briskly around the desk. "That key I gave you, do you still have it?"

After a moment more, Wolfram raised his head and shook his wrist where the key slipped out and dangled on the tie of his cuff.

Fionvar grinned, a fierce and angry sort of grin that Wolfram had never seen before, and yet one that felt familiar—like his own.

Stooping to the bottom shelf of his bookcase, Fionvar brought out a cask he stuck under his arm, picking up his goblet with his other hand. "Then follow me," he told Wolfram. "And bring your cup."

Chapter 36

WITH WOLFRAM wondering at his heels, Fionvar led the way to the trophy room, a long hall filled with mounts of exotic animals along with swords and helmets taken from their various enemies, including both King Rhys's sword that had belonged to his father, and the sword the Usurper had carried, a near replica of the other. The windows down one side showed a magnificent sunset, bands of red and gold behind the mountains lighting the room with eerie crimson highlights. Red—the color of death. Wolfram shook himself and padded after Fionvar to the far end. Here stood a few old chests that held various bits deemed too valuable for open viewing. Fionvar stopped and turned to Wolfram, holding out his hand.

Hesitating, Wolfram stared at one of the chests, where he caught a whiff of the tiger pelt. After being cleaned and cured two weeks ago, it still smelled rank to him.

He noticed Fionvar watching then and untied the key to hand it over.

"You really do smell it, don't you," Fionvar mused, bending to the chest.

"Can't you?"

He shrugged. "A little, but it's not strong. I have to really pay attention."

"In the mountains, you have to smell your prey before it smells you."

"You must be an excellent tracker." The lock clicked, and he lifted the lid.

Wolfram laughed. "Not by their standards."

"Here." Fionvar handed over the cask he had carried, and pulled the heap of fur into his arms. With his goblet in hand, he set out again. "In the princess's room, you said you smelled monkeys."

"I said that, yes."

"It's not like you to mince words." Sticking the stem of his goblet under his belt, Fionvar took a torch from a wall mount and brought them to a door by the temple. Inside, they could hear the singing of evening prayer. The small door took them into a narrow, triangular courtyard with a well, and to another door opposite. This one required Fionvar to put down the tiger and work a series of locks.

"I did smell monkeys," Wolfram replied at last, "but you didn't believe me."

In the darkness, Fionvar faced him, holding up the torch. "I didn't know any better." He frowned down at Wolfram's feet. "You have no shoes."

"I've gotten used to the dirt."

Making no comment, Fionvar led the way out, shutting the door behind them.

On a small flat plain uphill from the temple, overlooking the refugee encampment, he flung the tiger skin on the ground. In the camp, fires leapt high, and Hemijrani voices sang out with drink and joy. Their strange stringed instruments whined into the growing night, and Wolfram wondered what their dances might look like. Men and women would not dance together—perhaps women did not dance at all, as in the Hurim culture. On the edge of the camp, they were busily erecting more tents. The spices of their roasts tantalized him from a distance. Putting them from his mind, he turned to Fionvar.

Fionvar planted the torch in the earth. "Cask?"

Wolfram handed it over.

"Are you sure you don't want this thing as a rug or an archery target or anything?"

"Quite."

Fionvar's teeth gleamed briefly. He struggled to pull the cork from the cask and doused the skin with a long splash of dark liquid. Placing the cask on the ground, he took up the torch, and offered it to Wolfram.

Glancing at the skin, then at Fionvar, Wolfram accepted. He leaned over and touched the flames to the fiery stripes. After a moment, they singed and caught, crackling and hissing and giving off an even more foul odor. Wolfram coughed sharply, wincing at the pain in his side.

Fionvar stuck the torch back in the ground and motioned for Wolfram to come to that side of the fire, upwind. He poured them each a draught from the cask and held up his goblet. "I've been saving this for a special occasion. Goddess walk with you."

"And with you," Wolfram replied, and both tossed back their drinks. The stuff was thick and sweet and warm. Wolfram grinned. "What's the occasion?"

Swirling the goblet, Fionvar considered, then said, "We are both overcoming our fears, in spite of the cost."

Silent, Wolfram considered his own goblet. "Tell me the story, my lord. Maybe it'll help me get through this night."

"It's been a long time coming. Best make yourself comfortable."

Carefully, Wolfram settled on the ground, his bare feet before him. One night in the garden, Deishima had spread her hair to keep his feet warm. He pressed his hand to his mouth, feeling a sudden burn in his eye. He shuddered with the effort of quelling his emotions.

Sitting close by, Fionvar asked, "What's wrong?" a note of urgency in his voice.

Shaking his head, Wolfram took a long time to reply. He could not speak of Deishima, not now. "Do you love my mother?" he asked.

Watching him with some concern, Fionvar answered, "I do. I always have. It may surprise you that—contrary to anything you may have been called—you're no bastard." He smiled a little, and Wolfram found himself returning it.

Wolfram took a swallow of the liquor to steady himself. "Go on."

"I hardly know where to start," he said. "First of all, I should say that I'm no lord, and never have been. I'm peasant stock, farmers, to be precise. Our father died early, and, as the oldest, I was left with the family. During the usurpation of Lochalyn, my brother Orie fought in the battle to win Duchess Elyn's keep. She and the last of her family escaped, with his help. Orie scaled the wall to let the gate down and let them out at the same time. When the Earl of Gamel's Grove fell in battle, Orie was given his holdings in return for his act of bravery." Fionvar shook his head and drained his goblet, pouring another for both of them. "He made it possible for Lyssa to become a sculptor, and set the rest of us up in one business or another. I got to be his steward—I think he enjoyed ordering me around for a change." He rolled the goblet between his fingers.

"Orie eventually married Melisande?"

"Don't get ahead of me," he chided with a smile. "You've been to the manor where Elyn and Brianna hid for those twelve years."

Wolfram nodded. "A long time ago."

"I used to serve as our liaison. Brianna was away at an academy for most of the time, but she came one day to deliver a message. I was playing violin in the grove, waiting for the messenger." Smiling ruefully, he watched Wolfram's reactions.

"I remember now: you played at my bedside when I was down with the fever."

"I was afraid to leave you." Fionvar looked toward the smoldering skin. "Anyhow, we knew that we'd never be allowed to marry—she was betrothed to this absent king we were supposed to find or invent if need be. I was a farmer, elevated only by my brother's service. At that time, she wanted to defy her grandmother and married me anyway, in secret." He laughed. "Brianna was bold enough to marry me, but not to tell the world. By the time we found King Rhys, she was already with child." He ran his eyes over Wolfram's face. "Just as her grandmother wished, by the way."

"How about Rhys?" Wolfram asked quietly. "Where was he?"

Taking a deep breath, Fionvar plunged on, "The rumors of castration were true. The Usurper cared too much for Rhys, so he killed his elder brothers but sent Rhys to a monastery. Later on, he got worried and burned the monastery to the ground. I was the one who found the records and connected this young court singer, Kattanan DuRhys, with the missing prince. I wanted to be sure—Orie was furious when he found out what I'd suspected. By that time, Kattanan was in Princess Melisande's household as a courtship gift from a rival suitor." He seemed about to say more, but took a swig of drink instead. "Kattanan had the misfortune to fall in love with her. Orie realized it about the same time that Kattanan did, I think. Jordan—the Liren-sha—had joined our side, and got Kattanan away before Orie could do something stupid."

Grief passed over Fionvar's face as he spoke of his brother, and Wolfram wondered if he knew it and what he was holding back.

"Much of the legend is true. Rhys learned courtly manners from the duchess and her loyal barons. You know the story of your namesake—most of it, anyway. When he was brought before King Rhys, we didn't think he'd live. The moment that Rhys claimed him for a friend, that was the first time he dared defy his grandmother and take any of his due as king. That was when I became his man. I had been a little reluctant to swear fealty to someone who would steal my beloved."

"Understandable." The liquor was starting to take effect, making Wolfram feel light-headed and agreeable.

"Rhys figured out quickly enough whose child Brianna was carrying. She actually tried to put him off by acting the fool, but he saw through that as well. The whole time he swore up and down that he wouldn't marry her. After that legendary battle— the one where he raised the dead and flew over the heads of the enemy and subdued the Usurper single-handed, all true, by the way—I went to Bernholt to keep track of my brother. Orie had married Melisande in a rush, then came to be sure our battle was going as planned. He wanted a child of mine on the throne, someone who shared his blood—he was the Wizard of Nine Stars' apprentice, and I think he had some plan for you." Fionvar broke off and prowled the darkness for a moment, finding a long stick to prod the fire back into flame.

Waiting quietly, Wolfram started to pick through what he had been told and the way Fionvar seized up every time he came near to his brother's story. He felt strangely distant from the tale, as if he were not the child in question, heir to a throne, but merely an interested onlooker, learning more about Fionvar than he might have cared to reveal.

"I was there when Orie became a full wizard. He broke his bond with Alswytha after she'd healed Jordan. The other Wolfram had given chase, along with his guard Rolf. Rolf actually had Orie by the throat at one point." Fionvar stared into the distance. "If I had it to do over," he murmured, then looked down.

"You let Orie go."

"Remember what I said earlier about things that we regret?"

Wolfram frowned. "He was your brother."

"I raised him from the time he was nine; in a way, he was also my son."

"Even so, you're not responsible for the things he did, any more than you are responsible for me."

They stared at each other for a long time.

"That doesn't stop me from being plagued by doubts, does it? One day, you'll see what I mean." Fionvar prodded the fire again.

Studying him, Wolfram allowed himself a little smile. All his life, he had seen this firm, quiet man, his mother's Lord Protector; it had never occurred to him that Fionvar could have doubts. He pointed out, "You haven't finished yet."

"Ah, yes." His voice seemed subdued as he continued. "I had followed Orie to ask him what he was up to. Prince Wolfram arrived, defending his sister's honor. Orie used me. He paralyzed me with magic and used my blood to start healing himself, giving himself strength." Slowly, avoiding Wolfram's curious gaze, he rolled up his sleeve. A slender line marked the back of his forearm, a bare stretch where the dark hairs didn't grow. "It was a magic wound." He traced the line with a fingertip and gave a grim smile. "Nothing to match any of yours," he said.

Wolfram looked up. "None of mine went quite so deep."

Nodding slightly, Fionvar rolled the sleeve back down. "He died to save me; that's the unforgivable part. Why would he do that? We barely knew each other, but he looked at me, dropped his sword, and let my brother suck the life out of him." Tears streaked his face, and he crushed them away with one hand. "I'm getting drunk," he said. "I don't do this very often."

Laughing, Wolfram said, "I know all the best places."

"They all came to Bernholt to force King Gerrod to honor his son and eventually succeeded. Melisande and Rhys were reconciled, Jordan and Alswytha fell in love, Lyssa decided to let go of Jordan for herself, and I—I had to bury my brother."

Wolfram choked on a swallow of liquor and took a little while to stop sputtering. "You buried him?"

"I couldn't bring myself to cremate him; I didn't know what to do, really. I took him to the grove . . ." He stared into the dying glow of the tiger skin.

"Melody wondered about that, when we passed by Gamel's Grove."

"I should tell her, too; she deserves to know the truth. King Rhys came back here and made sure Brianna was still in love with me. He gave her back to me. Before the wedding, he took me aside—in that study where you found me—and asked me to trust him. It worried me, but I did. He named me as his Lord Protector, to guard queen and castle in his stead. The rest I didn't find out until much later. Lyssa created a diversion while Alswytha traded places with him, making him look like her and vice versa. It was the wizard who walked up the steps and proclaimed Brianna as the queen. The wizard stepped into the sky—to the stars, as most people believe. Rhys took his bodyguard and rode quietly away. He spent some time recuperating at Gamel's Grove, then went to be with his princess. As I was left with my queen."

They sat in the feeble glow of the guttering torch, neither one speaking, and Wolfram drained the last of his goblet.

"That is some story," he said at last.

"It is," Fionvar agreed. "I wish it had not taken me this long to tell you."

"The worst part was feeling that everyone was lying to me, that even my own hair was a lie."

"Great Lady, Wolfram, I hope—" Fionvar started fervently, then broke off.

"If you can't use my given name, who can? After all, you gave it to me."

"Does that mean I am forgiven?" he asked softly.

Wolfram flopped onto his back, looking up at the stars. The demon was at rest for the moment, but eighteen years of history was hard to overcome. "I don't know. Ask me in the morning." Then he laughed. "No, I'll be busy getting over this stuff." He waggled the goblet. "Ask me in a few days."

"I'll do that."

Silence descended again, and the torch flickered and died.

Fionvar spoke from the starlight. "Thank you for hearing me out. I thought, by the time it came to tell you, that the anger would overcome you."

"The demon," he said. "I thought so, too." Catching Fionvar's puzzled expression, Wolfram went on, "Ever since I was a child, I've felt as if something else lived inside me." He tapped his temple with one finger. "When something upsets me, this monster tries to escape; it tries to tear its way right through me and I . . . I go mad. I scream, and hurt people, and break things—and ruin everything." He gave half a smile. "My demon."

Fionvar gazed up at the new stars. "Is there anything else you need to tell me?"

As he lay considering the question, Lyssa sprang to his mind, kissing and caressing him. He cringed as he answered, glad of the darkness. "No."

After a moment, Fionvar asked, "Are you lying to me?"

302   ELAINE ISAAK

Wolfram sat up. "Yes."

"That's an interesting answer." Fionvar's voice grew hard.

"Sometimes it's not about me," Wolfram told him. "I'm not the only one who does things he regrets, remember?"

"I think I'll regret saying that, actually. Great Lady, Wolfram, I thought something was happening here." The ground crunched as Fionvar rose, his figure blocking the stars. "You can track your way home, I trust?" Without waiting for an answer, Fionvar crunched off into the night toward the temple.

Wolfram tried to think of another answer, another thing to say to keep Fionvar from leaving, but there was nothing, not without betraying Lyssa to her own brother and giving Fionvar another thing to feel guilty about, no doubt. The night grew suddenly cold around him, despite the burn of liquor in his throat. It was not the first time his father had left him, but somehow, it seemed the hardest. He couldn't howl anger to the sky this time. He couldn't storm off claiming not to care, claiming this time would be the last because he would do the leaving from now on.

No, this time Wolfram knew that he did not want him to go. And yet, he was powerless to stop him.

Pulling his knees in close to his chest, Wolfram felt cold, and small, and all alone.

Chapter 37

IN THE darkness, Fionvar made his way to the temple. At this hour, the congregates had left, and the priestesses had retired to their quarters. Only one light burned, a lantern visible under the curtain that still concealed the unfinished family chapel. Led by starlight, Fionvar found his way to the altar. He made the circle sign of the Lady and raised his arms before the altar. After a moment, he walked quietly to the outside wall and began to walk a circuit of the room. His footfalls seemed as thunder to him in the darkened space, covering the scratchy sounds of rats digging beneath the floor, complementing the ting and strike of Lyssa's hammer.

Fionvar walked three circuits and sat on a back bench, near the Cave of Spirit. The smoke lingered from a few candles lately gone out, and he wondered who else had prayed here tonight and what they had prayed for. He had been so open, just now, so ready to take Wolfram wholeheartedly into his life. In the tale of Wolfram's birth, he had told things he never voiced to anyone save Brianna. He laid himself bare before his son, and found himself unprepared for the blow so quietly delivered. He should have expected Wolfram to keep secrets, of course he would, and hadn't Fionvar himself asked the next question? What had he hoped for, that his suspicion was unfounded, or that Wolfram would lie again in an attempt to assuage his feelings?

Brianna was right—even if Wolfram changed, too much would be the same. He might grow up, but still never control his urges or reveal himself any more than he had to. "Bury it," Fionvar muttered.

For this young man, he had forsaken his love and his queen. All his bold words dissolved like mist, leaving him alone. Would Brianna take him back after all he had said to her? Would he be humble enough to ask? She would marry again, get new heirs. There would be no Lord Protector. There would be no place for him.

"Oh, bloody earth!" Lyssa shouted suddenly from behind her curtain, accompanied by the crash of falling tools. "Bury it and lose the grave!"

Fionvar was halfway there before he considered what he was doing. Inside, he was that same boy too young to be a man, trying to hold his family together.

"Lyssa? Are you all right?" He pulled aside the curtain and found her sitting on the floor, nursing her thumb.

"Blast it," she muttered, sticking the injured thumb back in her mouth.

"Cursing in temple? Not like you, Lyssa." Fionvar crouched beside her, smiling. "What can I do?"

"Go away." She glowered, examining her thumb. "Whacked it with the mallet—not bad, though, nothing broken."

"I'm so relieved." He let himself drop to the floor, picking up her fallen chisel and holding it out.

"What're you doing here anyway?"

He sighed. "Wolfram and I burned the tiger skin. I told him everything."

"You burned the skin? What on earth for?" She snatched the chisel and dropped it onto her leather tool carrier.

"He's been having nightmares—night and day, I guess—that the tiger's still after him. I thought that would help."

With her thumb in her mouth, Lyssa stared at him. "You don't think he's going mad?"

"No," Fionvar replied thoughtfully, then shrugged. "Maybe he is. Maybe he always was, I don't know."

"What happened to all your resolve? When we spoke a few days ago you were ready to throw away everything for him."

Running his fingers over one of the inlaid tiles of the floor, Fionvar examined his sister's work. Someday, the place would be beautiful. "He lied to me again."

She snorted. "Did you expect otherwise?"

Shaking his head, Fionvar told her, "This was different. Something happened to him today, something that scared him. He wound up outside my office." He paused. "My former office. He didn't mean to, I think, but he accepted my hospitality. I could tell he was rattled, but he wouldn't tell me what happened."

"Of course not."

"That's not the lie that bothered me. No, later on, I asked if there was anything he needed to tell me—confessions, I mean, and he understood that. He said no."

Lyssa blinked, wiping off her thumb and shaking it gently. "Naturally."

"I asked him if he was lying, Lyssa, and he said yes. Why would he say that? Why would he acknowledge my suspicion but refuse to tell the truth? 'It's not about me,' he said, like he could protect me from something." Fionvar traced the pattern of leaves.

"Mmm," Lyssa said, getting to her knees to start tucking away her tools.

"You don't think that's strange?"

Dropping the heavy case on her table, Lyssa said, "I don't know what to say. I don't know why it bothers you—he's still a liar, isn't that what upset you to begin with?"

Holding his arms about his knees, Fionvar said, "To begin with, yes, but I've been sitting out there in the dark. I made three circuits, and what I thought of was the way he looked at me when he said it. 'It's not about me,' he told me, then 'I'm not the only one who does things he regrets.' "

"Maybe you should let it go." She took a wide brush and started sweeping stone dust from the table.

Coughing, Fionvar arose, waving away the dust and frowning. "You don't have to do that now," he complained.

Eyeing him, she dropped the brush. "Maybe he is protecting you. Maybe whatever it was doesn't matter anymore."

Waving more slowly, Fionvar said quietly, "What was it between you, Lyssa? Why won't you talk to each other?"

"I told you." She looked away, leaning her powerful arms on the table.

"Something to do with him and Melody; but I put that forward, you just agreed."

She cupped her forehead with one hand, looking as if she'd like to have her long hair back, to hide her face. "Leave it alone, Fionvar."

Slowly, Fionvar walked around the table, and stared down at her. "Lyssa," he said, urgently, a tone of worry entering his voice. Suddenly he thought she might be right, he should leave it alone, forget it ever happened, whatever it was; but it was too late for that.

Her head propped up by her elbows, Lyssa's strong shoulders shook. Silently at first, then with a growing keening terrible to listen to, she wept. Tears streamed down her arms, carving channels in the dust and splashing on the tiles below.

Fionvar stared. When Orie had died, she had not cried. When Wolfram was born, when Jordan was married—not since she was seven years old had he seen Lyssa cry.

Now she wept in great wrenching sobs, her face buried, the whole of her powerful body given over to this grief.

Across the table, Fionvar straightened, and felt himself turn to stone as he realized the truth.

After a long time passed, he exhaled. "How far?"

"Not that. Just . . . I never meant . . ." She sobbed, then shook her head. "Great Goddess, Fionvar, you have to know—"

Weak-kneed, Fionvar let the wall support him. "Did he know?"

"Not then, later that night. I swear, Fionvar, I never meant for anything to happen." She looked up at him at last, her eyes swollen from tears, her face a mask of misery. "I was so glad to find him alive, to be able to save him. He was in pain, he needed . . . comfort."

"But you knew, Lyssa. You knew who he was to you—even if he wasn't the prince. Even if you weren't a priestess."

Wiping futilely at her eyes, she admitted, "He's been after me for years. I couldn't discourage him. I didn't want to push him away."

"All those years of stone-carving lessons and swordplay," Fionvar breathed. "Why didn't I see it?"

"You never saw him clearly; Great Goddess, Fionvar, by that time you were barely allowed to see him at all. I was his friend."

He gazed up toward the ceiling. "You were flattered. Here he was, all full of admiration, smitten with you like no one since Jordan."

"What could I do? I thought he'd grow out of it—I knew he'd taken a lover, I thought—"

"Then what?" Fionvar barked. "You thought you'd let him live out his fantasy, to see that you weren't as great as he believed?"

"It wasn't like that! After the leopards, we fought back-to-back, he was hurt, and I had him brought to my room. I thought he would be safe there."

Rounding the table, Fionvar looked her in the eye and felt her hot breath. "In your bed."

Pressing a hand over her mouth, Lyssa wilted beneath his gaze, the tears seeping slowly down her cheeks.

He drew back, the fury and agony coursing through him. "After I finish cleaning out the study, I'm going to the manor. If anyone cares, that's where I'll be."

"You can't leave, not like this—"

"Shut up, Lyssa!" He turned his back on her and strode for the silence of his abandoned place.

LOOKING BACK toward the castle, Wolfram saw the dark outline of the tower with the observatory at its top. With the sliver of moon in the sky, Dylan should still be there. He rose and went to the stairs, climbing their endless turns until his bare feet were cold and bruised with walking.

Knocking on the lower door, he waited. When he banged a little louder, he heard scrambling inside, someone making his way down the ladder.

At last, the door creaked open, and Dylan's pale face peered around. "Wolfram, it's you," he squeaked.

Frowning, Wolfram nodded. "Let me in; I need to talk to someone."

"Now? But the moon—"

"You can watch and listen at the same time, can't you? This is really important, Dylan."

With a sigh, Dylan pulled the door open the rest of the way, closing it as Wolfram mounted the ladder to the roof. Dylan followed resignedly, shutting the trapdoor when he reached the top. By his post were a small, hooded lantern and ready quill on top of a parchment already dark with notes and calculations. Next to his chair stood a tall clock, its brass works ticking away, gears ratcheting the tiny hands forward.

"That's the new clock?" Wolfram went to peer at it more closely, but Dylan jumped before him, nearly knocking over the delicate machine.

"Don't touch it!"

"I wouldn't; I know how long you all were working on it." Still, he retreated a few steps, then turned to overlook the landscape. "How can you make any measurements at this hour anyhow?"

"The mountain peaks, and a few standing stones. I have a chart with everything measured out to compare." Dylan dropped heavily onto his chair. "What did you want to tell me?"

Wolfram turned back to his friend. "I finally heard the whole story, the truth behind the legend of King Rhys."

"What's that?" Dylan leaned over to peer through a brass tube toward the horizon.

"Well, for starters, he's not dead."

"Of course not."

"What?"

"He was taken into the stars; he wasn't really alive, but a guise of the Lady," Dylan explained, then frowned. "You know all that, I mean, he's your . . ." He shrugged and turned back to his tube.

"No, he isn't," Wolfram said firmly.

Dylan was silent, not looking at him.

Nervously, Wolfram started pacing the circular rooftop. "You should go to Hemijrai someday, to see the observatory there. They have this dome, a full sphere, really, and you can go inside. There are paintings on the walls that show great events in the sky and in their religion, and all these little holes where the sun or moon shine through. They think they can predict when their god and goddess will be reborn." He stopped, considering the idea as he stood before the clock again.

Dylan, with his back turned, didn't see Wolfram bend down to take a closer look. Two dull metal weights hung from a thin chain, clicking over their gears with the time. Shadows edged the chain links like dried blood, and Wolfram flashed to the chain at his throat and the two metal beads that gave purchase for the hands that would have killed him. A bolt of horror shot through Wolfram. "It was you."

"What did you say? I didn't catch—" Dylan turned and froze, his face eerie in the tiny, flickering light.

Wolfram surged to his feet and caught a handful of Dylan's robe, knocking over the chair, dragging him down close to the candle to see his face. "It was you," he shouted, jabbing a finger at Dylan's face. "I broke your nose with the back of my skull."

"What are you talking about?" Dylan bleated, his scholar's fingers grappling with Wolfram's strong hands.

Yanking him to his feet, Wolfram pushed him back against the wall. "Why did you do it? Why did you try to kill me, Dylan? You are my best friend." The demon ripped at the inside of his skull even as grief welled up in his throat.

"Please, Wolfram, let me go, please," Dylan gasped. "Your Highness."

Growling like a mad dog, Wolfram heaved him off his feet, pulling his back over the low wall, leaning over him. "Why'd you do it?"

"She told me he wasn't your father, that you were an imposter," Dylan choked out. "She said it was mine, Great Lady, Wolfram. I loved her—I love her."

"Say something that makes sense, Dylan!"

"Asenith. I love her, Wolf—please!"

Tugging Dylan back from the edge, Wolfram let him drop to the floor as he sank on top of the trapdoor. "Asenith."

Nodding desperately, Dylan stroked his throat, red hair flopping over his eyes.

"The baby is yours," Wolfram said.

"She said so, I don't know, Wolfram. I don't know if I can trust her. I did then. Sweet Lady, I thought she loved me. She was beautiful, older—she wanted me. She's encouraged me so much . . . Sweet Lady." On his hands and knees, he bowed his head, still trying to get his breath.

"You're babbling, Dylan, tell me straight." Wolfram kneaded his temples, practicing his breathing as he stared at his would-be murderer.

"Don't kill me," Dylan pleaded.

"I won't kill you, Dylan." Throwing back his head, Wolfram laughed out loud, even as he wanted to weep. "You're my best friend, remember?"

Dylan sank down so that his forehead touched the stone. "I met her at a talk about the observatory. She was so interested, and she sought me out—me! I found out what she did—I wanted to marry her, Wolfram, but she wouldn't. I don't have any money.

She had a plan, she said. That's when she told me about you, that you are a bastard, that you should never inherit the throne. What would it matter, she said, if we played you along to get money. Then we could marry."

"The meeting in the tavern, where she was being beaten, you set that up, didn't you? You knew I wouldn't let it happen." He flipped up the eye patch and rubbed the ridge of bone around the empty place.

"She made the plans. My role was to get you there, a little drunk if possible. She would be grateful, you would be flattered."

Wolfram wrinkled his nose. "You let me share your woman? Good grief!"

Glancing up, Dylan saw the scars on his face and looked away again. "What could I do, I was desperate. When I worked the nights, you were with her. During the day—" His shoulders drooped, and he finally sat up, curled against the wall.

"Then she got pregnant. One last big take, she would tell you; am I right?"

Staring into the darkness, Dylan nodded. "We could finally be together."

Wolfram shook his head. "I was such a fool, Dylan. You had me all the way." Miraculously, as Dylan talked, the demon crept away.

"She wasn't supposed to come to the castle. I was scared out of my wits when she came to my room. Wolfram's running away, she said. 'I told him about the baby, and he hit me, Dylan, he knocked me down and said I'd get nothing from him.'" His voice grew distant as he recalled her words. "I'd never been so angry before, Wolfram, I didn't know what to do. You had as-saulted a pregnant woman."

"It wasn't true," Wolfram said.

From across the miles between them, Dylan studied him. "You'd been angry all that night. I didn't know what to be-lieve."

"I offered to acknowledge the baby, Dylan. I gave her the proof she wanted to hold over the queen. She never planned to run away with you. She used me to avenge herself on my parents; she used you to get to me. With me dead, she had the only heir."

"No," Dylan protested, "that's not all it was. She was so interested in my work, she knows all about the moon, how to watch, what measurements to take. She even asked for copies of my notes for her to study."

"Why would a whore need all of that?" Wolfram mused.

"She had another plan; she always has, I can see that now." Unexpectedly, Dylan started sniffling. "I am so sorry, Wolfram, please believe that. Great Goddess, I didn't want to hurt you. I've been so confused and miserable."

"I know," he said, with a calm he had not felt since Deishima's breathing lessons. "You didn't try very hard that night. A little harder, and you might have done it."

"No, I don't think I could, really. I wanted you to win."

Wolfram inched closer and touched Dylan's arm. Dylan jerked away, the whites of his eyes glinting. "I won't hurt you, I swear."

"I'm sorry," Dylan repeated.

"It's a long time ago, now."

Dylan took a deep breath. "It's not just that, Wolfram."

His headache faintly returning, Wolfram asked, "What else is there?"

"I know about the tiger that's still stalking you, Wolfram. She told me they'd kill you, her friends. They need you out of the way. I wanted, I couldn't, oh, Great Goddess," he moaned, dropping his head to his hands.

Wolfram reeled, the night suddenly colder than before. "That day in my chambers. You were so nervous, and I couldn't figure it out. Every time I asked a question, you jumped. You put a spell on me." Then he grinned as the relief washed over him, it was neither madness nor mistake. "Will you lift it?"

His lips trembling, Dylan spoke a few strange words.

Wolfram felt the tension go out of his shoulders, as if he need not keep looking behind. He gave a deep sigh.

"She's dying, Wolfram," Dylan murmured. "After all of this, all I've done; she is dying anyway. Poisoned, she says. I'm not skilled enough to find out."

Climbing to his feet, Wolfram stared down. "You tried to kill me—your best friend, your prince, no less—then you made me fear my own shadow, for a woman who used you, and now she's dying."

Dylan curled into himself, hugging his knees. "Will you ever forgive me?"

"I don't need to hold it over you, Dylan," Wolfram whispered into the night. "How will you ever look me in the eye again?"

Leaving his friend whimpering on the rooftop, Wolfram let himself down and wandered, unmolested, to his room and slept well past dawn without hearing a sound.

Chapter 38

WAKING LATE, and feeling fuzzy-headed, Wolfram decided to pay some visits. He dressed well, even replacing the coronet someone had returned to his room after he'd abandoned it in Fionvar's office.

The first visit must be to the privy, and, as he stood, glancing at the hole through which wastes fell into a fenced pit a few stories down, Wolfram had the beginning of a plan that might confirm his suspicions. It might also ruin all his hopes, but that he could not control.

Before he could set his plan in motion, it was high time he paid a call on his mother at court, uninvited though he might be. They should see him speaking and acting as fair as he could, in case he pulled off his scheme and could finally share all the secrets he was keeping. The court hall was close by the Great Hall, but lacking in most of its grandeur, equipped with rows of cushioned benches. A few of these were the same that they had used in exile at the manor in Gamel's Grove and were reserved for the finest of their citizens and visitors. Entering quietly, he found a place on a back bench, beside a rather surprised merchant. Wolf-ram smiled pleasantly and nodded a greeting to the man, who fingered his many rings as he bowed his head in return.

"I believe there are more of them every day," a thin woman was saying to the queen, who tapped her fingers together as she always did when she was losing patience. The woman wore sturdy clothing, nothing fancy, and as she paced, Wolfram caught the flash of a badge at her hip—a new guild mistress for the jewelers. "I don't want them selling their wares, they've not paid dues, nor been licensed."

"Yes, I understand, Mistress Weylin, the city guard have already been instructed that the Hemijrani are not to sell anything. They are doing their best to enforce the law."

"But when will these people be gone? They should be routed!" She slapped her fist into her palm.

Queen Brianna replied, in the weary tone of the thousandth retelling, "They are gathering here for a feast day of their religion, after which they will be gone. The ships are already at harbor in Freeport to take them home. Just a few more days." She straightened and addressed the room. "If anyone else here has a complaint against the refugees, please take it to the guard captain." As her eyes scanned the faces, she stopped at Wolfram's, her lips turning down.

Duchess Elyn, at her side as ever, heaved herself up on her cane, doddering a few steps down the aisle. "What're you doing here, boy?"

With a throbbing in his head, Wolfram rose and bowed to his mother. "I do not believe I have been banned from court, Your Majesty. If I am mistaken, I will go."

"You have fourteen days," his mother replied. "Do with them what you will."

"I thank you for your patience, Your Majesty," he said, meaning it lightly, but her lips tightened.

"You've told him, haven't you?" Elyn rasped, coughing into a cloth.

Wolfram examined the shaky figure that had once terrified him. "Told me what, Excellency?"

"About the marriage, the suitors." Elyn flapped her thin hand to take in the full range of possibilities.

"I have," said the queen. "My heir should be aware of such things, I believe."

Turning back to the throne, Elyn cackled. "Fourteen days to prove himself, no, Your Majesty, you've given him a fortnight to kill you!"

The hush of the room grew deeper.

Wolfram felt heat rising in his face and all the eyes of the assembly upon him.

"Think, Brianna!" the old woman exhorted. "Think! If you can't go through with it, or if you're dead, we're left with him and his bastard."

Fury tightened his shoulders, but Wolfram stood his ground, flexing his fingers to prevent them making fists. "I am trying to live up to the bargain, Your Majesty. I have no wish to be crowned before my time."

"In eight days," Elyn crowed, thrusting out her stick, "your time is up!"

With all his heart, Wolfram wanted to stay. He wanted to prove his own patience by sitting back down, but one more word from the duchess would send him into a rage he could not control. Bowing curtly, he turned on his heel and left, the door standing open behind him.

Ignoring his aches, he walked off the anger, taking a long route around the several galleries and surprising a few scullions in the kitchen. Then, still stoked with this gathered energy, he found the room they had given Asenith. A maid sat outside the door, darning an old pair of hose. She jumped up and bowed.

"Let me announce you, Your Highness." She knocked timidly on the door, darting him glances.

"You do that," he said as she opened the door, "but tell her I'm coming in however she feels about it." He grinned his most feral, and the maid nodded quickly, her eyes round.

A low murmur began in the room, the maid's voice pleading, Asenith's weak yet insistent.

Growing impatient, Wolfram pushed the door open, and strode in, taking the bedside seat as if he'd been expected. "Thank you," he told the maid. "You may go."

She bobbed a curtsy and scurried out.

For a long time, he studied the figure in the bed, even as she studied him. Her hair, growing out blond, was brittle and thin, framing a drawn and empty face. All the curves of her body had dwindled to nothing, leaving the bones of her shoulders and hips clearly outlined by the thin sheet that covered her. Every breath lifted the sheet a little, revealing her ribs, then sank back again. Her breath smelled rotten, and he turned away from her for air.

"After so long." She sighed, her voice the merest exhale. "What do you want?"

"Is your revenge as sweet as you had planned, Asenith?"

"Some parts . . . sweeter than others." She gave a wan smile, a ghost of her seduction. "Did Fionvar tell you all?"

"Most," he said. "All that mattered, I think."

"Did he tell you of the birth? How he held my arms?" A strange expression crossed her face, regret perhaps, or a sudden wistful mood.

"It didn't come up."

The next question she whispered, eyes shut. "Did he tell you that he kissed me?"

No wonder the queen had been so hostile to her lover, but he had not spoken of it to Wolfram—regrets indeed.

When he did not answer, she opened her eyes again. "I can still surprise you. Good. Have you seen the babe?"

Discomfited by the question, which had not crossed his mind, he said, "Not yet."

"She looks like you." She smiled to see him squirm. "I'm dying, they must have said."

"I'd heard that you were poisoned. It's taking a long time, isn't it? Maybe you just couldn't handle the birth." He watched the flutter of pulse in her neck.

"I handled everything, my lord." She laughed without sound. "I handled you."

"Nevertheless"—he tilted his chin up to scratch near the scar around his throat—"I'm still walking around, and you're unlikely to ever leave that bed."

Watching him gravely, she asked, "Did you do it?"

"What?"

"Poison me, somehow, some agent of yours." Suddenly, she jerked upright in her bed, her eyes open. "Was it Dylan? Did he do this for you?"

"It was probably your own friends. What was the arrangement, that you or your child would rule here while she rules in Bernholt? Why would she do that when she could take both?"

Asenith let herself drop back to the mattress, pulling up her sheets with feeble gestures. "I don't know who you mean."

"How long have you been planning this?" Then he considered more deeply. "Why now?"

"You speak nonsense." She sighed again. "Leave me in peace."

Wolfram rolled a few other questions around in his mind, but he did not want to give Dylan away. Killing the prince, no matter that he was on the outs with the queen, would raise suspicions, but if a young astronomer fell from his tower, who would question that? "Very well," he said at last, and rose. Staring down at her, wasting away in the bed, Wolfram felt a touch of loss. He stooped again and kissed her very gently on her withered lips.

Asenith gave a little moan, and her vacant blue eyes tracked him as he left her.

Outside, Wolfram stood a moment just breathing, clearing the scent of her dying from his lungs. Curious, he followed the passages to Fionvar's study and found it empty of all the Lord Protector's things. Even the great desk had been removed and the small rosewood table returned to its place. With a dark foreboding, Wolfram sprinted through the halls to Fionvar's quarters, finding a servant with a broom by the door.

"Where's Fionvar? I have to see him."

The man bowed, and answered, "Gone, Your Highness, just now."

"Bury it, he can't leave now!"

"If you're quick to the stables, you may catch him."

Taking off at a run, Wolfram reached the stables just as Fionvar's tall bay horse was brought round. Dressed in traveling clothes, with a pack already slung on the horse's back, Fionvar prepared to mount.

With a nod to the groom, Wolfram took the reins and steadied the horse, patting its broad neck as it snorted down at him.

Noting the change, Fionvar glanced over, his hands already on the saddle. Immediately, he turned his face away, with a quick breath.

The energy leaving him, Wolfram rested his head on the horse's neck, his arm wrapped around, fingers entangled in the dark mane. "You know."

"Yes." Fionvar adjusted the stirrup leather.

"I did not know who she was to me," Wolfram said.

"I know that, too."

"Bury it," Wolfram muttered. "I couldn't just tell you. Great Lady, I didn't know what to say. It wasn't my secret." He rubbed the twitchy skin beneath the patch.

Under lowered brows, Fionvar shot him a look.

"I'm sorry. Is that what you want? My apology? I'm sorry I didn't tell you. I'm sorry for every day of the last eighteen years." He shook, biting the inside of his lip.

"All right," Fionvar said, sticking his foot in the stirrup and swinging himself up. "Did you come here to stop me going?"

Wolfram buried his head beneath the horse's neck, stroking its warm cheek, its breath steaming his neck. Why had he come after all? He looked up into his father's face. "I came to warn you."

"What is it this time?" Fionvar bit back whatever else he might say, taking control of the reins as Wolfram stepped back.

"I'm about to put my foot in it. I'm about to do something reckless and rash and stupid, and it might get me killed, certainly I'll be exiled." He shook his head, tilting it to the right to maintain his gaze. "I thought you should know."

Leaning on the front of the saddle, Fionvar asked, "It's no good warning you off is it?"

Wolfram gave a crooked smile. "I'm afraid not."

Fionvar kicked the horse, which sprang forward, forcing Wolfram's quick retreat. "Then thank the Lady I won't be here to see it," he called back, riding hard for the gates.

Head bowed, Wolfram kicked at the dirt. That sinking feeling had returned. All those years, he had been disappointing some distant legend, flouting his royal father's blessing, while his true father stood in the shadows watching every moment of defiance and holding every hurt. He had tried, he had wanted so much to succeed this time. Now, what did it matter?

"Bury him. Bury them all." This escapade might well be his last, but his first one for all the right reasons. Turning his feet for the streets, Wolfram went in search of the equipment he needed, charging it back to the household, knowing he would pay in other ways.

Chapter 39

ALL THAT day, Wolfram sat in his room tying knots. The rope was stout, and should hold—Lady willing—and ended in a hook half again as long as his arm. When the sliver of moon had set, he rose and wrapped both rope and hook in a long, light cloak. Shoeless, he crept through the halls to the battlement stairs. The wing that housed official guests thrust out dark and square to the back of the keep. He headed straight there, ducking into alcoves as the men of the watch made their rounds. When he reached the guest wing, he peered down the wall. Far below, water gleamed, and he caught the scent he was after though it turned his stomach.

The castle privies were old-fashioned, small simple rooms sticking out from the wall, with open bottoms and wooden seats. Year upon year, the queen spoke of updating them, or at least enclosing them and concealing the pits below. Her generals, especially those who had fought the Usurper, argued against it. After all, those open holes allowed them to drop nasty surprises on would-be invaders. Halfway down the wall, a privy stuck out from the guest quarters where Faedre and her entourage were lodged. Wolfram had had some time to consider how and where they must hold Deishima and how to get in without arousing suspicions. Most of the rooms had windows, large and relatively accessible, but the privy's antechamber, stocked with bathtub and basins, had none. She would be safe from prying eyes. Or so they thought.

Wolfram crept along the wall a little farther and found what he wanted, a loop of metal stuck into the floor to tie down defensive artillery. He made fast the rope, and slipped the long cloak over his oldest clothing. Draping the hook over his shoulder, he played out rope over the wall, with knots every foot. Too bad they didn't have vines here as in Deishima's garden. Checking again for watchmen, Wolfram climbed over the battlement and clung to his line. Slowly, he began the descent, knot to knot, working carefully. His mind and heart he did not altogether trust, but he knew his own strength and the strength of his determination.

Hand over hand, he let himself down, his bare feet finding purchase in the worn stones and gaps of missing cement.

At last, the privy loomed beside him, then he was below it, listening.

He pulled up a bit of rope and tied off a loop to brace his foot, then unslung the hook.

Saying a prayer that no one would feel the urge in the next few minutes, Wolfram held the hook by its end, pushing upward until he shoved loose the wooden seat. Pulling the hood over his head, he took a deep breath and held it.

Carefully, he climbed up his line and grabbed the edge of the stone base, heaving himself over it onto the floor.

The smell was partially masked by strong herbs, but still made him retch. He forced himself to stillness and listened again.

In the antechamber, something rustled, breathing as carefully as he.

Wolfram slipped out of his protective cloak, folding it to the inside to be ready when it was time to go. Then he opened the door.

A whimper and furtive movements told him he was not alone, and the scent of cloves and Deishima's sacred leaves washed over him.

"Deishima," he whispered, keeping close to the floor. "It's me, Wolfram."

The movement ceased, then began again, edging closer.

From his pouch, Wolfram plucked a stubby candle and his flint and steel. He struck a spark and saw the huddled figure, her eyes glinting in the new light. Dripping some wax on the floor, Wolfram stuck down the candle and crawled to her side.

She wore no veil, and had been given a heavier gown for night. Her glorious hair fell in a tangle about her shaking shoulders.

Gently, Wolfram reached out and took her bound hands, his fingers working at the knots until she was free.

Shutting her eyes, Deishima bent her head forward, letting him remove the gag and cast it aside.

Looking on her in the flickering light, Wolfram bit his lip, his throat aching. "I told you I'd come. Did you hear me?"

"I heard you," she whispered, her voice hoarse, "but I have been too frightened to believe it was true."

Rubbing his knuckles with his palm, Wolfram held himself in check. "I wish I knew how to comfort you. If you were from Lochalyn, I could take you in my arms and keep you warm and tell you all the lies I can think of."

Deishima hugged herself, bowing her head. "You might pretend that I am."

With a soft cry, Wolfram gathered her into his lap, his arms wrapped around her tiny form, her dark head pressed close to his chest so that her tears burned and tickled through his shirt. He stroked her hair, her back, her small, cold hands. "It's all right," he murmured, over and over, wishing he could believe it.

She held her hand over his heartbeat. "You should not have come, Highness," she mumbled into his arm. "If they find you here—"

"I don't care," he answered fiercely. "I couldn't leave you here alone. Sweet Lady, I wish I could take you out with me, but I cannot carry us both that way."

Raising her head, Deishima slipped her hair back behind her ear. "You are like no one I have ever heard of."

He grinned. "They'll make new stories for me," he said, giddiness welling up in him. "Stories to frighten their children to behave."

She gave a ghostly smile in return and slipped from his arms to sit close by him. "Why have you come here?"

Wolfram grew serious again. "I think I know what they're about. This ritual, it's for the rebirth of your Two, am I right?"

Deishima nodded. "It has never been done before. We have been waiting for the sign and for Their earthly elements."

"Melody and Alyn."

"Over my country at the time of their birth the sky went dark and bright, for the sun and moon came together. Everywhere was searched, and no such pair was found."

"But Faedre knew about the twins in Bernholt. She came home telling the Jeshan they had been born, but far away."

Surprised, Deishima blinked at him. "How is it that you have learned all this?"

"There's more," he said. "In a few days, all of your refugees are gathering here—something else will happen—darkness again?" This earned him a full-fledged smile.

"The rebirth will be complete, and the Two shall again take form."

"Do you really think that will happen?"

The smile slipped away, and she watched the candle for a moment. "I do not know. The Holy Father, he believes with all of his being that it will be. The Holy Mother . . ." She trailed off and frowned.

"Faedre's not here for religion, she's looking for revenge."

The frown grew deeper. "I do not wish to believe this. Before we came here, I believed that she was true to Jonsha in all ways. When the tiger came—" She broke off and glanced at him, at his scarred face. "Forgive me; I shall not again mention it."

"It's not your fault."

"No, you were correct, the tiger came for me. She would have me die lest I should speak to anyone about this ritual."

"But she kidnapped you back instead." He hugged his knees, their arms close and warm. "Because they need you. She convinced Esfandiyar that you could be cleansed."

"Yes." The single syllable was faint, and she searched the darkness.

Wolfram swallowed, and said, "I know you use sacrifices in your rituals—the monkeys that Esfandiyar keeps."

One hand pressed to her mouth, Deishima nodded.

Reaching out, he gently touched her far cheek, turning her to face him, their noses inches apart in the darkness. "But such a great occasion calls for a great sacrifice, a worthy, pure, unsoiled sacrifice. It's you, isn't it?"

She did not want to meet his eye. "All of my life, I have been taught for this moment. The signs of my birth showed that I am to be the one, that my life will be most of service in this way. I have always known that it would be my place to die for the glory of the Two."

"You are not meant to marry anyone, you told me," he breathed.

"I am meant to consecrate the moment of their rebirth."

Wolfram let his hand fall and leaned his head back against the wall, looking at the distant ceiling. He did not want to ask what must come next, but it was the telling point. *Sometimes it's not about me,* he thought. "Is it still your wish to have that fate?"

She was silent.

"When we spoke of marriage, I thought I could make you a queen. They've given me fourteen days to do something stupid, to give them the reason to throw me out, and this is it. If anyone finds me, I'm an exile at best. Even if I could get you away, I have nothing to offer you." He steeled himself for the hardest thing he would ever say. "Tell me now, Deishima, if you don't want my help—you said you couldn't resume the life you left, but now you have, by whatever means—if you want me to leave you, I'll go. I'll hide my head on that day, and stay as far away as I can, and you can"—his voice broke, but he plunged ahead—"you can die for your faith, if that's what you want. I will let you go."

"I do not know what I wish," she said, her voice a quiet song of anguish. "This is not how I imagined it to be. And the Holy Mother cares little for the sacred things. These are the people of my faith who have taken from me both voice and peace."

Wanting to rage and storm and make her his own, Wolfram covered his mouth, squeezed shut his eye. The power of this desire went beyond any lust, beyond the need for flesh or fantasy. It filled the hollow places and it terrified him.

From the gloom, Deishima spoke. "Sixteen years I have dedicated myself to the moment that awaits me. For sixteen years, I did not question that it was so, that my birth had been for this, to bring the Two back into this world. I did not leave the women's places, I did not speak to man or heathen, I had no interest in the world, but in the spirit only. Sixteen years, then you came. You came to me and touched my hair."

Wolfram stifled a giggle.

"And I did not know why. Why has he done this thing? Why has he defied the laws of my people to enter this garden, to dare to touch me, the consecrated one? I wondered."

"Because I'm an idiot," he supplied gruffly.

"Do not say that!" she hissed so fiercely that he looked upon her. "A fire burns in you, Wolfram, a spirit so remarkable that even you cannot contain it."

Bowing his head, he said bitterly, "If it's true, then you're the only one who sees it."

She set her hand upon his ruined cheek. "Then I have been given a gift beyond measure, Wolfram, that you love me. And if you are a prince, or an exile, or a beggar in the street, it shall not make me love you any less."

Wolfram lifted her hand and pressed it to his lips.

"You need offer nothing more than yourself, and I will think myself a queen."

Tears ran down his cheek and soaked the cuff of her gown, and he pulled her again into his embrace. This time, she slipped her slender arms about him, and he felt the throbbing of her heart with his.

Outside, he heard a noise and tensed, then pulled away. "I have to go."

"Yes, yes," she urged him, flicking away her tears with her fingertips.

Impulsively, he said, "Come with me—I can tie you to the rope, I can pull you up. There's got to be a way."

"We have no time, Wolfram. You will find another way." She grabbed the scarves which had bound her.

As he reached the door, he turned back. "Dawsiir—where is he?"

"They overcame him. He lives, I know nothing more."

Wolfram nodded. "I love you." He slipped through the door, shutting it behind him. Gathering up his cloak to pull it on, he heard another door opening and froze.

A Hemijrani voice barked a loud question and Deishima stumbled over the answer. Another voice joined the first, then Melody said, "Why's her gag off? What's going on?"

"Someone has been here," Faedre reported, with a nasty edge.

"There is no one," Deishima pleaded. "I have freed myself. How could anyone be here aside from me?"

A heavy tread crossed the floor. "What about this?" The stripe of candlelight under the door suddenly faded.

Faedre murmured, "You little fool, did he come to you? Tell me!"

There was a sharp sound of a hand striking flesh, and Deishima cried out.

Wolfram ground his teeth, strangling the cloak with both hands. He had to leave, this was his chance, but the demon roared. He grabbed the edge of the stone seat, steadying the hook.

"Tell me!" Faedre shouted again, and someone struck the wall hard. Deishima moaned and did not answer.

Snatching up the hook, Wolfram spun about. Throwing open the door, he lashed out with the cloak, a war cry issuing from his throat.

Slumped on the floor, with a trickle of blood at her forehead, Deishima cried, "They will kill you!"

Wolfram flung the cloak over Faedre's head.

Faedre yelled, bringing two more men into the room, sending Melody tripping out of their way.

Swinging the hook in a wide arc, Wolfram sliced open one man's arm and kept the others at bay a moment longer.

He bent and scooped Deishima over his shoulder, dragging the knotted rope behind him.

The attackers stumbled and cursed.

Bursting through their midst, Wolfram ran for the door. His shoulder struck the opposite wall.

Dropping the hook, he ran on, yelling at the top of his voice.

When he reached the entrance to the quarters, he kicked it hard into the startled faces of the outside guards.

Freed from the cloak, Faedre and her minions pursued him down the hall, only to meet a group of hurrying castle guards coming to the commotion.

"Catch him!" Faedre shouted.

Wolfram clung to Deishima a moment longer, then slid her down to kneel on the floor and stuck his hands in the air. "I'm unarmed," he called out as they caught him.

Quickly, Faedre grabbed Deishima and pushed her behind, into the waiting arms of her men. "He broke into our quarters," she told the new arrivals. Her smoldering gaze had turned to fury. "You'll not get away with this, Your Highness."

Panting, he grinned back at her. "I'm not dead yet, Faedre. You'd better watch yourself."

Two men held him tight, already binding his wrists with someone's belt. He did not struggle.

Faedre drew close to him, then wrinkled her nose. "You smell like shit, Your Highness."

"So do you."

Shaking her head slowly, Faedre said, "You could have had anyone, why waste your life for her?"

Summoned from his nightly rounds, Gwythym arrived with

a scowl. "Oh, Your Highness, couldn't you last even a week, then?"

Glancing to Gwythym, then back to Faedre, Wolfram said, "After all the fights I've won and lost, I finally found something worth fighting for."

Chapter 40

PAUSING TO light a sixth candle at the Cave of Body, Lyssa made the circle of the Lady over her breast and stood a moment in silent prayer. She resumed her walk, the last circuit she would make. The first night, she had thought only of her crime, her penance, what she might do to atone for such an appalling lapse in judgment. As she walked, her thoughts turned first to her brother's fury and his shame. She did not know if he would ever look her in the eye again. All those years growing up, she wished he would leave her alone; now he finally had, and she missed him terribly. Tonight, Wolfram filled her thoughts. If she had betrayed her brother's trust, how much more had she betrayed his son? Never mind that he had been all too willing, she had knowingly brought him to her bed.

Lyssa passed the Cave of Death and came again to that of Spirit, where she lit her sixth candle. The two opposing Caves of Body and Spirit glinted in the cavernous darkness. Although Lochalyn was not a large kingdom, thanks to the Usurper they now possessed the largest temple dedicated to the Lady. In an attempt to atone for his own sins, he had hired the finest engineers and masons, including the master who had taught her to carve. In six days, the place would be full of Hemijrani heathens, celebrating their holy day in the only room large enough to hold them. The idea rankled her, but the chief priestess had some progressive notion that the heathen deities were in fact foreign saints, subservient to the Lady, and that Finistrel would permit this outrage. She supposed she should confess to this woman and seek duty from her to assuage this guilt, but she could not bring herself to do it. If she kept up her prayers, surely the Lady herself would show the way She could be appeased.

Even as Lyssa crossed before it, the entrance to the temple flew open, and someone ran in, momentarily befuddled by the darkness. "Mistress Lyssa?" Lady Catherine's voice called.

"Here," Lyssa answered, striding out to touch her arm.

Despite the warning, Catherine jumped.

"What's going on?" Lyssa drew the other woman back into the hall, where torches provided a bit more light.

Catherine wore her nightgown, with a robe flung inside out over her shoulders, the sleeves flapping. Her cap sat askew on brown hair braided for sleep. "Oh, Mistress, it's the prince. Will you come?"

"Of course, lead on!" They hurried down the hall, then took an unexpected turn into the old temple and made for the hidden door at the back of the Cave of Life.

"Where are we going?"

"Queen's room, Mistress. Don't ask for more, I don't yet know it." Taking the secret steps two at a time despite her short stature, Catherine said, "You're brother's gone, is he?"

"Yes, to the manor. He wanted some time away, I think."

"And who'd blame him?" They reached the top landing, and Catherine knocked.

From within came a muffled, "Enter," and the pair pushed through the door beneath a tapestry.

"Where's Fionvar?" Brianna demanded, stepping up to meet them.

"Gone to the manor. What's happened?" Lyssa touched Brianna's arm, encouraging her back to the parlor where fire and drink awaited.

Disheveled with sleep and disturbance, Brianna rubbed her arms and grunted. "Why'd he go now, doesn't he know when he's needed?"

"More than most, I'd say, but there's nothing to be done for it, is there?"

Back to the fire, Captain Gwythym stood waiting, the only one fully dressed and alert from his night watch.

Collapsing into a seat with a tall mug of mead, Brianna waved her hand at Gwythym. "Tell them, tell them the worst."

"Aye, Your Majesty."

Lady Catherine took a post beside her mistress, ready and attentive, while Lyssa took her ease in a seat by the fire. Two nights on her feet had begun to take a toll.

"In brief, and to tell you the worst, I've had to arrest the prince. The charge is unlawful entry, and we're expecting further accusations."

"What accusations?" Lyssa asked.

Gwythym ran quick fingers through his hair. "Assault and rape."

Her jaw dropped, and she leaned back to stare at him.

"An hour or so past, he left his room and tied a rope to the battlements. He climbed down and through the privy—"

Letting out a burst of laughter, Lyssa said, "Great Lady, only Wolfram." She shook her head. "Go on, sorry, go on."

"He found the room of that princess, the priestess's acolyte—"

"Deishima."

"Aye, Deishima. He's apparently beaten her, from what I saw, and who knows what else. Faedre and her lot came on them, ready to take him, but he snatched the girl and ran for the door, knocking down my own men and yelling like the dogs were on him. I was on duty myself and heard the commotion with a few others. We found him in the hall, this bloody girl on his shoulder—and I mean that truly—with the Hemijrani host at his heels. He set her down right off and threw up his hands for us to take him. I sent him to barracks for keeping, and came straight here. Oh, it's a mess like I've never seen, Mistress, Your Majesty."

"He went to all that trouble to rape this girl?" Lyssa blurted. "Why not take to the streets like he usually does?"

Groaning, Brianna pressed a hand to her forehead. "Get me some ale, this stuff's not strong enough."

Lady Catherine bustled out, ignoring the robe that dropped from her shoulders.

"He claims she agreed to marry him," Brianna said.

Lyssa frowned. "Is that his excuse?"

Gwythym shook his head. "He's said naught tonight, except to trade some words with Faedre. 'I'll wait for my hearing with the queen,' says he."

"Shouldn't we get dressed then?" Lyssa asked.

Uncovering her face, Brianna turned grim eyes to Lyssa. "Not tonight. I'll not give him the upper hand that way. No, let him stew in the dungeon until the queen's pleasure." She sighed. "Not that I'll get any pleasure from this."

Focusing on Brianna, Lyssa narrowed her eyes. "What does the girl say?"

Gwythym dropped into a chair. "I've only seen that glimpse of her, bloody on Wolfram's shoulder. It's Faedre doing the talking, and mind I was here when she tried to kill the king, so I don't place great stock in her words. But if it comes to her word or the prince's . . ." He gave an eloquent shrug.

"Fionvar's turned in his chain and left me, and now this," Brianna muttered. "What was in Wolfram's head? Can anyone tell me that?"

"Maybe he thought to force the marriage, or thought she'd not reveal him, since he's royal," suggested Gwythym.

Lady Catherine returned with a jug and refilled Brianna's mug, then poured a smaller one for herself and drank it in a gulp.

"If it's rape, he could hang for this. Do I hang my own son? Finistrel be with me." Brianna pressed her fists to her face, tremors bouncing the hair on her shoulders.

Shutting her eyes, Lyssa bowed her head. "Lady be with us all." She drummed her fingers together, then said, "I'll ride for Fionvar."

"No, I need you here. Send somebody, though, Gwythym."

With a quick bow, he went to the door and spoke briefly to someone outside, leaving Lyssa to conceal her relief.

Letting Brianna gather herself, Lyssa accepted her own mug, then said, "You've already brought up banishment, Brianna. That should be the first option."

Sidelong, Brianna eyed her over the rim of the mug she clutched like a shield.

"Unless there's more, something I don't know," Lyssa coaxed.

Licking her lips, clearing her throat, Brianna looked at each of the three in turn. "This does not go beyond us, not until I've had time to consider it all."

Lady Catherine nodded fervently, never one to reveal her mistress's secrets. Hesitating, Gwythym glanced to Lyssa, and asked, "Who else knows what you're about to tell, Your Majesty?"

"Only Fionvar and the prince himself."

"Aye, we'll keep it so." He knelt before her so she need not raise her voice.

Chilled, Lyssa leaned closer.

"The night he left, when the refugees fought our guard at the western gate? It was Wolfram who killed Erik."

Catherine made the sign of the Lady, while Gwythym swore softly. Lyssa stayed still as stone, waiting for more.

"He claims someone tried to kill him, that he thought Erik was in on it. Then he as much as admitted that Erik had nothing to do with it."

Nodding slowly, Lyssa said, "He told me of the attempt when we were—" She shied away from the memory, but continued, ". . . overseas. But nothing of Erik. You say he admits it?"

"The day Fionvar cleared the court, Wolfram told us." She took a quick swallow. "Finistrel knows why Fionvar turned in his chain. He didn't have to, I never made him."

"We know that, Brie," Lyssa assured her, not pointing out that the threat of her remarriage forced the choice as surely as his ill-advised defense of his son.

"He swore he'd stay beside him, that, no matter what Wolfram did, Fionvar would be there. Two days later, he's gone."

"Strange, that," Gwythym mused. "He's never been one to quit on an oath."

Silent, Lyssa searched her conscience and found she could not tell them the truth, not now. With Fionvar gone, someone should stand by the prince, someone should at least try. She felt a sudden lightening of her heart; perhaps this was the way the Lady had prepared, that she should work for Wolfram's forgiveness by being his advocate. "We fought before he left, Brianna. It wasn't you or Wolfram who drove him away, it was me."

Brianna studied her. "What quarrel could make him abandon his vow?"

"I don't believe he's abandoned it. He wanted space to consider it, all the implications." Lyssa forced herself to silence, afraid her talk might give her away. "You know he's been working on the translation of the old woods chapel."

Nodding, Brianna said, "He ever did find solace in study. Or in music." She sighed, brushing at her eyes. "It's been an age since I heard him play."

Turning a little pink, Gwythym walked a few paces off, suddenly very interested in one of the tapestries.

"He will come home, Brie, when he hears of this. You need not be alone."

"But he's resigned his commission. He no longer has any official status here, and we dare not reveal the truth. Oh, Lyssa, I've ruined it, haven't I? I have taken the best thing in my life and broken it, and it will never be remade."

Grief welled up in Lyssa as she sat, reaching to hold Brianna's hand. The question cut too close to her, and she dared not answer.

"Elyn's always been here," Brianna murmured. "She's been my closest advisor because she knows the ways of leadership and I never have. When she spoke of remarriage, she sounded so reasonable. It's what any queen would do in my position, with such an heir. It's what I should have done years ago. My people would forgive me the offense against Rhys's memory—I know many of them are as worried as I am about this, especially now that Asenith's had her baby. If he could've stayed out of trouble for these two weeks, now that he's home, mayhap we'd find him a wife. If he would be governed by us, he could be schooled to kingship, I'm sure"—she laughed, shaking her head—"Lady knows he's smart enough, and with spirit enough for two kings. Now this."

Scooting from her chair, Lyssa knelt beside the queen and

pulled her into a strong embrace. "You need sleep, Brianna. You can think on this in the morning. At the very least, give Fionvar a chance to come home. Let Wolfram have the rest of his fortnight, even if he lives it out in the dungeon. Let's find the truth of this mess before you decide."

"Yes, you're right," Brianna mumbled. "You're right."

Lyssa lifted her to her feet and walked her back to the bed. "Catherine will stay with you tonight, and I'll return by morning. I'll see if Wolfram will speak to me."

Lying back, Brianna shut her eyes, her face grim.

"Try to rest, Brie. No more thought tonight."

"I will try, Lyssa," Brianna replied, and Lyssa knew the promise would be broken before she'd even left the room.

Gwythym walked with her down to a small holding chamber in the barracks where they found Wolfram, marked with blood and still stinking, his wrists chained to a loop in the wall while four guards kept uneasy watch.

At the sight of Lyssa, he brightened, squaring his shoulders as best he could. "Thank the Lady!"

"Will you give me some time with him?"

Scrubbing his weary face, Gwythym said, "Might as well. We've got to transfer him before too long anyhow."

"I'm for the dungeons then?" Wolfram asked, sounding almost jubilant.

"Aye, Your Highness." Turning to Lyssa, he said, "I'll be right outside. Stay out of reach, would you? I don't fancy having a hostage taken under my nose." He shot a sharp glance to Wolfram and ushered the guards outside.

"Yes, you're for the dungeons. What were you thinking?" Lyssa demanded the moment they were alone.

"She has been kidnapped, Lyssa." Through the grime on his face his grin flashed. "I got her alone two days ago and pulled off her veil. They've had her gagged since they got back and her hands bound so she can't use her Ashwadi."

"They could do that," she said slowly, "show her off like that."

Eagerly, Wolfram nodded. "They need to discredit me. As if I needed any help. I had to talk to her, Lyssa, and this seemed like the only way."

"Even with your title in the balance, Wolfram?"

"How deeply have you loved?" he asked. "How deeply have you feared?"

Caught off guard, Lyssa thought of Jordan, who had loved her, then of the night she had forsaken him. Praying in a temple for the spirit of her brother, Lyssa had knelt at the Cave of Death. When the moon rose full over the opening, it shone behind her, casting her own shadow onto the words of the Second Walking, carved into the wall. The light from her candle turned the letters warm and luminous. *"Long She wept and tore Her hair, and from these things were women born, and they were a comfort to Her."* The words had called her so clearly, and the moonlight was the Lady's hand upon her shoulders. Lyssa stared at Wolfram, a lump growing in her throat. The one night she wanted to seduce him had ruined the Lady's love, and she feared never to feel it again.

His eye seeming all the sharper for its loneliness, Wolfram watched her. "Then you know that I had to try anything, and my title means nothing beside that love."

With growing wonder, Lyssa gazed at him. Wolfram leaned against the wall, his right side bent, his eye patch scuffed, and his clothing threadbare and dirty. With his scarred face, he more resembled a pirate than a prince. Chained to the wall and about to be taken below, he would lose all light and freedom, and just might lose his life. And yet he grinned as if he had been given the crown and the Lady's blessing to boot. This boy had dogged her steps for years, his tempers driving her mad even as his affection drew him nearer. He'd always had the title and the coronet to go along, but Lyssa had never considered him as the prince, as the heir to a kingdom. In a week, she might see him hanged. Fionvar's words returned, that it might take a miracle to save his son. And what kind of priestess was she if she could not believe in miracles?

Lyssa nodded. "My brother vowed to stand beside you, Wolfram. In his absence, you're stuck with me. What can I do?"

His smile turned toward sadness. "Deishima is the only witness in my defense, but she will not be allowed to speak. She told me Dawsiir is still alive, or was when we spoke. I need you to find him. He was there when they took her away. He might know more than that as well."

That determined grin infected even Lyssa, so that she laughed. "You want me, a priestess and a woman, to search their camp? I'll stick out like a sword among stones."

His grin turned wistful. "You ever have," he told her gently.

A rush of warmth flooded through her like the Lady's touch, and she basked in his forgiveness.

Chapter 41

A CHAIN about a foot long joined Wolfram's wrists, while another bound his ankle to a sturdy loop set into the stone wall of his new quarters. The leg chain gave him enough slack to pace most of his narrow cell, but not enough to touch the grate at its end. Cells radiated out from a central chamber where three or four guards played cards and swapped jokes. Torches between the grates provided some light, but little heat so far below the ground. He thought fondly of the tiny chamber he'd been given in the Hemijrani prison, with its daylight and breeze. Down here, his own stink was lost in that of the other prisoners.

Across from him he could see three Hemijrani spaced with empty cells between them—to prevent their conspiring, he supposed. A few other cells were occupied, but he couldn't tell anything about the occupants. He had slept sitting up against the cleanest wall, his hands tucked into his armpits for warmth. Once, long ago, he'd been given a tour of the dungeon, for it would be part of his domain. He remembered saying it wasn't near dark or foul enough. His mother replied that Lochalyn was a civilized country, even to its prisoners. Jordan had been held here, after covering Lyssa and Fionvar's escape from the Usurper, and had his fingers broken one by one for secrets he would not reveal.

Wolfram studied his hands.

A sound on the stairs above brought him to his feet. Two servants carried trays, and the guards assisted in delivering bowls of lukewarm porridge to the inmates.

As he reached for the bowl they slid under his grate, Wolfram called out, "Sir, may I have water to wash?"

"Crown prince, is it?" the guard sneered. "Don't you care for the smell?"

His temples throbbed, and Wolfram gritted his teeth. "I have my hearing today, sir, and I still have shit in my hair."

The guard laughed at that. "Cold water, that's what you get."

"That's all I'm asking," Wolfram replied. "Sir." His blood boiled to strike away the man's smile, and he knew why the chain came up short of the door.

After a while, a basin was shoved under the grate, and he bent over it, using the licked-clean porridge bowl to pour the frigid water over his head. He shivered and cursed, shaking out the rest of the water from his hair.

"Enjoying your bath, Your Highness?" the guard called out, making his mates laugh.

Wolfram surged to his feet, and stopped, fists clenched, the length of chain taut between them.

Deliberately, he turned his back and walked toward the back of the cell. He braced his hands against the wall and took a deep breath. The cell in Hemijrai had taken his freedom, but left some measure of dignity. Here, he felt like an animal. In his mind he saw the tiger Rostam pacing, always pacing that little cage that had brought him across the sea. It had only been one night, and already Wolfram was ready to tear someone's head off.

Toward the back of the cell, the stench increased, so he moved slowly forward again, and sat on the ground, his back to the guards. Crossing his legs, he cupped his hands together in his lap and shut his eye. He focused on the pounding in his skull, the angry swell of his pulse that heated his fingertips. With each breath, Wolfram worked to force back the demon, to spread out his awareness as he had done before.

"Wolfram duRhys!" a voice shouted from the stairs, and Wolfram popped his eye open, scrambling to his feet.

Two guards came for him, one of them waiting outside the cell with an armed crossbow while the other entered with the key and freed his ankle.

He met the guard's eye and saw coldness there as the man jerked him forward. Together with two newcomers, they brought him up the long flight of stairs into the hall above. Wolfram's feet stung as he walked the feeling back into them. The presence of the bear claw beneath his shirt reassured him, as if he had not lost it all.

They turned not for the audience chamber he'd been in before, but for the main court hall. Guards stood at attention outside and in, along the path toward the dais where Queen Brianna sat, her eyes sunken, lips drawn tight.

When they reached the open space of floor before her, the two guards shoved him to his knees. One of them bent to unlock his left wrist, and Wolfram smiled at this unexpected reprieve.

Grinning in return, the guard jerked his arm behind him, and locked them again, this time adding a short chain that bound his hands to the shackle still at his ankle.

Effectively hog-tied, Wolfram bowed his head before his mother, then looked up, searching for her gaze.

Brianna gazed somewhere just over his head. "Bailiff, read the charges."

Stepping forward, the bailiff spread out a scroll and began to read, "The accused, Wolfram yfBrianna duRhys of the house of Rinvien, crown prince of the sovereign kingdom of Lochalyn, stands accused—" At this, Wolfram let out a short laugh, his shoulders drawn back by the chain which held him down—"of the following crimes: perjury, kidnapping, criminal endangerment, reckless conduct, conduct unbefitting the crown, flight in an attempt to avoid justice, assault, assault upon a royal woman, assault upon a member of a religious order, assault upon a guest of the crown, assault upon an officer of the crown, unlawful entry, attempted kidnapping, rape, rape of a royal woman, rape of a guest of the crown, rape of a member of a religious order. So read the charges of the crown." He gave a short bow and withdrew to his place.

On his knees, Wolfram swayed. The blood rushed out of him, leaving him cold and shaky. After a moment of gasping, he finally drew breath.

A single charge of rape could get him branded, marked for the crime, aside from a sentence of years. But the additional charges, especially that the victim was royal, and religious—could get him hanged. With the weight of all the other counts, the queen could elect summary judgment and call for his execution within the hour.

The small group of nobles allowed to witness the hearing buzzed with dismay.

"How pleads the defendant?" His mother's voice had never sounded more regal, or more distant.

"Innocent," he breathed, looking up. "I am innocent."

She swept her imperious gaze back to the bailiff. "Proceed with the witnesses."

One by one, they called the guards who had caught him last night. They described the madness in his run, the blood on his clothes—the clothes he yet wore—and on the girl he had carried. Gwythym gave his testimony as well, including the threats against Faedre, and all with a sort of coldness Wolfram had never seen before.

Last night, these men had been his unwitting saviors, the defense he sought against Faedre's people simply slitting his throat. Now, they stood ranged against him, their faces showing their contempt.

"Lyssa yfSonya DuNormand, Mistress of the Family Chapel, and member of the Order of the Sisters of the Sword," the herald intoned.

Tall and powerful, Lyssa rose from her bench and stepped forward. "Present."

"Mistress Lyssa," the queen said, "you have previously told us about your journey to and in Hemijrai, and your return from that country. I would ask only a few questions for the record."

"Yes, Your Majesty." She held her wrist behind her, shoulders straight—unknowingly mimicking the posture enforced by Wolfram's chains.

"On the day of your landing at Freeport, were you invited by the Hemijrani delegation to join them in returning here?"

"Yes, Your Majesty."

"Did the prince agree to that course?"

Lyssa hesitated, glancing again at Wolfram. "No, Your Majesty."

"Why not?"

"He believed that the delegation were dishonest in their dealings, that they wished to keep him against his will. He had heard them plotting about keeping him."

"Please tell us what happened that morning on the ship."

"Goddess's Tears," Lyssa murmured, bowing her head for a moment. "He, the prince, snatched Faedre's acolyte, a girl called Deishima. He had a boar knife from the Woodmen, which he held to her throat, threatening to—threatening harm if they didn't let us go." She faltered, then said, turning toward the audience, "I went along with it. I helped to carry the girl off. There had been some signs that he might be right."

"Was any attempt made to stop you?"

"I thought some of the men looked suspicious."

The queen narrowed her eyes. "Mistress, was any attempt made?"

"No, Your Majesty. We got off with no trouble." Lyssa hung her head. "When we reached the gate, Wolfram wanted to let her go, but I was the one who said we should take her. If he was right, then she might be able to tell us what was going on."

"Thank you, Mistress, that's all for the moment."

Lyssa bounded before the queen, "But I'm responsible, too. I helped him get her off the boat; we wouldn't be here, now, if it weren't for me!"

Taken aback, the queen put out her hand. "I commend your loyalty, Lyssa, but answer me this, did you hold a knife to that girl's throat?"

Lyssa deflated. "No, Your Majesty."

"Then I'll ask you to step aside."

Turning away, Lyssa met Wolfram's gaze, and tears shone in her eyes. "What can I say, Wolfram?" she asked in a whisper.

He shook his head. As he had listened, the astonishment began to wear off, and he could see the way Faedre would try to get rid of him.

"Lady Faedre DalRakesh, chief priestess of Hemijrai," the herald summoned her.

Wolfram turned back to see her approaching up the aisle. Tight beside her limped Deishima, and Wolfram's blood ran cold.

Dressed in fresh wrappings of silk, Deishima walked with her face unveiled. Darkness blackened her eyes and blood trickled from scrapes on her forehead and cheek. Blood seeped between her cracked lips as if she tried to speak. Beneath her dark skin bruises showed at her throat.

Faedre held one of Deishima's hands, supporting her beneath her shawl with her other arm as the two slowly progressed between the rows of onlookers. Men turned pale and women looked away, tugging out their kerchiefs.

As they approached Wolfram, Deishima's head dropped to Faedre's side, her entire body racked with sobs.

"I should have left you," Wolfram mumbled as they passed. "I should have left you. Oh, Sweet Lady, Finistrel forgive me."

His last words slipped into the silence of the room like assassins, and he could not call them back.

"Pardon me, Majesty," said Faedre, turning them both to face the room. "Pardon this dramatic entrance. I have unbound her wounds, and revealed her face lest you should not be aware of what this monster has wrought upon an innocent child."

In Wolfram's head, the demon roared. "What have you done?" he cried. "You bitch, you might have killed her. She's done nothing to you, nothing! How could you do this?" Tears streamed down his face, his throat burned. He could not turn from Deishima's battered face.

"What have I done?" Faedre asked, blinking back tears of her own. "You, Highness, you crept to her room in the dead of night, taking her in your arms—can you deny it?" She buried her face in Deishima's straggling hair, hugging the girl closer.

For an instant from his perspective, Wolfram saw the way her other hand, hidden by the shawl, gripped Deishima's wrist with brutal strength. He strained at the chains, twisting his arms, while an inhuman growl issued from his clenched teeth.

"You see what he is like, Your Majesty, we are only seeking justice."

On her throne, Queen Brianna looked faint. The dutiful Lady Catherine had covered her face, and even the bailiff had grown pale at the sight of Deishima.

"You beat her." Wolfram yelled. "After they took me. You'd already hit her, and you threw her against the wall. If I had one hand free, I'd tear out your heart."

The guards stepped closer, and the herald banged his staff for order.

From the throne, his mother's voice came as a hiss, "And you claim innocence."

"I have never touched her in anger, never!"

"Even when you took her with a knife at her throat?"

He faced his mother, desperation warring with fury in equal measure. "Can't you see what they've done? They want me dead. They have to know you'll never hear me."

"You expect me to believe"—she said, rising to her feet—"that they beat their own princess? That they did that to her just to get at you? Look at her, Wolfram! She can't even speak, she can barely stand."

Clamping shut his eye, Wolfram lowered his head, his chest heaving with anger and tears, his head pounding with a wild thunder he had not heard since the night he'd left. And he could do nothing.

"Strelana has seen her, Wolfram," the queen continued, barely controlling her own fury. "Do you know what that means? What has happened to this girl is unspeakable, do you hear me?"

Wolfram strained until the cuffs tore at his skin and howled his helplessness. The guard grabbed his shoulder before he collapsed, holding him with an iron grip.

He pulled up his head and twisted to look at Deishima through the veil of tears. "I'm sorry," he said. "I am so sorry." Every word sounded his death knell, but he knew now that it didn't matter. They would have slain him in the night, but this moment handed them victory more surely than his murder could ever do. They would have his head, and have his own mother for their executioner. "By all that's holy, Deishima, I wish I'd never gone to you. I am so sorry."

Despite the clutch of Faedre's hands, Deishima turned her head a little, and gazed down at him from her wounded eyes. Almost imperceptibly, she shook her head, just once. She shifted her eyes down.

Between her fingers, she held a lock of hair, stroking it with her thumb.

Her eyes pleaded, even as her lips could not, and he heard the message as if she whispered in his ear. She did not regret his coming. She did not regret that he had held her in his arms, that he had come into her garden and stroked her hair. Even as she stood before him, beaten and defiled, Deishima forgave him.

He would die tomorrow, or today, and she within the week, at the hands of her teachers, her tormentors. If the Lady had a care for the condemned, She would leave him the memory of Deishima's hair to warm him as he rotted in the cold, cold ground.

Chapter 42

BARELY KEEPING herself to a walk, Lyssa fled the courtroom. She had watched Wolfram go from a confident prince to a broken prisoner and could bear no more. Whatever Brianna decided to do, Wolfram's evident confession would bury him more readily than any further testimony they might hear. Unless she found Dawsiir, or someone else willing to support Wolfram's claims. The more she watched, the more she became convinced that Faedre was lying, at best, and may in fact have beaten her own acolyte to discredit Wolfram. She did not know what Brianna might be thinking—surely the sight of the battered girl had put to rest any doubts the nobles might have had. But Brianna would wait until Fionvar's return, whenever he could be found. Given good weather and a willing horse, the ride to the manor could be made in four days. He'd had a day's start on their messenger already. Lyssa found herself praying for rain, anything to slow him down and bring him home.

In the meantime, she knew her charge: to find Dawsiir, the only independent witness Wolfram might have. The Hemijrani had no reason to help her, or to allow her anywhere near their camp. Acting too rashly would probably get the man killed. She needed a plan, and quickly.

Suddenly she wondered what Wolfram would do. No matter the straits he found himself in, he always seemed to find a way, whether that meant using the privy to gain access to the guest quarters or deliberately bringing on the guard to get himself back out again. Then she grinned, remembering one of his other solutions.

Swinging by her chambers to change, Lyssa felt a sort of fevered energy overtaking her. It had been a long time since she had gone into battle, and, though this was a game of wits more than swords, she welcomed it. Finding one of her best bodices, and a fighting skirt she could strip down to her leggings with a stroke, she dressed. Over the top, she slung her belt, with the sword at one hip, the hammer at the other. Finally, she donned a ceremonial sash with the arms of the queen.

The Hemijrani camp bustled with cooking, washing, and a row of tents with the acrid smoke of their smiths at work. They made charcoal fires in shallow pits and pumped small bellows with their toes while they hammered out whatever was needed. For the first time, Lyssa paused here and watched one of them at work on a long knife. The next man, too, had a knife, and Lyssa's senses went on alert. In the seven months they had been living here, they could have amassed a stockpile of such weapons. Nothing so conspicuous as swords, at least, not by day. City guards patrolled the tents, but had no cause to scrutinize what they saw.

Lyssa laughed at herself. How had she gone so quickly from a doubter to a believer, seeking the proof of Wolfram's suspicions? She spotted a pair of guardsmen strolling up the aisle toward her and walked more quickly.

"You, there, Ulric is it?" she called out.

The two men joined her, bowing briefly. "Aye, Mistress, what's on?"

"Queen's business," she said shortly, for it was near enough the truth. "I may have need of you."

"We're with you, Mistress." They shared a look and a smile, hoping for some relief to the tedium of the watch.

"Right, then. We're looking for the man in charge."

Ulric replied, "That'll be Ghiva, little chap with naked feet."

Lyssa rolled her eyes as another short Hemijrani passed, his feet as bare as all the rest. "Any idea where to find him?"

"Come on." He led the way between the vivid tents to a large open area ringed by cook fires. At one end a pile of dirty stones had been arranged into a sort of tower about as tall as Lyssa herself. Bits of feathers and fur surrounded it, and she frowned.

"It's a shrine, I think," Ulric explained. "Offerings and what?"

She stared at it. Something about the structure disturbed her. Probably it was the idea of this heathen shrine so close to their own temple. She shrugged off the feeling and pivoted to study the tents all around.

After a moment, one of the small men emerged from a tent and hurried forward. He bowed over his hands immediately and smiled his gold-toothed smile. "I am at your service, sirs, and lady."

"Ghiva?" she asked.

The little man bowed again. "Indeed. You are perhaps needing a translator? There are few enough of us who have been able to learn your speech."

Lyssa cut him off. "I'm looking for someone." She crossed her arms, mustering some of the anger that had driven her from court. "You know of the break-in at your ambassadors' chambers and the resulting trial."

"Yes, indeed." He lost his grin. "What a terrible thing to have occurred, and yet upon the eve of our ceremony and subsequent departure."

Nodding her agreement, Lyssa said a silent prayer for the Lady to guide what happened next. "I am Mistress Lyssa, one of the queen's close advisors. There was a man whom the defendant knew in Hemijrai, a groom, I met him on one occasion." To let them know she would recognize the man. "We have reason to believe that the prince gave this man a writ of free passage." With a quick, stern look to the guardsmen, she plunged on, "You are probably not aware that the prince has no authority to provide such a writ. If it's true that this man has one, that's another charge against the prince and may influence his eventual sentencing."

Though they squirmed a little at the lie, Ulric and his companion had read her look well enough to hold their tongues.

"I see, yes, Mistress." Ghiva nodded vigorously.

"It is vital that I see this man, Dawsiir, and ascertain if he received such a writ. I will, of course, require your translation."

Tilting his head to one side, Ghiva considered, squinting against the sun.

Lyssa held her breath. Would he take the opportunity to pile another charge against the prince? If Wolfram was right, they would do all they could to stop him.

After a moment, Ghiva said, "I believe that I would know the man you are seeking. He has unfortunately been injured and may be unable to provide the information you require, Mistress."

Though her heart fell, Lyssa held her expression. "Has he been searched? Do you know if he possessed a writ?"

The man's face twitched, and he brought his hands together. "I do not know of this, Mistress."

"Then perhaps you can take us to see him and find out?" She planted her hands on her hips, in easy reach of the weapons that hung there.

Ghiva's eyes flicked to the sword and back to her face, his gaze suddenly more alert, shrewdness crinkling his brow. "You will permit me, Mistress, to determine first if he is even well enough to be receiving visitors."

"Lead on," she said. "The queen will be pleased by your eagerness to assist."

Bowing again, he walked before them. As he did, Lyssa watched the way he stepped, almost too lightly, with a wiry bounce to his stride. The markings on his painted feet were those of a priest, but his walk was that of a soldier. He possessed an economy of movement and a well-schooled grace that betrayed him. As he gestured for them to wait outside a tent, she noted the bulge of his muscular arm.

Lyssa's smile grew. Once you knew to look, the evidence supporting Wolfram's case was all around.

"What are we about, Mistress, if you don't mind saying?" Ulric muttered.

"Finding a witness, and taking him to the castle. By force, if necessary."

They nodded their understanding as Ghiva held back the curtain.

"Perhaps," he began, with a flash of his golden teeth, "your men might wait outside as the space is rather small."

Lyssa met Ulric's eye and raised her eyebrow.

"Aye, Mistress, we'll be waiting," he told her, with a wink.

As they ducked inside, Ghiva said, "After these several months among your people, still I have some difficulty in accepting women outside of their place, if you will forgive me, and I am hoping this difficulty is not revealed for you, Mistress."

She paused, shaking her head. "No, I haven't noticed."

"You are a woman, and yet also a warrior are you not?" Ghiva let the flap fall behind them. "As a man of the spiritual as well as of peace, I am sure you can see my difficulty, Mistress, and so I ask that you would forgive my reluctance with you."

"Think nothing of it," she said. "Which way?"

She had to duck as she followed him down a narrow path between rows of cots. Their occupants groaned or whimpered, with bandages and herbs obscuring them. All were men, as were their attendants.

Ghiva bowed his head, and said, "We were somewhat unprepared for your winter here, and many of us have developed the fever, or have passed from the world as a result, Mistress. Even we are unable to find the plants that we would use to heal them."

"I am sorry to hear that," she told him.

With one of those powerful arms, he indicated the last in the row of beds.

Dawsiir lay with his head bandaged, his eyes glassy with fever. As they crouched beside him, he turned a little, frowning at Lyssa and mumbling something.

"You can see that he is not a well man, Mistress."

Nodding, Lyssa felt a shiver of doubt. The man looked feeble, on the verge of death or madness. "Ask him about the writ."

Ghiva made an inquiry in Hemijrani, with Lyssa paying close attention. She did not get it all, but caught the terms for royalty, and parchment. So far, the soldier-in-disguise was fulfilling her request.

Again, Dawsiir frowned at her and muttered something unintelligible.

Meeting his fevered gaze, Lyssa nodded slightly, unsure how to reassure him that he was helping Wolfram, not betraying him.

Ghiva spoke again, with an angry tone, and Dawsiir swallowed and shut his eyes.

Then the sheet rippled slightly as his hand moved. From beneath his body, he edged a stained and crumpled page.

Immediately, Lyssa snatched it up. Wolfram's hurried letters filled the sheet. For a moment, Lyssa studied it, considering whether to go through with her plan given Dawsiir's sorry state.

"Is it indeed what you seek in evidence?" Ghiva asked, his smile sharp and expectant.

She slipped the parchment under her belt. "Indeed, Ghiva, I've found just what I was looking for," she replied, then, bending over as if to thank Dawsiir, she slid an arm under him and pulled him up over her shoulder.

"Mistress! This man is very ill! He should not be moved, please," Ghiva said, then added something in Hemijrani.

Drawing her sword, Lyssa turned to the aisle and saw the attendants down the row bounding over the cots toward her.

She feinted right, slicing toward Ghiva's throat. He easily ducked and dove away from the backhand.

With the way cleared, Lyssa lunged forward, her blade ripping through the fabric. "Ulric! Guards!" she yelled, shoving through the opening.

They ran up heavily in their mail, swords drawn.

"Back to the castle!" She ran, Dawsiir clinging to her belt, all the way in, pounding up the stairs to the infirmary with her guard at her back.

Once inside, she lowered her captive onto an open bed as the healers hurried over. "Who's this? What is his wound?"

"His name's Dawsiir, and I trust you to do all that you can." She grinned her triumph.

"As well we must, Mistress," the healer replied. "For he'll be lucky to last out the night, as hot as he is."

Lyssa stared down at Dawsiir's closed eyes and sweaty brightness. "Oh, Goddess's Tears, he has to live!"

Another healer approached with a basin of water and shooed her out of the way. "We'll save him, Lady willing, but how long's he been like this?"

"I don't know." She counted back in her mind. "Perhaps a week, no, longer."

"No telling, then," he grunted, starting to strip the grubby bandage. "Even if he lives, he may never recover."

The energy fell from her as Lyssa knelt beside the still form. "Dawsiir," she whispered, then, in Hemijrani, "Do you hear me?"

He made no sign.

Dropping her head, Lyssa fought back her defeat. She pulled the parchment from her belt and curved his hand around it. "You've got to live, Dawsiir, Wolfram's life may depend on you."

One of the healers cleared his throat. "Mistress, we need space."

Reluctantly she rose and stepped back. Wolfram's best hope lay in that bed and might never rise from it again. She could do no more good here. Despair welled up in her, and she sheathed her sword at last.

Chapter 43

LEANING BACK against the altar in the tiny chapel, Fionvar stared at the round wall before him. He had come here with Brianna when the manor had hosted Duchess Elyn's court-in-exile, and with King Rhys in his early days. Over the years since then, he had cleared the vines that had obscured the door and the opening above the altar. He had reset some of the stones in the floor to make for more even footing, then began the tricky work of Strelledor translation. On the wall all around him, the last priestess of this place had written her visions and ramblings in the sacred language of the Lady. Some of her words were barely scratched, others gouged into the stone, making it hard to follow the thoughts. Times when Fionvar needed to get away, he came here. The Sisters of the Sword, his own sister's order, allowed him to come, provided he did not enter the manor that was their academy and their convent. Last night, he had slept in the Cave of Life and had the best night's sleep he'd had since Wolfram left. Or perhaps even before that.

Now, dawn touched the carved words that snaked over the wall. Sunlight gleamed on the handles of axes and the hilts of swords protruding between the stones. If one of the Sisters left the order, she left her weapon as well.

The translation was done, except for some fine-tuning, and he had given the work to the Sisters of the Sword as payment for their permission. Still, Fionvar loved the solitude and let his mind wander over the words before him.

Some of her predictions were clear, though often only in hindsight, while others made no sense to him, no matter how he poured through religious texts. The words that occupied him today were one of those passages.

"Ware the dark sun," she had written, *"for it falls upon the Lady's altar. A woman stands calling the darkness. An army she calls to bury a crown. Praise the dark son! The skin burns, the voice drowned, the heart burst. O, hear me true! The Blessed one is fallen as it should be. O hear me true, there is but one, not two."*

The words nagged at him, as he began to glimpse their meaning. "But one, not two"—a reference to this religion of the Hemijrai, of course. "The blessed one" was Alyn, who saw the Lady's visions, but why should his falling be "as it should be"?

Then he was faced with the curious echo words—the dark sun, the dark son. If he had not translated the passage himself, he would have suspected a simple misspelling, a clerical error in two phrases meant to be the same. "Ware the dark sun, praise the dark son."

Rolling it over in his mind, he thought of Wolfram, and Alyn's childhood prophecy that the sun would go dark. Fionvar glowered, trying to concentrate. He had come here for peace, to leave behind the mess in the castle and puzzle over a different mystery. Instead, the two mysteries bound together, and he cursed himself for not noticing the similarity before. Fionvar traced the wandering letters. "The dark son," could be Wolfram. The blessed one's fall, Alyn's fall, if he were right. He suddenly wondered if Alyn's childhood vision foretold not Wolfram's evil nature, but Alyn's own danger—that Wolfram would be present at his own fall. The woman calling—Faedre?—calling an army to bury a crown. The passage had no sense of time—it could refer to now, or years from now. A chill blew through him, and he touched the words again.

The next instant, he scrambled to his feet.

He had done the translation himself. What if she meant not skin, but pelt? Not man, but animal. How could she know? What did it matter, for the certainty overcame him. "The voice drowned." It was Wolfram, it had to be, and Fionvar hadn't listened.

Quickly, he gathered his few things into a bundle and climbed out of the chapel to find his horse. He cut the hobble and strapped on his bundle. Even as he mounted, he heard another horse approaching fast.

On a mount wheezing with exhaustion, a royal messenger galloped up. "My lord Fionvar!"

"Here, is it the army?" Fionvar demanded.

Confused, the man shook his head. "It's the prince. On trial for rape."

Stiffening his back, Fionvar stared. He recalled Wolfram holding the reins. *"I'm about to do something reckless and rash,"* he had said. *"It might get me killed."* Fionvar mounted his horse. Anger swamped the urgency he'd felt just a moment before. "Bury it, what did he do?"

"Broke into the guest quarters, m'lord, and went for the girl." The messenger circled his exhausted mount, himself drooping with weariness.

"Deishima? But he loves her."

With a weak smile, the man replied, "Not from what I hear— her blood was on his clothes. Queen's asked for you."

Bile rose in Fionvar's throat, and he dropped the reins, lowering his head. Perhaps all the evil of Alyn's prophecy was about to come true. "Sweet Lady, couldn't he even run away and let her out of the decision to hang him?"

He wasn't sure he had spoken aloud until the man replied, "He did run, straight to our own guards with the girl on his shoulder. Right gleeful he was, I hear."

"It doesn't make sense," Fionvar muttered. He recalled the scene in his office.

"Back then," Wolfram had said, *"I still had the option of running away."*

"Don't you still?" Fionvar had asked.

"Not if I am ever to be worthy of the crown."

After sneaking in, Wolfram ran to the castle guards? He wasn't insane. He was convinced Deishima had been kidnapped. For a moment, Fionvar let himself believe that his son was right. If that were the case, Wolfram was no rapist, he was a rescuer. That day, he'd come to warn Fionvar that he might be caught, that he might be shamed more even than he had been. He had come to try to save Fionvar that shame upon himself.

Fionvar caught up the reins. "Has the queen passed judgment?"

"She'll wait the week," the man returned, then added, "that was four days ago."

"Goddess's Tears!" Fionvar bent low and kicked his horse to a run. He had three days to make a four-day ride, and he could not afford to be late.

TRAPPED AGAIN in darkness, Wolfram lay on his belly on the floor, his head as close to the grate as he could get.

"The trouble is, Wolfram," Lyssa was saying, "I'm the only translator we've got, that we can trust, that is. And you all know I'm no good. Half the time he isn't even coherent. I think Ghiva's no priest, but that's not proof, and those blacksmiths haven't made so much as a bloody fishhook in four days."

His chin propped on his fist, Wolfram stared. In the weak light, he could make out her form, but little else. Still, with the weariness in her voice, he didn't need to see her face. "Then I'm sunk." He sighed. Since that day in the courtroom, he had struggled with despair. He shut his eye and saw Deishima's battered face. The queen had allowed him the full fortnight, but it could do him little good in the dungeon. Only two days remained before the Hemijrani ceremony, and he had no way out. His wrists, still sore, were bandaged beneath the manacles, but he had his bear claw. At the worst, he controlled the time of his own death. If he could learn when the hour was upon her, he could die at the same time. How poignant. He laughed without humor.

"What is it?" Lyssa, his only visitor, sat on her side of the grate, seeming naked without the sword and hammer the guards were holding for her.

"I'm going to die in the darkness," he murmured. "I came so far, Lyssa. So far you wouldn't believe it"—another laugh, for who ever believed him?—"to die in a dungeon for a crime I did not commit."

"You won't die." She kicked the grate. "Bury it, Wolfram, don't talk like that."

He sat up, not bothering to dust himself off. "How should I talk? Like I'll be pardoned? Like someone will come forward to defend me? Two days, Lyssa—in two days, everyone will know I'm right, and it won't matter anymore."

"Look at it this way," she snapped. "If you're right, then the Hemijrani will be in charge, and there won't be any point in killing you."

"Won't there?" He pulled the chain taut between his hands. "If I live, then this is all the freedom I will ever have."

Lyssa hung her head. "Maybe it's time to start praying," she said.

Running the links between his fingers, Wolfram didn't answer. After a while, he heard her go, her steps sounding hollow in the darkness. His eye ached, but he had stopped crying. After the first two nights, he had even stopped raging, earning him the gratitude of the other prisoners. He couldn't breathe properly, for the darkness stifled him until he thought he might choke on it. Somewhere far above him, Deishima lay in her own darkness. There was none to save her but him, and he had finally run out of ideas.

Every day, Lyssa visited, telling him things that he already knew. Every day she left him feeling a little more defeated, rolling it over in his mind, finding no way out. Since she had seen Deishima's face, his mother wouldn't even read his petitions. Some days, the guards pushed his porridge bowl in just out of reach, and laughed at him for hours. Although he had been stripped of rank and title, they dared not touch him, not yet. But in two days, the queen's justice wouldn't mean a thing. Wolfram knew it, and so did they.

Through his thin shirt, Wolfram touched the bear claw. If it could pick the locks, or smuggle him up the stairs, or—what? But even if he could escape the dungeon, what then? He wouldn't get within a mile of Faedre's rooms again, or even the temple where they would hold their bloody ritual. Unless he could fly, he was no good to anyone.

He played the chain links over his fingers, then froze, and started to smile.

Dropping the chain, he scrambled closer to the grate. "You, there! Guard!"

"I'm busy," the man shouted back, earning the laughter of his mates.

"I need to see the captain!"

The man plucked a card from his hand and slid it onto the table. "Cap's got better things to do, hasn't he?"

"I think he'll see me," Wolfram persisted, some of the old fire returning. "I think he'll be madder than a snake if you don't tell him I've asked."

The men snorted to each other and went on with their game.

"I don't have time for this," Wolfram muttered. He prowled to the back of his cell where the stench was strongest, and picked up a handful of muck. Approaching the grate, he took careful aim, and threw the handful. It passed the bars, but struck harmlessly some yards to the left of the table.

The guards laughed uproariously. "One-eyed rapist pitching shit!" the leader called over.

Roused, the demon dug in its claws, and Wolfram gave a nasty grin, going back for two more handfuls. The next one struck a little short.

The guards laughed again, but one of them glowered at Wolfram over his cards.

Gauging his aim and compensating for the missing eye, Wolfram threw again.

Splat! The gob hit the leader's shoulder, spattering his face and cards. He surged up, drawing his sword. "You little bastard!" He wiped the stuff off as he charged.

Quickly, Wolfram threw another.

Ducking, the guard slipped and went down. Suddenly, from across the way, another blob flew through the air, hitting the table.

Hemijrani voices cheered from their own darkness. Shit flew through the air from all directions.

"You lot calm down!" one of the guards roared.

"I want to see the captain, now!" Wolfram yelled back.

"Captain! Captain!" the other prisoners began to chant, glad of some distraction.

Running with his arms over his head, one man made for the stairs, while another snatched up the bucket of cold water kept handy. He trotted up and flung it through the bars of Wolfram's grate.

Stung by the cold, Wolfram yelped. Then, with the demon pounding inside his head, he called, "Thanks for the bath!" and got back in the game.

By the time Gwythym appeared, the remaining guards had taken cover on the stairs, shouting their threats and insults.

"Watch out, Captain! He's armed!" the leader shouted.

Wolfram got to his feet. "Leave him be!" he called to his backers.

A few more stink bombs flew halfheartedly, but they settled down at Gwythym's shout, "You want to be flogged or fed, it's your choice!"

Glaring, Gwythym came up to the grate. "Inciting a riot, eh? Can't you just leave well enough alone?"

"I need to see Dylan," Wolfram said urgently.

Gwythym smacked his forehead. "Oh, for pity's sake! Queen asked for him to test the truth at your trial, but she let me keep him back—keep him as far from you as may be. And who needs testimony, with that girl before them?"

"Please, Captain." He knelt so his face would not be in shadow. "I'm a dead man, you know that."

"Aye, for what you've done, you will be." His jaw clenched on the words.

Wiping his hands on his knees, Wolfram said, "This I did not do."

"If it weren't this, it'd be something else, don't you think?"

The unaccustomed sarcasm made Wolfram flinch, and he narrowed his eyes. "You know, don't you?" he asked softly.

Gwythym crouched down to meet his eye. "Aye, that I do. And if you think I'd let my son anywhere near you, then you're mad as well as doomed."

"He's your son, but he's not a child. Tell him we've spoken and let him decide."

"Bah!" Straightening, Gwythym crossed his arms. "If I hear you've been at this again"—he waved a hand to the soiled chamber—"I'll beat the shit back into you, hear me?" He turned on his heel and left, barking orders for the place to be cleaned, and any further incident severely punished.

Wolfram sank back on his heels, the fury leaving him empty and shaky as it always had. Pray, Lyssa had suggested. He prayed that it would be enough. But the hours wore on in darkness, and the guards didn't even bother with his porridge, and even that prayer grew hopeless.

Chapter 44

CRAMPED AND shivering, Wolfram roused to a sound outside the grate.

Clearing his throat again, Dylan shifted nervously from foot to foot. He wore clean, long robes and stood well back. Over his shoulder, the figure of his father loomed.

"Dylan!" Wolfram cried, relief flooding through him, nearly bringing him to tears. "Thank the Lady you've come."

"Somewhat against my will," Dylan pointed out. "What do you want?"

"Please, Dylan, I need to talk to you. Can you come closer?"

His eyes flaring, Dylan stepped back.

Wolfram held up his hands. "You're safe. I haven't been fed all day, and I'm fresh out of shit."

"You?" Dylan cackled. "Never!"

"Please," Wolfram said softly. "Your father doesn't need to hear everything."

Gwythym grumbled something, but Dylan, after a glance back,

came up and put one hand on the grate. "Are you threatening me?" His pale face looked even more anxious than last time they'd met.

"I'm out of options, Dylan, this is the only way I could get you to hear me."

"I'm not afraid," Dylan returned. "Who'd listen to you anyway? Look at you."

Nodding, Wolfram said, "I know all that. But I do have proof, kept in a safe place." He held up his arms so the chain crossed his throat, his face still and serious.

Gripping the bars, Dylan blanched.

"I don't want to threaten you, Dylan. I don't want to reveal you, and I don't know if it would matter if I did, but I need you." He emphasized the last few words.

"After what you've done, how could I possibly help?" Revulsion twisted his lips.

"Listen closely. I did not rape her, I did not beat her," Wolfram said, noticing the other's flinch at the mention of the word. "Dylan, I love her."

Dylan gave a queer laugh. "That's an odd sign of affection, I think."

Inwardly, Wolfram cursed. "You were ready to kill me for the woman you love, ready to try, anyhow, am I right?"

A glance over his shoulder and a quick nod.

"Would you ever hurt her, or force yourself on her?"

"Of course not!" The blood rose in Dylan's face.

"I love Deishima, and I would kill for her, but I swear by this scar around my throat, Dylan, I would never hurt her, do you hear me?"

Slowly, Dylan nodded. "But if you didn't . . . ?"

"Then her own people did." Wolfram let this idea sink in a minute, then said, "They'll kill her, Dylan, as part of this ceremony, and I'm the only one who can save her."

"Do you think if I told about Asenith and the tiger spell, they'd reopen your trial?"

"I'm not sure she'd back you; and they would all think I'd got you on my side."

Solemnly, Dylan sank to his knees, his face close to the bars. "What do you need, Wolfram? What can I do?"

"I think you can get me out of here."

Already, Dylan was shaking his head. "There's no escape from this place, Wolfram, everything's been tried—they even searched me at the door."

"Did I say escape? The day of the ceremony, that's the day you find out if your calculations are correct, yes?"

An eager nod. "If I'm right—"

"If you're right, the sun and the moon will come together in the sky."

Dylan's eyes widened. "Yes."

"So here it is. That's the biggest day of your life, Dylan, and I am—or at least, I was—your best friend. I'll probably be hanged the day after that, one way or another."

Looking away, Dylan sighed. "I'm sorry, Wolfram. Sweet Finistrel, if I could undo everything these last six months . . ."

Wolfram shut his eye, refusing the tears that filled it. "It means a lot to me, that you would say that."

"Tell me the plan, Wolfram, and I'll do what I can."

WHEN FIONVAR'S horse dropped beneath him, he barely escaped a broken leg of his own. He left the poor beast in a farmer's field and paid far too much for a new one to get him the last few miles. He had not slept in three days, had only allowed himself brief rests. His legs and his chest ached and just about everything in between, but he'd made it on the day of the Hemijrani ritual. There would still be time, there must be.

Outside the temple wall, a horde of refugees milled about, with little knots of city guards lurking around them. Fionvar paused a moment to stare at them. They wore rags and traveling clothes, but most were young and uninjured. How could there be so many? Wolfram's phantom army had indeed materialized, and he knew the queen had no force to match it.

In the bailey, he swung himself down and staggered as the

groom led away his horse. "Are you well, m'lord?" one of the men called out, but Fionvar shook him off.

"I need to see the queen," he panted.

"Aye, m'lord, she's been waiting on you."

Taking the steps two at a time, Fionvar ran as best he could, skidding toward the queen's court only to find it empty. "Where is everyone?"

"Queen's garden," a maid replied, with a curtsy. "One of them wildmen came, but wouldna set foot indoors. Was't even a man? I'm not sure, my lord."

Not a man? Fionvar frowned. "Maybe a man with a stag's head?"

Making the sign of the Lady, the maid nodded. "Met him in the garden, they did."

So Quinan had come here. Fionvar didn't have time to muse about that, he'd find out soon enough. Chest heaving, he ran as far as the queen's quarters and burst in unannounced.

A small gathering stood in the sunlight, facing a strange figure: Quinan in his shaman's robe, with the antlers still topping his head, shook a long stick covered with the beaks of birds and claws of owl. At Fionvar's appearance, the Woodman fell silent.

The others turned to him, and Fionvar made a tiny bow, brought up short by the pain. He gritted his teeth, and said, "Sorry, ridden all day."

"Get him a drink," the queen said, gathering her skirts and coming toward him, but she stopped a few paces shy, her expression concerned yet wary.

"I've been to the manor," he gasped, but she shook her head and put out a hand.

"Rest a moment, Fionvar, we're not going anywhere."

Shaky with exhaustion, Fionvar dropped onto one of the benches. Lady Catherine pressed a mug of water into his hands, drawn up from the little well at the garden's center. Taking a long swallow, Fionvar tried to relax, listening to their talk.

"Dark people build house of dirt," Quinan said. "Many house. You give those woods for my people. Why this?" He shook the stick so the beaks rattled together.

"I am sorry," Brianna told him. "We didn't know they were building. They went to the woods as we do, to hunt or find herbs."

"Not so!" He stamped, the beaks clattering like a flock of angry crows.

"They're going soon," she said, frowning, her own fatigue showing at the corners of her eyes. "This is their last day here, then they are all of them going away."

"I don't think so," Fionvar said.

Annoyed at the interruption, Brianna glowered.

"There are too many of them, all waiting outside the temple." His breathing was still ragged, but his throat no longer burned. "I've been studying the woods chapel again, Your Majesty, the prophecy warns of a day the sun goes dark, and a woman will call forth an army. I believe that day is upon us."

"Now you bring me prophecy as proof, Fionvar?" Her lips trembled, her eyes close to tears. "What shall I do with that? Alyn told us he was evil—my son went dark a long time ago."

"What if Alyn saw his own fall—not Wolfram's evil at all! Evil comes not because of our son, but because Alyn didn't heed the warning. Bury your proof, Brianna, where is your heart?" He thumped his own aching chest and rose. For a moment, they two were the only people in that garden.

"My heart has been betrayed too many times of late." One of the tears slid down her cheek. "If you had seen her, Fion, if you had seen what he did."

"Then where is she? I'll see for myself."

"In the temple, I suppose, with the others."

He caught her shoulders. "They've already begun?"

"Fion, you're hurting me."

A man of her personal guard came up beside her, his hand on the hilt of his sword, searching Fionvar's face.

Releasing the queen, Fionvar stepped back. "I believe he loves that girl, Brianna. Do you know where they were when he asked her?"

Numbly, wiping away the tears, she shook her head.

"The Grove of the Heart's Desire. Not that it wouldn't be the first time such vows have been forsaken." He wished he could take back the words, but they had gone.

"You don't know everything that's happened, Fionvar. You weren't there."

"Then I was a fool to leave him," Fionvar said. "It won't happen again."

"He is lost to me, Fionvar; he has done that to himself." She swallowed, and added, "And so have you."

A pain stabbed at his chest, and Fionvar's head shot up. "He's in the dungeon?"

Lady Catherine, with a glance at her mistress, nodded.

Fionvar strode for the door. He turned on the path and faced Quinan. "I will smoke with you. Before this day is out, Wolfram will prove worthy of his name."

Across the well, Quinan stared, his eyes overshadowed by the stag's antlers. He let out a small cry and lowered his staff. "No, friend. I think I will not smoke with you."

A retort formed on Fionvar's lips, but he saw some terrible sadness in the Woodman's rough features, and he held back. To Brianna he said, "What about Lyssa?"

The queen turned away, and Lady Catherine was left to reply, "She's been with him, my lord. Last I saw, she went to the infirmary; she has a Hemijrani groom there."

"She's found Dawsiir?" Anger turned to confusion. "Can't he support Wolfram's story?"

Carefully, Catherine said, "She tells us that he does."

Fionvar nodded. "I see. And Gwythym?"

"Is about some personal business. I've not seen him."

"Personal business? We're about to be at war!"

Over her shoulder, Brianna tossed, "So you say."

"Mark my words, Your Majesty, if we do nothing, we will be lost." He gave a short bow. "When the sky goes dark, you'll know where to find me." So saying, he turned his back on the queen and fled from her garden. On the table where they used to share their meals, he saw the long boar knife in its leather sheath, the knife that Wolfram had laid at his mother's feet. Fionvar snatched it up and stuck it into his belt. He would see that it was returned to its rightful owner.

The infirmary surrounded a garden of its own not far off, and he found Lyssa there, deep in conversation with a Hemijrani man.

His head bandaged, the man sat on the edge of a bed, clothed in ill-fitting local garb. Both looked up at Fionvar's precipitous entrance.

"She was kidnapped, wasn't she?" he asked.

Flustered, Lyssa leapt up. "Yes. They struck him. Once they had the princess, he didn't dare disobey them."

"Holy Mother. Wolfram's been telling the truth." He slumped onto the facing bed, wiping sweat from his brow.

"You, of all people, shouldn't look so surprised," she replied.

He studied her, even though she would not meet his eye. "Part of me still hoped he was wrong, that it wouldn't come to this. We need to stop that ceremony."

At this, Lyssa looked up. "We?"

Quietly, he told her, "I need you on my side, Lyssa, as much as he does."

She bit her lip.

"If there is one thing I've learned from this mess, it's that everyone deserves a second chance."

"Thank you," she whispered.

"Come on, we'll go to the temple, maybe we can get to Faedre."

Shaking her head, Lyssa said, "I've been. They've got guards on the entrance, ours and theirs. Nobody gets in. Even if we stormed them, there've got to be a thousand Hemijrani on the inside, we wouldn't get close."

Unsteadily, Dawsiir rose, speaking in his own tongue.

"They've been digging, he says, night and day."

"Yes," Fionvar said, "I've seen them with shovels. What of it?"

"They were making a womb to the goddess," Dawsiir explained through Lyssa. "If the temple is to be proper, the womb will be underneath."

Clenching his fist, Fionvar recalled the houses of dirt in Quinan's forest; it had to come from somewhere, and suddenly he heard the echo of what he had taken for rats, scratching every night beneath the temple floor. "They've made our temple into their own, is that it?"

Dawsiir, edging away from him, nodded. "Yes, but this may also be the way in, if it can be found. A Hemijrani temple has a tower, a round chamber, and a womb, with hidden doors between."

Considering the dark man, Fionvar asked, "You know that we're after your people. Can I be sure you are with us?"

"I have been their prisoner in my sickness. Highness Wolfram, through this lady, has been my deliverance. He and his princess have need of me."

"His princess?" Fionvar raised an eyebrow.

With a sudden light in his eyes, Dawsiir placed his hands together, fingertips to wrists. "She has told me they are to wed and gave me the blessing of her smile."

"Ah, Wolfram, I have been so blind." Fionvar sighed. But they had no time for regret, not now. He got once more to his feet. "Let's go then." He gave Dawsiir an arm to support him and the three left the infirmary as quickly as they could.

Chapter 45

HIS HANDS tucked between his knees, Wolfram huddled against the wall. The dungeon guards' withholding his food had left a gnawing in his guts, and he suspected even his demon had starved. Darkness and light ebbed before his eye. If he shut it, the empty socket showed him visions of Erik's death, Deishima's bloody face, Lyssa's hard, forbidden body. The tiger's breath burned him, the leopards' snarls drew him awake when he longed for sleep. The tiger roared, and Wolfram jerked, his body rigid.

Something had hold of his ankle, then the chain dropped away.

"On your feet," Gwythym snapped. "Come on, then."

Pushing himself up along the wall, Wolfram squinted. "Is it today, my hanging?"

"Not yet," the captain said. He turned Wolfram to the wall, and unlocked one hand, bringing them together again behind him. With a firm hand, he guided Wolfram out of the cell. "You've got your wish, an hour outside. Whatever it is Dylan's so keen to show you, I don't know. I don't know what your hold is over my son, but I'll tell you I don't like it."

Wolfram laughed, but it made no sound. Dylan had done his part, but Wolfram had no idea if he was strong enough to follow through. He hadn't counted on the toll the dungeon was taking, the way it sapped his will with every hour. "Thank you, Captain."

Two guards marched beside him, with four more behind. With his arms linked at his back and the cuff still about his ankle, Wolfram doubted there was much he could do, but the group seemed tense nonetheless. At the top of the stairs, Dylan waited, leaping forward when they emerged. It had been weeks since Wolfram saw a mirror, but the look on Dylan's face was all the reflection he needed. He tried a smile. "Dylan. I have been blessed to have you as my friend."

Swallowing hard, Dylan looked away. "Come on, there's not much time." He led the way down halls and up stairs to the base of the tower, where his key gave them entrance. As they walked, the servants and lords froze in their activities to watch them pass, and Wolfram hung his head beneath the weight of their contempt.

He stumbled more than once on the long, long stair, with one of the guards muttering oaths as he propped him back up and kept a grip on his elbow.

In the study room of the observatory, Gwythym called a halt, looking up the narrow ladder. Gasping for breath, Wolfram was glad of the rest. He didn't need to pretend to be weak and harmless. The chain dragged him even as the stench of his clothing and his unwashed hair still held him prisoner. He had given up on praying.

"We have to go all the way up," Dylan said, "or he won't be able to see."

"I don't like it," Gwythym said again. "I do not like anything about this, Dylan." His voice held a warning edge.

Wolfram let his weariness take over and shut his eye. Either the captain would let him up, or he would fail. Even if Gwythym let him make the climb, he had no guarantee, only greater risks. Now, he swayed on his feet and winced. "Forget it." He sighed. "I'll stay here. I'll die, it doesn't matter."

"No, Wolfram, it does," Dylan urged him.

Wolfram raised his head a little, and saw Dylan reach out, only to have his arm restrained by his father's strong grip. "It's no use, Dylan. You did your best," Wolfram mumbled.

"We'll get you up in the sun, the wind. Just being there will do you good." He pushed the red hair from his face and pleaded with his gaze. "Come on, Wolfram, don't give up now."

"No, mayhap he's right. This should be far enough." Gwythym gestured to the windows all around. "Open those, if you want a breeze."

"Aye, we could use some fresh air," one of the guards grumbled, waving a hand before his nose.

Wolfram's right side spasmed, and he fell, his knees striking heavily as his shoulder caught on the ladder.

This time, Dylan ducked around his father and came to Wolfram's side. Cupping the back of Wolfram's head, he brought his mouth to Wolfram's ear. "She needs you, Wolfram, have you forgotten that? Sweet Lady, Wolfram, you've got to try."

"I don't know if I can," he whispered. "I've got nothing left."

"You've got her."

He blinked, sighed, and finally nodded. "Help me up, will you?"

Slipping an arm around him, Dylan drew him to his feet and held him there. "Where's the key?"

"Dylan," Gwythym began, but Dylan cut in, "He's got to climb that ladder, where is the key?"

"I cannot do that, lad, and you know it." The captain's face was grim. "He's got something on you, and I'll not have your life in danger for it."

Setting his jaw, Dylan squared his shoulders. "All right, Da, so here it is. I tried to kill him. That scar around his neck? It's mine. The night he was leaving here, I went for him. Now, he has nothing on me."

Gwythym gaped at his son. "You tried . . . ? Dylan, lad, I don't understand."

Fighting back tears, Dylan said, "You don't have to, not right now. What you have to do is unlock that chain."

Gwythym let a slow whistle between his teeth. "It's madness, Dylan, after all that he's done."

"We don't have time for this, Da. Would you want to die without once more feeling the sun on your face?"

"Captain," one of the guards said, his tone insistent, but Gwythym ignored him.

From his belt, he drew the key, tapping it against his palm as he regarded his son.

"Don't do this, Captain."

"He can't overpower us, look at him." Gwythym's face grew a little warmer, his gaze a little softer as he studied Wolfram.

The man moved forward, gripping his sword. "It doesn't matter, he's a criminal."

"Wait in the hall, men," Gwythym said.

"Have ye gone mad?"

"If I have, then on my head be it. Lock the door, there's none at risk but the three of us." Then he walked to Wolfram's back and fitted the key into the lock.

Still grumbling, the men did as they were commanded.

Unlocked from the left, the heavy chain hung at Wolfram's right wrist. He rolled his shoulders and let out a breath. "Again, thank you, Captain."

Fixing him with a cold stare, Gwythym replied, "It's not for you, it's for my son."

"Can't you take off the chain, just for now?" Dylan asked.

"Different key. That's to be sure that he could take any one of us and not get himself free."

"It's all right, Dylan," Wolfram murmured. He straightened and looked up the ladder. "Best I go first, I guess."

"Get on with you, then." To Dylan, he said, "You owe me a thousand words on this, or more, lad."

"Aye, Father, I know it."

Hand over hand, Wolfram climbed the ladder and flung back the trapdoor at its top. The sun fell upon his face, and he rose into it. Dylan had been right; the warmth of the sunlight gave him solace, while the wind blew away the darkness he had carried with him. Crossing to the wall, Wolfram took a deep breath and held the springtime inside him before gently letting it out. The trapdoor banged shut. Wolfram faced father and son, and smiled. "I've never been so grateful for a day, even if it has to be this one."

"What d'you mean by that?" Gwythym asked, standing foursquare on top of the door, sword at the ready.

Dylan, crossing to his post, stopped with one foot in the air, his face turned to the sky. "Finistrel and all the saints," he murmured, "it's coming."

Squinting, Wolfram looked to the sun. At one edge, a sliver of darkness encroached. As they watched, the darkness grew, nibbling away at the golden heat.

"What is this?" Gwythym breathed, lowering the sword.

"The moon," said Dylan with a grin, "the moon and the sun, together in the sky. I did it!"

"You did this? What, with magic?"

"No, Da," he replied, with a laugh, "I did it with numbers, and with these." He gestured toward the new clock and the tubes of his equipment.

Wolfram peered over the edge toward the roof of the temple far below. "How long do I have?"

"Less than an hour now," Dylan said. "Are you up to it?"

"Up to what? What's going on?" Gwythym demanded.

Heedless of the captain, Wolfram asked, "Did you get what I asked for?"

Kneeling, Dylan popped open the case which ordinarily held his parchments, pulling out a great coil of rope and a pair of riding gloves. Handing them over, he said, "Are you sure of this?"

"She needs me." Wolfram strung the rope through one of the brackets made for Dylan's equipment.

In two strides, Gwythym stomped on the rope. "Hold there and tell me what you're on about."

"Bury it, Captain, there's no time! Deishima's down there, and they're going to kill her." His head beginning to ache, Wolfram squinted up at him.

"How do I know you're not trying to escape?"

"Like this?" Wolfram's grin returned with a vengeance. "I'd have to be a madman."

"By all accounts, you must be," Gwythym replied. "But you're in my keeping now." He let the point of his sword rest on Wolfram's shoulder.

Blood boiling, Wolfram gritted his teeth. "And if I escape? At least my mother won't have the worry of hanging me. Would that be so awful?"

Slowly, the sword withdrew, and Gwythym, after a moment more, stepped away and turned his back.

Quickly, Wolfram bound the rope about his waist, hampered by the chain at his wrist. He gathered the rope in his arms and dropped it over, watching it snake down the side of the tower and pool up in the crevice of the roof below. Again, his side cramped, and he doubled over.

"Wolfram," Dylan sprang to his side. "You're weaker than I thought. You're not up to this, are you?"

"I have to be," he said through clenched teeth. "If I can't make it, she dies, and an army will tear down this place and everyone in it." His head throbbed, and the pain in his side eased, leaving him pinched and aching. Dylan was right, he'd never make it—not down there, not to do whatever came after. He stared down the rope, then put his back to the wall and sat, his hands in his lap.

"Wolfram?"

"Just let me breathe." He sighed, trying to force back the doubts, to cage the demon. He conjured the vision of Deishima's face, hidden behind the veil. Her dark eyes beckoned him, and those two little lines formed between them, the lines of her concern. He went deep within himself, into the dark places, into the places her acceptance had filled. The body he had so depended on was failing him, so hurt that he could barely see straight. "Sweet Lady," he whispered, "if ever there has been a time I needed You, this would be it." He drew a deep breath. It carried the heat of the sun, the power of the wind, the strength of the stone around him. He could smell the springtime in new flowers on the breeze. If he must die, better it be in the open, striving for something worth his life.

After what felt like ages, Wolfram opened his eye. A sense of calm filled him, the urgency of his mission echoing around him.

"How are you, Wolfram?" Dylan crouched before him. "You look . . . better."

"I have to go," he said, pushing himself up. The hunger and weakness lingered, but he kept them in abeyance as he pulled on the gloves.

Bouncing a few times on his toes, Wolfram said, "If I don't manage this, Dylan, get him to send the soldiers, right?" He nodded toward Gwythym.

"I will." Dylan gave a half smile. "Come back, though, Wolfram? Without you, my life would be deadly dull."

Wolfram lightly punched his shoulder. "You'll not get rid of me this easily." Taking up the dangling rope, he grinned and lowered himself over the wall into the wind to begin his terrible descent.

Chapter 46

EMERGING THROUGH the little door by the temple, Fionvar felt a chill to the air that had not been there before. At first, he thought he imagined it, then he noticed the guards around the refugee camp. To a man, they stared at the sky. A few had removed their helmets and stood bareheaded and gaping. Their lips moved in prayer, and their fingers made restless circles, hoping to ward off doom by repeating the Lady's sign.

Although he'd had the warning of the woods chapel and Alyn's prophecy, the sight of the sun still rooted Fionvar to the spot. A chunk of darkness wounded it like a terrible bite. A broad crescent was all that remained and even that seemed to be dwindling. Shadows below were consumed by this great shadow, changing into unfamiliar forms.

"Holy Mother preserve us!" one of the guards shouted. He dropped his helmet and ran. Several others followed, tearing for the woods.

"Fionvar, look!" Lyssa pointed toward the Bernholt road. People and animals fled down it, wagons pelting along heedless of what was before them. Shouts and crashes echoed over the wall, and already a black smoke rose near the merchants' row.

"What's happening?" she cried.

"The prophecy spoke of a dark sun and the calling of an army."

"How do we stop it?"

Looking down the slope, Fionvar said, "We have to stop them." Where the camp had been most of the tents lay heaped in piles, the cook fires scattered. The Hemijrani, too, glanced to the sky, but they did not run. They smiled and cheered, shaking their fists.

Beside him, Dawsiir murmured something, and Lyssa translated, "It is true; this is the day they are coming."

"What does he know?" Fionvar demanded, as darkness steadily ate away the sun.

"This is the moon, our lady, coming to the sun, our lord, as on the day of their birth."

Incredulous, Fionvar pointed. "That is the moon?"

Dawsiir nodded.

"Ask him—" Fionvar began, but Lyssa interrupted. "We don't have time to understand, Fion, our men are panicking, and theirs are celebrating. Not good at all."

"The outside entrance," Dawsiir explained, "is for workmen only when digging. None but the most holy can enter there since the womb is complete." He peered down the hill into the Hemijrani host and shook his head.

Fionvar sighed. "He's got no idea, then."

She shook her head. "No, it's worse than that. They'll defend it. Someone down there knows where it is and will do anything to prevent us finding out."

Squatting down, Fionvar let his head and arms hang limp. "Is this how you felt when you stormed the castle?"

Coming down beside him, Lyssa grinned. She'd argued against that folly when she found herself behind the enemy line with King Rhys, the wizard, and Jordan, newly risen from the dead. It had become the stuff of Rhys's legend. She wondered if this, too, would be made into tales: the day that three confronted the Hemijrani horde and won entrance to their own temple. "No, Fionvar, there were four of us that time."

❧◦◦◦❧

WOLFRAM BEGAN to think the climb was getting longer, the rope stretching below him into the very heart of the earth. He dare not look down but could only creep along, the rope turned about his arm in case he lost his footing. Not that it would help much given how weak he already was, but if he grabbed on tight enough—again he steered himself away from that thought and concentrated on finding the next crevice. Inches from his nose, the granite sparkled in the remaining sunlight, his shadow at first in sharp darkness, now strangely doubled and shaded away as the sun disappeared.

Sounds of panic rose from the city, though he could catch the tune of evening prayer desperately sung. Fitting, for this nightfall at noon. Something burned, and he hoped the fire brigade hadn't fled beneath the awful sky. He reached a narrow slot cut into the stone and clung to the edge, resting, the chain at his wrist an unwelcome weight.

Wolfram allowed himself only a moment, trying to recapture that breath of peace he'd felt above, before he continued his treacherous descent.

Let the rope slide about his arm. Wriggle the left foot down to find a crevice. Let the right foot follow, the toes scraped and throbbing. Watch the twin lines playing out above him.

Sweat soaked the lightweight old shirt he'd chosen for the last climb. Wind chilled his shoulders and bare feet until his teeth chattered.

When the sound grew too much, he clenched his mouth shut and rested his cheek against the stone.

In the channels of mortar, the wind whistled, calling him like a dog to go home.

Wolfram started, popping his eye back open, gripping the rope tighter.

He had been climbing forever, an insect inching along the tower face. The light still shone, what little of it there was, so he had time, but not much. When the sun ran out, so, too, would Deishima's life.

Again let out the line, walk backward, feet seeking purchase.

He wished he knew the tower better, how many arrow slits cut into it and when he would reach the last one. There must be another soon, he needed that tiny respite.

Let out the line, reach downward—then his toe struck something warm, and the line slipped.

He barely had time to cry out as the rope tore along his arm and he fell, full length on his back on the roof below.

For a moment, he fought for the breath that had been knocked from him. At last, he sat up. He had stepped into a bird's nest, spilling feathers and twigs along the roof junction.

Wolfram laughed without breath. His shoulders stung from the impact, and his arms ached from the effort of getting him down. Eyeing the vertical wall before him, Wolfram cursed his own madness and gazed up. High above, a tiny figure waved. Dylan. He waved both arms, and the rope came tumbling down in a heap.

Somewhat recovered, Wolfram untied himself and gathered the rope, dragging himself to his feet. He stood on top of the lesser hall, with only its pitched roof between him and the temple courtyard, its confused guards keeping to their doors. They might spot him now, but they'd never reach him in time. He circled to contemplate the temple itself. The vast round space was roofed over with slate, steeply laid. Ribs of stone arched out from it to the surrounding buildings and to a secondary wall on the outside.

Carefully, he crossed over on one of the buttresses, his arms outstretched, holding his breath. For one moment, he glanced down, and found his shadow slender and doubly dark. He wavered, licked his lips. "Bury it!" He ran the last few steps, flinging himself upon the roof.

Tying off the rope to the buttress, Wolfram began a new sort of creeping, hunched over, diagonally up the steep slates.

Ridged with decorative stones, the hole suddenly lay open before him. The bear claw chafing his chest, Wolfram lay flat and snuck a look.

Many torches lit the temple interior, their smoke tingling his nose. Dark Hemijrani men filled the rows of benches, standing up, with long knives held in their fists. They filled all the space from altar to wall, even squeezing into the sacred caves, overturned candles littering the niches. A guttural chant reached his ears, topped by a keening wail, which rose and fell, its words lost in ululation.

On the altar directly below him, Deishima sat between a pair of curving swords. Legs crossed, hands cupped together in her lap, she wore no veil, and her hair gleamed with strings of beads.

To her left hand Esfandiyar led the chant. To her right hand stood Faedre, crying out strange words. Behind her, Melody held her hands together, joining in the song.

His pale hair a beacon in the sea of darkness, Alyn faced Deishima. Where the others were still and intent on their purpose, he stirred, looking side to side. Once, he looked up, his face fearful in the glimpse Wolfram had as he rolled to the side.

As he lay with his face to the sky, darkness consumed the last golden edge of sun.

Chapter 47

THE THREE crouched on their hill, searching the milling mass of Hemijrani. The darker the sun grew, the bolder grew the refugees, many slashing the air with wicked knives or calling out taunts to the few city guards remaining. Several of the tents still stood, and Fionvar couldn't tell which might hide the tunnel they sought.

Suddenly, Lyssa nudged him with an elbow. "It's there!" She pointed into the midst of the throng, where the stone pile and one small tent stood. "That's a shrine, a miniature of their own temples. I thought it was funny the other day—the stones aren't clean, they're still covered with dirt. They haven't been exposed for long, see?"

"I see," he agreed. "I see about a thousand men between us and it."

"We have the element of surprise."

"They will have seen someone moving up here, but I doubt they expect an attack."

Beside him, Dawsiir frowned, looking to his companions, then the camp. He flashed a brief grin and held up a hand, then took off down the hill, keeping low.

A moment later, he returned with an armload of the cast-off cloth. Dropping the bundle, he started talking so fast that Lyssa couldn't follow him and grabbed his shoulder to get him to stop.

Catching his breath, he explained more slowly. If they wrapped themselves, draping their heads, and walked hunched over, they might pass for women.

Fionvar and Lyssa exchanged a dubious look, then she shrugged. "What else do we have, really?"

With Dawsiir directing, they dressed themselves in the ragged lengths of fabric until only their eyes could be seen. Fionvar shook his head. "I don't know about this."

"It's just to get close, then I'll create a diversion. You go for the tent."

"Three against a thousand is bad enough, but one?"

Her green eyes twinkled. "I have an advantage. I really am a woman."

Dawsiir led the way, walking boldly now, his bandage disguised by a head scarf. He started a running monologue, sounding irritated, and earning knowing looks from the men they passed. They worked their way through the edge of the gathering, cutting a diagonal course toward the woods that would bring them near the stones.

A harsh voice cried out to them. Someone pushed through the crowd, and they hurried farther, Dawsiir turning to face the newcomer.

His feet clean of markings, with a curved sword in his hand, Ghiva confronted the groom, shouting angrily.

"Go, Fionvar," Lyssa urged.

Ducking and running, Fionvar slipped through the crowd, which turned to watch the commotion. He found the little tent and crawled under the flap. Inside, a steep tunnel opened into the earth. Stripping off his disguise, Fionvar drew his sword and plunged into the darkness.

GHIVA CAME on, shouting, "Who are you? Where have you come from?" Keeping his head bowed, Dawsiir explained, "These women, they have been at the temple door, thinking perhaps they could watch the ritual, and it has taken me some time to convince them they must not wait there. A thousand pardons, o great warrior."

"And shall you punish them yourself, little man, or do you require help with that as well? No one who does not fight is allowed to be here."

Dawsiir made a derisive noise. "I shall punish them and fight as well. Which would you have me do?"

His sword held high, Ghiva turned on Lyssa, who kept her face averted. Growling, he turned back toward Dawsiir. "Look at me, boy! By the Two, I'm sure I know you."

"As you know all those who serve the Two." Dawsiir's voice held a trace of doubt.

Under her loose garments, Lyssa took the hilt of her sword.

As Ghiva reached for Dawsiir, Lyssa swept off the cloth and let it flutter to the ground. Setting her stance, she grinned. "I, too, would fight, but my cause is different."

Drawing back, Ghiva studied her. "Our Two have struck the light from your kingdom, woman. Return to your place and await the coming of truth."

"My place?" Lyssa lost her smile. "My place is defending the Lady, against any who attack Her."

Darting a glance to either side, Ghiva shouted, "You were three. Where is the other?"

"There is no other, Ghiva. You're wrong."

In Hemijrani, he called out, "Find the third one!" but his own people, gawking at the woman with the sword, did not heed him.

Ghiva flashed his golden teeth. "You cannot stand against us, we are an army."

"Of men," she amended. "Will they fight me? Will they dare?"

"I will not need them; no woman is strong enough to defy me."

"Not alone," Lyssa said. "For the Lady stands with me, Ghiva, even in the dark."

Placing both hands on the hilt of his curved sword, Ghiva sneered. "Her temple stands for us today. Submit yourself to me, and you may not die."

"Submit yourself to the Lady and save me the trouble." Taking her hammer in the left, Lyssa aimed a slash to his middle.

Ghiva leapt back, and his own blade clanged against the hammer's shaft.

With a gasp and a jabber of their own tongue, the crowd fell away, leaving them circling as the sun went dark.

⚜

ON A BENCH of stone beneath the trees, Brianna sat in her garden, examining the first blooms of lavender by the gravel path. When Fionvar came, she had thought he would be with her. Surely, with Wolfram accused of rape, he could admit his mistake and return to her. Even if he could not admit it, there would be no shame in his release from that foolhardy vow. Why stand with a son who betrayed him, time and again?

Even with only the rumor of her remarriage, she had received three offers, princes younger than she with hopes of kingship. Lochalyn was a small kingdom to be sure, but better than the little estates they might get when their siblings ascended to reign. She set aside the letters and the portraits and could see only Fionvar's face before her. When she brushed her hair at night, she felt his hands, and she awoke in the morning missing his warmth. She knew he understood the need for a worthy heir, and the more he resisted, the more she insisted until she could not acknowledge her own heart.

There must be a compromise. If she exiled Wolfram or had him branded for the crime—but then these Hemijrani would get more angry than they already were, and they had every right to be. She had called up conscripts from the villages to strengthen the city guard in case the trial sparked a riot, but there had been no violence thus far. Not from them, anyhow.

Gazing at the path, she watched the shifting shadows of the leaves. Rounds of sunlight rippled and distorted into strange shapes, and she frowned.

The chill reached her back almost as it reached her heart, and the queen looked up. Overhead, a dark stain marked the sun, growing bit by bit.

The blood rushed from her face, and she tried to rise, but stumbled.

"Your Majesty!" Lady Catherine, her gown choked in both hands, ran up the path. "Have you seen? Sweet Finistrel in the stars, what's happening?"

"The sun goes dark," she breathed, and her son was locked in a dungeon while Prince Alyn joined in a heathen rite. "Oh, Fionvar, what have I done!" She swayed, and Catherine caught her. Together, they tripped down the path, meeting a contingent of guards coming up it.

"Your Majesty." Randall, Gwythym's lieutenant, bowed, then breathlessly began, "It's the city, there's a panic on, and people demanding entrance to the temple, while the rest run about like mad things."

"Get your men down there—where's the captain? I want that temple open and those refugees contained."

He frowned as he fell in beside her. "Contained?"

"It's an army, lieutenant."

"Well, we've got men on them, the ones outside, that is."

"And inside?"

He glanced away. "Orders were to let them have it, Majesty."

Brianna made the sign of the Lady. "Then take it back."

"Aye, Your Majesty. Best stay in your quarters, and I'll put some men on you."

"Not on your life, Randall. I'm for the dungeon." She stopped, sweeping the table with her eyes, but Wolfram's knife was gone. "Someone's got to free my son."

CROUCHING TO avoid the low ceiling, Fionvar sprinted down the tunnel. They had shored it up with timbers hewn from Quinan's forest, and the floor was packed by long use. He saw dim light ahead and finally burst out into an open space. In an instant, his feet lost purchase on the dirt, and he slipped.

Gasping, Fionvar flung himself backward and caught hold of the last timber.

He breathed hard for a moment, then pulled himself back into the tunnel. Sitting up, he got his first look at the womb they had dug beneath his own Lady's temple.

Perhaps twenty feet across, the pit extended in both directions from where he sat, with a spiraling path of packed dirt going up. A structure of stones and timbers supported the temple above, though they were bound with ropes and seemed precarious at best. Below, the path had already disintegrated as water welled up to fill the pit. How deep it went, he could not tell.

Fionvar smiled to himself. A people running out of water had probably not counted on the flooding of their womb. Still, the satisfaction of their surprise was short-lived. The pit undermined the very foundations of the temple above, and he dared not imagine what it would take to fill the thing in and be sure the temple was safe. How ironic, that the temple the Usurper's pride had lifted would be usurped by new invaders.

Dusting himself off, Fionvar drew his sword and started up the path, keeping close to the earthen wall.

As he drew nearer, he heard the sound of chanting, a sort of low drone, with high, wailing notes floating over all. Unlike the careful melodies of Strelledor, this music grated on Fionvar's nerves. He would put a stop to it and to the whole perversion of the Lady's way.

Slowing his pace, Fionvar reached a trapdoor, propped up with a long stick. He tried to hear if someone might be on top of it, but there was no way to tell. Supporting the door with one hand, he eased the stick away.

The heavy wood nearly got away from him; red stone tiles camouflaged the top side of the door. Gently he brought it down and pushed it to one side. Above him, on sturdy legs of marble, stood the altar of Death, a red cloth draped over the whole. No wonder they had been able to keep it secret this long.

Fionvar pulled himself up, bumping his head on the altar, but the chanting was loud enough that he doubted he could be heard. Hunched on the floor, he lifted the edge of the cloth and peeked out. Dark bare feet surrounded him, a thicket of legs.

Behind the altar, he found the narrow space clear and decided to risk it. Carefully he slipped out from under the cloth and got up on his knees, peering among the legs of those who stood on top.

With his back toward Fionvar, Alyn stood by the altar, facing a delicate woman who sat atop it. Folds of rich fabric fell all around her though her head was bare. Long, black hair shimmering with jewels draped her shoulders. Her face showed the yellowing of healing bruises. For an instant, she looked directly at him, as if she could feel his eyes upon her. Her face lit with an inner fire that quickly died away, leaving tears coursing down her cheeks.

In that moment, he saw the beauty and grace that had captivated his son. He wanted to go to Deishima and carry her off on Wolfram's behalf, but he dared not move. That she saw Fionvar and spoke no warning confirmed all that Wolfram had said. He had asked for her hand, she had given it, and now waited without hope for her hero's return.

The chanting receded to a whisper, and Faedre's ululating cries rang out in the temple. She raised her hands to the darkening sky. Calling the darkness, as the prophecy had told him. Opposite her, a Hemijrani priest shook scented water on Deishima's head. From the far side of the main altar, Melody stepped up, with a flash of silver in her hand.

Fionvar leapt up onto the altar of Death, knocking down the men already there. "Your Highness, Melody! Stop! You don't know what you're doing!"

The chanting ceased, and all faces turned toward him.

"Thank the Lady." Relief washed over Alyn's face. "Where are the guards?"

"Right outside," Fionvar claimed, but Faedre laughed.

"Outside indeed," the priestess said. "Running from the power of the skies and the strength of the Two. They are outside, Fionvar, and they will stay that way."

"Don't you see, Your Highness? She's no friend of ours—she's here to usurp this kingdom again. Whatever she wants from you, don't do it."

Deishima bowed her head, and Melody took her hand.

The displaced Hemijrani grabbed him all around, knocking the sword from his hand.

"You should have stayed home, my lord," Melody said, her face alight with an unholy smile.

Staring at her, Fionvar realized his mistake. It was not Faedre who would bury the crown. "No! You can't do this!" He struggled, but the men jumped up around him, dragging him to his knees, a dozen knives pricking at his skin.

Turning Deishima's palm to the sky, Melody sang a harsh song, and cut a slender line of red across the exposed wrist. Blood seeped from the wound and trickled down, making a scarlet stain on the upraised palm.

Chapter 48

HEARING THE commotion, Wolfram froze, expecting to hear someone coming for him, but the shouting died down after a moment, and he stole another glance into the temple. Melody touched her fingertip to Deishima's blood and stroked a line of red down each cheek. She moaned in a way almost ecstatic, her body arching, and the light in the temple shifted, a chill wind rushing down over Wolfram's back, down to the altar. The women's garments fluttered, gems tinkling together, sending flashes of light that danced across Deishima's dark skin. Faedre laughed, raising her hands as if welcoming an unseen presence. When Melody again drew breath and lifted her head, her hair rippled and shimmered, silver with the light of the absent moon.

With a hard smile showing her teeth, Melody held something out to her brother. Warily, Alyn looked over his shoulder, where Wolfram couldn't see, then to her. "This has gone far enough, Melody, your tricks and your teasing. I'm through."

"But you promised me, on our Name Day, you promised we could stand together."

"So I did—I promised to pretend, but this has gone beyond make-believe."

"Are you frightened? You, the Voice of the Lady? But there's nothing to it, is there? We cannot be the Two, you and I. It's all in fun. Take up the knife. Do you doubt that the Lady will prevent anything . . . unwholesome?"

In answer, he looked at Deishima, and Wolfram tensed, seeing the blood that pooled too quickly in her hand.

Staring back at his sister, Alyn said, "It's not a game, it's a sacrifice."

Melody laughed, the gemstones of her elaborate headdress shaking off sparks of torchlight. "What is the life of one heathen, more or less? Will you call down the wrath of the Lady upon me? Do you have that power, Alyn, or has She left you, here in the dark?" She reached the knife across the altar, level with Deishima's shoulder, to tap her brother's chest.

Alyn flinched, but did not step away. "She speaks through me, Melody, She does not act, nor force my actions, you know that."

"I can feel the power already, Alyn, flowing through me," she said, her body seeming to glow in the darkness of the temple. "Jonsha is here, within me. She will grant me all that I desire. Let Ayel become you, and you and I can be gods upon the earth!"

"No," he shouted, "Melody, no, listen to yourself, oh, Finistrel in the Stars, you have been so deceived."

She drew back the blade, changing her grip. "No, my brother, it's you who have been deceived."

On the roof, Wolfram waited for her to strike, but she did not.

Alyn's expression grew somber, his hands gripped together. "This is why I lost you, why I can't feel your presence, even now, even when I am looking straight at you, Melody, I do not see you."

"You never have," she spat back, adding something in Hemijrani.

Two men stepped from the ranks and caught Alyn's arms. He struggled, but only briefly—he'd refused even to be trained with a sword. "You said I could not be forced."

She merely smiled.

Much as he would like to see something horrible happen to Alyn, Wolfram knew the time had come. As Melody raised her hands, Wolfram dropped his rope.

For a moment, all eyes were again on the sky, then Deishima curled and rolled from the altar, the rope coiling on it and spilling over. Catching hold and wrapping one knee around it, Wolfram let himself down.

In a barely controlled fall, he slid down the rope and landed on all fours, raising his head with his best grin. "Have I missed much?"

Lunging forward, Faedre called out, but Wolfram leapt up. His foot caught Alyn in the chest, knocking him back into their arms, out of range of Melody's blade.

Beyond them, he caught a glimpse of Fionvar, held by many hands, ringed about with knives, and clamped his teeth shut on an oath. It didn't matter, he told himself, whatever happened, it had to be done.

Wolfram spun to face Melody. "I've been waiting so long to do that."

"Take him," she said, her voice deep and strange, but Wolfram held up his hands.

"You didn't want him, did you? You never wanted him, Melody." Sinking back to his knees, Wolfram murmured, "Can you forgive my blindness, sister, in not seeing you?"

Her hard gaze wavered. "Why should I? The way you've gone after that girl, Wolfram, why should I forgive you anything?"

"Do not listen to him, Melody, you know what we must do," Faedre urged, her hands upon the altar now.

Esfandiyar rose up then with Deishima in his arms. She sagged against his grip.

"There she is!" Melody crowed. "Don't you want her now?"

Wolfram kept his gaze upon her, roving over her body until his very silence became an answer. "This power you offered, Alyn doesn't need it. He doesn't need to strike down his enemies, he has no wrongs that cry for justice. Give it to me, Melody, let me stand beside you. There is nothing I have ever wanted more than this."

From the Cave of Death, Fionvar howled, "Wolfram, no!"

Faedre hissed, "Silence him," but Melody raised a single hand and the moon impossibly glowed in her eyes.

Again, Fionvar had ruined everything, his concentration most of all. Wolfram could not turn to be sure if his father was alive or dead. Silence throbbed in his ears.

The pulse beating at her throat, Melody stared at him.

In his skull, the demon tore and ranted. His body ached with stillness. Tension knotted his shoulders as he awaited her words.

But she gave him no words. Instead, a dizzying smile grew on her lips, her features suddenly alight.

Released, Wolfram jumped to the floor and straightened, the heat of her body so near he burned.

In a soft and thrilling voice, she told him, "All your enemies, brother, your queen, your father, anyone who's ever hurt you, we will take such a revenge that the stars will shiver to hear them scream."

He reached out and wrapped his arms around her.

For the first time, he held her close, every curve of her melting into him, his face buried in the soft darkness of her hair. The heat within him stirred, and the demon howled. Too long she had sought this embrace, and he had denied her. Wolfram brought his lips to hers, kissed her gently, then passionately as she trembled.

Her arms enfolded him, the flat of the blade pressing along his spine. The chain clinking softly, his hands roved over her body, his left hand crept up her thigh and stroked her waist, then cupped her breast.

Melody whimpered at his touch, an exhalation of fire on his cheek.

Wolfram's fingers inched between their heartbeats and found a small lump keeping them apart. He shut his eye.

With one swift, short stroke, he slipped the bear claw free and tore it across her throat.

***

UNDER THE dark sun, Ghiva, small and light on his feet, danced away from Lyssa's blade and started a high-pitched chant.

In the circle all around them, others took up the chant, a paean to their sun-god. Its rhythm swelled with stamping feet, and Lyssa shook her head, trying not to be drawn in.

She leapt a low swipe at her legs, but felt a stinging slash across her thigh as she spun to the attack.

Gleeful, Ghiva skittered away.

More like a game than a duel, the bout circled first one way, then the other.

Used to fighting men of her own height or more, Lyssa found herself cutting high, then with too much force, passing him by.

Whenever she missed, the little man gave a call of victory that his audience took up until it echoed all around her.

Still, their relentless rhythm pursued her. Her legs moved to its beat, and she cursed.

Ghiva again ducked her blade, blocking the hammer with his sword as he rolled below her defenses.

Catching her ankle, he toppled her to the earth and sprang up, the audience hooting their delight.

Lyssa tumbled, hitting hard, but letting the roll take her away from him a moment. In the dark sky, a ring of fire shone, with stars glittering all around it. "Oh Lady of the deepest seas," she murmured, quoting the Morning Prayer. "Sweet Finistrel wake my heart at dawning."

Rising, she smashed the hammer against the flat of her sword, a ringing blow that shocked the ears and shook the chanters. Her ears, never the best, echoed with that blow, and she sang out her own song, the Lady's prayer.

Snarling, Ghiva came on.

Oblivious to the sounds around her, Lyssa submersed herself in the fight, watching the enemy, the way he bounced foot to foot.

Bringing her sword in short, she cut him a backhanded blow to his arm, and his face twisted with curses she could not hear.

Lyssa laughed.

Tumbling and bounding like an acrobat, Ghiva tried to draw her eye.

Watching his middle, Lyssa maintained her focus, singing louder.

Unlike her king, or even her brother, Lyssa had never been

musical. The notes and the voices meant nothing to her. She mumbled her way through the prayers even to this day. Fortunately, no one expected her to lead a congregation with her brash, too-ragged voice. Now, with daylight turned to darkness, her voice rose in its defiance. All the strength in her body backed the words, and yet more, for her voice carried from the castle to the trees.

High up on his tower, Dylan's spirit soared to hear her. The desperate throng on the Bernholt road halted their flight, and those who huddled in the city temples took up the prayer.

Gwythym, gathering his men to assault the temple, hesitated and looked to the sky, which seemed full of song even in its darkness.

Then the prayer gave way to cheering. Overhead, the darkness ringed with fire began to ebb away, rays of sun shooting free to warm the day.

Heedless of the cheering, Lyssa saw her shadow growing, springing out from her feet as if it would join her in battle. Laughing aloud, she leapt again to the offense.

Stumbling, Ghiva ducked her and hacked at her arm.

Her sword flew wild, clattering to the ground.

Blood spattered the earth, and Lyssa fell.

As he came on, she thrust the hammer out with both hands, deflecting the killing blow, and rolling out of the way.

He kicked her as she rolled, then dropped to his knees, catching her leg.

Breathing hard, Lyssa tried to twist away.

Then the sword was back in her hand. The hammer blocked, and she forced herself up, driving the sword through his chest.

The shout of triumph died in Ghiva's throat as Lyssa pushed him back.

From beneath her doom she rose, shaking him off her sword and raising her chin.

Hemijrani men, unused to even looking at a woman, feared to meet her eyes. The sun warmed her back as she turned a slow circle, the men falling back, their knives wavering. Dawsiir, still on his knees where he had found her sword, gazed up at her with something like awe.

Seeing his face, Lyssa laughed. "Thank you." Sticking the hammer back in its loop, she thrust out a hand.

Cringing at first, Dawsiir looked her up and down. Then he accepted, his dark hand sliding into hers, and she drew him to his feet.

Grinning to the crowd, she said, "So, who's next?"

Chapter 49

BLOOD WELLED between them, and still Wolfram held Melody to his chest, his face buried. For a moment as her heart still beat, he felt a terrible rush of power, as if all the fire of the sun coursed through him, and he lifted his head.

Her lips gasped blood onto his shoulder. Anguish wrenched her face, and her eyes searched for a savior.

"We have no time for this!" Faedre shouted.

Melody's brown eyes, as warm as summer evenings, drained of beauty even as he stared, and Wolfram shuddered, letting his hand fall, the bloody claw dangling again between them as he lowered her to the floor.

For a moment, the Hemijrani host gaped, their upraised knives gleaming like vicious grins.

Slowly, Wolfram rose, turning to the altar.

"You," Faedre whispered, her face gray. "You killed her."

Barely breathing, Wolfram gave a single nod.

"But she was Jonsha—she carried the power of the moon. How could this be?"

The silence of the gathering broke into cries of fear and anger. On the altar of Death, Fionvar knelt with the knives at his throat, his face drained of color.

"Oh, by the Two, I have said that something terrible would

occur today!" Esfandiyar wailed, pulling Deishima closer as if he clung to her for comfort.

"Quiet!" Faedre shrieked, but Esfandiyar's head shook as his body quivered.

"It will not matter, you said, if the offering would be injured. We shall cleanse and heal her, you have told me. You made me torture her. The things you made me do to her—even Ayel cannot defend me!"

"You bastard," Wolfram growled. Flipping the chain into a loop around his fist, he smashed the priest's face.

Deishima tumbled aside as Esfandiyar coughed blood, a gold tooth flying free to strike the floor.

Shocked into motion, the dark soldiers lining the benches sprang down and moved as one against him. For a moment, he glanced down at Deishima. "Hide," he told her, and she scrambled under a bench, clutching her cut arm to her chest.

Turning, he leapt again to the altar and took his rope in hand. Catching up one of the golden swords, Wolfram pushed off from the altar, swinging into the faces of his enemies.

Whooping like a madman he flew at them, sweeping the sword in great swaths.

Someone caught the end of the rope, but Wolfram dropped free, landing hard amidst the benches and rolling under.

At the Cave of Death he rose, flashing his father a grin as his captors jumped to the fight.

Wolfram smote off a hand, the knife still in its grip and spun, putting his back to the altar.

Freed, Fionvar jumped down beside him, snatching his sword back and skewering the man who'd held it.

At the center, Faedre called out her orders, even as her followers gathered to her, clamoring for explanations and blessing.

A wobbly head rose from the floor, and Alyn drew himself up, a hand pressed to his forehead.

"Go for the doors!" Wolfram yelled.

Alyn swung around in a circle, a storm gathering in his eyes.

Hacking one of the soldiers, Wolfram shouted, "Run, you bloody fool!"

At last, Alyn responded, vaulting the fallen benches and eluding the distraught soldiers.

From outside, something boomed against the barred door.

"Thank the Lady," Fionvar muttered.

At the altar, Faedre spun to the door, eyes wide, then disappeared into the fray. By now, some of the Hemijrani had dropped their weapons, beseeching aid from above, where the sky grew ever lighter. Some crowded the doors, pressing too close to allow them to open while others struggled with the deserters or thronged at the Cave of Death, eager for a try at the obvious enemy.

Esfandiyar, borne up by his followers, shrieked in pain, flailing and spewing blood.

The doors boomed again, causing new cries from those packed against them.

Pushing back his attacker, Wolfram ducked a blade and crouched, searching for some sign of Deishima.

Suddenly, the floor was pulled from beneath him, and he fell, his head jarring on stone, his last view was the threshing of dark legs and a far away splash of crimson silk.

HIS BREATH in short bursts, pain building with each stroke of his weary arm, Fionvar cursed under his breath. He should have kept his mouth shut, then maybe Melody didn't have to die. Gwythym shouted outside the doors, trying to organize his crew. The small courtyard afforded little room for a battering ram, but they were doing what they could, praise the Lady.

Bumping hard against the altar, Fionvar cursed, then felt a cut to his upper arm. Quickly he glanced to the side.

Wolfram had vanished, a scowling Hemijrani in his place.

Fionvar ducked and drove upward with the sword, slashing the man's leg open. Beneath those bare feet lay the golden sword Wolfram had used. Blood streaked the floor back beneath the cloth.

Yanking it up, Fionvar dove underneath, tumbling into the tunnel.

"Goddess's Tears!" He coughed in the cloud of dirt his entrance had sent up. Rolling onto his knees, he rose, aching in every joint, his chest heaving. "I'm too old for this," he muttered. "Wolfram! Blast you, Wolfram, are you here?"

An ominous groan shivered the supports around him and Fionvar froze.

The precarious construction of branches and stones quivered.

Holding his breath, Fionvar crawled out onto the path, his eyes slowly adjusting.

Down below, he caught a flash of movement. A figure draped in cloth bent to the ground, then rose.

As she turned, he caught the glint of Faedre's eyes and her slender, nasty smile.

Staring directly up at him, she stuck out her foot and tilted it this way and that, like a new dance step.

Wolfram lay senseless at her feet.

Fionvar scrambled up.

With a laugh, she set her foot against Wolfram's ribs and shoved him over the edge.

"No!" Fionvar launched himself down the slope.

Wolfram's legs rolled over the edge, and for a moment he dangled, his right arm caught up somehow.

Fionvar's heart jumped to his throat.

The chain at Wolfram's wrist had been bound to a tall support staff. Even as Fionvar ran, the staff jerked free of its moorings and tumbled over the edge.

The structure shuddered.

With a shout of laughter, Faedre turned and ran for the tunnel.

All around him, branches and stones began to fall, smashing into the sides of the pit or splashing below.

Throwing down his sword, Fionvar leapt. Joining the rain of debris, he struck the cold, dark pool and went under.

In a moment, he found the surface and took a great gasp before plunging in again. Something hit his back, forcing out the breath, and he gagged, sucking in the muddy water.

To the surface again, narrowly avoiding a falling timber. Fionvar took a deep breath and dove in, stroking hard toward the unknown bottom.

His outstretched hand struck on a slender pole, wedged sideways. Keeping his grasp, he swam along it.

A spasm of horror flashed through him. A cold hand had brushed his face.

Fionvar found the chain, knotted through with a bit of cloth. His numb fingers worked at it. His head buzzed, and his concentration wavered. Still, he clung to the chain. Just as he cursed his abandoned sword, Fionvar recalled the knife. He jerked Wolfram's boar knife free from his belt, hands shaking as he sawed at the cloth.

At last, it separated. Grabbing Wolfram's limp arm, Fionvar kicked off for the surface.

They exploded out of the water, Fionvar gasping as he pulled Wolfram, resting his son's head on his shoulder. Hugging his son to him, Fionvar found the disintegrating path. Screams from above echoed all around him as the floor gave way.

Tiles and bodies filled the air, smashed aside as the main altar plunged through them, sending up a wave that threatened to shake Fionvar into the water all over again.

Crawling, then staggering, Fionvar dragged Wolfram up the path, down the tunnel, at last into open air, collapsing outside the little tent.

Choking, he spat out mouthfuls of mud, then pushed himself up and rolled Wolfram over. The old shirt he wore had torn, exposing the scars on his chest and the discolored marks where the tiger's teeth had sunk deep. He had lost the patch, leaving the smooth skin vulnerable, connecting the trio of scars that cut his eyebrow and cheek. Mud smeared his face and his false blond hair. Manacles enclosed both wrists and one ankle.

Fionvar pulled his son into his arms, rubbing his back, then slapping. "Breathe, bury you, Wolfram, just breathe!" Warm trails of tears streaked down his cold cheeks. The dirt in his mouth tasted of death and failure. The screams and rumbles from the temple faded away as he hunched over Wolfram's still, cold form.

Chapter 50

LYSSA STOOD over Ghiva's body, the bloody sword raised above her. In her loudest voice, she cried, "The Lady stands!" she cried out again, in Hemijrani, this time, "The Lady stands. Your gods have been undone. Fall to your knees and pray that She forgives you!"

A few long knives clattered to the ground, then more. In waves all around her, the soldiers dropped to their knees, pleading with her to preserve them.

In the sunlight, Lyssa laughed, casting back her head to let it echo all around her. At her side, Dawsiir, knelt as well.

"I would serve the Lady who gives such power," he told her, his eyes shining.

She grinned. "And so you shall, my friend, and any of you who forswear the Two shall be welcomed into the Lady's arms!"

Suddenly, the tent flaps stirred, and someone darted out. Faedre, her garments dirty and askew whirled, staring at her soldiers.

"Arise!" she shouted. "Now is the time to strike! The temple of the false goddess is falling!"

A rumble arose from the earth as she spoke, and Lyssa looked to the temple wall. Nothing happened. Again, she laughed. "You have no army, Faedre. Only your lies defend you."

"Where are the Two?" Dawsiir asked, rising to his feet. "You have promised they would be here, that this was the hour of their birth."

"Treachery," Faedre said. "They have been undone by betrayal from our very ranks."

"If they were betrayed, Holy Mother," he said, "it was by your abuse of the sacred princess."

"Betrayed?" Lyssa asked. "How can you betray what never existed? You are not here for religion, but revenge. You abused the girl because you knew the ritual was a fraud. You lied to bring these people here to fight and die for your revenge. There are not two, but one!" She raised her arm, the sword struck with the golden rays of sun, the very earth roaring beneath their feet. The eyes of the audience reflected the glowing figure she had become. A thousand men had gathered here to witness the rebirth of their gods. From the rapture on their faces, she knew she had embodied a Goddess of her own.

Gathering her skirts, Faedre ran.

With a cry, Dawsiir started after her. Behind him, the Hemijrani host arose and followed, howling and shouting as they dashed past Lyssa, past their dead general, knocking down the stones of their shrine as they ran. The tent fluttered to the ground in their wake.

Spinning, Lyssa watched them go, but already the furor was dying away. Her body trembled, as if her strength departed. "Wait!" she shouted.

Faedre had nearly gotten to the trees when the first ones caught her.

"The Lady abhors needless death." Lyssa's voice was lost in the wailing behind the walls. She ran after them, cursing her own words.

Screaming and clawing, Faedre fell beneath her army, then her screams were heard no more.

GAGGING AND sputtering, Wolfram fought the arms that held him. He beat his fist against the strong shoulder, but his own strength had fled, and he shivered with the cold.

In answer to his attack, the arms tightened, his captor shaking with sobs. "I'm sorry, Wolfram. Sweet Lady, if I could start all over, I swear I would never leave you."

Recognizing Fionvar's voice, Wolfram stiffened. "It wouldn't be the first time you made that vow," he said, pushing away, trying to sit upright under his own control. He shook all over and pulled his hands under his arms for warmth.

Fionvar made no reply, and Wolfram glanced over. His father sat with his knees drawn up close, his clothes dripping wet, mud streaking his gray hair.

The shivering took over again, and Wolfram shook back his hair. "What happened? Why are we wet?"

"Faedre pushed you into the pit tied to a bar." Raising his head, Fionvar ran his gaze to the chain dangling from Wolfram's wrist. "The floor caved in."

Studying him, Wolfram said, "You came after me."

"I had to, I can't let you die until you forgive me for every time I wasn't there."

Wolfram looked away. He took in a deep breath, and let it go. That peace he had found on the tower grew within him. "You're here now, aren't you?" he whispered, his throat aching as a tear stung his eye. "You came back when I needed you most."

They sat quietly a moment longer, then Wolfram said, "I killed Melody."

"I know," Fionvar told him.

"I didn't know what else to do. I couldn't think—"

A warm hand gripped his shoulder. "I know," Fionvar said again, calmly.

Wolfram went on, "When she died, I could feel that power—it was as if something else had taken her already, something that blew through me at her death. I could have taken it, then, and done whatever I would."

"And yet you let it go."

He let out a hollow laugh. "I wouldn't trust myself to use it well."

Still with that strange calm in his voice, Fionvar replied, "I would."

"You'd be alone in that."

"No. I saw the look on Deishima's face when she thought I was you."

Wolfram gasped. "Deishima!" Stricken, he turned to Fionvar. "Did the temple come down?"

"The floor at least, I don't know."

"Oh, Sweet Lady!" He scrambled to his feet, swaying as dizziness swam in his head. Waiting for it to clear, he rubbed his forehead.

Trying to stand, Fionvar winced. A ragged gash marked his back.

Looking down at him, Wolfram sucked in a breath. "You're hurt."

Raising his chin, Fionvar gave a crooked smile. "Aren't we all?"

Squatting, Wolfram thrust out his hand.

Fionvar clasped it in his own, and together they rose. Over their clasped hands, their eyes met, then Fionvar pulled him into a fierce embrace.

Once again, Wolfram felt the solid warmth of his father's arms. He had forgotten how much he missed that comfort. Pulling away, he said, "All those things I said to you before I left? I'm sorry about that."

Laughing, Fionvar said, "Why? You were right!"

Together, they walked up the hill, both weak, both aching, each hoping the other wouldn't notice.

The small door by the temple stood open, and they entered the narrow courtyard with its well. They let themselves into the chaos of the temple court, a half-round strip of space now full of arguing castle guards.

"Make way!" Fionvar shouted. "Where's Gwythym?"

He shoved a path through the crowd toward the temple doors. A great log lay nearby, battering no longer.

Swiping the sweat from his brow, Gwythym turned from the door and stopped, his jaw dropping open. "Fionvar, Great Lady, but I thought you were gone! It's the prince, oh, Goddess's Tears, Fion, I've made such a ballocks of the whole thing."

Placing his hand on Gwythym's shoulder, Fionvar stopped his words and stepped aside.

Weary and ragged, but still on his own two feet, Wolfram blinked at the guard captain. The day had drained him so that he could summon no anger.

Shoulders sagging, Gwythym fell to his knees. "Oh, Your Highness, Sweet Lady, I cannot begin to beg your forgiveness." He hid his face in his hands. "Bury me beneath a pile of stone, Your Highness, that's all I deserve for being such an idiot."

Glancing to Fionvar, Wolfram sighed. "I could grow sick of apologies, even."

Fionvar offered a smile that felt like Wolfram's own.

Turning back to Gwythym, Wolfram told him, "You can't be blamed for mistrusting me, nor for believing the evidence they brought you. You didn't need to set me free. Thank you for your compassion."

Gwythym's head jerked up. "Oh, Great Goddess, Your Highness, don't be thanking me! That I can take least of all."

Wolfram laughed. "Then it shall be your most fitting punishment. That and a few nights in that bloody awful dungeon." That said, he looked up at the door. "Why's this still standing?" On the other side, voices moaned and murmured, and a few cried out in Hemijrani.

Rising slowly, Gwythym dusted off his knees, then took a quick glance at the state of Wolfram's own clothing and grew red to the tips of his ears. "Something's jammed it inside, Highness. With the people there, we daren't try to bust it back. I've sent men for bars to break off those hinges."

Wolfram's mouth went dry. "Didn't anyone get out?"

Gwythym shut his eyes, giving a slow shake of the head.

Pushing past to the door, Wolfram smote it with his fist. "Alyn! Alyn, you bastard, are you there?"

After a moment, a weak voice called back, "Wolfram? Is it you? By all that's holy, I'll see you buried for the work of this day."

Tilting his head back, Wolfram grinned. "He'll be fine." He leaned close to the door. "But you'll have to get out of there first, Alyn. What's at the door?"

"They jammed it with a bench, and some of the stonework's come down to block that in. There's a few dozen heathens up against it now, and me, trying not to fall in the pit."

"Is Deishima there? Is she with you?"

"Great Lady, Wolfram, should I care?"

Wolfram slammed his fist against the door.

"Careful," Fionvar said. "There's still hope. We'll have to wait until they get it open."

But he avoided Wolfram's eye, and Wolfram said quietly, "She was by the altar, last I knew. Did you see it fall?"

Now, Fionvar met his gaze and nodded. "I'm sorry, so help me, if I could have saved her . . ." The words trailed off, and Wolfram heard the truth in them.

His heart seemed dead and hollow, recalling the last glimpse of her ceremonial robes—rich crimson, the color of death, and blood pooling in her small, dark hand.

"We'll find her, one way or another," Fionvar breathed, touching his shoulder.

Shaking off the hand, Wolfram looked up toward the roof. Then he backed away a few paces and started looking around. His rope still snaked up the side of the roof. If he could get inside, he could look around for himself.

"Wolfram, I don't know that you're up to climbing—" Fionvar began, but Gwythym took Wolfram's arm and pointed.

"We've a heap of barrels by that wall, Highness."

Both men trailed him to the barrels, and Wolfram clambered up, his breathing more labored now, his clothes clinging with water, thankfully clean of Melody's blood.

For the second time, he crossed over the court, all the men's eyes upon him. Carefully, he crept up the slates and came to the edge.

Dust swirled inside the temple, backed with the blackness of the pit that opened below. Tracing the walls, he could see the Caves and niches still standing, packed with terrified Hemijrani who regarded him with dazed expressions. He scooted to one side, and could make out the pile of debris at the doors and the flash of Alyn's bright hair where he clung to a column.

A cloud passed before the sun, removing the glare of the dancing dust, and his eyes followed the path of the rope. Then he laughed aloud.

Halfway down, where the altar would have been, Deishima

clung to the line. Her arms and legs were wrapped around it, her right arm bandaged with a strip of red silk.

At the sound of his laughter, she looked up, squinting into the new sun. "Can it be you?"

"Sweet Lady, you're alive!"

"By the Two," she called back, "so are you!"

He caught hold of the rope and strained to pull her up, his torn palms throbbing.

Voices rang out behind him, and suddenly the rope slid backward. Down below, a dozen guards hung on to it and hauled at Gwythym's command. Fionvar sat back on a barrel, one hand at his chest as he watched.

Slowly, Deishima rose beneath him until Wolfram caught her up in both arms and brought her over the edge. The men below let out a cheer as Wolfram embraced her. She slid her arms around him and sighed. "They have taken me from darkness to darkness, Wolfram, until I had forgotten there was light."

Wolfram stroked her dark hair and did not trust himself to speak.

"Then you fell from the sky like a star," she whispered, "and I was lit up by your glow."

Chapter 51

RELUCTANTLY LEAVING Deishima in the hands of the healers, Wolfram slowly made his way back to his room. His wrists were raw after days in chains, and his muscles protested every movement. After sending for a meal from the kitchens—a big, hot meal dripping with flavor—he finally walked to the bedroom.

Wolfram stripped out of his ruined clothes. Over his head, he slipped the bear claw on its thong, watching it twist in the air before him. Placing it on his night table, he touched the straw mattress on his bed. The clean linens lay folded back, awaiting his homecoming. Just for a minute, he would sit. Then the bed enveloped him, and Wolfram fell into a deep and dreamless sleep.

By the time he awoke, the sky was growing dark again. He could smell cold roast lamb and parsnips, and his stomach growled. Stiffly, he arose and dressed. Ravenous, Wolfram attacked the meal left for him. When he was sated, he paused, then returned for his coronet, then hesitated again. First, he washed his hands and face, adding a splash of rosewater. He tried to comb out his hair. This called for a bit of cursing, but he finally got it in order. Rummaging in his wardrobe, he found a belt of golden leaves and added the boar knife Fionvar had returned to him.

Watching himself in the mirror, he placed the coronet on his head. He had lost his patch, so the scars showed plain. It was a serious face, with no trace of the mischief it used to hold. He fingered the scars and the edge of the empty socket. At last, he smiled. He could have two eyes or one, dark hair or blond; and Deishima still loved him.

As he passed through the halls, servants bowed, and nobles looked away, the shame clear in their eyes. Under other circumstances, they might have come tonight to watch him hang. Wolfram made it a point to acknowledge every lord or lady, by name if he could. The demon kept to a low rumble of satisfaction at every flustered reply.

At the infirmary door, a phalanx of royal guard drew themselves to attention, and Wolfram frowned. He passed between them, then pivoted. The man on the end turned scarlet and focused somewhere over his shoulder. He had been the lead man that day in the dungeons, the day that Wolfram had gotten his meeting with Gwythym, the last day he had been fed.

Wolfram stared at him hard. The demon gnashed its teeth, longing for blood. Wolfram's grin tightened. "You are dismissed, sir. Turn in your arms and go."

Startled, the man met his gaze. "I—uh, forgive me, Your Highness."

Shaking his head, Wolfram kept his voice low and even, "I

believe I gave you an order. If you fail to obey me, there is room in the dungeon these days."

"Aye, Highness," the man mumbled, making a half bow.

The rest of the guards exchanged worried looks as the man broke ranks.

"One-eyed Highness pitching shit," Wolfram said, watching the man's back to be sure he was gone. Then he opened the infirmary door and shut it firmly behind him.

A new temporary infirmary had been established in an outbuilding to tend to those wounded in the temple. Lyssa's small army of Hemijrani converts tended their fellows, describing the miracle they had witnessed and the mighty arm of the Lady who slew their general. Here in the castle rested only a few. Thankfully, Alyn had already been released after his head wound was deemed a minor scrape. A curtain shielded the last bed, with its two windows overlooking the garden, and Wolfram cleared his throat before he let himself in.

Deishima was sitting up in bed, and her face broke into a smile at the sight of him. Several layers of silk had been removed, leaving her clad in a short, tight-fitting bodice and long, pleated skirt. She cradled her wrapped arm, her hands slathered with healing lotion for the rope marks across them.

Her visitor rose and stared. Wolfram faced his mother a long moment before she stepped aside, letting him pass toward the head of the bed.

Queen Brianna looked weary, her eyes rimmed with redness and shadows, her hair more gray, but then he had not seen her since he went to the dungeon.

Turning his back to her, he pulled the chair nearer and touched Deishima's cheek. "How are you?"

"Tired," she answered. "Otherwise, better than I have been in some time." She cut her eyes away toward the queen.

Wolfram bit his lip and released it. "I wish things had been otherwise for you."

Deishima glanced out the window, a tear trapped in her dark lashes. "We have been through terrible things, you and I." She laid her hand gently over his.

"There will be joy for us, I promise. Such joy as I can provide, it will be yours."

The queen made a small, helpless noise behind him.

"I believe you," Deishima said. "You have yet to break a promise to me."

A bubble of happiness welled up in him, and he grinned. "Then I promise that this will not be the first."

"Your Highness—" the queen began, and both turned to look at her, losing their secret smiles. Ducking her head, Brianna addressed Deishima. "Your Highness, you must forgive me for what has happened to you under my roof. If there is any way that I can redress the wrongs done to you, you have only to name it."

Deishima's face looked solemn and empty of warmth. "The boon I shall ask of you is this, that when Wolfram would speak to you, you would listen. That his word will be enough for you. That you shall not suffer him to lie in chains when it is in your power to set him free." Her small dark fingers curled around his hand.

Beneath those words, the queen withered, her eyes vacant. "What you ask is no more than my duty to my son. A duty I have neglected for far too long." Then she looked up, and a radiant smile lit her face. "Your Highness, of all that has come and will yet come of these events, the only thing I do not regret is that my son has found you. I know now that you were a light to him in the darkness. You believed in him when the rest of us cursed his name." She looked to Wolfram then, with those bleak eyes. "I do not expect your forgiveness, Wolfram. My crimes against you are too many for that. You have changed, these past months, and I hope you will grant me the chance to change as well. Tomorrow will be as if we met for the very first time." The queen hesitated, then went on, "I would like the chance to know you."

Letting out a pent-up breath, Wolfram regarded his mother. She stood meekly before him, awaiting his answer. "Shall I join you for breakfast, Your Majesty?" he said lightly. "We'll want to get an early start."

Her smile broke into laughter, and she wiped at her eyes with the heels of her hands. "Yes, yes, we must do that." She turned to go, then said, "Oh, I have called a court after Evening Prayer. I hope that you both will attend?"

"It will be a pleasure to attend your court in freedom, Your Majesty," Deishima said, "for both of us, if I am not mistaken."

The queen inclined her head. "In the meantime, Wolfram, I should tell you that my grandmother's condition has worsened. I know that you and she have not gotten on well, to say the least, but she has a visitor you should meet."

"We will stop in on the way," he told her.

With a swish of the curtains, she left them alone.

Wolfram brought Deishima's hand to his lips and kissed it. "I can only imagine what a terrible time you've had, Jeshnam. If anything I do or say pains you, just—"

"Ah!" She brought up her hand. "It is not you who have wounded me, Wolfram. Indeed, I believe it shall be you who heals me."

"There is so much you don't even know about me." He sighed. "Or I about you."

"We shall have time for all of that."

Shaking his head, he said, "Some things shouldn't wait that long, now that you're here in the castle. I should be the one to tell you, not some servant or lady-in-waiting."

Her dark eyes fastened on his face. "I am listening."

"I mentioned that I have known other women. There is one in the castle, Asenith is her name. Her father once usurped this kingdom, and my father—that is, not really my father—" He shook his head and laughed. "That's another story entirely. Anyhow, I—she entrapped me, trying to have my child. She succeeded, but now she's dying. I've seen her only once since I got home."

"I can understand this, Wolfram."

Watching the sunset, he frowned. "I have a daughter I've never seen."

Smiling, Deishima said, "I wonder if she resembles you."

He laughed. "I hope not!"

Outside, a bell rang in the city, calling the citizens to pray.

"That's Evening Prayer." Wolfram rose. "If I'm to visit Elyn, I should go soon. Will you come?" His eyebrows inched upward, longing for her company, afraid to say too much.

"I shall."

He put out an arm for her, and she leaned on him as she slid off the bed. Looking down, he laughed again. He had forgotten to put on any shoes. Their bare toes fidgeted on the cool tiles, hers as dark and delicate as the rest of her, his long, pale, and lumpy in comparison. "Everyone will think we belong together," he said.

"And shall they be wrong?" she asked.

He knew the way to Elyn's chambers because he had been avoiding it for years. The honor guard outside her door he expected. The sound of song beyond it made them pause: the Evening Prayer in Strelledor, flawlessly accented despite the climbing pitches and soaring notes of the singer. The voice had a crystalline perfection, clear, beautiful, and stirring, lifting up the listeners even to the stars of which it sang. The masterful stroke of a violin buoyed the singer's voice. Not daring to break the spell, Wolfram and Deishima waited outside until the song died away again to silence.

"Well, I'm afraid I need to dress for court," Fionvar's voice said, "so I'll leave you be." The door opened inward and he met Wolfram's eye, tucking his violin under his arm. Glancing back over his shoulder, he smiled. "Go on," he said. "It's about time."

Wolfram stepped into a chamber rich with carved oak and warmed by a roaring fire. Elyn lay in her enormous bed, her hands shaking on the coverlet, tears trickling down her cheeks. The singer stood with his back to her, arms folded, studying a painting.

"I am not crying, you fool," Elyn rasped. "'Tis the smoke. So, will you stand there all night, or aren't you coming in?" She glared at the newcomers.

Startled, Deishima shot him a look, but Wolfram just laughed. Elyn was an old lady, a decrepit, wrinkled little woman trapped at last in her bed. She no longer held power over him. "We have no wish to interrupt."

At this, the singer turned. "You are interrupting nothing, my lord, my lady." He gave an elegant bow and straightened, his handsome face suddenly still.

"Your Highness is the title, is it not?" Elyn cracked. "I assume she's reinstated you. Don't you recognize your own son, Rhys?" She cackled until her voice broke, and she took a swallow from her ever-present tea.

Wolfram stared at the singer, the man who had been King Rhys. The eunuch who was supposed to be his father. "I don't believe we've met."

King Rhys stepped around the bed and came nearer. "Once, in Melisande's garden. I thought you were someone else. A ghost."

"Orie," Wolfram supplied.

Rhys nodded. "I did not expect you to look so alike."

"Sit down, the lot of you," Elyn said. "I hate to strain my ears."

Obligingly, though they did not look at her, the three settled into leather seats by the bed. "This is Her Highness, the Jeshnam Deishima. She's my betrothed," Wolfram said, for the first time aloud and in her presence. Deishima lit up with a shy smile.

Gazing at her, Rhys said, "We are well met. I used to be King Rhys. Now I am a simple master of music."

"Simple?" she asked. "You are a master indeed, but simple, I think not."

"It's a good thing you're marrying her, Your Highness; otherwise, I might have to, prior devotion notwithstanding." Rhys lifted a mug from the table beside him. "I assume you know the whole story by now, Highness."

Frowning, Wolfram nodded. He wet his lips and sniffed the air, then shot out his hand to snatch the mug away. "Don't drink it!" Wolfram said, taking another sniff. "It doesn't smell right."

"It is Terresan tea, is it not?" Deishima inquired, leaning over. "And yet it is not. I believe you are right, Wolfram. Do you fear poison?"

Suddenly, Elyn began to laugh, deep and hearty.

They turned to look at the frail woman in the bed.

"Oh," she gasped, "the little minx said she would get me! Every day I met her, she wished to tear out my eyes. It's her, I am sure of that." She waved her mug. "Who drinks the stuff, save myself? And you, of course." She gestured toward Rhys.

"Asenith?" Wolfram ventured.

"The Usurper's daughter," she sputtered between fits of laughter that threatened to crack her ribs.

Wolfram shut his eye, resting his forehead in his hand. "How did you do it, Duchess?"

"The candles." She laughed. "I left the candles for her chamber, with quicksilver at the wicks. Oh, I have not laughed so much since . . . I do not believe I have ever laughed so much." Her voice died away, but the sheets stirred with her laughter as the three stared at the would-be murderer, herself a victim of the same venom.

"Aren't you glad now, that you came home?" Wolfram asked.

Tilting his face to look at the man who was and was not his son, Rhys answered, "I am glad that I have met you. Fionvar's letters used to sing your praises. Even when you were driving him mad. Speaking of Fionvar, we should be on our way to court." He looked again to Elyn. "Lady walk with you," he told her, but the old woman's eyes were already closing.

Chapter 52

THE NOBLES in the Great Hall fell silent at Wolfram's arrival, turning to bow and to stare, as much at the woman on his arm as at himself. The red clothing would cause a stir, but Deishima had little else, and she certainly looked regal enough with her dark hair flowing down her back in waves. Her head did not even reach his shoulder, but she walked with her chin held high, only her grip on Wolfram's arm betraying her tension.

Rhys slipped away to where Prince Alyn stood and took him in a quick embrace.

Alyn, too, wore red, the crimson of his mourning for his sister. Aside from that, and a bruise on his forehead, he looked as if the events of the afternoon had been years ago. Wolfram wondered if Alyn bore any scars at all, either on his skin or in his heart. Then the prince caught his eye and the confusion and sadness on his face gave the answer. He reached for Rhys's hand and looked away.

As they came up the aisle, the queen rose. She wore a gown of autumn colors that set off her graying hair, and a band of red about her arm, with the crown to show a royal loss. Descending the two steps before them as Wolfram bowed, Brianna proclaimed, "I give you my son and heir, Crown Prince Wolfram yfBrianna duRhys, of the house of Rinvien, without whom we would not all be here at this moment."

Wolfram straightened to thunderous applause. In another step, his mother embraced him. He returned the gesture, unable to remember the last time she had held him close instead of pushing him away.

"I give you also, her Highness the Jeshnam Deishima, and my son's intended bride."

They were seated beside her, but the queen remained standing. "I know you are all wondering about this court, after Prayer, at the end of a very long day." She glanced over to Wolfram, then to Alyn, her smile taking on a hint of sadness. "I have only two items of business, so I shall not keep you long from your rest. The first is to announce that all charges against Prince Wolfram have been found to be without merit."

The audience grew still, listening, not entirely welcoming him, but at least listening.

"As to the second . . ." she began, her face clearing with the words, all sadness swept away. She kept her eyes upon her son as she spoke, her face both eager and hesitant. "You all know that, in weeks past, I have considered remarriage, forsaking my widowhood for a new husband."

His eye beginning to twitch, Wolfram frowned. He felt the brush of Deishima's hand upon his arm, and took it in his own.

The Herald intoned, "Her Royal Majesty, Queen Brianna of Lochalyn, summons to her court Fionvar DuNormand."

It still felt strange to Wolfram to hear Fionvar's name with no title, nor honor. Perhaps she would return his chain. Certainly he deserved that much. Fionvar approached from a seat toward the back. He bowed slightly, his face betraying a twinge of pain from the wound to his back where the falling brick had struck him as he dove.

Still, he met Brianna's gaze, and said, "I am here at your will, Your Majesty."

"Wolfram?" she said, not turning aside.

Confused, he rose and went to her.

With both hands, Brianna lifted the golden crown from her head. She ran her fingers over the leaves, then held it out to Wolfram. "Hold this for me, would you?"

Reverently, he accepted it, the crown resting on his palms.

Bowing her head, the queen sank down on her knees at Fionvar's feet. "You were born no lord, nor prince, nor man of high estate. You came to me with nothing but your honor and your service. Lately, I have abused them both."

Already shaking his head, Fionvar reached down to draw her up, but she merely clasped his hand in both of hers and looked up into his face. "I cannot wed you as a queen," she began.

"Brianna, don't do this," he murmured desperately. "Stand up, Brianna."

Biting her lip, she shook her head. "If you would have me as a woman, sir, if, after all of this, you would have me to wife, there is no man in the stars or under them that I would have but you."

Sighing, Fionvar bent and swept her up into his arms, pressing her cheek to his, stroking her hair. "Of course I will have you, Heart's Desire. I will have you."

He stood a moment with the uncrowned queen in his arms, clinging to him with all of her might, then he cast a glance to Wolfram and grinned through his tears. With a little bow, Fionvar turned on his heel and strode off down the aisle, the queen's gown trailing at his feet.

All heads turned silently to watch them go as the door banged shut behind them. Slowly, the eyes pivoted back to the head of the hall where Wolfram stood, crown in hand. He blinked a few times, then shut his mouth, then laughed. In a bound, he topped the dais. "My lords and ladies, it must be time to retire for the night. In my mother's absence, I bid you take your rest." He stared at the distant door through which they had disappeared. Then he held up the crown, and shouted, "Long live the queen!"

Gwythym took up the cheer, and the room erupted into cheers and startled laughter as they rose up from their seats. Slowly then, they filed out through that same door.

"Wait here," Wolfram told Deishima and trotted to where Dylan stood.

He caught Dylan to his chest, lifting him from the ground, swinging him around, and setting him down again, if a little unsteadily. "For everything, I thank you."

"I should have done more, and sooner." Dylan's face flamed at the attention.

"Next time, my friend, I'm sure you will act swiftly. Say—your calculations were correct. That must be a thrill."

"Aye, 'twould be, if they hadn't been put to such a purpose." He bowed his head.

Wolfram lightly punched his arm. "Is that what's bothering you?"

"It's Asenith. They don't think she's got much time left. After all that she's done, sending on my numbers, the baby, all of that, I know I shouldn't care, but . . . I would have given her everything, if I could, but she wanted what I could never offer." His blue eyes searched Wolfram's face, glanced to the crown in his hands, and back again.

Wolfram rubbed his finger over a golden leaf. "I have an idea. I'll meet you at Asenith's room. Get her out of bed and dressed."

"I don't know, she's not strong."

"Call her weak, and I think you'll find her strong enough." He fairly skipped back to Deishima and drew her to her feet. "There's something I have to do. First, I'll see that they find you a room. There's one not far from mine, if you don't mind."

After he had her safely installed in the nearest guest room, with two maids to see to her wishes, Wolfram gathered a few things, then made his way to Asenith's chamber. Thin and pale, her fingernails showing blue, Asenith stood fully clothed in her best gown, though it hung from her bones. She leaned on Dylan's arm and glared at Wolfram. "Why have you gotten me from my bed?"

Supporting her other arm, Wolfram smiled. "If you'll come with me, my lady."

With numerous pauses to rest, they brought her to the Great Hall. A few torches transformed it into a cavern of shadows, the banner above creating subtle movements of darkness and light. Wolfram led them to the head of the hall and stopped a few feet short of the dais. There, he left Asenith's side and went to stand behind her. "You were right about the poison, my lady. It was Duchess Elyn—the candles in your room."

Breathlessly, Asenith laughed. "She'll outlive me, she will outlive us all."

"Despite your best efforts," Wolfram put in. "I know about the tea."

Asenith grew still. "Is that what this is about?"

Seriously, he said, "I don't believe there is time left to punish you, Asenith."

Her thin body trembled. "No, I don't believe there is."

Standing back, Wolfram shook out his official cloak of state, long and green, of velvet with golden leaves embroidered at its hem and a golden clasp at its throat. He draped it about her shoulders.

Her eyes narrowed at him. "What do you mean by this?"

"Kneel," he told her solemnly.

With Dylan's gentle assistance, she did as he bid her, staring up at him, her lovely blue eyes faded and dull with pain. Holding out the gleaming crown, Wolfram said, "Your father seized this crown by force and deception. But for tonight, I give it to you freely." Carefully, he lowered it onto her head. "Arise, Queen Asenith, momentary monarch of Lochalyn—or at the least, of this hall."

Swaying, she got to her feet, her face pinched as she snorted. "What sort of queen am I, with only two subjects in my little kingdom?"

Bowing, he offered her the throne. "One of us is the crown prince," he told her. "And the other is the man who loves you."

The lines eased away from her face, and Asenith held herself straight, lifting her elbow from Dylan's grasp. She picked up her skirt in her withered hands and walked up the steps, head held high. Turning gracefully, Asenith lowered herself onto the throne, savoring every moment. Her face shining, her eyes roving the vastness of the hall, she smiled, and sighed.

Below, the two men got down on one knee and gazed up at her, then Dylan's head bowed, and silent tears splashed to the floor. Wolfram touched his friend's shoulder, drawing his look; the wonder on his face was gratitude enough. He took the coronet from his own head and placed it on Dylan's. "Sit with your queen," he said.

Dylan mounted the steps, bowing over Asenith's hand. Then she put her hand on his cheek. "Oh, love." She sighed, and he stopped her with a kiss.

"I would have given you all this, if I could."

Her smile trembled. "I know, Dylan," she breathed. "I know."

He sank down beside her, laying his head on her lap. Her skeletal fingers touched his face, his hair, his shoulder, and relaxed as her head leaned back against the throne, the crown glittering over her brow, her eyes fixed on the unseen stars.

Chapter 53

AFTER THE pain awoke him, Fionvar lay for a long time, watching the new dawn find gold in the gray of Brianna's hair. He wondered about the barons this morning, arising, considering their queen's rash proposal, and the way he had carried her off. He hoped it would do no harm to Wolfram at least.

He rose and paced to the window, the stone cool beneath his

feet. Outside, late spring shimmered green in the garden, small birds chattering as they bounced among the last leaves of fall. The grassy path by the gate was a field of violets.

"Fionvar?" Brianna started up from bed, then settled when she saw him there. "I thought you'd gone again."

He crossed to her and knelt on the bed. "No, love, still here. You can smell the spring out there," he said, smiling. "Walk with me?"

"In my nightclothes?" She laughed. "Besides, Wolfram's coming to breakfast, and we're rising late as it is."

"Just a little while." He slid back off the bed and held out his hand. She hesitated, then sighed and took his hand, letting him draw her up. Hand in hand, they stepped out of the door into the remaining chill of dawn.

Brianna giggled as her bare toes hit the gravel path. "This is foolish. We'll catch our death of cold."

"Bosh!" he said, dropping her hand. "I'll race you to the orchard."

"Fionvar, you're wounded." She propped her hands on her hips.

"Then you'll have to give me a head start!" He sprinted along the path, dodging the well at the center, grinning at the sound of her feet behind him. He ran down to the garden gate, flinging himself against it with a triumphant whoop. In the next minute, he sucked in a breath as the pain once more clutched his chest.

Landing with a shout beside him, her palms to the wall, Brianna panted, then she frowned. "Are you well?"

"Tired," he said, "still tired after those three days with no sleep."

"You have a right to be," she said. "Why are you smiling like that?"

For Fionvar stood looking through the bars, out toward the forest, a wistful sort of smile playing about his lips. "Quinan said something yesterday morning. I think I understand now what he meant."

Fionvar broke away from her and flung himself down in the violets. After so short an exertion, he had a hard time catching his breath. Worry etching her face, Brianna settled in the new grass, taking his head on her lap. "I love you," she said.

Fionvar reached up to touch her cheek. "I know."

WOLFRAM CARRIED the crown in his hands to his mother's door, glad he had taken the chance when it came to him. Wolfram knocked and heard no answer. Puzzled, he knocked again. After a moment, he shrugged and pushed the door open a crack, peeking inside. The curtain to the bedchamber stood open, as did the door to the garden, and his parents were nowhere in sight.

Letting himself in, he crossed the sitting room and looked out the door, then set off on the gravel path.

When he drew nearer, he saw the queen with Fionvar's head in her lap, bending over him. His face flushed, and he was about to go when she looked up. "Sorry," he said. "I didn't mean to—"

Tears streamed down her cheeks, but, unlike last night, there was no joy in her eyes. "Wolfram," she cried.

He covered the last steps at a run and fell to his knees beside her.

Fionvar's face looked gray and drawn, his eyes searching the distance.

"Father," Wolfram whispered.

The dark eyes flickered toward him, and Fionvar smiled weakly. "You have a beautiful daughter, did I tell you?"

"Yes, you did. I haven't seen her yet." Wolfram's eye stung.

"I hope you will love her as deeply as I have loved you."

Wolfram grabbed his hand. "Don't die! I've only just found you."

"I have been here all along." He gazed up at them. "I will be here still." Then he seemed to look beyond, alert, as if someone had spoken his name. "Yes," he said at last. "Lady, I will walk with you."

The dark eyes, a match to Wolfram's own, gazed off into that distant place. Brianna began to shake, tears streaming down her face until she bent her head over her husband's, her loose hair hiding little of her grief.

Wolfram sat back on his heels, face to the sky, where the sun rose over the garden wall. Gently, he lay his father's hand upon his chest. With careful fingers, he touched his mother's shoulders, but the gesture set off a wave of sobs, and he drew back. He felt hollow, as if those places in him had at last been named, then abandoned. Quietly, he rose and turned away, leaving the queen her last moments with the man she loved.

Shutting the garden door behind him, Wolfram straightened his clothing and took a deep breath, letting it out slow. At last, he opened the outside door.

As expected, Lady Catherine sat there on a little stool, dropping the pretext of her embroidery as she curtsied low. "Is everyone up then, Your Highness? Ready to break the fast?" Her cheeks were slightly pink, her hesitant fingers clasped.

Wolfram forced himself to take another breath. "Lord Fionvar DuNormand is dead," he told her, calm and quiet. "Please see that arrangements are made."

The color fled her cheeks as she looked to the door, then back to his face. "Oh, for love of the Lady." She sighed, then glanced back to the door. "Oh, Your Majesty."

Wolfram touched her arm. "Leave her be a little longer, Catherine. Then I think she will have need of you."

Catherine nodded promptly. "Of course, Your Highness." She matched the calm of his own demeanor until she turned away, stuffing her things into her basket, pricking her hand upon the needle. "I'll see to the arrangements, of course." Her voice quavered, and she sank back onto the stool, hiding her face.

Retreating from her grief, Wolfram backed a few paces down the hall, then began walking, the aches of yesterday's adventures gone numb even as his mind seemed empty.

At the door, he raised a hand to knock, then lowered it, his head bowed. He knocked at last, and entered at a word. Inside, an older woman sat in a chair with slats upon its legs, creaking back and forth, and murmuring a wordless tune. She looked up at his appearance. Gripping her burden a little tighter, she made as if to rise.

"Don't get up," he told her. "I just thought . . . it was about time."

Nodding, she relaxed into the chair and slipped aside a corner of the soft blanket. Wolfram took a few steps nearer, gazing down. Inside her swaddling clothes, his infant daughter gazed back, her eyes a deep blue, wide and unblinking for a long moment.

"Bend down, Yer Highness," the nurse advised. "She can't see far."

Wolfram came up beside the chair and knelt, moving aside the blanket around her face. Asenith claimed the child resembled him, but who could tell? He smiled a little. Perhaps she was Dylan's after all; perhaps all the bother had been for naught.

"Would you care to hold her, Highness?"

"Oh, no, I don't think—" But she took his hand, molding his arm to support the baby's head.

"Just like so. You'll do fine."

The baby was warm, and lighter than he expected. One of her arms wriggled free. It waved in the air as her face took on an expression of intense concentration. Then the tiny hand covered and uncovered the painted eye patch. Cold, damp fingers patted his cheek so gently that it tickled, and he let out a nervous chuckle.

The baby's face split into a huge grin, bare of teeth, with her tiny nose crinkled up in devilish glee.

Wolfram laughed aloud. Something about the cheeks and the chin—it was his smile as it had been before the demon tore away such innocent pleasure, before the scars had reshaped his face. His smile. And his father's.

The breath escaped him in a rush. Tears welled up in him, spilling over his cheek, splashing on his daughter's face. He pulled her close, embracing her warmth, her soft head tucked against his chin, and they wept together in uncomprehending abandon.

Epilogue

WOLFRAM AND Deishima wed at midsummer, needing a celebration after too much mourning. She wore a gown of local style made from a gleaming green silk from her native land, woven with leaves of gold. A circlet of gold gleamed on her midnight hair, but could not match the glow in her eyes when she looked on her husband.

Since the Hemijrani converts had yet to finish repairs to the great temple, they married in the old chapel, as King Rhys had done, the ceremony spoken in Hemijrani as well as Strelledor, with Lyssa officiating. She grumbled over this but had to agree as the only priestess who could speak both tongues. Every member of the wedding and their guests wore sashes of red for Fionvar DuNormand, and Bernholt's Master of Music performed "A Blacksmith to his Lady," weeping as he sang.

Hemijrani rose wine sweetened the joyous feast, but Queen Brianna's crown weighed heavily upon her, and many said they should not be surprised if she yet chose to step down and quietly retire.

Wolfram taught Deishima a few of the latest dances, which she took to with some grace, although he had to shorten his exuberant strides so as not to leave her behind. More than once, he simply swept her up in his arms and spun them both around the floor.

At last, with a cheery wave to the guests, the bridal couple departed, Wolfram leading the way to their new chambers, a fine suite of rooms where they could overlook the queen's garden—not so dissimilar to the one Deishima had left behind.

Shutting the door behind them, Wolfram paused a moment before he turned. He felt giddy with wine and nervous as well. He rested his head against the wood, trying to calm his beating heart, shifting his leather eye patch to rub the skin beneath.

"Shemhiraz," Deishima murmured, "is something troubling you?"

He turned to face her, still leaning. "What did you call me?"

She ducked her head, shining like an emerald in her wedding dress. "Shemhiraz—it means, 'shooting star.' It is how I think of you."

Smiling, he told her, "I'm fine. It's just, I'm nervous. I did not expect that."

Her fingers folding together, she turned her head. Her gaze drifted toward the bed, new linens folded back to greet them.

"Not as nervous as you are, I guess," he murmured, coming to stand beside her. "If you . . . aren't ready, I won't touch you. I can be patient."

She raised an eyebrow. "I was not aware you possessed that virtue, Wolfram."

The three syllables her voice made of his name stirred a warmth deep inside him, and he reached out a gentle finger to slip back a lock of her hair. "Sweet Lady, Deishima, I want you more than anything. I am not good at patience, but I can learn."

"Only one man has ever . . ." Her words died away, and she swallowed.

Wolfram faced her and sank to his knees, taking both of her hands in his. "If I can learn to breathe again," he said. "If I can learn to hold my anger, then I can wait for you. You are worth every moment."

Slipping one hand free, she stroked his right eyebrow, her finger catching on the scars that cut through it. "I am afraid," she whispered.

"I know," he said. "I understand."

Deishima cupped his cheek, then let her hand slide slowly down, her fingers playing with the hairs at the lacing of his shirt.

"If you can face a tiger for me, then I can surely be brave enough to face a man."

Looking up at this unexpected answer, Wolfram laughed, and was rewarded by her smile. He embraced her waist, drawing her into the warmth of his arms. And growled.